Don't Forget to Breathe

Melinda Harris

Copyright © 2013 by Melinda Harris

Cover Design by Kara's Kreative

Don't Forget to Breathe

Published by Triple "S" Publishing

ISBN: 978-0-9893306-3-3

All rights reserved. No part of this book may be reproduced or transmitted in any form or by any means, electronic or mechanical, including photocopying, recording, or by any information storage and retrieval system without the written permission of the author, except where permitted by law.

This book is a work of fiction. Any similarities to real people, living or dead, are purely coincidental. All characters and events in this work are figments of the author's imagination.

*For Kristi, boots and three-piece suits
– a few of my favorite things.*

TABLE OF CONTENTS

CHAPTER 1 4

CHAPTER 2 14

CHAPTER 3 21

CHAPTER 4 27

CHAPTER 5 35

CHAPTER 6 43

CHAPTER 7 57

CHAPTER 8 69

CHAPTER 9 74

CHAPTER 10 87

CHAPTER 11 94

CHAPTER 12 103

CHAPTER 13 109

CHAPTER 14 115

CHAPTER 15 128

CHAPTER 16 137

CHAPTER 17 145

CHAPTER 18 160

CHAPTER 19 175

CHAPTER 20 186

CHAPTER 21 202

CHAPTER 22 212

CHAPTER 23	217
CHAPTER 24	224
CHAPTER 25	231
CHAPTER 26	241
CHAPTER 27	251
CHAPTER 28	262
CHAPTER 29	268
CHAPTER 30	276
CHAPTER 31	290
CHAPTER 32	302
CHAPTER 33	321
CHAPTER 34	331
CHAPTER 35	342
CHAPTER 36	349
CHAPTER 37	367
CHAPTER 38	377
CHAPTER 39	390
CHAPTER 40	397
CHAPTER 41	406
CHAPTER 42	420
CHAPTER 43	429
CHAPTER 44	437
CHAPTER 45	446
CHAPTER 46	454
EPILOGUE	463

CHAPTER 1

Seriously?

I slap at my alarm clock as it buzzes annoyingly beside me. It can't be morning already. No way.

With one eye still closed, I glance at the offending piece of technology and see that it's a quarter past six. That makes a cumulative seven hours of sleep I've gotten in the past two days. Awesome.

I love my job. I love my job. I love my...

Oh, whatever. That chant is quickly losing its luster.

I pull the covers over my face, stubbornly trying to avoid the inevitable. I used to love my job. I truly did. It was absolutely perfect, until my new boss lady, Señorita Bitchface, came to town and started ruining the one thing I look forward to when I wake up every morning – *Andrew.*

Deep breaths, Jules. You can do this.

I will not let that skank ruin my life. I still have Andrew. That's all that matters.

I eventually make my way to the shower and try my best to keep pleasant thoughts of Mr. Andrew Mercer, Jr. on my mind – the way his hazel eyes shine in the sunlight from his office windows when he looks up at me, or how his hair is always slightly damp when he comes in every morning.

Damn, I'm so smitten with that man.

When I finish my shower, I make my way to the kitchen for some painkillers and a large glass of water. The two bottles of wine I drank last night in an effort to wind down have left my mouth feeling everything short of a cactus and some tumbleweeds.

I turn to the cabinet to grab a glass, frustrated by the fact that my hangover is clouding my daydreams of Andrew. Before I know it, Bitchface has popped back into my head, pairing well with my aching brain. I knew she was bad news the minute her Louboutins hit the elevator lobby a few months ago.

Damn her, and her overpriced and extremely perky tits! And did I mention she's only a couple of years older than I am? Stupid slut.

I continue to scowl as I pop the pills in my mouth and fill my glass with water from the sink. I seriously need a nap.

The painkillers have thankfully kicked in by the time I finish my make-up, but I'm still moving slowly as I make my way to my closet. I'm thinking black needs to be the color of the day for me – should match my mood nicely.

I grab a pair of black pants and a black short-sleeved sweater. My dark curls are especially unruly today, but I couldn't care less at this point.

I look down at my shoe selection and huff. I refuse to wear heels today because I may fall on my face. Flats are in order. Andrew's dad – or Mercer Senior, as I prefer to call him – can get the hell over it.

I give myself a last look in the mirror. Not great but not awful. My once bright and shining green eyes are slowly losing their sparkle, not to mention the dark circles forming underneath. Even though I'm thinner than ever, my extra work hours are taking away from my gym time, and I'm starting to feel a little flabby.

What happened to me? I used to be relatively attractive.

God, I need a new job.

And a nap.

Definitely a nap.

I pull my hair into a messy bun, having to use around fifty bobby pins to tame the long, nappy mess but I finally get it looking halfway decent. I leave the bathroom, knowing that's as good as it's going to get today, and start to slip on my favorite black flats. I sigh as I look down at my feet and reluctantly grab a pair of heels to carry with me. Mercer Senior can be very scary.

As usual, my roomie, Abby, isn't awake when I leave. She still has her job from college, which is working as a bartender at Marlow's in the Highlands. Abby is actually a very talented artist, but she refuses to give in to "The Man". So, she keeps her shitty paying job at a run-down Jazz club and does some painting now and then. I've tried to get her to take her artwork seriously, but she refuses. Stubborn mule.

Good grief, Jules! Get yourself out of this funk! Now!

I pull into my office building parking lot around seven-thirty, my usual arrival time.

As the assistant to Mr. Andrew Mercer, Jr., and now, unfortunately, Ms. Victoria "Bitchface" Hamilton, I have lots to prep in the morning before everyone arrives.

Luckily, Ms. Hamilton isn't high maintenance when it comes to her morning routine. But throughout the day, she thoroughly enjoys yelling at me, treating me like a five-year old and springing things on me at the last minute. I'm forced to stay in the office late nearly every day finishing up crap that I could have been doing for her sorry ass during work hours, if she had the decency or brain capacity to organize a freaking thought every once in a while!

But I digress...

I walk out of the elevator and see the lights are off in the lobby. Good. That means no one's here, which is typically the case, but I definitely need a few minutes of alone time today to try and get my head straight. What I would really like to do is go into Andrew's office and curl up on his cozy leather sofa for a couple of hours, but that's not going to happen, so I drop my things at my desk and head to the break room to get the morning started.

After I finish making the coffee and placing our daily continental breakfast order with the café downstairs, I do my usual morning tasks for Bitchface, before making my way toward Andrew's office to make it ready for his day.

I'm so grateful Mercer Senior is now working at the Midtown office. He used to run me ragged, even with two other full-time assistants catering exclusively to him. I swear the man can't do anything on his own, except make people cry. And he does that very well.

Bitchface took over Mercer Senior's office when he left, which moved her farther away from me. I was excited at first, but unfortunately, it hasn't stopped her from visiting my desk every five minutes. Most of the time, she's not coming to see me anyway.

The only people on our side of the building are the accounting team and Andrew. Bitchface certainly has no interest in accounting – or I would guess any math at all, for that matter – so that leaves whom? That's right.

My Andrew.

Brainless tramp.

I wipe the scowl off my face – semi-permanent now, thanks to my skanktastic boss lady – by thinking of Andrew.

Mmmm. Much better.

I've been Andrew's assistant for almost two years, and those two years have not been without a few bumps in the road. However, we eventually arrived at a good place, which makes my life much easier than it was when I first started.

Plus, the fact that I've fallen madly, deeply, whole-heartedly in love with him helps too.

I go to my desk to grab the items I need for Andrew's office, and head that way. I unlock his office door and turn on the light. I open the blinds on his wall of windows, place his newspapers on his coffee table, turn on his computer, put his messages in his Inbox and turn on his "soothing sounds" waterfall by his desk; which I want to make fun of daily but wouldn't dare. Andrew loves the outdoors, so that's supposedly why he bought it – makes him think of waterfalls and nature, which help him relax. Personally, I think the thing is ridiculous, especially knowing what he paid for it, and honestly, it just makes me feel like I have to pee.

All that's left is to make sure I have coffee ready for him when he gets in, so for now, my job here is done.

When I get back to my desk, I do all of my personal stuff first – check my emails and scroll through my social media accounts to make sure no one got married or pregnant in the last twenty-four hours – then start in on work around eight-thirty.

I've been slammed this week trying to help with the upcoming garden party the company's hosting for potential clients this Saturday. It's actually being held at the Mercer Estate, which I've visited several times over the past few weeks to help organize the party – not my taste, but it truly is a beautiful place.

My voicemail and email are full of RSVPs, which I hurriedly add to the attendee list. Andrew's been requesting an updated version every day when he comes in, so I want to make sure it's ready for him.

Bitchface the Great has also requested that I provide detailed research about each guest, including everything but what type of toilet paper they use. That's what has been consuming most of my time this week. Of course, Andrew thought it was a great idea, like he does with all of her ideas. Yuck.

Speaking of the She-Devil…

I can hear the clicking sound of her stilettos in the lobby all the way down the hall. The sound always sends chills up my spine, like the Grim Reaper has arrived to take me to Hell.

"Ms. Greene." She comes immediately to my desk when she walks in, her voice loud and irritating.

"Yes ma'am?" I don't look up at her. I just continue looking at my computer screen.

She clears her throat. "Ms. Greene?"

I pull my head up slowly, making sure my fake smile is front and center. "Yes ma'am?"

"I assume you have the updated list for this morning?" She looks impatiently at her gaudy watch, then back at me. Her face is as condescending as ever.

I have a college degree, asshole! I'm not a child!

"I'm working on it now," I say sweetly, ignoring my inner monologue for the moment.

"I need it as soon as you have it updated," she demands. "And I think I'd like some hot tea this morning. My throat's feeling a little scratchy."

Oh, I could have a field day with that one.

"Absolutely," I promise, once again suppressing my evil side, resurrected recently by Bitchface herself.

My friend, Adrian, looks at me from across the hallway as soon as The Evil One leaves. Her look tells me she's sorry I have to deal with that. At least I'm not the only one affected by that lady's wrath. Poor Adrian is the assistant to our accounting group, but since her desk is the one closest to mine, Bitchface uses and abuses her from time to time when I'm not around. The woman knows no bounds and unfortunately, Andrew seems to worship at her alter, so it looks like she won't be going anywhere any time soon.

If I'm being completely honest, that's why I hate her most. I've had a job since I was fifteen, and since then, I've had a couple of terrifying bosses. Even Andrew used to make me cry myself to sleep nearly every night for the first few months that I worked here, but this lady's different. Not only is she a nasty bitch, she's encroaching on my territory and there's absolutely nothing I can do about it.

Fuck my life.

My morning goes by quickly, as I try to do thorough background checks on some of the new RSVPs. My eyes are starting to cross from staring at my computer screen for the last two hours straight. I could really use another cup of coffee.

A quick glance at the corny little Elvis clock on my desk – compliments of my equally corny mother – tells me there's no time for coffee. Andrew should be in any minute. My heart starts pounding with the anticipation of seeing him.

I'm so ridiculous.

Right on time, he comes walking down the hall at ten-forty-five. His meeting was scheduled to be over at ten-thirty. A fifteen minute ride to the office and here he is. Thanks to me, the man's schedule is bulletproof. Unfortunately, that seems to be the only thing he loves about me – my flawless organizational skills.

"Ms. Greene." Andrew nods without looking at me, as he walks past my desk and into his office.

This is pretty customary. He used to at least glance at me with his morning greetings, but that rarely happens anymore.

"Good morning, Mr. Mercer," I say to myself, as he closes his office door. He's wearing his dark brown suit today with a teal, paisley tie. He looks lovely.

If you listen closely, you can hear all of the quiet swooning that happens when Andrew walks through the office, but no one would admit to it. The man is ridiculously gorgeous – tall and lean, with panty-melting eyes and a head of hair that would be the envy of any proper frat boy. But let's just say that he's not known for his people skills.

My instant message startles me as it pops up on my screen.

Coffee?

Dammit! I forgot about his coffee. I was too busy daydreaming about Andrew and what's *under* that dark brown suit. I'm already standing as I type.

Sorry sir. Right away.

I rush to the break room, make his coffee as quickly as possible, and hurry back to his office.

"I'm sorry, sir," I repeat quietly, as I sit his coffee on the coaster on his desk.

"It's okay, Ms. Greene," he tells me, head down, reading his messages. "You've been busy lately. I understand."

"Yes, sir." It's pathetic what his voice alone does to me – all deep and manly and just *Andrew*. "I'll have an updated version of the guest list to you within the hour. I just want to get through a few more new additions."

"Thank you, Ms. Greene." He looks up at me with a half-smile. I somehow manage to keep my cool, but only on the outside.

His beautiful hazel eyes look teal today to match his tie, and his dark brown hair is perfectly coifed. Though I'll admit I prefer the less structured hair-style he sports some times when we work on weekends. I live for the days of dress pants, button-down shirts with no tie, loafers and unkempt hair. Simply mouthwatering.

"You're welcome sir. May I get you anything else?" I try to pull my eyes away from him but it's a challenge, as always.

"That's all for now. Thank you again."

Oh his voice is so silky smooth. I've asked him to call me "Julia" a few times, but he won't. He insists on calling me "Ms. Greene" which I hate. Like everything else between us, it's so formal, which is yet another sign that the man has zero interest in me personally.

Why do I do this to myself?

I walk out of his office and back to my desk. I slump back into my chair and sigh.

I really need to find a new job.

CHAPTER 2

"How old is he again?"

"He just turned thirty," I tell Abby for the hundredth time.

"Gross!" Abby is yelling over the music in the bar, but I can still barely hear her. "He's so old!"

"For God's sake, Abby," I laugh. "Thirty's not old. That's only a few years older than us."

Abby rolls her eyes. "Don't remind me."

"Besides, weren't you dating a forty-two year old last month?"

"Don't remind me about that either. And I wouldn't exactly call that *dating*."

I smile at my friend. "Andrew's not that bad."

"He's most definitely easy on the eyes," she says. "No doubt about that, but I can't get past the fact that he's a complete...ummm, what's the word? Oh right. *Asshole*."

Abby's lucky we've been friends basically since birth, and I love her like I do. Otherwise, I would have to fight her to the death for talking shit about my man.

"He's not that way with everyone," I say, defensively. He's never mean to me – at least, not anymore. "And you don't even know him. You met him one time, at my show, and you barely spoke to him."

Abby rolls her powder blue eyes at me once again. "Jules, from what you tell me, the guy is bad news - too many secrets and all around weird shit going on there. I don't think you need to be messed up in all of that. And don't even get me started on

Daddy Dearest. Besides..." Oh here it comes. "Are you serious about this guy? You've been worshipping him from afar for over a year now, and he's not even your type. What the hell?"

"I know," I laugh. "I've tried giving him up, but it never works. He just buys a fabulous new suit and then I'm done for."

"You're so ridiculous." Abby's laughing at me, and I laugh too. I know she only says these things because she cares, and it's not like she's lying.

"And he's so...*preppy*," she adds.

"Preppy?" I smile.

"Yes. I'm stereotyping. Sue me."

"Watch out or I'll call *my* Daddy Dearest," I smirk.

"Don't threaten me with your lawyer daddy," Abby winks. "But you know I do think your dad is total hotness, so you can send him my way any time."

"You're disgusting."

"And you're totally whipped...by a *preppy* one, no less."

I laugh again. "I can't help myself."

"So, is it his money?"

"Are you serious?"

"What?" she tries to look defensive, but her smile is giving her away. "I just thought you have something against your parents' money, but maybe you like his better?"

I laugh hard this time. "How do you come up with this nonsense?"

"What?" she laughs. "I don't know how the whole money thing works. I grew up poor...you know...walked to school, no shoes, in the snow, uphill, both ways?"

"Abby, we were neighbors at one time," I remind her. "You grew up in a middle class, suburban neighborhood...not exactly the backwoods. And it rarely snows in Georgia."

"Whatever," Abby brushes me off with a wave, and I smile at her. "I'm just trying to find reason in all of this."

"Why?"

Why does there have to be a reason, Abby? I just love him. Period.

"Because!" Abby's getting animated now, thanks to her third margarita. "You're a smart, beautiful, extremely creative and artistically gifted girl, wasting your time working at a commercial construction company as an assistant to a total douchebag and his Nazi counterpart." Abby shrugs her shoulders. "What gives?"

"He's special, Abby," I tell her, and by the look on Abby's face, I fear my answer may have come straight from the burning depths inside me that pine for that man. "Just trust me, okay?"

Abby's sad smile confirms my suspicions. I just accidentally unleashed the full potency of my love for him with my eyes. *Oops*. No more drinks for me.

"I'll leave it alone," she tells me. "Just be careful."

"I love you too." I wink at her. Abby is the best.

Abby leans back and sips her cocktail, obviously taking a break from our conversation to scope out the possibilities in the bar, and for Abby, the possibilities are usually endless.

Abby is a beauty, with her huge blue eyes, long legs, and creamy complexion. She typically has her pick of the litter when we go out. Even with her hot pink and platinum blonde hair color combo – currently pulled up in a very sassy ponytail – the boys still fall at her feet. I was against the hair color at first, but I'm not surprised to find she's totally capable of pulling it off. It was blue streaked a few months ago, which I also frowned upon, but it worked for her.

While Abby chooses her victim for the evening, I take the opportunity to indulge in my favorite pastime – thinking about Andrew. Not one guy in this dump holds a candle to him.

Abby's right. Andrew's definitely not my type. Most of my past boyfriends have all been plentifully pierced, plentifully tattooed, or both. But they've all been losers, so maybe a change of pace is a good thing…or not.

Andrew may be minus the piercings and tattoos, but he definitely doesn't have a reputation for being a super swell guy, at least not anymore. I've heard rumors about him before I came along. He apparently used to be friendlier and more down to earth. But the daily grind of corporate America can blacken even the purest of hearts.

"I'm leaving," I eventually say to Abby as I stand and grab my tiny clutch.

"Why?" Abby gives me her super sad face, but it won't work.

I'm exhausted, and this whole bar scene is just not working for me anymore. Sometimes I feel like an eighty year old, trapped in a twenty-four year old body.

"I'm tired," I say into her ear as I bend down to kiss her cheek. "You have fun. I'll see you at home later."

"Ok. Love you!"

Abby doesn't look too upset to see me go. She hops up and heads directly for some of her other friends on the makeshift dance floor before I've barely left our table.

I walk quickly out of the bar, even though my feet are killing me. Stupid Mercer Senior stopped in this afternoon forcing me to leave the office in my heels, forgetting my flats in my desk drawer. I could have gone home first, but I decided to suck it up. However, the idea of sweatpants and a t-shirt are so appealing right now. I think I could run home in these shoes.

I look up at the moon, thankful it's a nice night. The streets are still crowded with party-goers, since the old lady in me is crashing early this evening.

Part of me hopes to see Andrew somewhere in the crowd. Maybe if I got a few drinks in him, he would realize he loves me too and we'd go elope at some corny little chapel in Vegas with a fake Elvis as our witness. My mom would love it. The thought makes me smile.

It's a short walk to my place, which is great because my heels are getting less and less appealing by the minute. I've tried to talk Abby into finding a better apartment now that I'm making semi-decent money, but she still likes living in the party zone. Very much. Most of the time I hate it, but I guess it's nice to not have to drive home after you've had a few drinks.

I go straight to my bedroom for my sweats before I do anything else. *Ahhh*, the sweet relief of my fuzzy slipper socks.

I walk into the kitchen searching for something, but not sure what. A glass of water sounds good. I only had one drink tonight, but I don't think I've fully rehydrated from last night's wine bender.

I pull out my laptop at the kitchen table, deciding to take advantage of the next hour or so I have to myself at the apartment. My email has a few more RSVPs, but I'll deal with that in the morning. I'm not working late tonight. I refuse.

I check my "Andrew" folder and see twenty-three messages from him. *What?* Did I forget to do something before I left today?

I start with the first one sent, which was only an hour ago. He's sent me twenty-three emails in an hour?

Seriously, Andrew?

The majority are just "to-dos" for tomorrow. What a relief. Then I come across the last email sent, which was only three minutes ago. It's a question about the upcoming event. I click reply and start typing, but I don't get far. It's so quiet in the apartment that the beep of the instant message makes me gasp.

Ms. Greene? What are you doing up?

Oh my God! Andrew's talking to me via chat...after midnight...probably sitting at his house...in some sexy sweat pants...no shirt...

Okay, enough. I have to fan myself with a nearby notepad. It's really hot in my apartment all of a sudden.

I put down the notepad and start chewing on my nails. I have no idea what to say for some reason. Why am I freaking out?

Evening, sir. Just checking my emails.

Did that sound dumb? That sounded so dumb. I'm an idiot.

Actually, it's morning, Ms. Greene. Please get some sleep.

I smile. I can't help it. I do love him so.

Yes sir. Have a good morning then.

Was that flirting? I'm totally flirting. *Jules! Stop it!*

You too, Ms. Greene. See you tomorrow.

I'm smiling again. The way he affects me is absurd.
I wait for a moment to see if he adds anything further, but nothing pops up. I decide to leave well enough alone and close my chat.
There was nothing remarkable about that exchange, but for me, it doesn't matter. Abby's right. This man has me completely under his spell.

CHAPTER 3

"Are you kidding me with this?" Bitchface is nearly shouting at me.

Please don't cry, Jules. Please don't cry.

"I thought you wanted it separated that way?" I wish I had a little more conviction in my voice, but I'm not having a good week.

"And why would you think *that*?" Bitchface rolls her blue eye-shadowed eyes at me, looking like the MAC counter threw up on her face.

Maybe because that's the way you told me to separate it? You hateful hag!

"Perhaps I misunderstood," I say, looking back at my computer.

I will not shed tears in front of this woman. Not even angry tears. I won't give her the satisfaction.

"Ms. Greene?" I refuse to look at her. "Ms. Greene!"

Okay, fine. That's it.

"I'll correct it," I tell her, looking her square in the eyes. "But next time, I suggest you type out an email, detailing your instructions, so we won't have any further misunderstandings."

The look I get back from her is priceless. At first, I think she's going to storm back off to her office, but it seems she's not through with me yet.

"Excuse me?" Her slutty red lips form a hard line. "What did you just say to me?"

I smile sweetly up at her. "I just suggested that it may be better if we have things in writing from now on. That's all."

To my surprise, Bitchface tosses my spreadsheet at me, and then slams her hands on my desk. I quickly scoot backwards; honestly afraid she may hit me, and kind of hoping she does. Perhaps then they'll fire her sorry ass.

"Who the hell do you think you are?" She is seething, and Adrian is now staring at us, obviously wondering what the hell is going on.

I stare down my attacker, holding my ground. However, I'm not willing to lose my job at the moment, so I keep my mouth shut and my eager fists away from her plastic face.

"I know you think you own this place, being Andy's little pet and all, but if you think you can treat me like that, you have another thing coming."

She calls him "Andy"? Gross.

I brace myself, as she looks like she's about to have another go, when all of a sudden Andrew steps out of his office.

"Excuse me, Ms. Hamilton? A word please?"

And with that, he turns and walks back into his office.

I look back at Bitchface and a slow, satisfied smile stretches across my face.

She angrily grabs the spreadsheet from my desk and storms toward Andrew's office. Oh, if only I could be a fly on the wall. Was he watching our exchange? His door was open, so he must have overheard us. Is he reprimanding her? He looked angry when he came out of his office just then. Maybe he's angry with *me*?

The door is closed now, so I can't hear anything. Unfortunately, there's no shouting.

About fifteen minutes later, Bitchface leaves Andrew's office. She doesn't even give me a second glance as she walks back to her office. She looks pissed, but not that pissed, which is unfortunate.

Adrian looks at me and raises an eyebrow. I shrug. I have no idea what happened in there, but I'm thinking she didn't get fired. *Dammit.*

My instant messenger dings, breaking me from my reverie.

May I see you a moment, Ms. Greene?

Crap! Looks like I'm the one in trouble, but I didn't do anything wrong in this particular instance, and I'm more than happy to defend myself.

I stand and pull my cardigan off. The thought of getting in trouble is making me sweaty. I can't lose this job. Not yet.

"Yes, sir," I say as I step in the doorway of his office. "You wanted to see me?"

"Sit please, Ms. Greene."

Oh dear. Not good.

I take a seat on one of the chairs in front of his desk. I can immediately see on his beautiful face that he's unhappy, but at what? At whom?

I cross my legs to keep my right knee from bouncing. Nervous habit.

Andrew finishes what he's working on, and then turns and looks at me. *Really* looks at me.

"Are you okay?" he asks, and I stare in shock.

Huh?

"Ummm...I'm sorry sir?"

"I overhead the conversation you just had with Ms. Hamilton," he continues. "She was inappropriate, and I reprimanded her for it. I also wanted to make sure that you were okay."

"Yes, sir," I say quickly, still a little dumbfounded. And the fact that he's still staring at me with those lovely eyes has my heart beating like I just ran a marathon. "I'm totally fine," I assure him, although I'm feeling anything but *fine* at the moment.

"Good," he says, and then I see a rare beauty.

Andrew *smiles*.

I instantly smile too. "Thank you for your concern," I tell him. "I suggested to Ms. Hamilton that perhaps we should put things in writing from now on, to avoid any further disagreements."

Andrew is still smiling. *Wow.* "Yes, I heard that part too. A good suggestion, I think."

"Thank you, sir."

"You're welcome, Ms. Greene." Andrew then turns back to his computer, clearly dismissing me.

I stand, a little upset our pleasant exchange is over. "May I get you anything, sir?" I ask, not wanting to leave.

"No, thank you. I'm fine."

I turn to walk out, but as I approach the door, something comes over me. I'm touched by his concern for me and I want to make sure he knows it, even though I'm smart enough to know it's totally platonic.

"Mr. Mercer?" He looks up at me, his face confused. "Thank you again...for defending me. It means a lot."

I'm once again rewarded with a small smile. "My pleasure, Ms. Greene."

Did he just say *pleasure*?

My entire body reacts to that word like he just told me he loved me. *Dear God.*

I walk back to my desk on unsteady legs. I know I'm imagining things, but it felt like something just happened between us – some unfamiliar, wonderful thing.

It's not the first time he's ever done something nice for me, but it is the first time he's stood up for me like that, especially where Bitchface is concerned. And the way he was looking at me...particularly the look he gave me at the end, when I was standing by the door? It was in his eyes, those excruciatingly beautiful eyes.

Oh, who am I kidding? Looks like I'm approaching full-on delusional. Perfect.

I close my eyes for a second before returning to my work. I definitely need to find a new job and fast.

After pouring myself back into the grueling spreadsheet for another two hours, I decide to quickly check my emails before lunch.

The first one in the stack is from the boss lady. I stare in shock. Not only is it a full outline of her exact changes for the spreadsheet, but she also used the words "Thank you for all you do" at the very end, AND she's copied Andrew.

Wait, what?

As I sit wide-eyed still trying to process the impossible email, Andrew walks past my desk heading for his lunch meeting. I look up at him, and he gives me a sideways glance with a wink and a smile.

That seals the deal.

I don't care if I have to clean the toilets.

I'll never quit this job.

Never.

CHAPTER 4

By eight o'clock that night, I'm the only person left in the office, and the thrill of Andrew's wink from earlier has worn off. This is the last place on earth I want to be right now, but I don't have a choice. I'll just cry my way through this stupid spreadsheet all night until I can't cry anymore.

As I work through my ridiculous spreadsheet, my sadness starts slowly turning to rage – rage for my unrequited love, rage for Bitchface Victoria, rage for this stupid, annoying spreadsheet that should be handled by a second level assistant instead of me. But most of all, I'm just mad at myself.

Abby's words flash through my mind again. I *am* wasting my life away here. I hate this job, but I stay for *him*. How pitiful is that? I'm putting off my career, putting off what I love, for a man.

What's happened to me?

The sound of my phone ringing startles me. It's Abby. Do I want to talk to her?

"Hello?" I sniffle into the phone.

"Have you been crying?" Abby sounds pissed, which doesn't help my current mood.

"Maybe," I say quietly. "I'm just tired."

"You need to quit that damn job, Jules," she says angrily.

"I can't."

"Yes, you can. You're better than him."

"No, I'm not."

Abby sighs into the phone. "Jules, you know you're a knock out with your C cups and all of that exotic, Middle-Eastern swagger. And I'm sure Mr. Andrew Mercer, Jr. knows that as well. The fact that he hasn't made a pass at you in two years means he's obviously gay, so just move on, and start taking some pretty pictures again, okay?"

I laugh through my tears. "You're probably right. I haven't seen or heard of a girlfriend of any kind since I've been here. And he *is* a really good dresser."

Now Abby and I are both laughing. "Come home?" she pleads.

"I'll be home soon."

"I love you, Jules."

"I love you too."

I hang up with Abby feeling a little better, not much, but a little.

I start working on my nemesis of a spreadsheet and get excited when I hear the familiar ding of my instant messenger. *Maybe it's Andrew again!*

I click "save" on my spreadsheet before looking at the pop up.

> *Ms. Greene, I believe we have you working a little too much lately.*

It's Andrew! My heart starts pounding out its usual hip-hop number whenever Andrew is involved.

> *No sir. Just trying to finish up the attendee list.*

I'm always staying late at the office, especially lately, and he knows that. I wonder why the sudden concern?

> *I had planned to send you an email, but then noticed you were online. I wanted to see if you're available for hire for the garden party?*

Oh dear. *For hire?* All sorts of inappropriate things are flashing through my head right now.
Jules! Pull it together!

> *I'm sorry sir. I'm not sure I understand.*

Hire me? I'm attending, if that's what he means. Surely he doesn't want me to serve food or something. My heart sinks as I realize this is probably what he's referring to. He wants me to be part of a welcoming committee or the wait staff. I just know it.
I stare impatiently down at my instant messenger. He must be typing a long one. It's taking forever.

> *If I remember correctly, you graduated with a degree in photography. I feel like we need a photographer at the event, and although I'm sure you've already hired one (as you always think of everything) I would prefer the hired photographer be you. Interested?*

I read and re-read the message, just to make sure I'm not imagining things. Is he serious?

> Sir, I did hire a photographer, who is very well known and respected. Thank you for considering me, but he will do a fine job. I'm confident everyone will be pleased with the results.

Why is he asking this of me? I can't believe he even remembers my degree. I didn't think he remembered anything about me personally.

There was that one time when he gave me a gift card to a photography shop in town, but that was over a year ago. Oh wait. He also gave me the annual membership to the art museum for my birthday this year. Okay. That was actually a really thoughtful gift, now that I think about it...

The instant messenger chimes in again and breaks my train of thought.

> I'm sure the person you hired is wonderful, but I want you.

Ummm...*oh my*. I'm going to close my eyes and pretend like we're not talking about my photography skills for a moment.

> Honestly sir, I'm not sure I'm qualified. Perhaps you should take a look at some of my work. I don't normally do event photography.

I'm totally not qualified to do this. What if I mess up? What if I lose the memory card or worse, what if I forget to even put the card in the camera? I've done that before at my neighbor's baby shower, and I cried for days.

> *I've seen your work, Ms. Greene, and I feel you're more than qualified. Will you do it?*

He's seen my work? When? Oh right. I did ask the entire office to come to one of my art shows shortly after I started here. That was the first and last time Abby met Andrew. It seems like forever ago. It was the beginning of the end of my photography career, but I'm hoping to jumpstart that again soon. I still can't believe he came...

> *Yes sir, but may I ask a question?*

I have to know.

> *Please.*

Should I ask him this? What if I discourage him? As intimidating as the job may be, I actually could use the money.

> *Why are you asking me to do this? The photographer I hired is wonderful. Forgive me, but I don't understand your insistence.*

I have to know what brought this on. And why do I feel like I've spoken to him more than normal lately? I guess it's just this event. Perhaps we should have more events.

Honestly?

Uh oh. Is this going to be bad?

Please.

I wait eagerly for his response, but it takes a while. Just as I'm starting to think I may have lost him, his message pops up.

I happen to think your photos are very beautiful. I realize it's not a typical job you would take, but I thought you could use the extra money...for your trip.

I feel like crying again. How does he remember that? I mentioned my trip to Italy to him months ago, and it wasn't even directly to him. I was chatting with Adrian in the break room and he overheard. I remember him telling me he's been a couple of times and that I would love it. He was wearing his black suit that day with the red and black striped tie.
I have no idea how to respond – between his intervention this morning with Bitchface and now this? What's going *on*?
I'll just stick with professionalism. He *is* my boss.

Yes sir. It's much appreciated. Thank you again for your consideration and the compliment. I won't let you down.

I'm smiling from ear to ear now. He likes my photos. Why is it that Andrew liking my work is better than any compliment I could ever receive from a professional artist? I sigh. It's because I want him to like me so badly, I'll take anything I can get.

> *I know for certain you won't let me down. That's never a worry of mine, Ms. Greene. We'll talk about your fee tomorrow. Thank you for accepting the offer.*

Okay, his politeness is starting to worry me now. What's up? Should I be worried?

> *Sounds good. Thank you again, sir.*

I mean, he wouldn't be so nice to me if he was going to fire me or something, right?

> *Good night, Ms. Greene. I'll see you tomorrow.*

I stare at my computer screen a little while longer, but he obviously has nothing further to add.
Hmmm...what to take from this new development...
If I think about it, I guess it's not too strange he wants me to photograph the party. He probably knows I'll be cheaper than the guy I hired, but Andrew Mercer isn't typically worried much about money. So, why then?
Maybe he really does like my work. Is that possible? I don't even know if the man likes art at all. Perhaps he's a connoisseur and I don't know it. There are several nice pieces in his father's home.

Or maybe he just likes my pictures. I find that hard to believe, since no one else seems to like them.

Either way, I'm not sure I care. I could really use the money. Maybe he's just trying to reward me for the work I've done on this party. That has to be it. He really is a good person. I wish other people had the chance to see it like I do.

My phone rings again. I look at the clock on my desk. It's almost nine-thirty and I've barely done any work at all. *Dammit.*

I look down at my phone to see who it is. It's my mother. I can't handle her right now, so I ignore the call. Then I turn my phone completely off because I know she'll call about a million more times after this, even though she won't remember drunk dialing me. I'll call and check in tomorrow morning.

I kick off my shoes under my desk, and settle in to my relatively comfortable office chair. It's going to be another long night.

CHAPTER 5

"Good morning, Mom."

I'm not really in the mood to deal with my mom right now. I'd planned to call her this morning, but I forgot my laptop at home, and by the time I turned around to get it and came back to the office, I was nearly thirty minutes late for work. Andrew wasn't here, but Bitchface was, and I'm sure she'll be oh too happy to inform Andrew of my tardiness.

Plus, since I was all flustered from being late, I managed to spill coffee all over my skirt. Luckily, it's chocolate brown, so the stain is blending nicely.

"Morning, sweetheart," my mom slurs.

I roll my eyes. "Seriously, Mother?" I say through gritted teeth, as I get up to walk to the elevator lobby and talk with her. "It's ten in the morning."

"What?" My mom plays innocent, but she's obviously wasted.

I wonder what it is this time. Vodka? Maybe some pills? Maybe both?

"What do you want?" I ask quietly, trying to keep the tears of anger from overflowing.

"I just wanted to check on you. I miss you."

And there go my tears. "I miss you too, Mom. Where's Dad?"

My mom's quiet for a moment. "He's at work," she says. "You know...your father and his work."

"Maybe I'll come by and visit this weekend," I tell her.

I don't want to visit, of course. I hate that place, but my mom knows how to tug at my heart.

"That would be lovely." I instantly hear her mood elevate.

That settles it then. It's the Den of Satan this weekend in exchange for rest. Fabulous.

"Have some coffee, Mom," I tell her, hoping she listens. "I'll see you Sunday."

"Sunday?" she seems upset. "Not Saturday?"

I squeeze my eyes shut. She doesn't even remember, and I've told her about it a million times.

"I have my work party on Saturday, Mom," I remind her...*again*. "Mr. Mercer asked me to be the event photographer."

I can hear her pouring – and spilling – something in the background, probably no longer listening to a word I say.

"That's nice, dear," she finally says.

"See you Sunday, Mom." My face is going to be a wreck.

"I love you, sweetheart."

"I love you too."

I hang up with my mom and start dialing my dad. I'm not in the right frame of mind to deal with my dysfunctional family this morning, but I guess I have no choice, as usual.

"Mr. Greene's office. How may I assist you?"

"Rebecca, it's Jules. Is my dad around?" My dad's assistant is nice. Too bad I have to hate her, since she's his current mistress and all.

"Sure, Jules. How are you, Hun?"

Don't try to be nice to me, you home wrecker!

"Good, Rebecca, but I really need to speak to my dad."

"No problem. I'll put you through."

A few seconds later, my dad answers.

"Hey buttercup! How's my baby girl?"

Ugh. His cheerfulness is so revolting some times.

"Hi Dad. You have a minute?"

"Anything for you. What's the problem?"

I close my eyes, plop down on the floor in the corner of the lobby and stretch out my legs. I lean against the wall and try to figure out for the millionth time how to make my father understand.

"It's mom."

My dad's silent, which is a typical response. "What about her?"

"I just spoke to her and she's wasted. Again. I thought you were going to get her some help."

"I tried, Jules," he sighs. "She won't stay in treatment, and you can't force it."

Maybe if you were home every once in a while? Or maybe if you would stop BANGING YOUR SECRETARY?!

"I'm just worried about her," I say, trying hard to avoid a fight.

"Me too, baby, but I don't know what else to do."

"Really, Dad? " I'm trying to keep my anger at bay, but it's just dying to surface. "So you're just giving up on her? Why the hell are you two even married still?"

It's the same old argument, but it's one that I unfortunately have to have with my father over and over again because I just can't seem to understand it.

"Jules, do we really need to talk about this now?" He's using his parental voice, like that has any effect on me at all anymore. "I'm assuming you're at work, and so am I. We can talk about this later."

"No, we can't," I tell him, raising my voice a little louder than I should. I hope no one hears, but at the moment, I really don't care. "Because I'll never get it, Dad. It will never make sense to me. I'm done."

I hang up the phone and toss it down beside me. I can't take any more.

I put my head in my hands and start crying. This is not the best spot for this, but I don't have the energy to move. I'm just too damn tired.

Eventually, after many deep breaths and a heap of tears, I decide I better go back to my desk. Surely Bitchface has been looking for me at least once or twice this morning.

I wipe my eyes the best I can and move to stand up, but before I can get upright the door to the elevator opens.

Please don't let it be Andrew. Please don't let it be Andrew. Please don't let it be Andrew.

Of course, it's Andrew.

"Ms. Greene? Are you okay?" The alarm on his face is almost comical. "Did you fall?"

He offers a hand to help me up, and I take it. I love how large it is compared to mine, and it's nice and warm from being outside.

I stand up and brush off my coffee stained skirt. "I'm sorry, sir. I took a call out here. I was just heading back in."

Wow. This is really embarrassing. The good thing is that he doesn't seem angry. My face has to be eighteen shades of red though.

"Have you been crying?" Andrew asks. "Was it Ms. Hamilton again?"

Am I imagining the honest concern in his eyes? Oh my. Those *eyes.*

"No sir." My goodness, he looks pissed. "And I'm fine," I hurriedly say.

Oh God, just let me get the hell out of here.

Andrew hands me the handkerchief from the inside pocket of his dark beige suit. I wipe my eyes as he continues to stare at me. Eventually, I find I have to look down. I can't look into his beautiful eyes. They are too disarming and I don't want to cry again.

"Yes, okay then," he finally says, clearing his throat and looking slightly uncomfortable, before walking ahead of me to get the door.

He holds it open for me, as I walk through. I veer off and head directly to the ladies room. I need to make sure my face isn't a total wreck. Perhaps a splash of cold water will do the trick. Andrew continues past me to his office without a look back in my direction.

My eyes are a little red, but I wasn't crying long enough for my tears to do too much damage. I dab a cold paper towel on my face and pinch my cheeks to add some color back in. I'll add a little lipstick at my desk and then I should be good to go.

I take a few more deep breaths before returning to my desk. I can't believe it was Andrew of all people who found me in the lobby. Today is just not my day.

Yes, Andrew, I have a wonderful family. My father's a very powerful corporate attorney, who's currently having one of many affairs on my addict mother – a fact that everyone but me seems to be fine with ignoring. How about that Andrew? Falling in love with me yet?

My instant messenger pops up. For once, I'm kind of thankful it's not Andrew.

> *You okay?*

It's Adrian. I look across the way and give her a sad smile before I answer.

> *Just having a shitty day. Thanks though.*

Adrian answers back, quickly.

> *No problem. Victoria stopped by your desk a couple of times while you were gone.*

I assumed as much.

> *Did she look pissed?*

I know the answer before Adrian sends it.

> *Unfortunately, yes.*

I roll my eyes. I'm never in the mood for that woman, but especially not today.

Thanks Adrian. I'll see what she wants.

Let me know if there's anything I can do to help.

I look up at her and give her a more genuine smile. I really do like Adrian. She's been with the company a while and she was the first friend I made when I started here. We've gotten closer over the last several months or so. She may be quiet and kind of nerdy, but the girl's one of the good ones.

Dammit. Should I call Victoria to see what she wanted? Nope. She can come to me.

It's time for me to once again start to bury my head in this bitch of a spreadsheet, but I can't shake the embarrassment of having Andrew finding me drowning in my tears. I guess the one bright spot was how worried he looked when he saw me on the floor, but it was obviously him keeping an eye on Bitchface, rather than honest concern for me. Right?

Before I can think on that one any longer, I hear the sound of heels clicking down the hallway, heading in my direction.

"Ms. Greene," her nagging voice says as she approaches. "I stopped by a couple of times earlier, but you were out."

I reluctantly look up at her. "I had to take a personal call. I didn't want to disturb anyone."

She gives me her best fake smile. "Okay fine." She quickly skips over any personal exchange between the two of us. "How's the list coming? I haven't received my copy yet this morning."

Is she serious?

"I emailed it to you over an hour ago. Perhaps you should check your Inbox?"

Bitchface smirks at me. "Perhaps you should check your 'sent' items. I didn't receive it."

Now I'm annoyed. I click roughly through my emails to find it so I can prove her wrong. I start getting anxious when I don't see it at the top of the list. But I did send it, didn't I?

"Did you find it, Ms. Greene?"

I can tell she's smiling, even though I'm not looking at her obnoxiously beautiful face.

Where is it? I know I sent it!

Then I remember…I hadn't finished typing the message to her when my mom called. I look in my "drafts" folder and sure enough, there it is. *Shit!* I hate being wrong, particularly where Mega Slut is concerned.

I take a deep breath. Apologizing to her is going to take a lot out of me.

"I'm sorry, Ms. Hamilton. Seems I got distracted and never sent it. It's here in my drafts. I'll send it right now."

She doesn't say a word to me. Her horrible face says it all. This lady is happily recording every mistake I make.

You hateful bitch!

I slump in my seat as she walks away. Andrew reprimanded her for being mean to me, but if she starts reporting all my shortcomings to him, maybe he'll start second guessing his decision.

Oh, my life.

No time to contemplate my tired existence at the moment. I have some ridiculously boring and unimportant work to do.

CHAPTER 6

I take a second glance at my favorite Elvis clock, hoping my eyes are deceiving me. It's already nine o'clock? Unbelievable.

I look back at my computer. I have at least another few hours or so before I'm finished. Tears spring to my eyes yet again. Why am I doing this? This is NOT my job!

I start silently cursing Bitchface and all of her unfortunate fabulousness.

And Andrew likes her. A lot.

Sure, I know for a fact he was upset with the way she treated me, but of course he still likes her. He lets her call him "Andy". Gag me.

I pull a tissue from my purse to wipe my eyes. I've cried so much today, I realize I must look like death, so I take out my compact as well to check my face. Yikes. Worse than death.

I toss the mirror back into my bag and lay my head on my desk. What does it matter? I have no one to look nice for anyway. I have no life.

My phone ringing saves me momentarily from my downward spiral.

"Hello?" I sniff.

"Jules? You okay?" It's Abby. She sounds pissed...*again*.

"I'm fine." I don't even care if she knows I've been crying. "What's up?"

"Please tell me you're not still at work." She's furious. I'm unaffected.

"Okay, what do you prefer I tell you?"

"I would *prefer* you tell me you're leaving right this moment and coming to meet me and some friends at Copeland's." Abby pauses, waiting for my response, but I have nothing to say. "So, are you leaving, or shall we come pick you up?"

I sigh, so tired of this argument. "You know I can't," I say quietly. I don't have the energy for this. "Don't be mad at me, okay?"

Abby sighs too. "Jules, what are you doing? I can't believe---"

I cut her off and quick.

"Enough," I growl. "Abby, I'm tired, okay? I've had about negative ten hours of sleep total this week, and it looks like I'll be lucky if I get a couple tonight. But the longer I stay on the phone with you, arguing about the same thing for the millionth time, the slimmer my chances of sleeping become." I pause, but it seems I've rendered her speechless with my rant. Good. "Now, you guys have a fabulous time. I'll hopefully see you tomorrow and I promise you that tomorrow, I'll be knee-walking drunk within a half hour of me leaving this office."

With that, I hang up. I feel momentarily bad for yelling at my dear friend, but I have nothing more to say.

I look back at my computer and continue with the monotonous task of organizing and researching the attendee list for my new favorite person.

I'm nearly foaming at the mouth with disdain for my new so-called boss when I hear a crash coming from the lobby. Maybe near the elevators? It sounded like glass breaking. This can't be good.

I hurriedly reach into my purse and grab my mace – singing my lousy dad's praises for making me carry it – and start walking toward the lobby.

In my brief moment of panic, I have no idea what to do. Security's in the office, so should I dial them? If it's someone getting off the elevators, then they would have to have seen him or her. Surely they know someone is coming up here, so they'll be here any minute, right? Or maybe it *is* security?

I think about turning back to go for the phone. Instead my curiosity gets the best of me, which I realize is obviously some form of insanity caused by a mix of sleep deprivation and having to put up with my new bitchy boss lady.

I arrive at the lobby and stand up straight, armed with my police-grade mace, and aim it toward the door. Whomever, or whatever, made the crashing sound is definitely headed my way. I can see a silhouette through the smoky glass windows in our lobby.

My heart's racing. It's only been seconds since I heard the noise, but I've been through a swirl of emotions, and now my fight or flight instinct is leaning more toward the "flight" side, as the silhouette gets closer.

I hear a throat clear, and I nearly jump out of my skin. It's male, definitely male.

I'm standing there, poised and ready to spray, when my attacker finally reaches the lobby.

Wait, the door is locked. Oh, thank heavens.

Then I hear someone fumbling around with some keys in the lock. They have a key? Who would be coming in this late?

I think for a minute about spraying the second the doors open, but what if it *is* someone who works here, or a security guard doing a routine check? Instead, I simply brace myself, close one eye and hope for the best.

Needless to say, I'm a little shocked when my assailant stumbles into the lobby and nearly falls on his face as he trips over the posh Oriental rug.

Andrew? Is he drunk?

"Mr. Mercer? Are you okay?" Putting the mace in my skirt pocket, I run over to him, but he rights himself as soon as he hears my voice.

"Ms. Greene," he seems very confused, understandably. "You're here," he says, sounding rather...*relieved*?

He's trying not to slur his speech, but he's not succeeding. Normally, this would be a most pitiful sight – a grown man, completely obliterated, void of all control, helpless and alone. But somehow, Andrew still looks like a demi-God. His tall, lean body is dressed in dark jeans, a navy blue t-shirt, a gray hoodie and Nikes. His thick, wavy hair is an adorable mess, like someone's been running their fingers through it. I'm instantly jealous of those fingers.

I've never seen him this casual before. How can he look just as good in this outfit as he does in a three-piece suit – even better really, in my opinion?

I regain my composure, after ogling him for a second. Hopefully, he won't remember my lingering stare tomorrow.

"Y-Yes, I had to finish up the party list, sir," I stutter. "Do you need anything?" I immediately fall into my assistant role, as I try to assess the situation.

Andrew looks over at me then and his face is sad, but to my surprise his eyes are wistful and full of something resembling longing. It's the kind of look that could set my undies on fire, but at the same time, shatter my heart into a million tiny pieces.

I wait for a reply, but he doesn't say anything. After our awkward exchange, he just stumbles down the short hallway toward his office and shuts his door.

I stare at his office door, mouth agape. What in the hell just happened?

I slowly walk back toward my desk and sit down. I stare, still open-mouthed, at my computer. The screen saver has come on, and I watch the company logo bounce around for a bit as I clear my head.

What was with that *look*? That look he gave me was horrible and wonderful at the same time.

I've never seen him that vulnerable before. This is the same man that slashed nearly thirty percent of his workforce last year without blinking an eye – the same man that brings grown men to their knees with nothing more than a firm fist pound on a conference table.

Now he's drunk, dressed in jeans and sneakers and probably comatose in his office.

What. The. Hell?

I sneak a glance over to his office. He never turned the light on, which confirms my suspicions that he's probably passed out on his sofa.

I look back at my computer again. There's no way I can work now. I pull out my phone and see have five texts from Abby. I scroll through them quickly, rolling my eyes. They're all apologies for our conversation tonight, when I should be the one apologizing. I'll deal with that later.

It's now nine-thirty, and I have several more hours before I finish this report for the night. I quickly start thinking of possible solutions.

I could take it home and finish, but I shrug that idea off immediately. It's been a constant party at my place this week. Abby's had a few college friends in town visiting, which is why I've been working in the office so late all week instead of at home in the first place. But she's currently not home, so maybe that will work?

Or I could just come in early tomorrow and finish, but what if Andrew's still here? Surely, he wouldn't sleep in the office. Or does he do this often?

Okay, I need to figure something out quickly.

Think, Jules!

I close my eyes and take a deep breath. It's been a long day, and after what I just saw, I can't seem to concentrate. I sit for at least eight hours a day with that man in his office next to me, but this is different.

I finally decide to pack up and take the work home. I can hopefully get some work done before Abby gets home with whatever riffraff will be crashing in our living room this evening.

I finish packing up, and realize I should probably run to the ladies room before I leave. When I finally make it to the restroom, I'm frightened by myself in the mirror. I cringe, thinking about my recent encounter with the love of my life.

Oh dear God.

No wonder he looked at me like that. The longing I thought I saw was longing alright – longing for me to get the hell out of his sight looking like this!

I quickly try to fix my face, just in case he's up and moving about when I leave. My deeply rooted insecurities will not allow me to look like this in front of him.

My eye make-up is all but gone from crying, which I can't do anything about. So I put some lipstick on my cheeks for a bit of color, add a little powder, some lip-gloss and that's as good as it's gonna get. I look at myself and sigh. It doesn't matter anyway.

I tiptoe out of the bathroom, until I realize I'm being a moron, so I start walking like a normal person. There's no sign of Andrew. All is quiet in the lobby and the light is still off in his office.

I grab my laptop bag at my desk and start to walk back toward the lobby door, but I can't make myself walk through it. I have to know he's okay. I'll just go peek into his office. Maybe he needs a blanket.

I put my bags back at my desk and start tiptoeing again – like an idiot – toward his office.

Just breathe, Jules. Breathe.

I close my eyes and take a couple of deep breaths. I remind myself he has no idea I have feelings for him, so I can just act normally. Although it's hard to act normal around that kind of perfection, I do my best.

I try to see in his office through the narrow pane of glass by his door, but it's too dark. I decide I better knock before I enter, so I knock lightly, in case he's asleep.

I wait for a few seconds but hear nothing. Maybe he left when I was in the bathroom? I knock quietly again, and after a minute or so, I still hear nothing.

I think about leaving but my OCD, along with my overwhelming need to take care of this man, keeps me standing in front of his office door. With trembling hands, I try the handle and it's unlocked.

I open the door just a crack – again not wanting to wake him, but I still can't see anything. I open the door a bit more, and I can finally make out his sofa, but he's not on it. I look over to his office chair and he's not there either.

He has a private bathroom, so maybe he's in there? I'm so torn! Do I continue to invade this poor man's privacy, or do I just mind my business and go home?

While I'm contemplating, I hear something. My eyes dart around his office, as I open the door further. It's a little over half way open now, and my eyes are adjusting to the dark. Finally, I see him sitting in the corner, knees up and head down, in the back of his office.

I can't believe what I'm seeing. I'm witnessing one of the strongest men I've ever known cowering in the corner like a little child. And to top it off, I think he's crying.

Oh, Andrew.

Without hesitating, I walk over and sit down on my knees in front of him. I don't say a word, and he doesn't look up at me, although I'm sure he knows I'm here.

Now that I'm closer, I can see he's removed his sweatshirt along with his shoes and socks. Maybe he was trying to sleep but couldn't. What could've possibly happened? Tears come to my eyes yet again, but I stop them immediately. I need to be strong here, even though it's painful to see him like this.

I slowly reach my hand toward the top of his beautiful head. My heart's racing, wondering if he'll push me away or throw me out of his office, but at the moment I don't care. I just need to make him feel better. I need to make him strong again – for him and for me. I inhale as I place my hand in his hair.

Please don't push me away, Andrew. Please let me be here for you.

Andrew jumps when I touch him. I thought he knew I was here, but maybe I was wrong.

When he looks up at me, I instantly drop my hand and lean back a little. Not only am I afraid that he'll literally push me out of his office, but the look on his face is like an arrow through my heart. Forget slowly breaking into a million pieces, my heart just exploded violently in sadness.

"Mr. Mercer?" My voice is a whisper. I don't want to upset him further. "I was just leaving, and I wanted to make sure…" I'm feeling embarrassed now, like I'm seeing something I shouldn't be seeing. "I just wanted to make sure you were okay."

I wince and look down. I shouldn't have touched him. I've longed to run my fingers through his silky brown hair, but not this way. It was inappropriate. Suddenly my nerves kick up. Am I going to get fired?

When I don't hear a response, I dare a look back up at him. He's now leaned back against the wall, his hands over his eyes. I have to remind myself how drunk he is. He's not in his right mind, and I should leave him be. Hopefully, he won't remember the head touch in the morning.

"Good night, Mr. Mercer," I say as I stand. "I'll see you tomorrow."

I feel so ridiculous. I would run out of his office if I knew for sure he wouldn't remember any of this.

I'm nearly at his office door, within feet of my escape, when I hear, "Wait." I stop immediately in my tracks. "Don't go," he adds and I sigh.

His voice is husky and full of grief, but still the most beautiful sound in my world.

I turn slowly back to him, and he's staring at me with squinted eyes from his corner. I decide to try and keep it professional.

"Yes, sir? Would you like some water? Coffee maybe?"

There's an excruciating pause before he speaks again. I hold my position by his office door.

"No," he finally says, as he gets up and slowly stumbles his way to his sofa. "No, thanks."

I feel my cheeks flush as I watch him. He's so beautiful, even in this horrible state. I silently curse myself for the millionth time for loving him so much.

I watch as he basically falls into his plush leather sofa. He sits and places his elbows on his knees, his gorgeous face in his hands again.

I stand for a moment longer, waiting for him to say something more, but he never does.

In another moment of blind courage – or insanity, the verdict is still out – I move toward him once again. "Mr. Mercer? Sir?" I'm not even sure if he's still awake.

I'm standing in front of him now, only inches away, between him and the coffee table. I'm about to reach out and touch his shoulder, to see if he's still alive, when he looks up at me.

It's the same sad, pain-filled look he gave me a moment ago when I was sitting in front of him in the corner, and it's just as horrible to witness now as it was then. I quickly draw my hand back, trying to avoid a repeat of my inappropriate behavior from earlier.

Andrew watches my hand with rapt attention as it moves back to my side, and to my sheer disbelief, he reaches for it. I don't move an inch. My heart suddenly kicks into hyper speed and I have to concentrate very hard on not panting.

Andrew moves his hand slowly toward mine, a scowl on his face as he watches, like he has no control over his movements – like his hand has a mind of its own.

I continue to stay perfectly still, watching him, until his hand finally reaches mine. He lifts my now quivering hand to his face and places my palm on his cheek. He closes his eyes, and I shake my head in wonder. What is he *doing*?

I don't even get a chance to try and reason out what's happening. The next thing I know, he places his other arm around my waist and pulls my entire body toward him. He never looks up at me. His eyes are still closed, as he drops my hand from his face, puts both arms around me and hugs me close, his cheek resting on my stomach.

"Please stay with me," he whispers, and without hesitation, I put both of my arms around him.

"Sure," I whisper back, with one hand now slowly stroking his unkempt hair.

For so long, I've dreamt of this man touching me. He's grazed my fingers before while passing me paperwork. We've bumped into each other a couple of times in the hallway, and then today, when he offered his hand to me in the elevator lobby...even those slight touches send a thrill up my spine, stoking the always slow-burning fire inside me where he's concerned. I always thought that if he ever touched me the way he is now, I'd lose my ability to form coherent sentences and make a complete fool of myself.

But as I sit and hold this beautiful man in my arms, I'm not entirely surprised to find I feel more confident than ever.

I'm confident because this is what I do. I take care of people. I take care of him. Every day. And I love my job because of it. I will endure sixty-plus hour weeks until the end of time if it means I get to see his perfect face every day. He's my reason for waking up in the morning, and he's a damn good reason.

He suddenly pulls me tighter, and I feel the wetness from his cheek soaking into my blouse. I continue to gently run my fingers through his hair.

"It's okay," I whisper. "It's going to be okay."

I have no idea how long we stay locked together, but it's one of the best moments of my life. Too bad he probably won't remember it tomorrow.

Andrew's tears finally stop, and I feel his grip loosen, but he doesn't completely let me go. His eyes are closed, and he begins to sag against me. His breathing eventually starts to level and I smile when I realize he's asleep.

I unlock his arms from around my waist and slowly lay him down. It's no easy task, as he's nearly twice my size, but I somehow manage.

I go to retrieve his hoodie from the top of his desk and lay it over him. Then I take his drinking glass to his bathroom and clean it, before putting it and the whiskey bottle back in the cabinet.

I lean down over him and frown. I don't want to leave him. I know he'll never remember any of this, even though I want him to so badly.

Remember that time you were so sad and I comforted you? You needed me, Andrew. Remember?

I brush a piece of stray hair from his forehead before getting up and making my way to his door.

I lock it, just in case someone gets in early tomorrow. I wouldn't want anyone to see him like this. He could shower here, and no one would be the wiser. Maybe he stays here more often than I know. Is that why he always keeps a change of clothes here? I never thought of that.

I grab my bags and start toward the elevators. When I get there, I see what caused the crash I heard earlier. It seems Andrew dropped his whiskey bottle on his way in.

I sigh and head back inside. I lay my bags down in the break room and grab some cleaning supplies. I can't let anyone see this either, so I go back to the elevator lobby to sweep up the glass and clean up the spill. Now I smell like a bar, so I quickly wash my hands before leaving again.

As I ride down the elevator, I find that I'm smiling like a crazy person even though I just experienced a gut-wrenching moment with the man I love. Of course I feel awful for him, but I'll be living off that moment for a long time. He needed me. Not just for coffee or copies. He needed *me*. Deep down I know that in his drunken state, he probably would have settled for any warm body, but I'm going to pretend like he was looking for me. And I was there for him, just like I always will be.

Love me or not, Andrew Mercer. My heart will forever belong to you.

CHAPTER 7

Ouch!

I wince as I draw my hand back. I just smacked my alarm clock so hard I actually hurt my hand. Brilliant.

I stumble out of bed, my head foggy from another long night with zero sleep, but I'm feeling surprisingly well this morning. The reason? Andrew, of course.

In the morning light, what happened last night at the office seems very dream-like, but even with my clouded, sleep-deprived brain, I know it wasn't. I remember the way his arms felt around my waist with astounding clarity.

My roommate and her obnoxious friends came crashing in about an hour after I got home last night, and because I'm such a weakling, I let them talk me into a last call game of quarters.

Smooth move, Jules.

Now, I'm paying for it with a bit of a hangover, but nothing a little Andrew Mercer can't cure. I swear that man cures anything that ails me.

I eventually make it to my bathroom and fumble around with the shower until I get the water a decent temperature. I probably need a cold one to wake me up, but I opt for my preferable scalding hot version.

Despite my surprisingly good mood, I feel another panic attack coming on while I'm in the shower. They kept waking me up last night as well, regardless of the several shots I consumed during our late night quarters shenanigans.

What if he remembers?

What will I say to him?

And what was *wrong* with him last night?

I try not to let the panic set in, and let my favorite mint shampoo help wash away my worries instead, as I fall easily into my usual morning daydream about Andrew. I wonder what he'll be wearing today. I hope it's the tan suit. He hasn't worn it in a while, and it's so *springtime*. It looks amazing with his hazel eyes.

I finish in the shower and head for my closet. I hate trying to find something to wear. I'm in serious need of some shopping, but with trying to save up for my trip I just haven't had the money. And with the new boss lady at work, I haven't had the time.

I sigh, as I pull on my old faithful black pencil skirt and a cream-colored sleeveless blouse. I grab a cardigan too, since it's always so freaking cold in the office.

I finish getting ready and head toward the kitchen. If one of Abby's friends has eaten the last of my bagels I'm going to cut somebody.

Lucky for the slumber party, there's one bagel left, so their lives will be spared. I pop it in the toaster and start packing up my computer mess from last night, carefully stepping over snoring bodies as I do.

I did manage to get some work done before getting drunk, but I didn't put anything away.

As I'm getting my stuff together, Abby staggers into the kitchen. What's she doing up?

"Morning," she says through a yawn. "Did you make coffee?"

I lovingly roll my eyes at her. "What does this look like? Mel's diner? Make your own damn coffee."

She narrows her eyes in my direction. "Are you still pissed at me about last night? You know I just don't approve of the way that shit-hole company treats you. I *am* proud of you for landing the picture-taking gig though. Good girl."

I smile at her. "I know, and I'm not still mad at you."

If only Abby knew about what else happened last night, but I can't tell her. I can't tell anyone.

The toaster dings, so I move back to the kitchen to add cream cheese to my bagel, before wrapping it in a paper towel.

"But this whole I'm-in-love-with-my-asshole-boss-but-he's-obviously-gay-since-he-hasn't-asked-me-out thing should really be addressed, you know?" Abby adds, and I smile again.

"Yes, dear," I say, as I gather my things.

"Don't mock me, young lady." Abby's shaking her finger at me, which makes me giggle. "I'm not afraid to ground you. I'll take away your laptop and Blackberry for a week! What will your precious Mr. Mercer do then? Huh?"

"Goodbye, Mom." I shake my head at her before opening the front door.

"Make sure to wear your seatbelt!" I hear her yell as I'm locking the door behind me. "And no fornicating on the copy machine!"

Okay, that was a good one.

I'm smiling now, as I make my way toward my car. It's raining out, which I didn't know about before I left. *Dammit.* It's not like me to be so unprepared. This shitty week, and the whole thing with Andrew last night, is wrecking my brain.

I have no umbrella, so I run quickly to my car. As usual, the running does absolutely nothing to keep me dry. Instead, it makes me a little sweaty and causes my feet to hurt from running in heels across the parking lot.

And unfortunately, nothing can save my hair in this kind of weather. The normally untamed curls turn to frizz, which is never attractive. I'm sorry I even spent any time at all trying to fix it this morning. I look into my purse for my hair band once I get settled in my car. A ponytail it is.

I make my way to the office, which is a slow go from the rain-traffic, but I still manage to get there ten minutes early.

My heart starts pounding as I enter the elevator. I'm usually the first one in the office every day, but not by much. Adrian is normally in around eight, and sometimes John from accounting comes in early, but he's on vacation this week.

What if Andrew's still here? Surely he went home. It's rare he's ever in the office this early. He's normally the last one to arrive, but I know for a fact he works from home in the mornings. I've gotten emails from him as early as four-thirty. Perhaps he's an insomniac.

I wouldn't mind learning more about his nocturnal habits. I wouldn't mind at all.

The elevator doors open, and I see that the lobby is still dark. My heart rate instantly slows. *Thank God.* He must have gone home.

I walk into the lobby, noticing the light is off in his office as well, and my heart continues its descent toward an acceptable rhythm.

I set down my things, turn on my computer and then make my way to the break room to start my normal routine.

When I come out of the break room, I notice the light is now on in Andrew's office. *Oh dear God.*

I walk quickly to Bitchface's office and do a half-hearted job at preparing her office for the day, before walking back to my desk.

What do I do? Did he just arrive? Or did he spend the night here after all?

I have no idea how to handle this situation. Add what happened last night to the mix, and my heart is once again approaching maximum velocity.

I start to fiddle around with things on my desk, trying to look busy while I think. I want him to remember. I honestly do. But even if he does, will he remember it in a positive light? Probably not. He's probably been spending all morning trying to decide how to explain his moment of drunken insanity.

Shit! What the hell am I going to *do*?

I take a deep breath and decide to leave him alone. I'll go knock in a few minutes, maybe after some other people have arrived. Surely he knows I'm here, so if he needs anything, he'll ask. He's never been afraid to bother me early in the morning before.

As if on cue, my instant messaging pops up on my computer.

Ms. Greene, may I have a word please?

Oh hell. Am I in trouble? Why do I always feel like I'm in trouble?

Yes sir.

It's hard to type because my hands are shaking. I stand up and smooth out my skirt.
Just act normal, Jules.
He was so wasted. There's no way he remembers last night, and even if he does, he'll most likely never bring it up. Right?
I walk slowly toward his office, but then remember how annoyed he gets when he has to wait, so I pick up the pace. I knock before opening his door.
"Come in," he says, and I wince. Seems his typical boss man demeanor is back now in full force.
I take another deep breath before I walk in, and then I have to take my usual sweet-heavens-he-is-so-beautiful pause before approaching his desk. Oh, what this man does to me.
He's not wearing his tan suit today. He's wearing the navy blue one with red pinstripes. It's my second favorite. Nothing beats the charcoal colored three-piece he wears with his garnet tie.
"Yes sir?" I say, as I finally reach his desk.
"I have a meeting today with Somerfield," he starts, and I'm instantly trying to decide if he remembers, but he hasn't looked at me since I walked in. "Do you have their paperwork ready?"
"Yes sir. I printed it yesterday for you. I planned to have it on your desk this morning, but..." I trail off, not wanting to

remind him of last night, still feeling like I may be in trouble.

"I didn't expect you in so early, sir."

He clears his throat and I notice his eyes flick briefly in my direction before looking back up at his computer screen.

He definitely remembers.

"I have a lot to do today," he says finally. "Please get the paperwork to me when you can."

"Yes sir. May I get your coffee?"

"Yes, please."

"Coming right up."

I turn to leave his office and smile on my way out. He remembers. I can feel it. And the fact that he remembers *and* he didn't immediately land me with the drunken insanity excuse, gives me hope.

"Hi Jules." Adrian is already pouring herself a cup of coffee in the break room. "What's Mr. Mercer doing in so early?"

Of course she's curious. This is an abnormality for sure.

"He's just really busy with the event tomorrow and the Somerfield deal," I say.

Your secret is safe with me, Andrew. No worries.

Adrian shrugs. "Let me know if you need anything further for his meeting today."

"Will do. Thanks Adrian."

Adrian smiles before she leaves. I quickly move to make Andrew his morning beverage of choice – coffee, black with two sugars.

I head quickly back to his office, my heart racing again as I near his door. I wonder if he'll mention last night, or will it remain a looming secret between the two of us forever? I'll never tell, of course, but I'm dying to know what he's thinking. But as I reach his door, my train of thought brings me back to the more pressing issue from last night. What the hell was *wrong* with him?

I flinch as the memory of his tormented face flashes across my mind. That face could have easily been the death of me. The idea of someone hurting him is unfathomable.

My stomach is churning now as I bring his coffee into his office. I grab the coaster from its spot on the coffee table and place it on top of his desk, before putting his cup of coffee on top.

"I'll be right back with the preparations for your meeting today, sir."

"Thank you, Ms. Greene."

He still hasn't looked at me. Maybe he doesn't remember. He's obviously not going to say anything, either way.

I should be relieved I guess, but now I can't seem to get his tortured face out of my head. I would really like to know what's bothering him. I'd like to help.

I feel ashamed for thinking my normal impure thoughts about him this morning. What happened between us last night is probably the least of his concerns.

At my desk, I quickly pull his paperwork together, along with his messages from yesterday afternoon, and copies of the *New York Times*, *Atlanta Business Chronicle* and *Wall Street Journal*.

I walk into his office, and he still doesn't look up. I place his meeting paperwork and messages in his Inbox, and then move to place the newspapers on his coffee table.

"Anything else, sir?" I ask before leaving, wishing he would at least look at me.

I would love to see those hazel eyes, and maybe a small, reassuring smile. Something to let me know he's okay? That *we're* okay? That wouldn't be too much to ask for, would it?

Please look at me, Andrew.

"That's all for now," he says, eyes focused on his computer screen. I slump slightly before walking out of his office.

Despite my desperate hopes, it seems nothing's changed between us. And if what happened last night doesn't change things, nothing will.

How could you be so stupid, Jules?

I'm not surprised to find I'm on the verge of tears as I reach his office door, but I stop suddenly at the sound of his voice.

"Ms. Greene? Wait."

It's not quite as sorrowful as last night, but a touch of the desperation is still there.

I slowly turn to face him, making sure first that my tears are going to stay put.

"Yes sir?" I finally manage, as my heart tries to pound its way straight out of my chest.

Just keep this professional, Jules.

Finally, he looks up at me, and I'm momentarily lost in those gorgeous eyes. They look light blue today in his navy suit. Breathtaking.

"Ms. Greene, I just wanted to say..." He's uncomfortable, which is not something you see every day. I have to try hard not to smile. "I just wanted to say...about last night...."

Oh God, he's adorable. Absolutely adorable. And his awkward nervousness is somehow putting me at ease.

"It's no problem," I interject, putting him out of his misery. "I promise to keep everything to myself, sir. Please don't worry."

Andrew, I love you with everything I am, and I'm always here if you need me.

I watch as he sighs and his broad shoulders visibly relax. He looks down and then stares back up at me through those luscious lashes.

Keep breathing, Jules. Keep breathing.

"Thank you," he mouths, and I nearly come undone.

I say nothing. That look rendered me incapable of speech. I simply smile, nod and turn quickly, trying again not to sprint out of his office.

I glance back at him as I open his door, and I'm shocked to find he's still staring at me. I immediately look away, embarrassed I got caught.

What just happened? And what exactly was that "thank you" for anyway? Was he thanking me for being there last night or for keeping his secret? With that look to accompany it, it was hard to tell.

I stumble back over to my desk in a daze, as I remember the way those extraordinary eyes nearly penetrated my soul. *Good gracious.*

"Jules, you want to do lunch today?" I hear Adrian's voice, but it takes me a second to realize she's talking to me. "Are you okay, Jules?"

I look over at her before almost falling into my chair. "Fine," I try to assure her. "Totally fine."

Adrian smiles at me. "So, lunch then?"

"Right!" I smile back, slowly regaining my composure. "Sorry about that. Ummm, yeah. I can do lunch." I remember then I have to pick up lunch today for Andrew. "Can we go to Ruby's though? Mr. Mercer requested lunch from there today for his Somerfield meeting."

"Ruby's sounds great. Around eleven-thirty would be good?"

"That's perfect."

I do like Adrian. She's always in a good mood, and I'm thinking I could use a little more positive energy in my life.

I turn to my computer then and start on the arduous task ahead of me. I'll definitely be glad when this stupid event is over. This attendee list has put me so far behind with some of my other projects. I'm going to have to work late for the next six months to catch up.

The next thing I know, Adrian's at my desk. "Ready?" she asks when I look up at her.

I glance at my Elvis clock. Lunchtime already?

I hold a finger up asking her for one more minute. "Let me tell Mr. Mercer I'm leaving."

I press my ear to the door, but don't hear anything. Assuming he's not on the phone, I go ahead and knock.

"Yes?" he answers, so I open the door.

"Just leaving to grab lunch," I tell him from the doorway. "Do you need anything before I go?"

All I can think about when I see him is what happened last night. I hope that goes away. Soon. This is not good for our working relationship.

"No, thank you," he says, without looking up at me from his desk. I guess our moment from earlier has officially passed.

I don't say anything further. I just close the door and walk toward Adrian.

"Everything okay?" she asks, obviously reading my confused expression.

I quickly put a smile on. "Totally fine," I tell her. "Let's move."

CHAPTER 8

As promised, I meet Abby at Marlow's for drinks after work.

"So, shall we start with a couple of shots?" Abby asks. "I've been playing around with some recipes. I think I have one you'll like."

"Surprise me." I try to seem enthusiastic so I don't squash her excitement, when truthfully, I'm not overly interested in drinking tonight.

What's going on with me? I feel like an old lady.

Abby decided on Marlow's so we could drink for free. Her boss is completely in love with her, which is unfortunate, since he's married with two kids. Even Abby has standards, so she would never go there, but she gladly takes advantage of the free drinks.

"So, are you excited about tomorrow?" she asks as we choke down her first concoction. My tongue feels kind of numb afterward. That can't be good.

"I guess," I say, as I try not to worry about my picture-taking duties tomorrow. As if being in charge of the event wasn't enough.

"Elizabeth will be there to help, right?" Abby sees the worry in my face.

"Yeah, and she's great, so I'm sure things will be fine."

Elizabeth is our VP of Marketing. We used to have an event coordinator, but she got cut last year, so somehow this event fell on me. I don't mind. I actually like event planning, but it's undoubtedly stressful.

"So, what else is new?"

I sigh. "I have to visit my parents' house on Sunday."

Abby signals the bartender on duty for another shot. "I'm sorry. Mom on another bender?"

"Unfortunately, it seems she hasn't been off of one in a while."

"I really am sorry. Will your dad be there?"

Abby's known me long enough to understand a little about how my family works. It's not pleasant. It never is.

"I'm not sure. I'm just going to appease my mom."

"Maybe you can talk some sense into her." Abby tries to look hopeful, but it falls a bit short. "You've been successful before."

"True," I admit. "I've been able to get her into rehab, but no one can figure out how to keep her there."

"Damn pacifists. Screw that 'you have to want the help' nonsense. Addicts shouldn't have rights."

"I agree," I say, smiling.

"Do you want me to go with you?"

"No, thanks." Abby really is a good friend. "It will probably just be mom and me. I'm sure my dad will be off with Rebecca...oh, I mean, *working*."

Abby laughs. "I'm a little offended he's never hit on me, you know? Is it just his assistants he goes after? Is he hiring?"

"Gross." I smack her playfully. "You have no pride."

"No, I do not," Abby agrees, as she scopes the bar. "Speaking of...slim pickings tonight."

"Because this place is a dump."

Abby looks offended. "No, it's because it's happy hour, and only the lushy drunks show up for happy hour."

"Cheers!" I say, as Abby and I take down our third shot. "Does your tongue feel numb?"

"Yeah, I was afraid of that." Abby looks quizzically at her glass. "What the hell's in this stuff?"

"No worries friend, no worries." Abby brushes me off with a smile. "So, what's up with your love life? Do you only have eyes for your gay boss, or can I interest you in some other selections?"

I smile at even the thought of Andrew. "Although it's incredibly tragic, I only have eyes for one at the moment."

Abby looks disgusted. "A wretched tragedy, indeed."

"Did you have someone in mind?" I ask. Just curious.

Abby cocks an eyebrow. "Perhaps. Interested, are you?"

"Tell me who it is."

"I met him here, actually. Very nice. Owns his own bookstore downtown. His name is Nate. You'd love him."

"What does he look like?"

"Seriously? You're so into vanity now. What's that company doing to you?"

I hit Abby again, a little harder this time.

"Like I would set you up with a mutt? He's a hottie. Trust me," Abby says, as she rubs her arm. Oops. "He's twenty-eight, with an English degree. You should give him a shot."

I sigh. I can't do it. It wouldn't be fair to the Nate guy.

"I can't." I shake my head. "I'm hopelessly devoted."

Abby rolls her eyes. "If it hasn't happened yet, it's not going to happen, Jules."

I gasp. How can she say that to me? I have to bite back tears.
Abby, how could you?
But she's right.
"I know." I sigh. "I wish I felt differently, but the man has me wrapped."
"Well then, it won't hurt anything for you to go out on one little date, will it? If you hate the new guy, which I'm positive you won't, you always have your precious Andrew to run back to."
Abby's pissing me off. Maybe it's the strange shots we've been consuming.
"Why hate on him, Abby? You don't even know Andrew."
Abby looks at me in disbelief. "I don't have to know him." Her voice is slowly rising. "When you started that shitty job, you used to cry every day for months because of that asshole. And then you end up falling in love with said asshole, who for some ungodly reason doesn't love you back. I could know nothing about Andrew Mercer, and those things alone would be enough to make me hate him."
Touché, my friend. Touché.
"And," Abby continues, "that job's keeping you from the one thing that ever meant anything to you. You're staying there for him, Jules. That's kind of sad."
Okay, that's enough.
"For starters, Andrew has treated me fine after the day I told him off in his office," I quickly remind her.
I demanded his respect, and I got it. I wish his love came with it, but unfortunately, that remains one-sided.

"And I didn't quit photography because I wanted to or because of Andrew," I continue. "No one liked my work, Abby. Not one person."

Once again, I'm fighting back tears. How did we get on such a sad subject?

"That's not true and you know it!" I think something bad is in these drinks. Abby seems overly aggressive. "You only gave it one shot, Jules! One shot, and you gave up!"

Tequila maybe? I'm starting to feel rather angry too.

"Look, you're one to talk about giving it a shot. At least I tried. What have you done? I haven't seen a paintbrush in your hands for quite some time."

Abby looks hurt, and now I feel awful. What's this about?

"I'm sorry," I say. "That wasn't fair."

Abby sighs. "It's okay. We both have issues."

"True." I smile at her. Abby's literally impossible to stay mad at. "Friends?"

"Of course!" she says with a smile, before leaning across the table and planting a wet kiss on my cheek. "How about another round?"

CHAPTER 9

Oh my, oh my, oh my.
My nerves have peaked. Today's the day. And I'm running late.
Abby and I ended up staying way past happy hour last night, which was a horrible mistake on my part. In return, I feel bloated and sluggish with huge bags under my eyes and a pounding headache.
I'm speeding down I-75, hoping I have everything I need. I planned to get to the Mercer Estate a few hours before the party starts, but even at this speed, I'll be at least an hour behind my planned schedule.
I emailed Andrew this morning to let him know I would be a little later than planned. I lied and told him I was doing some last minute confirmations, when I was actually lying in bed, trying to get the room to stop spinning.
"Julia Greene with Mercer Construction," I say into the little box when I finally reach the front gate.
No one says anything back to me. With a beep, the gate opens. I pull down the long drive and eventually reach the turn around. I'm happy to see the valet company is already here. I give the guy my keys, and watch as he boldly appraises me top to bottom before throwing a rather unappreciative look toward my beat-up BMW. I take my ticket and scowl at him.
She may be old and run down, but she's mine!

"May I get someone to help with my things?" I ask sweetly, keeping my temper reeled in, while making a mental note to complain to the valet company about their unprofessional employees.

All three valets hop to attention, but I quickly move to grab my camera bag, afraid to let it out of my sight. It's cost me a fortune over the years as I've upgraded, added lenses, etc. It's like my child, and I'm rather protective of my baby.

"Jules? Is that you?"

Elizabeth finds me unloading near the front door. She's our VP of Marketing, and I've been enjoying working closely with her on this event. She's very nice and has been so grateful for my help, since our event coordinator was laid off last year.

"Sorry I'm late," I tell her as she hugs me.

"No worries at all! Looks like you were on top of things. I think all we're waiting on are the people to bring the tables and chairs."

"Right. Those guys were doing a wedding this morning, so I knew they'd be a bit late." I look at my watch. "They should be here in about thirty minutes."

"Then we're all set!" Elizabeth looks so proud of me. It's such a nice feeling.

Elizabeth helps me and the valet guys carry my things, as we make our way toward the garden. The French doors are already open to the patio outback, and the view is breathtaking. The Mercer estate is everything you would think it should be – oversized, pretentious and museum-like, on lakefront property, complete with mail order swans meddling around some severely ostentatious fountains.

I haven't seen Andrew yet, but that doesn't surprise me. Knowing Andrew, he's probably somewhere working.

Elizabeth leaves me to go speak to Mercer Senior, so I take a seat on one of the stone steps leading down from the patio and open up my small box of files filled with all of the vendor contacts and the background information for the attendees. Now that the painkillers are finally starting to kick in, I want to go quickly through my vendor list to make sure everything is in order.

"Good morning, Ms. Greene."

I turn to find a gorgeous Andrew staring down at me. He's wearing his tan suit. I love that suit.

"Morning, sir." I quickly stand to meet him.

"Everything looks like it's going as planned, Ms. Greene. Are you all set to take some pictures?"

I gesture to my camera bag at my feet. "All set," I say, but I notice Andrew seems upset about something. "Are you okay, sir?" I decide to pry.

"I'm fine," he says, but it feels more like a question.

Is he asking me if he's *fine*? Well...

"Please let me know if there's anything I can do. I'm just going to quickly run through this vendor list to make sure everyone has what they need."

"Sounds good. Thank you, Ms. Greene."

I smile, but he turns and walks away from me so fast I'm not sure he saw it.

That was weird. I wonder what's going on with him.

I'm about to sit back down when another voice sounds behind me.

"Good morning, Ms. Greene."

Oh great. It's way too early for this.

"Good morning, Mr. Mercer." I turn to find scary Mercer Senior, with my favorite person locked and loaded on his left.

She's wearing pale pink, which is an awful color for her skin tone. She'll look all washed out in pictures. The thought makes me smile.

"May I assume everything is in order?" He's so condescending. No wonder he and Bitchface get along so well.

I can tell Mercer Senior was probably a good looking man at one time, but not anymore. He's tall, like Andrew, but other than that, they look nothing alike. Mercer Senior has powder white hair, icy blue eyes and a face that looks like it was carved from creamed cheese. There's always a sinister, half smile plastered on his thin lips, and his overall demeanor makes me crave disinfectant. I have no idea how Andrew came from that man's loins. He must be 99.99 percent his mother's son.

"Yes sir." I try and give the terrible twosome a genuine smile, but man, it's hard. "The tables and chairs should be here any minute," I tell him. "Other than that, we are all set."

"Let's hope they make it. How awful would that be, if we had no seats?" Bitchface rather gleefully remarks.

I seriously hate her. That's right. I *hate* her.

Mercer Senior smiles at her pitiful attempt at a put-down, like it was the best line he's ever heard. Gross.

"I'm sure everything will work out perfectly," I assure them once again, but Mercer Senior just gives me a questionable smile.

"Let's hope so," he says, "for your sake."

I try not to gape as they both walk away from me. Great. As if I needed a little more pressure today.

Eventually, I shake off his asshole comment and take my perch once again on the steps. As I move to look through my files, a bad feeling comes over me. Something about bitchy boss lady's face was excessively evil today. Wait a minute...

I quickly find the number and make a call to the vendor bringing the tables and chairs. Sure enough, someone called and told them the party was starting at three o'clock, instead of noon.

I can't believe it! That bitch is trying to sabotage me!

I hastily apologize for the confusion, and lucky for me, the chair vendor is still able to show up within the hour. Crisis averted, but now I'm worried about everything else.

I pick up my Pendaflex file containing all the vendor contracts and agreements and start making my rounds.

After about forty-five minutes of checking, it looks like she only messed with the one vendor. *Evil slut!* Unfortunately, Andrew catches me still fuming.

"Is everything okay?" he asks, his face laced with concern and still a touch of the same anxiety that was there before.

"Fine," I huff, before putting on my fake smile. "Everything's totally fine. I just wanted to do a last minute check, but everything seems to be fine."

How many times am I going to say 'fine'?

Breathe, Jules.

Andrew smiles at me. *Yum.* That works to help take my mind off The Evil One, if only for a moment.

"You've done a great job, Ms. Greene, as usual. Thank you."

"You're welcome, sir."

Andrew turns to leave me again, and I move to return to the stairs. A quick glance at my watch tells me I need to start moving my things. We only have about an hour until the guests start arriving, and the table and chairs should be here any minute.

I pick up my file box and camera bag and head inside. Where do I put my things? I remember seeing a study toward the front of the house when I did the tour. Surely that won't be open to the public.

I move toward the door, and it's closed, but luckily unlocked. I drop my box and camera bag in the corner by the door, and I get out the items I need for my camera. I decide on my large zoom lens, so I don't have to get too close and bother anyone.

I put my camera around my neck, add a fresh coat of lip-gloss and head out the door.

I can barely believe I nearly ram into Andrew, yet again, as I exit the study. He's as startled as I am.

"Ms. Greene? I'm so sorry."

"I-It's okay," I stammer. I'm such a klutz. "I put my things in this room. Is that okay?"

"Totally fine." Andrew's flustered, and I don't think our near head-on collision is the sole reason. "Thank you again for today. Everything looks great."

"No problem sir." Now I feel awkward. "I better go see about the table and chairs vendor."

"Sure, sure." Okay, he's really flustered. "Do what you to have to do. I'll just…"

And with that, he walks away. Something's up. Andrew's acting really strange.

Is he nervous around me because of the other night? Is that what this is about? Oh God, I hope not. Maybe he wants to talk to me. He's kind of acting like he wants to tell me something. Should I talk to him?

No. No way. I'm not broaching that subject again unless forced. But could that be it? He wasn't acting this odd yesterday in the office.

Move on, Jules. This is none of your business.

I take the advice of my subconscious and make my way to the back patio again. I'm not there fifteen minutes when I see tables being brought out the double doors. I give them quick directions on where to set up, and they rush to get started, apologizing for the mix-up.

I follow the last set over to make sure they get the arrangement correct, and I see Bitchface standing with Mercer Senior under one of the awnings near the lake. I give her the least genuine smile possible, and the scowl on her face makes me so happy I could dance a jig.

Jules = 1, Bitchface = 0. Bring it on!

Guests start arriving shortly after the last table is set up. I immediately start making my rounds with my camera, snapping tons of shots. My confidence isn't what it used to be, so I want to make sure I have plenty of stuff to choose from.

I have the list of a few specific shots Andrew wanted in my pocket. I chose this dress specifically from Abby's closet for the pockets. I usually hate strapless, and flowers, but beggars can't be choosers.

I keep bringing out the list to look at it so I don't miss anything. Most of them are pretty straightforward. He wants me to concentrate a lot on his dad, which makes sense. That's what the papers will want to see most. It's the second person of interest I'm not too thrilled about. Bitchety-Bitchface. Super. I take comfort in knowing she'll look like hell on camera in that pink suit. Plus, I made it a point to catch her at horrible angles, and in not-so favorable positions – eating, slouching, etc. I'm pretty proud of my work so far.

Even though he didn't ask specifically for any shots of himself, I can't resist. Andrew looks amazing today, and as the party goes on, I notice he seems to lose the nervous jitters he had this morning. I watch, mesmerized, as some of the guests start to fall for the Andrew charm. I can't blame them. It happens to the best of us.

I pause and take a seat on a bench away from the party to take a look at some of my shots when the party has about an hour to go. Yikes. I took more pictures of Andrew than I thought.

I double check Andrew's list. I think I did a good job, and I still have an hour left. *Whew.* Now I can relax a bit.

"I'll need to approve any photos you send to the media."

Mercer Senior startles me as he seemingly appears out of thin air. God, he's so creepy.

"Absolutely, sir," I assure him, but Andrew specifically directed me to show him the photos first.

And I listen to Andrew. Sorry, Mercer Senior.

Mercer Senior looks me critically up and down. Yuck. Now, I need a shower. "Are you having a good time then, Ms. Greene?"

"Yes sir. I think everything turned out well. The guests seem to be having a good time, and you have a very beautiful home."

"Oh, well, thank you." Mercer Senior loves compliments. "I think today has been a success indeed." Something about the smile on his face is just not right. It's a little more evil than normal. That can't be good.

"Well, I better get back to my picture taking," I say, standing and holding up my camera.

"Yes, I'm sure my son is paying you a pretty penny for your work. I hope it's worth it."

Wow. Unbelievable.

"Yes sir. I'm sure he'll be pleased." I'm surprised to find I'm trying to fight back tears.

Good grief. I need some freaking sleep!

"I do hope so," he says, with another sinister smile, and walks off. Bastard.

I try to shake off Mercer Senior before returning to the party. As I start making my way back to the crowd, I see Andrew coming toward me from the house.

"Ms. Greene?" he yells, trying to get my attention.

I start walking quickly toward him. "Yes sir?" I say as I approach him. "Did you need something?"

He's smiling at me again. "No, I was just looking for you." *For me? Really?* "Did you get some good shots?"

Oh, he wants to inquire about the photos. Of course he does.

"Yes sir. I think so. I just took a minute to go through them to make sure I had some good ones."

"Great. We can review everything on Monday."

"Yes sir." I'm happy to see Andrew seems to be feeling a little better.

"I hope you've enjoyed the picture taking. It's nice to see you in your element."

Ummm...*what*?

"I've enjoyed it very much. Thank you, sir," I tell him, as I try and work out his last comment.

Did Andrew hire me because he wants me to start taking pictures again? Because he knows it makes me happy?

No. That can't be true. Me and my wishful thinking.

He continues to smile, as he walks away from me, back into the house. I start to move back toward the crowd, but I turn when I hear my name.

"Ms. Greene?"

It's Andrew. He's still smiling widely at me from the doorway.

"Sir?"

Andrew looks down, as if he's contemplating something, and then shakes his head and smiles before looking back up at me.

"Ms. Greene..." he pauses with a sigh, "I just wanted to say thank you again for today. Everything has turned out better than expected."

"No problem. You're very welcome."

I turn to walk away from him, but he calls to me again.

"One more thing."

I turn back to face him. Wait. Is he *blushing*?

"Yes?"

"I also wanted to tell you that..." he pauses again. He's definitely blushing. "I wanted to let you know that I think you look very beautiful today."

Oh. My. God.

Andrew smiles at me for a second longer, before finally turning away and walking back into the house.

I stare blankly after him, with a stupid grin, and manage to sit myself down on one of the steps. Andrew has never complimented me like that. Sure, he's complimented my work, but never my looks. Never, ever my looks.

I know I need to resume my picture taking, but I'm not sure I can walk. The compliment probably wouldn't have meant as much if he wasn't blushing. He was *blushing*! Andrew Mercer! Could he be any more appealing? I don't think so.

Shake it off, Jules.

I have to get back to work. It's nothing. He was just being nice.

But he was blushing!

Okay, enough. Must concentrate on work. Mercer Senior is right. With the check I get from the pictures today, my photography trip to Italy this fall is pretty much paid for.

Oh Andrew, how I love you so.

The next hour passes by in a flash. Most of the guests don't linger, except a few talking with Mercer Senior. It's the same group of sleazy-looking guys that have spent the majority of the day with him and Bitchface. I assume it's a big deal coming to fruition. I don't recall their faces from all of my research, but I honestly couldn't care less because Andrew thinks I look beautiful today! I'll pay Abby whatever she wants for this dress. It *will* be mine.

I clear up a few details with some of the vendors before making my way back to the study to get my things. Even though I went with flats today, my feet are killing me, and I'm absolutely exhausted.

"Great job today!" Elizabeth says as I pass her on my way in.

"Thanks." I smile, and give myself an imaginary pat on the back.

I actually pulled it off, even with that slutty ho's attempt at sabotaging me. I still managed to make it work. *Go, Jules!*

I'm smiling ear to ear as I approach the study. Once again, the door's shut, but not locked. I open the door and hope for a moment I can find Andrew again before I leave. Maybe he'll have another unexpected compliment for me!

Speaking of "unexpected", the site before my eyes as I enter the study is just that. Two people are making out in front of the desk. Even though her back's to me, I know immediately who the girl is from the yucky pink color of her suit. She has the other unfortunate person pushed up against the desk, her arms locked around his neck.

Even though I despise the woman with everything I am, I feel horrible for the interruption. Heaven be it for me to interrupt her closing one of her business deals.

The lovely couple breaks when they hear me enter. I try not to look as I grab my bag and file box from the corner. "I apologize," I say, as I get my bag on my shoulder. "Just getting my things."

Then I hear a snicker, which causes me to look in their direction – a decision I will surely regret for the rest of my life. Because the unfortunate man pushed up against the desk is Andrew.

CHAPTER 10

Move, Jules! Move!

I try, but I'm frozen – frozen in Hell.

All I can do is stare at Andrew for what feels like an eternity, and watch as his eyes widen with every passing second.

Oh Andrew. Say it isn't so. Not her. Please not her.

My not-so trusty fight or flight instincts kick-in, but my mind reacts before my feet.

Get the hell out of here, Jules!

That's all I want to do, but my feet just won't move.

I finally manage to pick up my file box and turn to walk out the door as quickly as possible. I have to get to my car immediately. I won't be able to hold my tears down for long.

No. No. No. Dear God, no.

The naïve little girl in me half expected Andrew to leave Bitchface behind and come after me. At least he could apologize for the unprofessionalism, but he never comes. I have to wait for my car from the valet for a good ten minutes, and Andrew never shows.

Hold it together, Jules. Never let them see you sweat.

But I'm just too tired. The tears have already started when the valet finally brings my car. Luckily, the ugly crying doesn't start until I pull out of the driveway.

How could he do that? No wonder he was acting so weird this afternoon. Maybe he was nervous about Victoria being there.

He must like her more than I thought. Maybe she hadn't returned his obvious affections until today.

The nice things he said to me earlier this afternoon now seem null and void. He'll never love me. How could he? Abby's right. He's not my type, and I'm certainly not his. The fact that he wants to hook up with Bitchface should probably make me think less of him, but I love him too much. I'm so pathetic.

The tears are flowing so hard by the time I reach my house, I can barely see. I wipe pointlessly at my eyes. It's no use. He loves her. The skanky ho. He loves the skanky ho.

I sit in my car for a few minutes, reluctant to go inside. I'm not ready to talk about this with Abby.

By the time the tears start to slow, I've been in my car for almost an hour. Maybe it was a nightmare. Maybe I'm sleepwalking. I'm tired enough that it could be a possibility.

I look down at my phone, which has been going off non-stop for the last half hour or so. I have a few missed calls and several text messages, all from Abby. What is she? My freaking mother?

Nothing from Andrew. Not one thing. I can't believe I actually expected him to attempt an explanation. He owes me nothing. It's his private life, and I'm his secretary. That's it. End of story. That's all I'll ever be.

I sit in the car for a few minutes more. My tears have stopped, but I'm sure that's not the last of them. I don't even bother to return Abby's texts, or any of her calls. All I want to do is go to my room and go to sleep – go to sleep and pretend like today never happened. But it did.

Andrew, how could you?

I open my car door. I need to make a move before I start crying again.

"Long day?" Abby asks as I walk in. I don't say a word.

"What the hell's wrong with you?" she asks, once she sees my face. "Holy shit, Jules. Are you okay?"

Do I look that bad? I feel that bad.

I keep on the path to my room, and as soon as I reach it, I slip off my shoes and crawl into bed. I don't even bother removing Abby's dress, which I now have zero affection for.

Lucky for me, Abby gets the idea, and doesn't say another word. She sits on the bed beside me, and starts running her fingers through my hair. I instantly start crying again.

The next thing I know, I'm waking up and it's dark out. How long did I sleep?

I look at my alarm clock, and I'm shocked to see it's four in the morning. *Good grief!* I've been asleep for almost twelve hours! I lie in my bed for a few minutes hoping to go back to sleep. But once the events from yesterday start trickling back in to my mind, I realize sleep isn't going to happen.

Plus, I'm still in this hideous dress, and it's not very comfortable.

First things first, I get up and find some more sensible pajamas. As I plunder through my drawer, I'm so happy to see my favorite gray sweatpants are clean. At least something good has happened in the last twenty-four hours.

I leave the flowery dress on my floor. It can rot there for all I care.

I try to walk quietly into the kitchen for some water. The floors in this old apartment are seriously noisy, and I don't want to wake up Abby. I wonder how long she stayed with me yesterday afternoon.

The water is cold and delicious. I sit at our tiny breakfast table and try not to think about yesterday, but it's impossible.

I don't really feel like crying any more, which is a good thing I guess. I actually feel kind of numb, but I know one thing for sure. I have to find a new job. Immediately.

"What are you doing up?" Abby asks through a yawn as she comes strolling into the living room.

I look at the clock on my laptop. "Better question is what are *you* doing up?"

It's nine o'clock, which is about three hours earlier than Abby's typical wake-up time.

She smiles at me. "I got a new job."

I nearly spit my water on my keyboard. "What?! When were you going to tell me about this?"

"I just started on Wednesday. It's at a new art museum on Highland."

I squeal in delight. I'm so proud of her!

"The guy that owns it teaches classes two nights a week," she tells me. "He agreed to let me attend the classes for free if I work a few days a week for him."

"Abby!" I feel like a proud mommy. "That's so amazing!"

"Thanks." Abby's smile is blinding. "A friend at the club told me about the opening, and I thought it was about time I get back to it. I miss it too much."

"Abby, you're a brilliant artist. Trust me when I say this is a step in the right direction."

"I knew you'd be happy." She smirks. "So, enough about me. What the hell happened to you yesterday?" She looks at my computer screen and frowns. "Uh-oh. That doesn't look good."

I never fell back asleep. I've been searching online for a new job since four this morning.

"Yeah. Well…" Am I ready to talk about this? Definitely not, but if anyone will understand, it will be Abby. "There was a bit of an incident at the event yesterday."

"Incident? Like you screwed something up?"

"Not really." How do I say it without crying again? "It seems Bitchface and Andrew…well it seems they are…ummm…" I can't even say it.

Thankfully, Abby can read my mind. "Oh God, Jules. No way."

I nod and bite my lower lip. My head hurts. I don't want to cry again.

"I'm so sorry," Abby says as she hugs me. "How do you know? Wait," she pulls away, "Do I want to know how you know?"

I shake my head. If I don't have to, I would rather not relive that moment ever again.

"Yuck. I'm so sorry girl." Abby's face is full of disgust, and I love her for it. "You're really going to quit?"

I bow my head. "I can't be around that, Abby. I can't."

"I understand," she says, grabbing my hand. "They don't deserve you any way, but you need to stick around until you get that check from your photography job. He at least owes you that. Stupid asshole."

I look up and manage a sad smile. "I just feel so stupid," I admit. "I was even stupid enough to think he would run after me, or call, or email, or something. I thought he would try…that he would want to explain."

"And nothing?"

"Nothing." I shake my head and feel a tear roll down my cheek.

"You don't need him, Jules. I know you love him, and it may take a while, but you *will* recover. To hell with them and their ivory tower. "

I reach up to hug her again. "Thanks," I whisper.

"Of course," she says, "and I'll be more than happy to find you another job. You just let me know how I can help."

I nod. "I appreciate it, but first, why don't you set me up with that guy you told me about."

Abby pulls away, shocked. "Are you serious?"

"I haven't had a date in months," I tell her with a sigh. "And although I can't make any promises, I think I need to give someone else a shot."

Abby smiles widely. "That's my girl."

I smile back. "What time do you have to be at work?"

"Crap!" Abby looks at the clock on the microwave. "In like twenty minutes. I gotta run."

"Go, I'll be fine," I assure her. "And I'm so happy about your job."

"I love you too," she yells back to me as she makes her way quickly back to her room.

I turn back to my computer and resume my job search. Am I ready for a new job? Maybe. Am I ready for a new guy? No way. But I have to move on. It may take months. It may take years. But I have to let him go. He never belonged to me anyway.

CHAPTER 11

I finished up my job search a little over an hour after Abby left, and then made my way to my room to get ready for a fun-filled day of family. It's been such a swell weekend for me.

I pull into my parents' driveway just before noon and see that my dad's car is gone.

Really, Dad? A freaking Sunday? As if you don't work enough during the week?

"Ms. Julia! Long time, no see!"

Our long time housekeeper, Bessie, greets me as I walk in. Even though she's not a blood relative, I still consider her my favorite family member.

I give her a huge hug. I've missed her. "I know, Ms. B. I'm sorry. How have you been?"

"Fine and dandy." Her typical answer. "Can't say the same for your momma. Been going through a rough patch."

"Yeah, I know. Where is she?"

Bessie gestures to the stairs. "Still in the bed."

I look toward the stairs with a sigh and then back to Bessie. "Thanks, Ms. B. Let's catch up when I get done, okay?"

"I look forward to it, sweetheart."

I give Bessie one more hug before heading upstairs.

I find my mom passed out in the fetal position in her huge bed. It would be fine if she actually shared it with someone, but unfortunately, my dad chooses to share beds with everyone *but* my mom.

Deciding not to wake her quite yet, I have a seat in the chair by her window and watch her sleep. She's lost weight again. She looks so tiny in her oversized bed.

While she sleeps, I can pretend that nothing's wrong. I can pretend she's normal. I can pretend my family is normal and my mom is just sleeping – not sleeping off what is probably a twenty-four hour bender. Maybe she's sleeping in because her late afternoon tennis matches wore her out yesterday.

I can pretend.

My mom finally starts to stir a little after noon.

"Hi, Mom," I say quietly from the chair, hoping I don't startle her. "Do you want me to have Ms. B bring you some coffee?"

"That would be great." Her voice is hoarse and deep. "I forgot you were coming today."

"Not happy to see me?" I tease her, when I really just feel like crying again.

"Of course I am," she quickly corrects, trying to sit up, but I know her head must be pounding. "What time is it?"

I get up and head to the bathroom. "It's lunchtime. Are you hungry?"

For something other than pills and booze?

I fill a glass with water and grab two aspirin from her overstocked medicine cabinet.

"Not right now." She's sitting up in bed when I return. "Thanks sweetheart."

My mom downs the water and the pills as I call Bessie for some coffee. "Coffee's coming," I tell her, once I hang up.

"So, what do you want to do today?" My mom seems like she's finally starting to adjust to the light. "Want to go shopping?"

"Sure."

I'm not in the mood, but shopping is my mom's cure for everything, and maybe I can persuade her into buying me a few things. I'll need them for my new job.

Bessie brings the coffee, and I watch as Mom spikes it using the flask on her bedside table. I shake my head, before going and grabbing the flask from her hands and pouring it down the bathroom sink, along with her take on Irish coffee.

My mom stumbles out of bed. "If you're going to act like that, you can just take yourself back home!"

I nearly burst into tears at the sight of her frail figure. I quickly avert my eyes to her face, which doesn't help. Her once bright green eyes are now heavy and bloodshot, as they stare back at me in question. Her cheeks appear hollowed, and her dark hair is noticeably thinner and hanging limply around her pale face.

Who is this woman? I barely recognize her.

I can't believe my dad is essentially sitting back and watching as she wastes away. He obviously doesn't care at all anymore. Bastard.

"Mom..." I try to stay calm. "How about this? How about no drinking or pill taking, while you're with me today? You can do whatever you want after I leave, just give me a few sober hours? Please?"

I hold my breath and wait for her answer. I've tried to barter before, but it's not always successful.

My mom slumps. "Fine," she says, hanging her head. "I'm sorry."

I walk over and take her tiny body in my arms. "It's alright, Mom. Don't start crying, okay?"

I can't take any more tears right now.

I pull her away from me. "Let's find you something to wear," I suggest. "Sound good?"

It's so hard to be chipper around this kind of insanity, but I do my best. My mom follows me to her closet, and we pick out a respectable skirt and blouse, and her favorite red flats to match.

She takes a quick shower, and I help her with her hair, while she does her make-up. So far, so good, she seems to be okay without the drugs or alcohol, but I know I don't have long. Maybe a couple hours, tops.

As soon as we have her dressed and ready, I call Bessie for someone to bring the car around front.

My mom looks like another person now, her secrets well hidden behind her Chanel make-up and Kenneth Cole blouse.

We spend about an hour at her favorite boutique, and then decide we could both use some food. I realize I haven't eaten since breakfast yesterday.

But let's not think about yesterday, Jules. One problem at a time.

Right now, I need to figure out how to keep my mom from drinking her lunch.

We decide on a small café near the boutique. I was aiming for the sandwich shop across the street, because they don't serve alcohol, but my mom claims she wants a sit-down restaurant so we can have more time to chat. I see right through her.

Sure enough, when we sit down and the waitress comes by, my mom orders a Bloody Mary without even looking at me. I tell the waitress I'll have a water, but little does my mom know, I'll be drinking her Bloody Mary, while she enjoys my water.

"You promised," I remind her.

"It's one drink," she scoffs. "I'm a grown woman."

"Exactly," I scowl.

The waitress returns with our drinks, and I immediately take the Bloody Mary from my mom. She gives me an angry glare, but I can tell she doesn't have the energy to fight.

"Let's just get through lunch," I tell her. "Then you can go back home and do whatever you want. You agreed."

"I know." She looks like she may start crying. *Dammit.* It's really bad this time.

"Mom..." This is not the place for this conversation, but it has to be done. *Again.* "I thought you were going to get some help. What happened?"

"Nothing helps. There is no help for me." She gives me a sad smile, which breaks my heart.

"That's not true." I grab her hand. "You can do this, Mom. You can get better."

My mom just shakes her head. "What for?"

Now I'm getting angry. "Great. Just give up then. Seems that's all this family is good at – giving up."

"Julia Anne Greene." Her pitiful attempt at being a mother nearly makes me laugh. "You stop that right now."

"No, *you* stop." I'm trying so hard not to raise my voice in public. I close my eyes and take a couple of deep breaths. "Can you try one more time? Can you just try?"

My mom looks at me, and I see it. I see hope in her eyes. It's there. She just has to hang on to it.

"Why?" she asks in a small voice. "Why should I?"

I know what she's getting at, and I hate him for it.

"You need to do it because you're better than this. You're better than *him*."

It's the truth. I will always love my dad because he's my dad. But he treats my mom like shit. Always has.

"You can get better," I tell her. "And you can get out of there."

"I love him." A tear rolls down her cheek, and I quickly move to wipe it away.

"I know." *I feel your pain, Mom. I truly do. More than you know.* "But he's never going to change. And Mom, I promise you that you're better than him. You are. You can do this."

I see it again. In her eyes. That flash of hope.

"I'll do whatever I can to help. I'll help you get through this." *Please Mommy?* "I just want you to try. Use his money to go to the best rehab facility in the state, and then leave his ass."

"Jules!" My mom's smiling while scolding me. "Language."

I smile too. "Please, Mom. *Please.*"

"I'll try." She smiles. "I promise I'll try."

I hug her. "I love you."

"I love you too."

We eat our lunch, and I enjoy my Bloody Mary. It actually works to take the edge off nicely.

"So, what's new with you?" Mom asks, as we wait for dessert.

"Nothing much," I lie. "I'm thinking of getting a new tattoo."

"Oh yeah?" She seems excited. You would think my mom would disapprove, but she doesn't. She's cool like that. "What's it going to be this time?"

"Not sure yet," I admit. "I have an idea. I'll let Abby sketch it out."

"I can't wait to see it."

I smile at her. "Thanks for putting up with your tattooed freak of a daughter."

My mom smiles back. "Your creativity is one of the things I love most about you."

"You mean my tackiness."

"That too." She smiles again. "I love you, no matter what."

"I know."

"I always will."

"Ditto."

Truth is, if my mom wouldn't have ended up with my father, she probably would have been a tattooed freak herself. Hiding underneath all of that uptight, attorney's wife exterior is a wonderfully eclectic persona, with a penchant for the cheesiest of Elvis trinkets – case in point, my desk clock.

I've seen glimpses of her alter ego over the years. Honestly, it's pushed me even harder to live my life the way I want to live it – not only for me, but for my mom as well.

When we return back to my parents' house, I call my dad as Mom heads upstairs. She tells me she has to use the restroom, but I'm not an idiot.

"Hey buttercup!"

Ugh. Tone it down, Dad.

"Hey, Dad. Do you have a minute?"

"What's up?"

"I'm at the house, with Mom."

"What?" My dad fakes appalled really well. "No one told me you were coming!"

I roll my eyes. "Sorry. Listen. Mom says she wants to try again."

Silence.

"Dad?"

"Are we going to go through this again, Jules?"

That's it. My hurt and anger from this weekend finally reaches its climax. He's lucky I'm not in his office.

"Yes. Yes we are, you fucking bastard! We will go through this again, and again, and again. We'll go through this as many times as it takes because she's my mother, and you're her husband, and I think we both know you owe her at least this." I can't believe I just called my dad a "fucking bastard", but I'm on a roll. "I want you to get her into the most expensive rehab your money can buy, and I'll do everything I can to make sure she stays there this time. And when she gets out? Clean and sober? I'll help her pack her bags and get the hell out of this house, like she should have done a decade ago!"

Needless to say, there's nothing but crickets on the other end as I pant from my shouting episode. I'll feel terrible for it later, but right now, I don't feel bad at all. Not one bit. My dad can thank my Bitchface boss lady for my new rage issues.

"Julia," my dad finally speaks. "For starters, I deserved that." *You're damn right you did.* "But I will not let you talk to me that way. I'm your father."

Oh no you don't.

"Well then act like a father! Act like a husband! Do something!"

My dad's quiet again.

"Look, Dad. I'm sick of this conversation, but I'm not going to continue to sit around and watch as our family crumbles to pieces. Life's too short. Just get her into rehab ASAP. I'll handle the rest. Good bye."

Enough of that.

All of a sudden, I hear a slow clap coming from behind me. It's Bessie and my mom. I didn't know they were listening.

Bessie's the one clapping. My mom's face is a mixture of pride and fear, but that glimmer of hope is still in her eyes. Maybe she can actually do it this time.

"I hope I don't get fired for saying this..." Bessie looks at my mom and then over at me. "But I'm so proud of you," she says, coming to give me a hug.

My mom laughs. She actually laughs.

"Thank you." My mom comes to give me a hug too.

I can smell the vodka on her breath, but that's okay. *Baby steps, Jules. Baby steps.*

CHAPTER 12

After the incident with my parents yesterday, I was walking in the clouds. I needed that. And as awful as I was to my father, he needed that too.

But now? Now the clouds have dissipated. I'm sitting at my desk at my office. It's eight o'clock. Andrew's here.

He hasn't come out of his office yet. He hasn't said a word to me. I've been here since seven-thirty, and his light was on when I arrived. Did he spend the night here again? Was he upset again?

Oh give it up, Jules! Good grief!

I didn't go in to set up his office this morning, since he was already here. I didn't even bring his coffee, and he hasn't requested it either.

I've been to the bathroom once, thinking I may be sick, but I just ended up leaning against the wall, trying to figure out a way to handle this, trying to figure out a way to be strong.

Andrew probably thinks I'm embarrassed by what I saw. He's probably embarrassed. I've decided that's how I'll handle it, if he brings it up. I'll tell him that there's no reason to be embarrassed. I'll assure him that his secret's safe with me, once again, and we'll just go about our normal routine...at least until I can get the hell out of here.

I've spent the morning going through the pictures from Saturday and putting them on a jump drive to give to him. I wonder if he'll even request them. At this point, I'm starting to wonder if he ever plans to speak to me again!

I finally get a call for him around eight-thirty. Here's the moment of truth.

I ring his office to announce the call. He answers immediately.

"Ms. Greene. Good morning." His voice is like a dull dagger through my heart – cold and indifferent.

"It's Mr. Barnes for you, sir." My voice is shaking.

"Send him through." And he hangs up.

I squeeze my eyes shut, trying to hold back the tears. Is he mad at me?

"I'm transferring you now, Mr. Barnes," I tell the caller and hang up quickly.

I can't do this. I can't be around him. It hurts.

I sit at my desk for a minute or two trying to push down my tears.

Not at work, Jules. Suck it up.

And then, as if my heart needed some additional punishment, I hear the clicking of heels in the lobby.

Really? *REALLY*?!

The next thing I know, Bitchface clambers into the hallway, yapping loudly on her cell phone.

Don't look at her, Jules. Just concentrate on work.

But I can't help myself. My brain is so fried from this past weekend, I was lucky to get my clothes on straight this morning.

Next time, I'll make sure to listen to my subconscious. I look up and watch an evil grin spread across Victoria's face as she walks past me, straight into Andrew's office.

My heart starts racing, and I can feel my face turning red. I have to get out of here. Now.

I open my emails and click "compose".

> Mr. Mercer,
> As I previously mentioned, I have a doctor's appointment this morning. I'm leaving now and should return before lunch.
> I didn't want to disturb you. Please call my cell if you need me.
> Ms. Greene

Andrew will never remember if I have a doctor's appointment or not. He never remembers anything, unless I put it on his calendar.

I wait to pack up my things before I hit "send".

I grab my purse and make my way quickly toward the elevators. I click the button but decide I can't wait and head to the stairs. I'll take the eight flights any day over spending one more minute in this place.

I walk out of the building reception area and into the sunlight. I take a few deep breaths. It feels good. I was suffocating in there.

I walk toward the parking deck, and I'm concentrating so hard on getting the hell out of this place that my phone ringing startles me.

Even more shocking? It's Andrew.

"Yes sir?" I try to sound calm, but it's not without effort...a lot of effort. Plus, I'm kind of out of breath from my trip down the stairs.

"Ms. Greene, I just received your email."

"Yes sir?" I can't deal with him right now.

"Which doctor are you seeing? I don't remember you telling me about the appointment."

Dammit!

"It's just a checkup, sir. Just a routine visit." I lean against the wall next to the parking deck elevator and close my eyes. He knows I'm lying. But do I care?

"Which doctor?" he asks again.

He definitely knows I'm lying, and no, I don't care.

"Does it matter?"

Oh God, Jules. That was so inappropriate. Calm down!

"It matters to me."

Wait, Andrew doesn't sound angry. He sounds...he sounds *sad*. Are we still talking about the doctor?

I don't say anything. I don't know what to say.

Keep it professional, Jules.

I put my hand over my eyes. "It's just a checkup," I repeat. "A physical with my regular physician, sir."

"Ms. Greene?"

"Oh my God!" I nearly have a heart attack. It's Andrew's voice, but it doesn't come from my phone. He's standing in front of me.

"Sir?" I say confused, still holding my phone to my ear.

Don't cry, Jules. Please don't cry.

"Ms. Greene..." He'll barely look at me. Is he upset? I need to see his eyes. *Look at me Andrew.*

As if he could hear my thoughts, he looks up, and I slowly pull my phone from my ear when I see his face. He's sad, definitely sad. But about *what*? Oh God. Is he going to fire me? Is he sad about having to fire me?

"Ms. Greene," he starts again, "I think we both know you do not have a doctor's appointment today."

"Ummm..." *Jules, find your lying skills, girl.* "Why would I lie about a doctor's appointment?"

Ugh. I am the worst liar. *Ever.*

Andrew doesn't say anything. He just gives me a meaningful look.

Nope. You're going to have to say it, Andrew.

"Ms. Greene, I think we should talk about what you saw on Saturday."

Oh Lord, here it comes. *Brace yourself, Jules.*

I try to speak, to go over my "your secret's safe with me" speech, but he starts in again before I can say a word.

"Ms. Hamilton and I, we..."

That's it. *Ms. Hamilton and I*? No freaking way.

"It's no problem at all, sir," I say quickly, forcing a smile. "I didn't see a thing."

I keep smiling, hoping he'll leave so we don't have to chat about this anymore, but he just stands there with a strange look on his face.

"You're not upset?" he finally asks.

Oh Andrew. What about that incident didn't upset me?

"No sir." I try to sound confident.

Andrew stares at me blankly for a moment before responding. I'm so uncomfortable around him now. I hate it.

"Well then." He clears his throat. "I'm glad everything's okay."

It's so not okay, but I'll smile anyway.

"Yes sir." I look at my watch, any place but his beautiful eyes. "I'm going to be late."

"Right. Please." He gestures for me to move toward the elevator door.

I force yet another smile, as I push the down button.

"Ms. Greene?"

WHAT?! I feel like screaming! Just let me get the hell out of here! I slowly turn toward him.

"Sir?"

"Please come see me when you get back?"

"Absolutely."

He turns and walks away from me. *FINALLY!* I can't help but admire the view as he walks away…light gray pants, gray vest and his green-striped tie. Is he trying to kill me?

I put my head in my hands, just as the elevator arrives. The thought of not seeing him every day makes my whole body ache. I instantly feel sick. I'm as bad as my mother. Do they have rehab for this?

CHAPTER 13

I return to the office around eleven-thirty. Fortunately for me, the "doctor's office" had a fabulous shoe selection. Although after about an hour of trying on at least thirty different pairs of stilettos, I decided retail therapy wasn't going to help. I just kept envisioning putting one of those heels in Bitchface's eye, up her nose, through her black heart...you get the idea.

I put my purse in my desk drawer and open my emails. I have several, so I scroll through quickly to make sure I didn't miss anything important.

As I'm scrolling, I see I have five new messages in my "Andrew" folder. Fine. Let's see what he wants.

There are a couple of "to-dos", which I print out, then there are two forwarded emails from clients bragging about the party. Whatever. I wish I could permanently erase that horrid event from my memory.

The last email is a reminder to stop by and see him when I get back. Might as well get that over with.

I stand up and make my way over to his office. I knock tentatively and quickly hear a "Come in."

Deep breaths, Jules. In and out.

"You wanted to see me, sir?"

"Ms. Greene. Please have a seat," he says without looking up at me.

I sit and wait for him to finish typing. I silently curse myself for allowing my eyes to linger on his long fingers as he types. I should hate him after Saturday! Why don't I hate him?!

"I have a proposition for you, Ms. Greene." He's still typing.

"Sir?"

What's this? Another photography job? Gee, thanks.

"I'm leaving tomorrow for New York." He flicks his eyes quickly to me, then back to his computer. "I have a meeting with a prospect."

I immediately pull up his calendar in my head. How did I miss this?

"Don't worry," he says, noticing my obvious panic. "I just decided on the meeting this morning."

Got it – must be with The Barnes Group.

"Okay." I nod. This is easy. Let's focus on your schedule. Yes. That's a good distraction. "So, I can move your meeting with J & G Realty to later this week, no problem." I quickly run through the rest of his schedule in my head. "And I believe that's the only major thing you have tomorrow. Will you be returning tomorrow evening?"

"No, we will be returning on Wednesday evening."

"We?" I quickly repeat, praying he's not taking Victoria. I look down at my notepad. I can't look at him and think about her. "Yes sir. You and Ms. Hamilton?"

I keep her schedule too, so I'll need to rearrange some things there as well.

"No," he says to my surprise. "You and I will be returning on Wednesday."

I'm sorry. What the hell did you just say?

"I'm not sure I follow."

I'm trying hard to not let the nervous laugh in my throat escape my lips, while Andrew is casually shuffling through some papers on his desk, as if he didn't just drop this bomb on me.

"That's my proposition," he says, looking up at me nonchalantly. "I would like for you to attend this meeting with me."

Okay, calm down, Jules.

This isn't the first business trip that I've been on with him. No need to act like this is a big deal.

Andrew's looking at me strangely now. *Oh dear.* I'm starting to sweat.

"Y-Yes sir," I stammer. "I can be available."

"Good." Andrew starts going through the papers again. "We need to leave out early tomorrow morning, returning late Wednesday night. I have dinner plans for Wednesday."

"Yes sir." Thankfully, my breathing has started returning to normal. "Will anyone else be attending?"

That's an acceptable question, right? I mean, I need to purchase the plane tickets, book the rooms...totally acceptable. Andrew looks slowly up from his papers. "No," he says, as a small smile forms on his beautiful lips. "Just the two of us."

My Lord, those eyes.

Be a professional, Jules!

"Yes sir," I smile, now with good reason. "I'll book our flights right away."

Andrew turns back to his emails. *Is that it? Dismissing me already?*

"Is there anything I need to prepare?" I ask. "Anything I need to bring for you?"

"No. I don't think so. I should have everything I need," he says, concentrating intently on his computer screen. "I would just like you there for support."

Support, eh?

"What about a hotel sir? Where's the meeting being held?"

"Just do the usual."

Translation: The Plaza. I can barely contain my excitement!

"Yes sir." I get up to leave, smiling widely as I walk to his door. It seems I have a trip to plan!

"New York?" Abby's face is making me laugh. "Freaking *New York City*? You have to be kidding me!"

"And The Plaza, no less!" I add, as I continue to try and find a semi-acceptable wardrobe for this trip.

I was able to talk my mom into a couple of cute skirts on our shopping excursion yesterday, but what about tops? Is it cold in New York in April? I have no idea. I've never been.

"And since when do you go on business trips with Preppy Mercer by yourself? This is a first, right?" Abby's pissed. I can tell she doesn't like this one bit. But is she pissed I get to go to New York, or that I'm going with Andrew? It's hard to tell.

"Yes, this is a first," I say from in front of my closet. *Dammit!* Where's my navy blue blouse? "But it's no big deal. He's my boss. I can't say no."

And there's obviously no chance of a romantic getaway. That dream was successfully shattered on Saturday, but that doesn't mean I'm going to turn down forty-eight hours alone with him...in New York City. I'm not an idiot. Or maybe I am.

"Can you handle this?" Abby asks, reading my mind.

I turn to her. "I can do it. Bitchface won't be there." I turn back to my closet and sigh. My damn navy blouse is at the cleaners. "I don't think I could handle her being there. But I can deal with Andrew alone. It's just work."

"Why does he want you to go?"

"Based on past work trips, he probably wants me to be available just in case – order lunches, make copies, answer emails, etc. That's my typical role on these trips." Although it is kind of odd he didn't want me to prepare anything ahead of time.

"Wow. Gopher girl. Sounds exhilarating."

I turn and toss one of my slippers at her. "It's my job. Thank you very much."

"Don't' get all sassy." She smiles. "But seriously, are you okay? I mean you were pretty upset on Saturday."

I stop my clothes hunt and join her on the bed. "I'm fine," I say, which I'm not of course, but that's okay. "The hardest part is that there's really no one to be mad at but me."

"What?!" Abby yells. "Oh I can find a million reasons to be pissed at that tool and his slutty lover."

I sigh. "I know, but what I'm getting at is that neither of them did anything wrong... at least not to me. They didn't do anything wrong to me."

Abby sighs too in understanding. "That doesn't mean they're not still pricks."

"True." I wish I could hate Andrew. I really do. Bitchface? No problem. "But I can't be mad at him, or her really. Not for that. I can be hurt, but that's my own doing. Trust me, I know it sucks, but that's pretty much par for the course for my life."

"Awww." Abby reaches to give me a hug. "You don't need him anyway. You're better than him."

I flinch at the same words I used with my mom coming out of Abby's mouth. I need to follow my own advice, I guess.

"I'll be fine," I try and assure Abby. "I'm still looking for a new job, and hopefully, I'll be out of there in no time. Meanwhile, I'll let Mercer Construction afford me a trip to New York City. Can't beat that."

"Good point," Abby says smiling, "And I hope you find a job involving cameras and pretty pictures and not douche bags in stuffy suits and sluts with bad dye-jobs."

I smile. "I'm working on it."

"Okay then. So, New York City?" Abby smiles back. "Yeah, I'm totally going to need a souvenir."

CHAPTER 14

Ready?

The ding of my Blackberry messenger startles me awake. It's Andrew.
I'd been snoozing, sitting up on my sofa. I was so nervous I would be late for our seven o'clock flight, I barely slept last night.
I quickly type him back.

On my way down.

I jump up to grab my bag and check my face in the small mirror by our front door to make sure I don't have mascara running down my cheeks. I'm pleased to see I still look relatively presentable. I guess falling asleep sitting up has its advantages.
The Atlanta airport can be a bear, so we have to get there at least a couple of hours early for our flight. Luckily, I don't live too far away.
Andrew offered me a ride, which I gladly accepted. I thought it was a nice gesture.
I make my way down my apartment stairs and see the sleek, black town car waiting in front of my building. It looks so out of place in my shabby little apartment complex. I think the nicest car in our lot is probably mine, which isn't saying much.

The driver meets me at the bottom of the stairs and takes my bag. "Good morning, ma'am," he says.

"Good morning." I try to be chipper as he opens my door, but it's super hard at this hour. I need some coffee. Desperately.

Or maybe a shot of Andrew, I think as I climb in. The car is full of his delicious, manly scent, and he looks up and smiles at me as I take my seat. "Good morning, Ms. Greene," he says before looking back down at the papers in his lap.

Oh yes. *Very* good morning to me.

"Good morning, sir." He has a cup in his hand, which I would guess is coffee, black with two sugars. It's all I can do not to steal it from him.

"It's chilly out this morning," he says. "I got you a coffee, although I'm not sure how you take it." He looks disappointed in himself. "So, there's plenty of cream and sugar."

The driver reaches over the back seat before we pull out of my apartment complex and hands me a warm cup of bliss in a cardboard cup holder that's loaded with cream, sugar, napkins and a spoon. It's like Christmas!

"Thank you so much." I gladly take the coffee gift and quickly pull the cup from the cardboard holder. I place the holder, along with all of the condiments on the floor at my feet. "Thank you for doing this. It's a very welcome gesture this morning," I say to Andrew.

"No problem." Why is he still smiling at me? *Stop it*. My frazzled brain cannot take that kind of excitement, especially not this early. "No cream and sugar?" he asks.

"No sir. Just plain old coffee for me," I tell him, feeling so happy to have the warmth – and the caffeine – in my hands. "I'm boring like that."

Did I really just say that? Am I flirting again? Oh forget it. I'm too tired to analyze it.

Andrew smiles at me then looks back down at his paperwork. What's he reading so intently? It would be rude of me to look, but I'm sitting right next to him in the backseat. A quick side of the eye glance will surely go unnoticed.

I decide to give it a shot. Hmmm...It looks like a bid proposal, but it's nothing like the ones I've done before.

Whatever. I need to mind my own business and enjoy my coffee – while also enjoying the close proximity of Andrew's leg to mine.

Andrew seems engrossed in what he's reading, so I don't bother him. I just spend my time switching my gaze between the front windshield and my side window. Since it's still dark out, I enjoy the city lights on the ride in. I kind of wish I had my camera.

About fifteen minutes in to the drive, my coffee thankfully starts kicking in, and I'm not feeling like I may pass out standing up while walking through the airport.

"Feeling better?" Andrew asks, as he places his paperwork back into his briefcase.

I look over at him. "Yes. Much."

"So, the meeting..." he starts, "there's actually not much I need from you today."

"No?"

Andrew keeps smiling at me. Damn him. "No, I have this one handled. So, just feel free to stay in the hotel, shop, sightsee, whatever you like."

Huh?

I let out a brief giggle. "Shop, sir? Sightsee?"

Andrew, please stop smiling at me. For the love of God.

"Think of it as a little present for all of the hard work you did at the event this past weekend," he says, matter of factly. Well, there goes my good mood. Did he have to bring up *that* day again? "I think you deserve a break."

I take a couple of seconds to process this. "Sir..." Let me see if I have this straight. "Are you saying that today is like a mini-vacation or something?"

Andrew looks hesitant now. I hope I didn't make him feel bad. It really is a nice gesture. Or is he just trying to make amends for Saturday? The thought instantly pisses me off.

"For you, not for me. " He looks out the front windshield and turns on his serious boss man face. *Did* I piss him off? "I just wanted to show my gratitude for pulling that event together so quickly, but if it makes you feel better to work these next two days, that's fine too. It's up to you."

I feel sick. How could I be so stupid? He's doing something nice for me – probably one of the nicest things he's ever done for me! New York City? The Plaza Hotel? Who cares if he's just trying to make-up for kissing that slut? He's offering me a vacation day in New York City, and I'm ruining it!

"Mr. Mercer," I turn slightly in my seat to face him. "I am so sorry if that came out the wrong way. I was just a little shocked by your offer, but please know that I am absolutely blown away by your generosity. I hope I didn't make you feel otherwise."

"I thought I may have upset you," he says, still looking out the front window, his eyes weary.

"No sir. Not at all," I quickly assure him. "Honestly, I don't feel worthy. It's really too much."

"Okay, that's enough, Ms. Greene." He turns back to me, his perfect lips forming a small smile. "It's not that big of a deal, and I wasn't that upset." *Whew*. Another crisis averted. "I just thought you may enjoy it. Have you ever been to New York City?"

"No sir. I haven't." I'm smiling now too. "I don't even know where to start."

"Well, I took the liberty of making a few arrangements, but we can talk more about that on the plane."

Arrangements?

We pull up at the airport, and Andrew hops out, once the driver opens his door. By the time I grab my purse and pop in a piece of gum to take care of my coffee breath, my door is opening. I step out, and Andrew's there, both our bags in hand.

"Ready?" he asks.

He seems awfully excited for a business trip, but I don't question it. His mood swings have been volatile lately. I better enjoy the good while I have it.

"Yes sir," I say with a smile. He looks divine today in his navy blue three-piece and pale yellow, diamond patterned tie. "I'm ready."

Andrew leads the way, and I follow him quickly into the airport. No matter how much money you have, unless you fly by private jet, no one is impervious to the grueling lines and security checks that Hartsfield-Jackson has to offer. But as with most things, Andrew amazes me as he manages to weave through the crowds with grace and confidence, likes he owns the place. I checked us both in last night and gave Andrew his boarding pass this morning, so I simply follow in his footsteps as he leads me to the line for the security checks. He's still managing all of our bags as well, which is probably a little unfair.

I look at my rolling bag, next to his small hanging bag, draped over his shoulder. Did I pack too much? I used the smallest suitcase I have, but maybe I should have just used my workout duffle or something. He probably thinks I'm a total diva.

"I can take my bag, sir," I say reaching for it, but Andrew simply pulls my rolling bag closer to him.

"I have it," he says.

"I really don't mind," I say, grabbing for it again, but Andrew holds up his free hand to block me.

"Why don't you let *me* do something for *you* for once?"

His eyes are soft, as well as his voice, rendering me absolutely speechless.

I pull my hand back slowly, mouth slightly open, in a state of utter shock. That was unexpected.

Andrew smiles at me again, which is happening more often than not these days. My mind drifts for a moment and I realize that all of his smiles may be the result of the new love in his life. I quickly push the thought away, but not before the bile starts rising up my throat.

Andrew's a first class flyer, so we at least get the short security line. We're through and on the tram to our terminal before I know it, and all the while, my mind's still reeling from what Andrew said in the car.

Sight-seeing? Isn't he being overly nice to me? I guess not. The little mini-vacation is really generous, but I suppose it's a suitable gift for my work on the party. Right?

Also, what the hell is he so cheerful about? He seemed very excited about his reading material this morning, so this must be a big prospect. He doesn't normally tell me much about the business deals, but I'm nosey and sometimes read the proposals. Speaking of, where did he get the one he had this morning? I didn't do it. I didn't even recognize it.

"Ms. Greene?"

We are now in the Sky Club longue, standing at the bar.

"Would you like a drink?" Andrew asks. "Water? More coffee? Vodka? It's up to you. It's your vacation."

I smile at him. "Water's fine," I say.

I look down at my watch. We have a little less than an hour before our flight. We made good time.

I relax into one of the comfy seats in the longue, and Andrew takes the seat next to mine. He places our drinks on the small table between us.

"Here's to some well-deserved R & R, Ms. Greene," he says, holding up his club soda.

"Thank you, sir." I grab my own glass and toast. "So, tell me about New York City," I say after I take a sip. "I've always wanted to go."

"You'll love it. I know you will." Andrew seems confident, and his is a confidence I rarely doubt. "As I mentioned in the car, I made some arrangements for you, since I knew you wouldn't have much time."

"I appreciate that." *Thoughtful, sweet Andrew.*

"However," he adds, "you're free to roam as you please, so if you would prefer to just walk around at your leisure, that's certainly fine too."

I smile at him. "Mr. Mercer. I think you know me well enough by now to know I'm more of a planner."

He smiles back at me. "Yes, Ms. Greene. I suspected as much."

"So, what's on my agenda?" I'm starting to feel excited now. What could Andrew have possibly planned for me? He doesn't even really know me that well. Maybe a couple of art museums, but what else? Some touristy stuff?

"Well, I had a friend help me put an itinerary together for you. I hope you won't be disappointed."

"I'm sure I won't." Okay, I'm definitely excited! "But what are your plans, sir? You have meetings both days? Are you sure there's nothing I can help with? Who will be covering your calls and such?"

As excited as I am, it's strange being with Andrew and not thinking about work.

"No. I'll be fine. You just worry about *you* for the next couple of days. I'll take care of my meetings." He takes another sip of his club soda, leaving his lips moist and delectable.

Stop looking at his mouth, Jules!

I try looking up at his eyes, but that doesn't really help. They are just as enticing. Lucky for me, I don't think Andrew notices my swooning.

"And Ms. Carter will be covering my calls and emails today in your absence," he continues.

Adrian? Really?

"You told her about the trip? I mean, your…ummm…*gift* to me?"

"No," Andrew answers quickly. "I told her you would be busy helping me with the meetings, and you would appreciate her help covering my desk." Andrew frowns. "Besides, this was rather last minute, and I wanted it to be a surprise. I told no one."

I'm once again speechless, this time it's mostly because I can't stop fixating on his wet lips.

"It's a very thoughtful gift, sir," I finally manage. "I think I may still be in shock. I can't believe I'm going to New York City!"

"I'm glad you're excited," he says. "It's really the least I can do. Besides the party, you've put up with me for two long years."

And I've loved every single minute of it.

"You're not that bad, sir." *You're perfect.*

Andrew cocks an eyebrow at me. "You're not a very good liar, Ms. Greene."

I smile at him. This is the longest conversation we've ever had that wasn't about a bid proposal or his schedule.

"Okay, so maybe the first few months weren't the best," I admit. "But you eventually came around."

"Yes," Andrew laughs, "I thought I better make a change before I got shot or something."

"It wasn't that bad," I scoff.

"If I remember correctly, you called me an 'immature bully' and told me you were 'not going to take my shit' anymore. Wasn't it something along those lines?"

Yikes. He really does remember more than I give him credit for. I had forgotten about the "bully" thing.

I cringe into my seat. "Yes sir. I guess that was pretty bad."

Andrew smiles. "No, it wasn't. I deserved it."

"Maybe so, but it was harsh and not very appropriate coming from your assistant."

"That may be true," he agrees. "But I still deserved it."

"Honestly, I was just tired of crying myself to sleep every night," I say smiling, but then I watch as Andrew's face instantly pales.

Oh God. What did I say *now*?

It feels like hours pass before Andrew speaks again. I exhale in relief when he finally does.

"I'm so sorry," he says quietly, staring out the window with a furrowed brow. He looks very uncomfortable.

Dammit! Can't I go ten minutes without completely screwing something up?!

"Sir, I was younger, and this was my first *real* job. It just took me a while to get used to how things work in the corporate world." I cross my legs to keep my nervous-bouncy-knee syndrome in check.

"I really made you cry?" There is no mistaking that he's appalled by this fact. "I had no idea."

Jules, you're an idiot.

How could he not have known? And why does he seem to care so much?

"Sir, please don't let my idiotic comment upset you. It didn't really have anything to do with you." I lie to him - anything to make this right. "I had a lot going on in my life at the time, and I kept making mistakes when I first started. Remember? You had a right to be upset with me all those times. I was a disaster."

I wait a moment for him to speak again...to look at me...anything. But he's still looking, thoughtfully now, out the window, staring at the skyline in the distance.

I close my eyes. "Mr. Mercer, I can't believe I've managed to upset you twice this morning already. I am so sorry ---"

I stop talking and my eyes pop open, when I feel a warm hand suddenly on mine.

Andrew leans toward me, across our small table. The closeness makes me lightheaded. Oh God, he smells so good.

"I have made my fair share of employees cry, Ms. Greene. I guess you could say it's in my blood." He looks up at me through those obscenely long lashes and I take a deep breath. This man could abuse me a million different ways and I would still keep coming back for more. "But I hope you know that it's not something I enjoy."

I'm trying hard to listen, but it's not easy with his hand still on mine.

"I do, sir," I manage, trapped in his steady gaze. "I know it's not who you really are."

He stares at me a moment longer before finally removing his hand, which is a huge relief. I was about to forget my own name.

Andrew straightens in his chair and clears his throat, as if shaking off what just happened between us. "I wasn't in the best place then either. What I'm trying to say is that I'm sorry," he starts again, "for everything."

I smile to try and lighten the mood. "Mr. Mercer, I think you're taking this too seriously."

Andrew, please don't feel bad about something that happened two years ago. Besides, I still love you with every piece of my heart.

"I'm a crier," I tease. "It's really not a huge deal."

Andrew smiles at me, but it's a half-hearted attempt. "I think we've already determined that you're not a very good liar, Ms. Greene."

I sigh. "You probably should have just fired me back then."

"Probably so."

"You would have saved yourself the heart ache of having to deal with me for the past two years."

Andrew laughs, as if I missed a private joke. "Indeed."

Okay...

"Friends again?" I ask with a smile, extending my hand for him to shake.

"Sure." He tries another smile, but this one falls short as well, before shaking my hand. Surely he's not that upset about my crying comment.

Okay, we need a subject change, and I need a new focal point, other than his lips.

"So, do I have to wait until we get there to see the itinerary, or do you have it now?" I ask, excitedly.

This seems to bring a more genuine smile to his lips, which makes me very happy.

"I have it, if you would like it now."

"Yes! I'm eager to see what my plans are for the day!"

Andrew happily goes into his briefcase, pulls out a piece of paper and hands it to me.

Wow! It's nearly the entire day mapped out to the minute. And the irony of Andrew giving me my schedule for today is not lost on me. It makes me grin.

"So, what do you think?" he asks.

"Honestly?" as I read over the itinerary, my excitement continues to build.

"Please."

I look up at him, smiling widely. "I'm glad I brought good shoes."

CHAPTER 15

Ding. Ding. Ding.
What the hell was that?
I open my eyes with a start. Oh, I'm on a plane. Right.
Oh no! I sit up straight and smooth my hair out of my face. I was lying on Andrew's shoulder.
No. No. NO!
"Guess the coffee wore off," he says.
I can tell he's smiling, but I can't look at him. Please tell me that did *not* just happen.
Oh God. Was I drooling?
Kill me now. Just kill me now.
"I am so sorry," I finally say, still not looking at him.
Andrew leans up, trying to see my face, but I look out the window. I'm so mortified.
"It's not a big deal," he says, before leaning back in his seat. I guess he got the hint. "You were up pretty early this morning."
"I'm so sorry, sir," I say again. "That was completely unprofessional."
I wipe under my eyes for any stray mascara. Lord knows what I look like.
"Ms. Greene," Andrew says in his boss-man voice, now commanding my attention. I reluctantly look over at him. "It's nothing. Really. It's forgotten."
Why does he look so angry?

"Yes sir," I say, looking back toward the window. "I just feel ridiculous." I start nervously wiping my eyes and smoothing my hair again.

"Don't," Andrew says, as he pulls my hand from my hair and places it in my lap. "And you look fine."

I turn back to him, and his eyes linger on mine a little longer than they should. This does not help my anxiety level at the moment.

"We should be arriving any moment," he says, eyes forward now. "Put your seatbelt back on."

I look up and realize the "fasten seat belt" sign must have been what woke me.

I put my seat belt on, and try to take some subtle deep breaths. *In. Out.* At least he didn't push me off his shoulder, I guess. I remember laying my head back and dozing as Andrew studied his proposals again. How long was I asleep? A quick look at my watch tells me it's been almost an hour. Oh good grief.

I turn toward my window after I get my seatbelt on and close my eyes. The stupid, freaking deep breaths aren't helping.

As we begin our decent into New York, I can finally feel my heart rate start to slow. Thank God. I need to shake it off. It's not a huge deal. It was an honest mistake. I apologized. He didn't seem too upset about it.

Move on.

Honestly, I wish I could have enjoyed that moment, sleeping on his shoulder. I wish he wasn't my boss. I wish he was *mine*.

There have been a handful of times over the past two years that I've thought maybe Andrew liked me too, as a little more than his assistant. But those brief flashes came and went quickly. There was always something to contradict my hopes – something he said or did that would make me see the reality of the situation.

The events of the last few days have been more confusing than ever, especially that late night in the office, but once again, my dreams were trampled on by the head tramp herself.

I lean my head back on the seat and sigh, as I gaze at the New York City skyline on our approach. He'll never be mine. I think it's about time I start to realize that.

"How do you like the city so far?" Andrew asks smiling, as we pull out of LaGuardia airport in another town car.

"I'm glad we weren't taking a taxi," I admit, remembering the chaos as we walked out of the airport. "That looked like an ordeal."

Andrew smiles and pulls out some more paperwork. I assume it's the same stuff he's been studying all morning, but I don't peek this time.

I pull out my itinerary for the millionth time, since Andrew gave it to me in Atlanta.

"If I didn't know any better, I would say someone is excited about their day," he says when he sees me pulling the paper from my bag.

"Guilty." I smile sheepishly up at him. "I forgot to ask earlier, but will I be taking a cab to all of these spots, or can I walk most of it?"

After seeing the madness at the airport, trying to hail a cab seems pretty intimidating.

Andrew smiles. "I've arranged for a car."

No. Way.

"You've arranged for a car?" I repeat because I can't think of anything else to say. The man has managed to stun me into silence multiple times today, which is a hard thing to do.

"Yes," Andrew confirms, looking back down at his paperwork. "Cab rides can get expensive. A private car was the more sensible option."

Good point. I'm pretty impressed that Andrew managed to get all of this together without me.

"I guess that makes sense," I agree, trying hard to not act like a kid at Christmas. I'm going on a chauffeured tour around New York City! *Oh my GOD!* "Thank you again sir," I add, not able to contain my huge grin.

Andrew looks up from his paperwork and smiles again. "You're very welcome."

He goes back to his reading, and I look out my window, excited to start taking in the sights.

We pull up to The Plaza right on time. Andrew's schedule-making skills are almost as good as mine...almost.

I follow Andrew into the lobby as he checks us in. I can't believe I'm standing in the lobby of The Plaza hotel! I start to immediately recognize things from movies and TV shows I've watched over the years. This is so cool!

"You look star struck, Ms. Greene," Andrew says with a huge grin, as he hands me my room key.

"I'm sorry, sir." I laugh. "I'm trying to be professional."

Andrew laughs too. "This way," he says leading me to the elevators. "We're on the sixteenth floor."

Andrew's walking briskly to the elevators, which is annoying me, but then I realize I have all day to look around if I want. So exciting!

"I apologize for the rush," he says once we reach the elevators, glancing at his watch. "My meeting's in less than an hour, and I want to get settled before hand. Plus, your car will be arriving in about fifteen minutes."

"No problem, sir. I understand."

When we get to our floor, Andrew points out that our rooms are across the hall, and a couple of doors down from each other. We reach my room first.

"I hope you have fun today, Ms. Greene," he says as he continues to walk to his room. "You should have all you need on the itinerary I gave you. I'll catch up with you later."

"Thank you again sir," I call to him, as he opens his door. "And good luck today."

He smiles at me, and then enters his room, and I stare after him like a love-struck idiot in the hallway. God, I love that man – even more now, if that's possible, which is unfortunate for me.

He went over his schedule for today briefly with me when we were on the plane. He has a morning meeting, then another after lunch. He said he didn't have dinner plans at the moment, but that could change if one of his meetings goes well.

I hate to say this, because of course I hope he closes a deal, but oh what I wouldn't give to have dinner alone with Andrew at some fancy spot in New York City. Just the thought of it gives me butterflies.

I shake off the wishful thinking. No need to get too excited about that now. The chances are probably pretty slim any way, and I need to drop my things off before I meet the car downstairs.

I open the door to my room, and stand in the entranceway for a moment, taking in the view. How many times will I be shocked silent today?

I don't have time for this right now though. I'll have to check out the fabulous room later.

Oh, but look at that amazing bed! And is that a bottle of wine on the table?

Later, Jules. Later.

I toss my briefcase on one of the chairs by the window – *It is a bottle of wine!* – and then I pull my rolling suitcase over to the bench in front of the bed. I quickly unzip it and pull out my make-up bag, so I can freshen up a bit before I leave.

Oh my God! The bathroom is incredible! Marble sinks? Gold-plated faucets? This could be heaven! I think I may be in heaven!

Wait. Nope. Not quite. Andrew's not naked in that unbelievable bed.

As I'm adding a little blush, my phone buzzes on the counter beside me. It's a text from Abby.

> *Just making sure you made it in one piece. Call or text when you arrive.*

Should I tell her? Not yet. I quickly type back.

I'm here. Busy day. Buzz you back later.

I'll wait to give her all the details after my sightseeing excursion. She's going to flip!

I head downstairs in a rush. According to my well-organized itinerary, my ride should be out front already.

I stroll leisurely through the lobby this time. I can't help myself. Why the hell didn't I bring my good camera? I snap a few pictures with my phone as I walk toward the entrance. The lobby area is better than a museum!

I finally make it to the revolving door, and when I come out on the other side, I literally feel like I've arrived. I see a sleek, shiny limo waiting with the door open, and I smile. I'm a rockstar. I'm a freaking rockstar.

I love you, Andrew Mercer.

I bound down the wide staircase, extending my hand to the driver.

"Julia Greene?" I question, to make sure he is, in fact, here for me.

"Yes, Ms. Greene," he replies and shakes my hand. "My name's Raphael. I'll be your driver today."

"I can't wait!" No need to contain my excitement around Raphael.

He smiles and closes my door once I'm inside. Raphael reminds me of a pudgy George Lopez.

I love George Lopez.

As I get settled inside, I'm shocked to find a chilled bottle of champagne waiting for me on a small bar, along with a few snacks and some bottled water.

"The champagne is compliments of Mr. Mercer, ma'am," Raphael says from the front seat. "Should already be open. Just pull the top."

Don't mind if I do, Raphael. Don't mind if I do.

I happily pour myself a glass, as Raphael pulls out onto Fifth Avenue.

"Did you receive your itinerary from Mr. Mercer, ma'am?" Raphael asks. "If not, I have an extra copy for you."

"I did receive a copy. Thank you." I'm the most excited about the first stop! "Looks like I get to see the museum at the International Center for Photography first?"

"Yes ma'am." Raphael has a nice smile. "The stop after this one can be pushed out a bit, if needed. Mr. Mercer said you may spend more time here than allotted. That's why it's first on the list."

Wow. Andrew really put some thought into this. I'm impressed.

I look out the deeply tinted windows of my *rockstarmobile* and take in the sights as we make our way to the museum. This city is fantastic. I grew up in Atlanta, which is not a small city by any means, but this...there are just no words to describe it.

I look down at my itinerary again, after I get over the shock of seeing Rockefeller Center out the car window. *Rockefeller Center!*

I know I'll probably want to pack my bags and move into the Center for Photography, but my next stop is lunch, which I don't want to miss. I had one of the granola bars in the limo, right after we left the hotel, but I'm still starving.

We finally arrive at the museum and Raphael's at my door in no time.

"I'll be back out front at eleven-thirty, ma'am," he tells me as I get out of the car and stare at the glass revolving door leading into the museum. I can't believe I'm actually here! "If you think you'll be later, please call this number, and let me know. I'll reschedule your lunch reservation."

Raphael hands me his card, and I take it with a smile. I'm pretty sure my smile will be a permanent fixture for the remainder of the day.

CHAPTER 16

The museum was everything I thought it would be and more. Andrew was right, I could spend days in that place, but I didn't want to miss lunch. At this point, my stomach is starting to eat itself.

I got a map when I went in to the museum, quickly decided on the exhibits I wanted to see most and stuck with that. I finished up right at eleven-thirty, and Raphael was waiting for me, as promised.

"Have you ever been to *21*?" I ask Raphael as we make our way there.

I can't believe it. Another legendary New York City spot, and I'm having lunch there. This *day*!

"No ma'am," Raphael responds with a chuckle. "But I'm sure you'll enjoy it. Pretty famous place."

"I still can't believe all of this," I tell him. I hope I'm not talking too much.

"Are you having a good time so far, ma'am?"

"You have no idea."

And I still have the Museum of Modern Art, Rockefeller Center and a tour of Radio City Music Hall to go!

"Glad to hear it." Raphael's smile makes me very happy. He's a nice compliment to my day.

We arrive at *21* and suddenly I'm panicked. Am I dressed okay? Don't they have a dress code here? I have on a new brown pencil skirt my mom bought me, my brown and pink striped button up blouse and my favorite pair of nude sling backs. But I'm not wearing pantyhose. Do you have to wear pantyhose? I don't know the rules!

"Raphael?" I get out of the limo and smooth out my skirt. "Am I dressed appropriately for this restaurant?" I ask, feeling kind of silly. Surely Andrew would have told me, if I wasn't.

Raphael smiles. "Yes ma'am. They used to be pretty strict," he says. "But they've gotten a little more lenient over the years. Just a little," he adds. "Not a lot."

"Thanks." I smile back at him.

"I'll be back in an hour, ma'am. Enjoy your lunch."

"Thank you, Raphael."

I walk toward the front door, and snap a quick picture of the little jockey statues on the staircase. God, I wish I had my good camera. If only I had known!

I walk, a little more confidently now, to the door and give my name to the hostess inside, as directed.

"Yes, Ms. Greene. Please follow me," she says in a very pleasant English accent.

When I walk into the dining room, I'm in awe...*again*. This has been one of the most exciting days of my life, and it's only lunch time!

I'm about to trip over my own feet while staring at all of the vintage toys hanging artfully from the ceiling, when I hear a familiar voice.

"Having fun yet?"

Andrew! Just when I thought this day couldn't get any better!

"What are you doing here?" I ask, and I don't even try to hide my enthusiasm. He looks so fantastic today, sitting in the booth in just his vest, tie loosened a bit and the top button of his shirt undone. Just...*wow*.

"I thought you might want some company for lunch." He stands when I reach the table and pulls out my chair. Such a gentleman. "Is that okay?"

Oh, it's more than okay. It's the best part of my day so far.

"Of course," I say as I sit down. Andrew resumes his seat in the booth across from me. "This place is..." I'm running out of adjectives at this point.

Andrew smiles. "I love this place. My mom used to drag me to New York with her at Christmas for her annual shopping trips. We always had dinner here one night on the trip."

I smile at the thought of Andrew with his mother. I never met her, but I've seen pictures, and everyone seemed to love her. She was apparently very nice and very beautiful, just like her son.

"I can see why you like it, from the atmosphere alone," I tell him, checking out the ceiling once more.

A waiter comes by to take our drink order, and I stick with water. The champagne in the limo, plus my lack of food, is making me a little lightheaded...or maybe it's Andrew.

"So, did you have fun at the museum?" he asks, after the waiter leaves.

"Mr. Mercer, it was one of the best experiences of my life. I kid you not."

"I thought you might like it," he says. "And please don't take this the wrong way, but I took the liberty of ordering your lunch beforehand."

"That's great. You've been here before, so I trust your judgment."

Why is Andrew ordering my lunch so sexy to me?

Oh. Right. Because it's *Andrew*.

"I did it for a couple of reasons," he continues. "I wanted to try and keep you on schedule, and I also wanted to keep up the tradition of you being pampered today. No need to think of anything. I have it under control."

Okay. Seriously sexy.

"Thank you again, sir." I laugh at my countless *thank you's* to him today. "Honestly, I'll probably be saying *thank you* every day for the next year," I confess.

Andrew laughs too. "No need. I'm glad you're having a good time."

He seems so relaxed. It should be strange, since I've never really seen him like this, but it's not. It's not strange at all. It's wonderful, and he's more beautiful than ever.

"So, how was your meeting?"

I'd nearly forgotten one of us was here on business.

"It went well," he says with a sigh, "But I don't think we're the right fit."

"I'm sorry to hear that," I say, secretly glad that I'm one down, one to go on the possibility of a dinner alone with Andrew tonight. However, I didn't anticipate the lunch date. I shouldn't be so greedy.

"It's okay," Andrew says. "I still have another meeting after lunch today, and then a couple scheduled for tomorrow, if this afternoon doesn't go as planned."

Wait a minute...if this afternoon goes well, then tomorrow....

"So, if you close your deal this afternoon, you'll have tomorrow off?"

Please tell me my luck is this good. *Please.*

"Yes," Andrew says smiling. "I thought you should maybe see Little Italy and Chinatown tomorrow. If I can, I'll tag along."

Oh thank you God. Thank you.

"You want me to take tomorrow off too?" I ask, tentatively.

Can I afford that though? I'm so behind. Oh, what am I talking about?! Andrew's going to possibly spend the day sightseeing with me? I'd blow off a meeting with the President of the United States for that opportunity.

"Why not?" Andrew asks, all nonchalantly. "Ms. Carter can handle my stuff another day. I think you deserve it."

I smile and take a moment to revel in the beauty and strength that is Andrew Mercer. He's so in his element here. Although, I'm pretty sure Andrew would feel confident most anywhere. The way he leisurely strolled into The Plaza this morning, like he does this sort of thing every day, which he kind of does, I guess. Nothing seems to faze him. That's why seeing him in that horrible state last week was such a shock for me. It gives me chills now just thinking about that night, and I still want to murder whoever did that to him. Pray they never cross my path.

"I'll check with Adrian...ummm, Ms. Carter this afternoon, just to be sure," I say. The control freak in me will start screaming around mid-afternoon. I'm sure of it. "She's totally competent," I add, not wanting to give a bad impression of my friend. "I'm just a---"

"Control freak?" Andrew interrupts me. "We can smell our own."

"Yes sir," I say smiling. "It's a merciless disease."

Andrew smiles, but before he can say anything further, our food arrives. I look at the cart with the uncooked meat and raise an eyebrow.

"Steak tartare," Andrew explains. "I hope you're not a vegetarian. It's delicious."

"Only carnivores here," I say excitedly. "Sounds fabulous."

Andrew and I eat our fancy lunch chit-chatting a bit about a few work related things, but a lot of the time is spent in comfortable silence and smiles. I find myself pretending more than once that we're just an old married couple, having a nice lunch together, enjoying each other's company.

My thoughtfully pre-ordered lunch ends with a chocolate soufflé that is to die for and a coffee with a shot of Bailey's. I could definitely get used to this.

"Let me take a picture of you with the jockeys," Andrew says, as we exit the restaurant. Raphael's already here waiting for me.

"Sure," I say, as I open my purse to grab my phone.

"Here, I'll take it with my phone," Andrew says, so I make my way over to the steps on my left.

I put my arm around one of the jockeys and give Andrew my best smile.

"Send it to me?" I ask, after he snaps the picture.

"Will do," he says. "Have fun, and I'll be in touch later this afternoon."

"Thank you, sir. Lunch was amazing."

Just like you.

"You're welcome, Ms. Greene."

I wave before I step into the limo, and Raphael closes my door. He and Andrew have a short exchange, and then I watch Andrew as we drive off, still standing in front of the restaurant, looking down at his phone and smiling. At my picture, perhaps? Probably not, but a girl can dream.

A couple of minutes after we leave the restaurant and Andrew's out of sight, my phone buzzes. It's from Andrew. It's the photo he just took of me at the restaurant.

Your professional opinion?

I laugh. It's actually not a bad shot.

Don't quit your day job.

I hesitate before I hit "send". Am I flirting again? Do I care? Nope.

I press the "send" button. A few seconds later, my phone buzzes again.

Don't worry. Still a good memory, nonetheless?

Wait, is he asking if I had a good time at lunch? Is he serious?

One of my best memories. Thank you.

I hit "send" this time, without thinking twice about it.

Enjoy the rest of your day, Ms. Greene.

I sigh and lean back in my seat. I think about sending the picture to Abby, but I don't want to piecemeal this trip. I'll wait until tomorrow when I get back so I can talk for hours about how amazing this has been.
Oh Andrew Mercer, how I love thee.

CHAPTER 17

My afternoon went by in a flash. After lunch, the remainder of my schedule kept me on my toes, but I enjoyed every second.

I got to see another museum, walked around Rockefeller Center and even got a quick, private tour of Radio City Music Hall. And sweet Raphael drove me through the crazy madness that is Times Square so I could take a few pictures. It was absolutely unbelievable!

Now, I'm sitting in my room, rubbing my poor feet. My favorite, comfy sling backs are no longer my favorites. I don't think I could have handled all the walking I did today in my sneakers, much less a three-inch heel.

I'm starting to doze off in my relaxing, baby blue hotel room, when my phone rings. It's Andrew.

Please say you're having dinner with me. Please. Please. Please.

"Hi, Mr. Mercer."

"Evening, Ms. Greene. I can only assume you are utterly exhausted."

I smile. "Yes, but it was worth it. I had a wonderful time."

"Glad to hear it," he says. "Do you have dinner plans? If not, would you like to join me?"

YES! YES! YES!

I realize that must mean his deal didn't go well this afternoon, but I honestly couldn't care less at the moment.

"No sir. I don't have any plans." I'm so glad he can't see my face right now.

"Great. Did you bring anything casual to wear?"

"Actually, no," I tell him. "I wasn't prepared for anything other than work."

"I assumed as much," he says. "Something will be delivered in about thirty minutes. Ms. Carter helped me, so I hope you like it."

Adrian? I'm starting to wonder what Adrian must think is going on here. She's a pretty sharp girl.

"You didn't have to do that, sir. I could've gone out and picked something up."

This is a lie. After my sightseeing today, I found out quickly that I'd need about four of my current salaries to survive here.

"Meet me downstairs near the front door in an hour," he says, ignoring my last statement. "I hope you like Italian food."

"Sounds great." My face is starting to hurt from smiling. "I'll see you then."

After we hang up, I jump out of the bed, sore feet all but forgotten, and head for the shower. I'm very curious to know what Adrian picked out for me. Please don't let it be jeans and a t-shirt. I wouldn't mind looking nice tonight.

I finish my shower quickly and start my make-up. My get-ready process is normally not a very long one, but tonight's different. I know Andrew's apparently off the market, but that doesn't mean I can't do my best to look exceptional.

As I'm finishing up my eye-shadow, I hear a knock at the door.

I grab a couple of dollars from my purse and give it to the bellhop after he hands me a white hanging bag, along with a shiny white gift bag that's closed with a ribbon on top.

I open the white hanging bag first and smile when I see what's inside.

Sweet Adrian, let's be forever friends.

Adrian has chosen a stylish pair of dark jeans, a deep green camisole with lace trim at the top, and a fabulous short black suit jacket, trimmed in satin. If I had a dozen outfits to choose from, I would have gone for this one. It's perfect.

I open the gift bag next and see a shoe box on the bottom. *Oh boy!* There's also another small cream-colored bag inside, which I open first. It contains a beautiful, long silver chain necklace with a bunch of fun charms all bunched together on the end and a pair of silver hoops to match. It also includes a small clutch that's deep, purple suede.

I open the shoes, praying I don't have to endure super high heels this evening. My prayers are answered. *Thank you Adrian!* It's a beautiful pair of black, patent leather flats that look as inviting as my fuzzy slippers back home.

I hurry back to the bathroom to finish my make-up and do my hair. I have another half hour before I'm supposed to meet Andrew. Plenty of time.

I spend some extra time on my curls, making sure they are silky smooth. I decide to leave my hair down and since I rarely ever wear it down, I'm surprised to see how long it is – hanging a little past the middle of my back. Perhaps a cut is in order when I get home. The plus side is that it will probably be pretty chilly tonight, with zero humidity, which equals a good hair night for me.

Now, time for the clothes. I looked at the sizes earlier, and everything was perfect. Adrian's good.

I slip everything on and go back to the bathroom for one final look. It all fits like a glove.

I put a few necessities in the clutch purse and check the clock. I have fifteen more minutes. I stare out the window at the busy street below as my nerves start kicking-in.

I've worked for Andrew Mercer for two years now. He was difficult in the beginning. It's true. But I quickly saw a softer side of him that no one else seems to be able to see. Every day I think about walking away. I *should* walk away. But then, just when I feel like I'm at the end of my rope – the crazy party I was asked to plan, the hiring of my new Bitchface boss lady, and then the ultimate blow from the afternoon of hell – just when I think I can't take any more, he gives me today.

But even before today...

I knew last week, when he came into the office that night. I knew as I held him in my arms that I would love him forever. No matter how things work out between us – which I fear will not be in my favor – I will never get over Andrew Mercer. I will never stop loving him.

I wipe the single tear that manages to escape my eye and laugh. I am becoming quite the crier.

I look at my watch and decide to go ahead and make my way down. It's never a bad thing to be a little early, is it?

As I leave my room and head toward the elevator, my anxiety starts slowly turning into excitement. I remind myself again that he has no idea I have feelings for him. I'm going to enjoy every second of this evening alone with him. Who knows when I'll have this opportunity again?

I step off the elevator feeling calm and confident in my fabulous new outfit, thanks to Adrian.

I stroll leisurely through the stunning lobby again, knowing I have a little extra time. I snap a few more pictures with my phone as I walk.

When I finally reach the doors, Andrew's nowhere to be seen. I check my watch and see – thanks to my doddling in the lobby – I'm right on time.

I take another glance around, and still nothing. Hmmm...where could he be?

As I'm searching, a sinfully hot guy in a worn leather jacket catches my eye. Andrew's the ultimate for me, of course, but that doesn't mean I can't appreciate the scenery every once in a while.

I still don't see Andrew, so I return my attention to the hottie in leather. His back's to me, and he's talking on the phone.

I watch him for a second, and then...wait a minute. *No way.* He's standing near a wall, long legs slightly parted, knees locked, and his left hand tucked in his jeans pocket. I can't believe it. I would recognize that stance from a mile away.

I walk slowly up to him, trying to catch my breath, but it's a challenge.

Dark jeans, what looks like a light blue button-up shirt underneath a faded brown leather jacket, and brown boots to match.

Sweet Jesus.

He's putting his phone away as I reach him, so I tap lightly on his shoulder. Lord he smells good, and his hair has that still-damp look I crave every morning.

Andrew's eyes widen when he turns and sees me standing behind him. *Oh no.* Do I have something on my face? I smile, embarrassed. Please don't let something be wrong.

"Ms. Greene." He clears his throat. "Sorry about that. Ready?"

He looks away from me quickly, and starts toward the revolving door, which probably means I do have something embarrassing going on. Lipstick on my teeth? Something on my nose?

I catch my reflection right before I go through the door. Nope. Nothing on my face or my nose. Thank goodness. I wipe my teeth with my index finger, just to be safe.

I follow Andrew outside, and it's chillier than I thought it would be. We have to wait a moment for the valet to get us a taxi. Andrew won't look at me. *What's going on?*

"So, where's this restaurant?" I ask while we wait, trying to ease the tension. He seems startled by the sound of my voice.

Good Lord, he looks absolutely beautiful this evening. Andrew in a three-piece suit is a sight to behold, but Andrew in a leather jacket is like sex personified.

"Little Italy," he says, before looking away from me again.

"That makes sense, I guess." I try to joke, but he's obviously very tense. Perhaps something happened on the call? Or this afternoon?

"How did your meeting go today?" I ask, fishing for some information.

Andrew seems to relax a bit. "It went very well. I think it's a done deal."

"Great news!" I say excitedly. "A successful trip then?"

And do I still get to spend all day tomorrow with you? Please?

"So far, so good," he says, looking over at me now, but there's something in his eyes...it's that look again, that look of wistful longing he gave me last week in his drunken stupor, but there's no sadness there this time. Oh my Lord. I don't think my undies can take it.

"I'm glad things went well," I say smiling, trying to extinguish the fiery feeling I now have between my thighs.

Finally! Taxi cab to the rescue!

The valet opens the door, and I scoot in. Andrew slides in beside me. He gives quick directions to the driver for the restaurant, and we're on our way.

I'm honestly still full from lunch, but how can I resist Italian food from Little Italy?

"If I may, Ms. Greene, you look...very nice this evening."

I feel the heat rise in my cheeks. Did he just compliment my looks again? Was that what the pause was about when he saw me? *I wonder...*

"Thank you, sir." I'm hoping the dark cab is hiding my blush.

"You and Ms. Carter did a great job."

"It was mostly Ms. Carter," he admits. "I did suggest the shoes though."

"That's my favorite part." I smile. How thoughtful is he? "And you look nice as well," I add. "It's strange seeing you out of a suit."

"Believe it or not, I prefer it," he says smiling. "Perhaps it's time to bring back casual Fridays?"

I laugh. "Great idea."

Andrew in jeans and leather jackets every Friday? Yes, please!

"So, tell me about the rest of your afternoon." Boss man Andrew seems to be coming back to me a little now. Good. I'm not sure how many more of those looks or compliments I can bear.

"It was fantastic," I say, feeling myself calm a bit as well. "I wasn't sure what to expect from the Radio City tour, but that may have been my favorite part of the day."

"It's great, isn't it?" Andrew's smiling again. "I wish we had time for a show. It's a lot of fun."

"I'll make sure to add that to my list for next time."

"Oh, have I gotten you hooked now?"

Oh Andrew, you had me hooked long ago, my love.

"Definitely! I'm having the best time."

"Good. I hope you enjoy dinner."

"Italian food happens to be my favorite," I admit, and it's true. I'm a sucker for pasta and pizza, any way you slice it.

"This place is a little more laid back than *21*," he says. "And the atmosphere is kind of rustic, but the food is excellent."

I smile at him. "Sounds perfect."

The taxi pulls up at the restaurant, and I hop out first, as Andrew pays for our fare. I start to feel guilty about what this trip must be costing him. Other than a couple of bottles of water, I haven't spent a dime.

Sure, he has the money, but I have a thing about people spending money on me. I blame that one on my dad, since he spent the majority of my life trying to buy my affection.

I totally need a therapist.

"Let's go," Andrew says, as he steps out of the cab.

Andrew made reservations, so the hostess escorts us immediately to a small dining area in the back of the restaurant.

Andrew was right, the décor is rather rustic, but I love it. The lighting is dim, and the whole place is wood – the floors, the walls, even the ceiling. The walls are covered in an eclectic mix of photographs and paintings in various styles of frames, some just nailed directly to the wood. It's beautiful, really.

"Do you like wine?" Andrew asks after we're seated.

We're not in a completely private room, but our table is very secluded in a corner. It's surrounded by some more of the beautiful artwork I saw as we walked in that I can't seem to take my eyes off of, and that's saying a lot, based on what's sitting across from me. The man is definitely a work of art.

"Yes," I answer, as I continue to scan the walls around us.

"Red or white?"

"Red."

"Do you mind if I choose?"

I smile at him. "Be my guest. Your selections at lunch were excellent. I trust you."

"When it comes to food." He laughs, and then orders a bottle.

"Not only when it comes to food," I add, after the waiter leaves. "I rarely doubt you."

"Oh no?" Andrew cocks a perfect eyebrow at me, and I smile.

Screw it. Let the flirting begin.

"Because you typically make good decisions," I say. "You hired *me*."

"Wow." Andrew tries to look appalled, but his smile is giving him away. Adorable. "Were you drinking in your room earlier?"

"What are you saying, Mr. Mercer?"

Andrew looks at me, and it's not just any look. *Holy Lord.*

"Best decision I ever made," he says confidently, before looking back down at his menu.

No way that just happened. *No. Fucking. Way.*

The waiter brings our wine, and I quickly look down at my menu trying to regroup. Okay, so I was flirting. No doubt about that. But he's flirting with me too. Andrew is flirting with me! Oh. My. God!

Now I'm nervous and don't know if I can keep it up. Besides, doesn't he have a girlfriend, or sex-buddy, whatever the hell he's doing with her now? I swallow hard. The thought of them together...I just can't seem to keep it down.

The waiter asks for our order, and I'm still studying the menu. I have no idea what to order. I've read the description for the eggplant parmesan twenty times now.

"Do you know what you're having?" Andrew asks.

I take a deep breath and look at the waiter. "I'll have the eggplant parmesan."

"Excellent choice, ma'am." The waiter looks to Andrew.

"I'll have the same."

"Fantastic. It will be out for you shortly."

After the waiter leaves, I find I can barely look at Andrew.

No need to be awkward now, Jules. You're no amateur in this arena. Just make the best of it.

I take a couple more subtle deep breaths. I still have every intention of finding a new job as quickly as possible, so what do I really have to lose?

Game on.

"So, you're free tomorrow now?" I ask.

"Looks that way," he says with a smile.

"You know, if there's one thing about today I could have changed, it would've been to have someone to share it with," I admit, truthfully. "All of the incredible things I saw…it would have been nice to have someone else there to experience it with me."

Andrew looks disappointed. "I'm sorry," he says. "I would have joined you, if I could. That's why I tried to be available for lunch. I wanted to make sure everything was going well. "

I wave him off. "Mr. Mercer, please don't be sorry. Today was amazing. I only said that to say it will be nice to have someone to sightsee with tomorrow."

"We'll have a good time," he says. His eyes are bright and shining in the dim light. "So, did you speak to Ms. Carter this afternoon?"

"I did speak with her briefly," I admit. "She assured me all was well and told me to have a good time. I assume you told her about my little excursion today?"

"I did," he says. "She agreed it was well deserved."

"I can't wait to tell my roommate." Abby is going to die! "She told me to bring her back a souvenir. I'll have to find something tomorrow."

"What would she like?"

I laugh. This wine is delicious. "For Abby? The cheesier the better. I was thinking about one of those 'I heart NY' shirts, or maybe a foam Statue of Liberty crown."

"Did you buy any souvenirs today?"

"No sir."

"Too good for souvenirs?" he teases.

"No." I laugh. "Just didn't see anything that caught my eye."

"Nothing at all?" And there's that look again. Oh my.

I have so many possible responses on the tip of my tongue, but the coward in me backs down. Bitchface and the scene from Saturday pass through my mind.

What are you doing, Jules?

"No sir," I say, with a touch of sadness. "Nothing that felt right."

"I see." Andrew doesn't even try to hide his disappointment. "That's too bad."

Subject change, Jules. Subject change.

"So, what were your bids for this morning? Are we going to build in New York?"

Perhaps that will be a good excuse for me to come back for some work-related reason. I really do love it here.

Andrew hesitates for a moment and studies me. "Could I ask a favor?" he finally asks.

"Of course."

Anything for you, Andrew.

"Can we be friends tonight, rather than co-workers?"

I'm confused, while Andrew's face seems eager and sincere.

"Sure," I manage.

"Great," he says, a big smile stretching across his face. "You can start by calling me Andrew, not Mr. Mercer."

I nearly choke on my sip of wine. "Sir?"

Andrew cocks his head at me. "My friends do not call me *sir* or *Mr. Mercer*," he says. "They call me *Andrew*."

"Okay...*Andrew*." I give his name a try, and it feels better than expected coming off my lips.

And to my delight, Andrew seems to react pleasantly to it as well. His smile is wide as he leans in a little closer to me across the table.

"And may I call you *Julia*?"

God, he's stunning.

I pause a moment, concentrating on the way my name sounded coming out of his beautiful mouth – my poor heart...and my poor undies.

I take another, rather large, sip of my wine.

"My friends actually call me *Jules*," I correct him, with as much confidence as I can muster.

"*Jules*," he says, letting it linger a bit on his smiling lips. "Jules it is."

I lean back in my chair, needing a break from the tension between us. If I make it through this evening without jumping his bones, it will be a miracle. What's going *on*?

"So, *Jules*," he starts again. I smile and automatically lean in with the sound of him saying my name. I could listen to that all day. "I have something to tell you, but I need you to promise to keep this to yourself for now. Can you do that? As a friend?"

"Yes sir...I mean, Andrew," I say smiling. Old habits die hard. "No problem."

"Good," he says smiling back at me. "I'm going to tell you something, but the main reason I'm telling you is so I can explain some things that have happened recently that I feel need to be rectified...as a friend."

I nod, wondering where the hell he's going with this. Andrew leans even closer toward me, and I follow.

"The company's in trouble. It has been for a while now," he says, and my sharp intake of breath is uncontrollable. *What*? I had no idea. "I've been trying to reinvent some things, push us in a new direction, but I'm not having much luck."

"What's happened?" I truly was unaware of any issues. Andrew and I are close at work, but I'll admit he keeps things on a "need-to-know" basis. This little confession is definitely out of the ordinary.

"The economy," he says, "among other things," he adds, under his breath.

Other things? What the hell's going on?

"I thought things were going well," I admit. "I've heard people talk about how much better things are, since you've taken over the day-to-day. You're a born leader, Andrew, and you've single-handedly put Mercer Construction on the map."

No one likes Mercer Senior. I'm not alone in that one. And most people aren't huge fans of Andrew either, but they all agree he is the better leader for the company. It's a fact.

Andrew is smiling at me. "Thank you," he says. "But I didn't do anything *single-handedly*, and even if that were true, it doesn't change the fact that the company is in trouble. Let's just say I don't have the easiest job at the moment."

I feel sad for some reason. Is that why Andrew is so closed off and withdrawn? He hates his work?

"I'm sorry," I tell him. "I honestly had no idea."

He smiles again. "Haven't you ever wondered why I'm such an ass at work?"

I smile too. "I just thought that was your personality."

"Nice. Thanks."

"What?" I tease. "I thought that was your *work* personality. How's that?"

"Better, I guess."

If he doesn't stop all this smiling, I'm going to come across the table and attack his mouth with mine.

"I'm having an issue trying to get investors for my new ideas," he adds, and his beautiful smile disappears. Dark and withdrawn Andrew now sits before me. His face is similar to the one that haunts me from last week.

No, Andrew. No.

I hide my hand under the table, as it's anxious to reach out to him, to comfort him again.

"What's wrong?" I whisper.

Please don't be sad, Andrew. Not tonight.

He shakes his head. "I think my father's trying to sabotage me."

CHAPTER 18

Okay, the news about Mercer Senior isn't as shocking as it probably should be, since that man is a complete dick, but how could he do something like that? He's Andrew's *father*!

"I'm not totally sure yet," Andrew continues, "But I have my suspicions, and a recent development that points some fingers at him." Andrew laughs in disbelief. "As of a few months ago, he was all for my ideas, but something's changed. I have to find out what's going on. I haven't looked into too much yet. Honestly, I just haven't wanted to believe it's true."

"Andrew, I'm so sorry." My eager hand is nearly at his leg under the table. I can't control it. My need to love him, to comfort him, is overwhelming.

Andrew looks up at me with that look – this time it's the sad and desperate one from his office last week. My heart breaks all over again, and I have to try hard to keep my tears down.

"Is that what last Thursday was all about?" I ask him.

It would make sense. Finding out your own, trusted father is working against you would be enough to bring even the strongest man to his knees.

Andrew looks down and nods. "I'm sorry about that, by the way," he says, looking back up at me. "I found out some news that night that was pretty unsettling. I was…devastated, to say the least, but as your boss, even as a friend, my actions were inappropriate. I'm sorry."

"Please don't apologize for that," I tell him.

Oh Andrew, please don't apologize for giving me one of the best nights of my life. Please say it was one of yours too.

"I have another apology," he says, but before he can begin again, the waiter shows up with our food.

How am I supposed to eat *now*?

The waiter leaves and Andrew ignores his food for the moment, so I do as well. I keep my eyes on him, encouraging him to continue.

"Please let me get this out, before you say anything, okay?" he asks, and he looks very uncomfortable. I instantly know what's coming.

I look down at my lap and close my eyes. *You can do this, Jules. You can take it. You're strong enough.*

I look back up at him, my confidence on shaky ground.

"Okay," I say, but I hear my voice tremble, and I'm sure he does too.

Just let me get through this without crying. Please God.

Andrew takes a deep breath. "I have to apologize for last Saturday with Ms. Hamilton. But selfishly, I want to explain what happened, for my own sake, probably more than yours."

As directed I don't say a word. I just listen, using every bit of strength I have to hold back my stubborn, unruly tears.

"As I'm sure you may have noticed, something's going on between Ms. Hamilton and my father," he starts. "I haven't really gotten to the bottom of that one yet, either. She came on to me at the garden party, and I played along, for my own reasons. I want to tell you those reasons, but I'm so scared you'll think less of me."

Wait. *Played along*? What does he mean?

"I won't," I assure him. "I promise."

As much as I hate to admit it, nothing will ever change the way I feel about you, Andrew. Nothing.

My words seem to be enough. He takes another deep breath before starting again.

"My father's a cunning business man, as I'm sure you know. If I am going to find out anything about his plans for the company, I'm going to have to take an indirect route." I stay quiet so he'll continue. "My father hiring Victoria is just one of several things that have raised an alarm for me over the last few months. I've played along with Victoria from the start because I thought if I could get close to her, perhaps she would help lead me to some answers. I'm not sure it will work, since she's turning out to be even more devious than my father, but she's my best bet at the moment. Plus, keeping her happy can only work to my advantage right now."

I start blinking rapidly. *Pull it together, Jules!*

Is he saying that he doesn't really like that hag? Is he saying that he's using her to get information on his dad? Could this day get any better?

I should be appalled. I should be disgusted. But I'm not. Not one bit.

I can't speak. This changes everything. He doesn't love her.

"Jules?" Andrew clears his throat. "Ms. Greene, say something. Please."

"I'm sorry," I say, shaking my head. I need to clarify this, before my heart pounds out of my chest. "So, you plan to use Bit---Ms. Hamilton to try and find out what your dad is up to?"

"Yes." Andrew looks so uncomfortable. It's the cutest thing ever.

And I can't even describe how it makes me feel that he's this concerned with how I may react to this news.

"So, you two are not really seeing each other?" This is turning into such an inappropriate conversation, but I have to hear it. Point blank. From the horse's mouth.

"God, no." Andrew shakes his head, his face full of disgust. "You honestly think I would associate myself intimately with that woman? I would hope you of all people would think better of me than that."

Me of all people? What the hell does that mean?

Andrew's smiling again now, seemingly feeling better since he found out I'm not horribly upset about his devious seduction plans. Honestly, I couldn't be happier. He can seduce me any time he wants.

"Jules, I feel like you know me better than most people," he continues, "Probably better than a lot of my closest friends. How could you think I would fall for someone like her?"

"I'm sorry," I say, feeling like I'm getting scolded.

"You said you rarely doubt me," he reminds me.

The comment catches me off guard. He's right. It's one of the first times I've doubted him, but only because I let my own insecurities get in the way.

"It won't happen again," I assure him, and it won't.

"Good," he replies, still smiling. "So, you're not upset about me...*using* Victoria for information?"

I smile too. "Not at all," Am I being too obvious? *Back it up, Jules.* "Should I be? I mean, it's truly none of my business."

"Well, it's probably not the most gentlemanly thing I've ever done, but I'm desperate," he says. "I'm glad you're not upset with me."

"Mr. Mer…I mean, Andrew…" Man, this name thing is tougher than I ever thought it would be. "I'm sure you can understand this news is rather shocking to me. I mean the company being in trouble is one thing, but then your own father working against you? I don't know what to say."

I'm trying to avoid the Bitchface conversation with all my might. I need time to process.

"I want you to know that I'm here to support you, as a co-worker and as a friend, whatever you need," I add.

I will always be here for you Andrew. I only wish I had the guts to tell you how much you really mean to me.

"Thank you," he says. His eyes are soft and inviting. "That means a lot to me."

I smile, feeling a little embarrassed now about the whole conversation. Did I give away too much?

Andrew grabs his fork and takes a bite of his dinner. My stomach is in knots, but I make an attempt to do the same.

We both give each other a sort of sad smile as we chew.

"Are you very hungry?" he asks, after he finishes his bite.

"Not really," I admit, as I finish mine.

"Do you want to get out of here?"

"Very much."

Although the setting is kind of romantic, my buzz from the wine is making me even less hungry than before. And with the news Andrew just dropped on me – and the strange chemistry between us this evening – the tension is so thick it's smothering. I think we both could use some fresh air.

"Great," Andrew says, his eyes excited, as he signals for the waiter.

"I feel bad leaving all this food."

"So do I, but I couldn't be less hungry."

"Same here," I agree.

Andrew chugs the remainder of his wine, and I finish mine as well, as he takes care of the check. I stand and wait as he puts the dreamy leather jacket back on, and then we head for the door.

Andrew's able to hail a cab fairly quickly when we exit the restaurant, and I'm excited to hear the destination when he tells it to the driver.

"The Empire State Building?" I repeat. "I'm glad we're going there. I was wondering why you didn't include it on my list today."

"It's better at night," he says. "Trust me."

We don't say much in the cab, and I'm honestly not sure what to think. With the unexpected declarations at dinner, the palpable tension and meaningful stares, there's definitely something strange going on between the two of us. If I didn't know any better, I would say Andrew has flirted with me a few times tonight, but I can't allow my head to fully go there. I'm too scared for my heart.

When we arrive at the Empire State Building, I have a brief touristy, fangirl moment.

"I can't believe I'm here!" I tell Andrew once he steps out of the cab behind me. "I just don't know if I'll ever be able to thank you enough."

The sound of Andrew's chuckle warms my insides, which is a welcome feeling. It's getting kind of chilly out, and this silk camisole is not the warmest piece of clothing imaginable.

"I think you've thanked me enough," he says. "You deserve this, Jules. You really do."

I find myself staring at his luscious lips. Will I ever get used to him saying my name? I don't think so.

I break my stare, but not before I notice a huge smile spread across Andrew's face.

It's the wine. It has to be the wine. My poise and self-control seem to be abandoning me in a time of dire need!

I walk quickly toward the front doors. Andrew catches up and walks beside me. I can tell he's looking at me, but I keep my eyes straight ahead.

The confidence I had at dinner is gone. I close my eyes briefly as we stand at the counter and Andrew gets our tickets for the lift.

"Are you okay?" he asks.

Dammit! Why am I so nervous all of a sudden? *Calm the hell down, Jules!*

"Totally fine," I say, attempting a smile.

"You're not scared of heights are you?" Andrew's smiling at me.

Yes! There's a good out!

"Maybe a little," I lie.

"Don't worry," he says, as he grabs our tickets. "I'll keep you safe."

Oh, Andrew. You're not helping.

The elevator's crowded, which forces Andrew and me close together, but still not quite touching. He lets me in first, so his back is to my front. In a now thinning effort to keep things professional, I do everything possible to keep the distance between us, but I can't resist the smell. *Oh God.* That delicious smell – made even manlier tonight by the scent of worn leather.

I give myself a quick pep talk on the way up. It's the same deal as always: Andrew doesn't know I have feelings for him. Even if he suspects it, it's not confirmed. I can deal with that. I can always deny, if necessary.

I step out of the elevator behind Andrew, and follow his lead through the glass doors onto the observation deck. Good Lord, this is incredible!

An audible gasp escapes my lips, as we get closer to the side and look out. The view is so beautiful; I think I could cry again. Since when am I such a sap?

"Are you okay?" Andrew asks again.

I smile. He thinks I'm afraid. It's cute.

"I'm fine," I say, staring out at the breathtaking view, as we walk along the wall. "This is indescribable," I tell him, shaking my head in awe.

"Beautiful," he says, but I barely catch it, he says it so softly.

I look over to make sure I heard him correctly, and he's staring out at the lights, deep in thought.

And then I find I can't peel my eyes away. I know I'm staring at him, but I don't really care at the moment. This is by far the best view in town.

Out of nowhere, a shiver rocks my entire body. I want him in my arms again so badly it hurts.

Control it, Jules!

"Are you cold?" Andrew looks back over at me, and stops to take off his jacket.

I smile and nod. I'm so warm right now, I could probably set this place on fire if I concentrated hard enough, but I will not say "no" to having that jacket and his mouth-watering scent wrapped around me.

Andrew steps behind me and puts the jacket around my shoulders. I close my eyes, anticipating a finger to stray and caress my neck or shoulder, but it doesn't. He places the jacket on me so delicately; it's as if he's purposefully trying not to touch me.

Of course that's the case, Jules. When will you ever learn?

Feeling the cold – and disappointment – settle in now, I pull the jacket around me, and slump into it.

"Ms. Greene---"

"Jules?" I quickly correct him. "Still friends, right?"

"Right." Andrew lets out a nervous laugh. What's going on *now*? "I need to ask you something."

"Sure," I say, turning away from the view and toward Andrew. I watch in confusion as Andrew's eyes size me up, turning from absolute uncertainty to burning determination in a flash. The intensity of his stare nearly takes my breath away.

He moves closer to me, and I match his one step forward with one step back.

I can't concentrate when you're that close to me, Andrew.

We continue our dance, until my back is pressed firmly against the wall. His body and face are inches from mine, as he places one of his hands on the wall behind me.

"I just have a quick question," he starts. I can barely breathe. "When I told you about Ms. Hamilton tonight, I was very glad you weren't upset with me about my plans for her. You probably should be, but I'm glad you're not."

That's not a question.

I wait for more, but nothing comes. And then, all coherent thought completely escapes me as he places his other hand on the wall, leaving me trapped between his strong arms. His body is so close to mine that his shirt is brushing his leather jacket, which is still wrapped tightly around me.

"But I was a little confused by your reaction to the fact that I wasn't actually *seeing* her," he continues, trapping me now not only with his arms, but also his penetrating gaze. Oh, those gorgeous *eyes*.

I drop my arms to my sides, and he moves his body even closer so that it's just barely pressed against mine. That tease of a touch has me shivering again, but definitely not from the cold. Not this time.

"You seemed rather...*happy* that I wasn't dating her, Jules. And I would like to know why."

His smile is beautifully wicked, as he stands completely still, waiting for my answer. Can't he see what he's doing to me?

I'm pretty sure the blushing and panting have to be giving it away. I couldn't speak now if I tried.

"Jules?" he teases. "Cat got your tongue?"

Oh God. Did someone say *tongue*?

The word instantly draws my eyes to his mouth, but I look back up as quickly as I can manage. I'm hanging on by a thread here. This can't be happening. Can it?

My hair's whipping my face, blowing wildly with the wind, but I barely notice. That is until Andrew lifts his right hand from the wall to gently push a curl behind my ear. His thumb lingers at the top of my ear, and my eyes close. I can't take it. This is not happening. There's no way this is a happening.

"Jules?" I hear him ask again. "I'm waiting."

And the sweet sound of his voice is like a shot of adrenaline. Screw the professionalism. Let's try honesty. I think it's time to take a chance.

My eyes pop open, and the intense desire in his stare nearly breaks my resolve...nearly.

I stand up straight and move just a bit closer, so there's no longer any mistaking the fact that our bodies are touching. I exhale what feels like a breath I've been holding for centuries.

"Because I don't like the thought of you with her," I tell him, and take pleasure in the shock and awe that briefly cross his face.

He leans in and whispers in my ear. "And why is that exactly?"

I'm shivering again, as he puts his right arm around me and pulls me closer, burying his face in my hair. I leave my arms at my sides, still afraid to touch him, still afraid I may wake up.

"Because you're better than her," I say breathlessly into his ear, repaying the favor. I close my eyes again and press my cheek to his, then my lips to his perfectly chiseled jawline, just below his ear.

I feel Andrew tremble against me before pressing me hard against the wall. He has one arm firmly around my waist, and his other hand comes up to caress my face, his thumb landing on my quivering lips.

My eyes are still closed, breathing him in, when I feel him pull away from me slightly.

"And?" he says, caressing my bottom lip with his thumb.

I open my eyes and watch, as the intensity of his stare grows to the point where I feel like I may give in any second, but...

"I can't," I whisper. I'm able to push my tears down, but not before my voice breaks.

Don't make me do this, Andrew. Please don't.

Andrew doesn't let me go, which makes me extremely happy, but I feel my tears surface again as I watch him hang his head in defeat.

He wants you, Jules! He can't make things more obvious than this! Just do it! Just let go! For once! LET GO!

My arms are still at my sides. I have no idea how to react. I want to tell him how I feel, more than anything I've ever wanted in my entire life, but I can't get past the thought of losing him. It would end me. I'm sure of it.

"Jules," he whispers my name. "I have a confession," he says.

It takes everything inside me not to reach up and touch his face, to comfort him, anything to get rid of that hopeless look in his eyes, but I can't. What if this isn't real? This can't be real. It can't be.

"That night..." he starts again. "Last week, when I came to the office...I didn't come for a place to stay. I came..." He sighs. "I came looking for *you*."

That's it. I'm officially undone.

"I needed to be with you, Jules," he says, looking down at me. His voice is breathless and full of desperation. "All I could think about was seeing you. I knew you would make it better. You always do. I needed you. I still need you."

I reach my hand up to his face, placing it gently on his cheek. I exhale with the relief of finally being able to touch him. His eyes close with my touch, and he takes a deep, shuddering breath. I slide my thumb softly across his bottom lip, and as he opens his eyes, I pull his face toward me with confidence and without hesitation.

He needs me. Just like I need him. And I can feel the intensity of that need as his lips move slowly but passionately against mine.

He grabs at my waist and pulls me even closer. His warm and tasty tongue explores my mouth, and his confident hands reach under my camisole and land softly on my bare back.

I can't think of anything but Andrew. Work doesn't matter. Nothing matters. Nothing exists, but Andrew – just me and my sweet, sexy Andrew.

He's the first to pull away, and we're both breathless. Not quite satisfied, I reach up for one last taste, and Andrew gladly obliges. But what was supposed to be a quick peck rapidly turns into more, until eventually I feel his mouth smile onto mine.

"Ready to go?" he asks as he pulls away again, his eyes now lingering hungrily on my lips.

I nod, as he takes my hand and leads me back toward the elevators. It's the first time I even notice there are other people around. Oh well. They just got a show.

Andrew puts his arm around me in the elevator – now a little less crowded than before – and I gladly snuggle into him. He kisses the top of my head, and I burrow even further in. Eventually, I'm going to wake up from this dream, so I may as well enjoy it while I can.

He keeps his arm around me as we wait for a cab outside. I can feel him shivering, and I feel bad for taking his jacket.

I pull away from him and start to take it off, when he reaches for me and pulls me back into him.

"Stop it," he says, and I put my arms around his waist, my face resting on his perfect chest.

"But you're cold," I mumble, and I feel him shiver again.

"I'm fine," he says, his voice deep and tempting. "Trust me."

I smile and pull him closer. *I'll keep you warm, Andrew. Don't worry.*

We finally get a cab, and Andrew leads me in first. When he slides in beside me, he immediately offers his arms for me to crawl back into, and I gladly take him up on the offer.

"The Plaza," he tells the driver, and we're off.

Andrew puts a finger on my chin and lifts my head so we're eye to eye.

"Are you sure you're okay with all of this?"

I smile at the genuine concern on his face. *Silly, silly Andrew.*

I decide there's no need for words. Instead, I sit up and pull his beautiful face to mine once again.

Making out in a New York City taxi cab can now be crossed off the bucket list. *Check!*

When we arrive at the hotel, Andrew continues to hold me close as we walk through the lobby toward the elevators. When the elevator arrives and the door closes, I'm relieved to see we're alone.

I'm even more relieved that Andrew decides to take full advantage of that fact. He backs against the wall of the elevator pulling me against him and I wrap my arms eagerly around his neck.

I want to believe this is happening. I want to believe that the soft hand moving tenderly against the small of my back is real. I want to believe that the fingers under my hair, gently caressing the back of my neck, are real. I want to believe the fact that we're so close together that I can actually feel his heart beating is real too. I want to believe, but I'm just so scared.

We have to take a break from our make-out session when someone gets on at the fifth floor. It's an older couple, and they give us a suspicious look, as we simultaneously wipe our mouths. Andrew and I both smile, and he squeezes my hand. I squeeze back as the elevator arrives at our floor.

Is he leaving me? Surely he'll stay, right? My self-confidence won't last through to morning.

Please stay Andrew. Please stay with me.

CHAPTER 19

We walk toward our rooms hand-in-hand, looking at each other periodically and smiling – both of us obviously in shock by the events that have transpired tonight.

As we near our rooms, we still haven't said a word to each other. If he doesn't ask, I will. At this point, what do I have to lose?

As if on the same wave length, we both stop and turn to each other in unison.

"I'm not ready to leave you," Andrew says first, with quiet sincerity, as he looks down at our interlocked hands.

"Good," I say, reaching up to kiss his lips again. They taste better than a chocolate sundae on a summer day. Chocolate sundaes are my favorite. "My room's closer," I breathe on to his lips, and he pulls me tightly against him.

Somehow we manage to reach my room, all tangled up with each other. I smile as he seems reluctant to let me go so I can fish out my key.

As soon as I have it in my hand, Andrew's arms are around my waist again and his lips are back on mine. *Sweet heavens.* Those *lips*.

All of this time, I thought his eyes were his sexiest feature. I was wrong. So very wrong.

Andrew pulls away and smiles. He reaches for my hand still holding the key, and then lifts my hand, using it like a puppet-master to insert the key into the door.

I smile shyly, feeling embarrassed. After that last kiss, I forgot where I was for a moment.

Andrew keeps a hold of my hand, as he opens the door and leads me inside.

A sudden wave of panic hits me like a gust of wind when we enter the room. This is Andrew – the man I have been lusting over, fanatisizing about, obsessing over and falling madly, deeply, hopelessly in love with for the past two years. Am I ready for this? Am I truly ready for *him*?

"Would you like a drink?" Andrew asks, his voice jolting me back to the here and now.

"Please." I remove his leather jacket and toss it and my small purse on the bench in front of the bed. "I'm going to freshen up a bit, if that's okay."

I need a moment – a long moment.

Oh God. Oh dear God.

"Sure." Andrew gives me an anxious smile, which tells me I'm wearing my emotions on my sleeve, as usual.

I slide off my shoes and hurry to the bathroom before I can cause any further damage. As soon as I close the door, I put my hands on either side of the marble sink.

Deep breaths, Jules. In and out.

I can't do this. What if he doesn't live up to my expectations? I've put this man on the highest of pedestals. What if he's not everything I thought he would be?

I immediately roll my eyes at myself in the mirror.

Of course he'll be everything you thought he would be and more, you dumbass! It's you, you need to worry about! What if he doesn't like you?

I'm breathing so hard I'm starting to feel light headed. Am I hyperventilating?

Inhale. Exhale. You can do this, Jules.

I look at myself in the mirror.

It's *Andrew*.

And I love him. I do.

Whether or not he loves me back is irrelevant. I will always love him. And there's no way I'm letting a night like tonight pass me by.

A few more deep breaths and my pulse is finally back to a semi-acceptable level. I have nothing to worry about. Andrew came on to me. He started this, and now I'm eager to finish it.

I pull my fingers through a few of my curls in an effort to untangle the nappy mess. It's wildly unkempt from the crazy wind on top of the Empire State Building, but thankfully, it still looks relatively decent.

I decide to add a little blush and some lip-gloss, before turning to face the door.

I *am* ready for this. I've *been* ready for this.

I exit the bathroom and find Andrew standing and looking out the window, a glass of wine in his hand.

I take a second to study how his shirt dips into the deep groove between his broad shoulders. His silky hair is perfectly tousled, just the way I like it – even more so now, since I know it was my fingers that have it looking so wonderfully disheveled. And the way his jeans hug his muscular thighs and his beautiful behind has my mouth watering like I haven't had a drop to drink in days.

He looks magnificent, and tonight, he's all *mine*.

Eventually, he turns his head toward me and smiles, and I'm disappointed to see the smile is laced with uncertainty. My thin layer of confidence immediately starts to wither.

Andrew puts his glass of wine down on the table next to the window. I move toward him, anxious to pick up where we left off before my insecurities officially strangle me, but he holds a hand up to stop me.

What's this, Andrew? Have you changed your mind? Oh please no. I don't think my heart, or my ego, can take it.

"I have something to say." He crosses his arms around himself, and looks at me with serious eyes. "I wanted you to know that I'm perfectly okay with taking things slowly."

Wait. Is he nervous too?

I feel my confidence swell again, as I watch him squirm.

God, you're so lovable, Andrew.

"I know I was forward tonight," he continues, "but I'm not sorry about it. I'm tired of pretending."

Pretending? My heart is racing, but I hold my spot next to the bathroom, my eyes fixated on him.

I watch him run his fingers through his hair, and I whimper quietly. My hands are burning now with the need to touch him again, and although I'm eager to hear what Andrew has to say, I know I won't be able to keep the distance between us much longer.

"Last week," he starts again, as he sits down in the chair next to the window, "when I came to the office, I was so relieved to see you there. I wanted to tell you how I felt. I never expected..." he pauses and looks down at his feet. "I never expected you to do what you did. When you came into my office…I just never thought…"

I back up to the wall by the bathroom so I can lean against it for support. My legs are shaking. I'm not sure I can handle this confession.

Andrew continues to study the floor, and I want to say something, but all of this is so surreal, so unexpected. I have no idea what to say. All I can concentrate on at the moment is trying to figure out how in the hell I'm supposed to keep myself from running into his arms and never letting him go.

And when he suddenly looks up at me through those beautiful lashes, I can't hold on any longer.

I walk slowly over to him, noticing he watches my advance with sad eyes.

Don't be sad, Andrew. Please don't be sad.

When I reach him, his eyes are still on me as I run the back of my fingers along his cheek, trying to comfort him, reassure him.

"In your arms that night, I felt so safe," he says, softly. "I've never needed anyone or anything the way I needed you that night, and you were there for me, like you always are. That night…that night made me think, or hope rather, that maybe…that maybe you might need me too."

Despite the intense moment between us, I have to stifle a giggle.

Oh Andrew. If you only knew.

Andrew stands abruptly, and I back away from him as he starts pacing.

"But then, with everything that happened at the party, I could see you were upset. I had no idea how to handle the situation. I had no idea what to say or do. I wanted to call, email, something, anything to make it right, but I just didn't know…" He stops in front of me, grabs my hand and stares at it a moment. "And then tonight, I started to hope again that maybe…" He trails off, still looking at my hand, playing with my fingers. "That's why I came on to you. I couldn't resist. I had to know for sure."

Andrew looks at me, and I can tell he's waiting for me to say something. His eyes are darting from my eyes to my mouth, so I decide I better not torture either of us any longer. I'm about to speak, but impatient as ever, he starts in again.

"And I just want to add that after everything that's happened tonight, I'm still unsure." I'm stunned by the tentative look in his eyes. Can he really not see it? "This is not some kind of silly crush for me, Jules. If you feel something for me, I want to hear you say it. I *need* to hear you say it. Please."

As hard as it is after that confession, I somehow manage to gather myself and make sure to speak quickly this time before he gets going again.

"You know, I just realized that I never really answered your question from earlier," I say, as I move closer to him, and take his other hand in mine, so I'm now holding both. "At least, I wasn't one hundred percent honest," I add to clarify.

"What question?" he asks, seeming genuinely curious.

"The question you had for me earlier, before you attacked me on top of the Empire State Building," I tease. "I assume you remember that?"

"Fondly."

His voice is hushed and breathless as I drop his hands and start to unbutton his shirt. I look up at him through my lashes – a taste of his own medicine.

"Ask it again," I demand.

When I finish with the last button, I take a moment to admire the beauty before me, as I run my index finger slowly over his collarbone, down his chest, over his perfectly sculpted abs to the top of his jeans. He inhales sharply, and I smile.

"Mr. Mercer? Cat got your tongue?"

Andrew clears his throat, which I'm starting to learn is apparently a nervous habit.

"Ms. Greene…" God his smile is so sexy. "You seemed rather happy tonight when I told you I wasn't seeing Ms. Hamilton. Please do tell me why."

I put my hands on either side of his face, look into his eyes and take a deep breath.

This is the moment of truth, Jules. After this, there's no turning back.

"Because I'm in love with you, Andrew Mercer," I say quietly, but with confidence, and I'm surprised by how good it feels to finally get it out.

And best of all? He's not running from me. As a matter of fact, his beautiful hazel eyes are warm and reassuring.

"I've loved you for a long time, and I don't think that's ever going to change," I continue, as he puts his arms around my waist and pulls me close, only encouraging me further. "I've tried to change how I feel," I confess. "Because I never thought in a million years that you could ever feel the same, but even when I thought there was no hope, I still couldn't seem to let you go."

Andrew moves a hand to my cheek, and I lean into him. I've waited for this day, dreamt about this day, for so long. So far, it's better than I could have ever imagined.

"That night…last week?" I start again and he nods as he continues stroking my cheek. "It was a privilege to take care of you, Andrew. And even though you were in such a terrible state, that night…" I sigh. *Oh, that night.* "That night was one of the best nights of my life. It was the first time I got to hold you in my arms. It was the first time I felt like you needed me, really needed *me*…for something other than coffee or messages at least."

Andrew chuckles before smiling sweetly at me.

"I love you, Andrew," I repeat it, and I want to repeat it a hundred more times. "Does that answer your question?"

Andrew pulls me even tighter against him, and I move a hand from around his neck to touch his face…his lovely, lovely face.

"That was…*perfect,*" he whispers, and I smile.

He leans down to kiss me, and I delight in how soft and warm his lips are and how perfectly they fit with mine.

And those perfect lips never leave mine, as he moves his hands up and pulls at the collar of my jacket, and I quickly put my arms at my sides so he can remove it.

As I pull away, I grab Andrew's hands and lead him to the bed. I push him gently down, and he sits on the end. I smile as I move between his legs, and put my hands on his bare shoulders, under his sexy blue shirt.

"I love this shirt," I say, as I move my hands down his smooth, muscular arms, successfully removing said shirt.

"I'll wear it every day," he says smiling, as he finishes taking it off, and I put both hands on his chest, appreciating the thrill of touching his naked flesh.

I was right. He's even better looking *without* clothes.

Andrew puts his hands behind my thighs, and pulls me to him. His hungry eyes look up at me through those succulent lashes, and his smile is sinful.

"Actually, my favorite is your charcoal-colored three-piece with the garnet tie," I admit, as I pull my camisole over my head and drop it on the floor.

Andrew kisses my stomach, and I arch my back in response. This man is going to be the death of me.

"Really?" he breathes as his mouth explores my abdomen. His hands move to unbutton my jeans. "I think my favorite outfit of yours may be this one."

He pulls my jeans down, and I step out of them, so I'm standing before him in only my lacy black bra and undies to match.

I grab Andrew's hand and pull him up so he's standing in front of me. He puts a hand on my cheek, and starts pulling at my bottom lip again with his thumb. "My beautiful Jules," he sighs.

My beautiful Jules? Are we taking ownership now? Sounds good to me.

I reach up to kiss him again, and I gladly trail my fingertips down his chest and once again over his tight stomach, stopping at the top of his jeans. He moans softly into my mouth as I start unbuttoning them. I smile to myself, although I'm still wondering when I'll wake up from this incredible dream.

He pulls me close to him, and my body starts to rapidly heat up as my bare skin presses against his. *Heavenly.*

Andrew moves his hands up and down my back as we kiss, stopping a moment to unclasp my bra, and I let it fall to the floor with the rest of our clothes. I'm nearly panting when Andrew pulls away and admires me.

"My *very* beautiful Jules," he says, and I smile shyly.

In one very smooth, confident move, Andrew picks me up, spins me around and lays me gently on the bed. He removes his underwear and mine, before joining me. His face is radiant, and I sigh deeply, as he lies beside me, one of his legs between mine, his long, lean body warm against my side.

"So…" he starts placing soft but sultry kisses all over my cheek, then my neck, as his hand moves slowly, feeling its way around my body. "Tell me again…How are you liking New York so far?"

I thread my fingers through his hair and close my eyes, as his relentless lips reach my breasts.

"It's okay," I tease, breathlessly.

I can feel him smile against my chest. "Hmmm…just okay?"

He continues his assault down my sides, along my stomach, and once again, my back arches in delight.

"Better than okay," I gasp, as I open my eyes. "I love this city."

"Is that so?" Andrew pulls away slightly, and the grin on his face has me nearly undone already.

To hell with foreplay.

I put my hands on his chest and push him onto his back. I crawl slowly on top of him, straddling him. The connection sends instant relief flowing through my body, warm and satisfying.

Andrew gasps and closes his eyes, as I start to move. "I don't care what city we're in," I breathe into his ear. "Just as long as I'm with you."

"Jules," he murmurs my name softly before putting his hands on either side of my face, raising my eyes to his. "I'm all yours," he whispers, and I pull his beautiful mouth to mine.

CHAPTER 20

"I can't believe you have a tattoo," I tell Andrew, as I run my finger along the black lines that sit low on his left hip.

"You're just noticing it now?" Andrew chuckles, and it shakes my entire body, which is thoroughly intertwined with his.

I laugh as well. "I was a little distracted."

Andrew's arms are wound tightly around me, as we lay naked on the floor of my hotel room. Our breathing has only recently returned to normal.

"I got it when I was eighteen," he says. "My mom took me."

I look up at him in disbelief. "Your mother took you to get a tattoo?"

"She did," he says smiling. "I think she did it because she knew my father would hate it."

I smile back. I think Mrs. Mercer and I would have been great friends.

"Your mom sounds amazing."

"She was." Andrew's face is so sad when he talks about her. It's obvious he misses her like crazy.

"I'm sorry she's gone," I say, as I push some of his messy hair away from his eyes. "It was cancer, right?"

Andrew nods. "Breast cancer. It was so hard watching her suffer."

"At least she's not suffering anymore," I offer, not knowing what else to say. I've never lost anyone that close to me. I can't imagine.

"She would have liked you," he tells me, and I can see the tears threatening his eyes, but he's holding them back.

You don't have to be strong all the time, Andrew. Not around me.

I lean down and kiss his lips. "I know I would have liked her too, especially after finding out about the whole tattoo thing." Andrew laughs, and I'm glad the sad moment has passed. "So, what does it mean?" I ask, running my finger again over the swirly black ink. It's shaped like a plus sign, but the ends are all tangled around each other.

"My mother's family was from Greece," he tells me, which I never knew. "It's an old Greek symbol for strength. I guess she thought I may need it to put up with my dad." Andrew laughs again, but when I look up at his eyes, they're still sad.

"Greece, huh? I didn't know that about your mom," I admit, trying to move the conversation far away from Mercer Senior. "I'm part Syrian. Did you know that?"

Andrew turns on his side, and I follow suit, so we're facing each other.

"No," he says, as he leans in to kiss my cheek. "It's a shame really. I feel like I know very little about you, personally."

"Well," I say smiling, as I scoot closer to him. "Let's change that. What do you want to know?"

"Ummm, okay..." Andrew looks down at me. "You're part Syrian...do you speak Arabic?"

I laugh. "A little. My mom hates that I'm not fluent. She tried forcing me into it when I was younger, and I chose to rebel. Surprised?"

"Not really," Andrew says with a smirk. "Say something to me in Arabic."

His voice is so soft and seductive; I instinctively cuddle closer to him. I smile shyly as I decide what to say.

"Bahibbak," I tell him and Andrew smiles as he pulls me even closer.

"I hope you didn't just curse at me," Andrew teases. "But honestly, even if you did, it was still sexy as hell."

"You need help," I giggle. "And no, I did not just curse at you."

"No? Then what did you say?"

I hesitate, even though this is not technically the first time I've said it this evening. But Andrew is yet to return my affections, so I'll keep him guessing for now.

"I'll tell you later," I say with a huge grin.

"Seriously?" Andrew pouts, obviously not pleased with having to wait. "You're kidding me, right?"

I laugh at his adorably pouty face. "I guess you'll just have to find some patience, Mr. Mercer."

Andrew narrows his eyes at me. "Not my strong suit, Ms. Greene, and you know that."

"Why yes I do, sir." I love teasing him. "And that makes this so much more fun."

"You're evil." Andrew tries to hide his smile, but he fails miserably. "Pure evil."

I reach up to kiss his pouty lips and he happily obliges. "What else would you like to know about me?"

Andrew lifts a brow, as if contemplating whether or not he's ready to move past my rusty Arabic. I grin as I trace the curve of his jaw with my fingertips, and he falls perfectly into my trap.

He closes his eyes briefly and sighs. "Fine," he finally relents. "You win. For now."

I smile up at him, and he kisses my forehead before pulling away slightly.

"So, how many tattoos do *you* have, exactly?" he asks, and then moves to kiss the one closest to him on my ribs.

I gasp. "That one's my favorite, actually."

Andrew pulls away and takes a closer look. "It's beautiful," he whispers, before kissing it again, causing flashes of heat to surge pleasurably throughout my body.

"The dragonfly is me," I explain. "And the music notes coming off her wings represent a lot of different things – loss, change, independence."

I close my eyes as Andrew runs his fingertips along the outline of the dragonfly.

Oh dear God. Will I ever breathe normally again?

"And the others?" Andrew moves to kiss the one on my ankle next.

I laugh. "That was my first," I say, smiling at the cheesy little flower. "I love daisies."

Andrew smiles up at me before gently rolling me over and kissing the next one, high on my left hip.

I prop myself on my elbows and smile back at him. "It's a desert beetle with a prayer inside, written in Arabic. Kind of a tribute to my mom and all of her...struggles."

Andrew's face turns serious. "What's wrong with your mom?"

"Long story," I admit with a sigh. "Maybe another time."

I certainly don't want to get into that mess right now, and thankfully, Andrew doesn't press the issue. He moves his hand slowly up my back and kisses the final tattoo, near my hairline on the back of my neck.

"Is this the last one, or are you hiding others?"

"That's it." I giggle. "It's Hindi for 'balance'."

"Are you part Indian too?" he asks, and I giggle again.

"No. I just thought it looked cool. I was nineteen."

Andrew smiles and I roll back over, so we're facing each other again. "Anything else you would like to know?" I ask him.

"So many questions..." he says, studying me for a moment.

"Well, at least I already know how you take your coffee."

"Which is very important."

"Don't mock me." He smiles.

"I'm not." I smile too. "The way a person takes his or her coffee can be very telling."

"Oh really? Do enlighten me."

"Are you mocking *me* now, Mr. Mercer?"

"Never." His smile is killing me.

Andrew, please. My heart.

"For example," I run two fingers along his lips, "you take your coffee black, with two sugars."

"Yes," he whispers against my fingers and smiles.

"So, to the average person, it would look like bitter, black coffee." I slip one of my fingers into his mouth and then place it in my own. I close my eyes briefly and suck. Andrew moans deep in his chest, as I remove my finger and rub the wetness along his bottom lip.

"But once you have a taste, you find out that underneath all of that dark, broody bitterness is actually a touch of irresistible sweetness."

Andrew kisses my fingertips before placing my hand on his chest and pulling me closer.

"Clever," he whispers with a smirk.

"I try, sir."

"What about you?" he says, before kissing me sweetly on my cheek. "You drink your coffee black, no sugar. But you're all sweet and no bitter. Your theory doesn't work."

"Yes it does," I say breathlessly, as he trails kisses along my neck. "I only drink coffee for the caffeine, not for the taste. So, you could say I don't mess around. I get straight to the heart of things."

Andrew looks down at me. "You certainly got to mine."

Please God, don't ever let me wake up from this dream.

"You're quite the romantic, Andrew." I smile at him. "I didn't know that about you."

"I try, Ms. Greene," he teases and kisses me again. "And I'm glad to know there's still a little mystery there."

I laugh. "You're still a mystery to me in a lot of ways. There's plenty more I want to know about you."

Andrew puts a finger on my lips. "In time. Now, it's my turn."

"Fine." I say, and pull his finger into my mouth. He closes his eyes as I suck gently before releasing it. "What can I do for you, sir?"

Andrew pushes me down on the floor and hovers above me. "My questions can wait."

The next morning I wake up to the sun shining brightly through the window.

"Breakfast?" I hear, as I start to stir in the comfy bed.

I open my eyes quickly to find the source of that amazing voice. He *is* real.

Oh thank you, God. Thank you.

Andrew comes to sit next to me on the bed, dressed in his jeans from last night and a white t-shirt.

Best. Morning. *Ever.*

He reaches to push my bushy hair out of my face. I probably look horrifying, but it's not bothering me at the moment. Nothing is.

"Good morning, Ms. Greene," he says, as he leans down to kiss me on the cheek. "Hope you like French toast."

"Who doesn't like French toast?" I ask, pulling his face back to mine so I can kiss him again.

Andrew smiles. "Just one more thing I need to learn about you – what you like for breakfast."

"You're looking pretty tasty this morning." I smile seductively back at him, and he laughs.

"You are insatiable, Ms. Greene."

"Yes," I agree. "But I'm also starving, so you'll just have to wait."

"We have all day," he says, kissing me one more time.

Mmmm...I love the sound of that.

Andrew stands and heads back over to the small table, where he's set out our breakfast. I sit up and decide I probably need to do something about this hair.

I get out of the bed, still naked, and smile as I watch Andrew's eyes follow me all the way to the bathroom. He winks at me before I close the door, and I have to brace myself on the sink once inside. No one should be that good-looking. It's just not fair to the rest of the male population.

I take a quick look in the mirror and laugh at my ratty head. My curls are going in all different directions, but I find I can't be upset about anything right now.

I grab a ponytail holder from my bag and put it up quickly. Then I splash some cold water on my face and brush my teeth. Damn, that feels good.

I wrap the fabulous, plush robe around me that's hanging on the back of the door, and make my way back out for breakfast. I laugh as my stomach growls at the thought of the French toast. We basically skipped dinner last night. Add in the marathon love-making, and now, I'm ravenous.

Andrew's sitting in one of the chairs next to the table, reading the paper, with glasses on. I didn't know he wore glasses. The man even makes nerdy look sexy.

I smile as I approach him. It officially looks like this is not a dream. I can't believe it.

Andrew puts the paper down on the table, as I sit across from him, and removes his glasses.

"I already ate," he confesses. "I was starving."

I take a bite of my French toast before I respond. Oh good grief, that's awesome.

"How long have you been up?" I ask, after I finish my bite. I'm quick to jam another one in my mouth. I don't think food has ever tasted this good.

Andrew smiles sheepishly. "A while."

"You didn't sleep at all?"

"Not much." A sad smile threatens his face now, but I refuse to let that happen.

"I didn't know you wear glasses," I say, before taking another bite of my delicious breakfast.

"Yes, well, my contacts were killing me, so I took a chance on showing you my geeky side this morning." He smiles, and I melt.

"You're geeky side is rather sexy," I say, smiling. Andrew smiles back and then yawns. "And your eyes are hurting because you're tired," I scold him, but he just smiles at me again.

Beautiful, beautiful Andrew.

I get out of my chair and move toward him. I plop myself down in his lap and give him a soft kiss on the nose. "We can stay in today, if you want. After last night, I think I've officially seen all of this city I need to see." I press my hand against his chest, and kiss his forehead.

"I'm fine," he says, pulling me close in his arms. "I actually haven't slept well for a while now. I'm getting kind of used to it."

"Andrew, that's not good for you." I've noticed him looking tired in the office lately. No wonder. "You need some sleep. Let's stay in today." I run my fingers along his jaw, down his neck, down his chest…

"Jules," Andrew laughs. "I have a feeling even if we stay in, I still won't get any sleep."

"And why's that?" I tease.

"Because I find you rather irresistible," he growls, as he nuzzles into my neck.

Andrew, I'm never gonna let you go. You're stuck with me. Hope you're okay with that.

I plant a quick kiss on his nose before hopping out of his lap to finish my breakfast.

"Fine," I say, as I sit back down in front of my yummy French toast. "Are we still going to Chinatown? I'm sure I can find something fun for Abby there."

"We can do whatever you want."

Hmmm…I have so many sarcastic remarks for that one, but I'll leave him alone for now. I can tell he's exhausted. "You've been to this city before, not me. You decide. I trust you."

"Then yes, I think we should give Chinatown a shot. I think you'll like it."

"Sounds fun! I'll get Abby a good knock-off bag. She'll love it." I smile.

Andrew smiles too, before going back to his paper, and I continue with my breakfast. This French toast is seriously good.

After I finish, I walk back over and sit down in Andrew's lap. He welcomes me into his arms with a smile. And even though he seems extremely tired, Andrew looks the happiest I've ever seen him. The idea that I may have even the smallest of parts in that happiness warms my heart.

I run my fingertips along the dark circles under his eyes, and he closes them at my touch. He must not have slept at all last night. I lean in and kiss under each eye, wishing I could erase the worry there.

"Andrew, please stay in today," I beg. "I'll go wander around for a while, so you can get some sleep. I don't mind."

Andrew opens his eyes and studies me. "I do."

"You do what?"

"I want to spend the day with you," he says, putting his hand on my cheek. "That's what this trip was all about."

Oh really? That's news.

"This trip was all about spending time with *me*?" I say, completely taken aback. "But what about your meetings?"

Andrew's face is adorably guilty. "I never had meetings planned for today," he admits, and clears his throat. I smile.

"So, if your little seduction scheme wouldn't have worked last night, what did you plan to do today?"

"No idea. I hadn't gotten that far."

"Oh, I see now," I say, raising an eyebrow at him, "This whole trip was designed so that you could get into my panties? You're pretty slick, Andrew Mercer."

"No. Last night was a bonus," Andrew says, smiling. "I really just wanted to do something nice for you, and I wanted a chance to explain myself for that night in the office and the unfortunate happenings at the garden party. I honestly never expected---"

I put a finger to his lips. "Don't lie."

He smiles against my finger before I remove it. "I hoped, but I wasn't sure. You're a hard woman to read. I felt like I was getting mixed signals."

I laugh. "Are you serious?" My love for him is probably the only thing I've been sure about in the past two years. It's so hard to think he didn't know. "You had no idea how I felt about you?"

Andrew smiles again. "Once again, I hoped, but I didn't know."

I lean down and kiss his sweet lips. "Well, now you know."

Andrew pulls me closer to him, prolonging our kiss until I'm breathless. God, I love this man.

He eventually pulls away and lays his head on me, breathing heavily onto my chest. I run my fingers through his hair as he holds me...perfectly content.

Andrew's breathing starts to slow and even out. Is he asleep? Just as I have the thought, he raises his head and his weary face is heartbreaking. *So tired, sweet Andrew.* I feel awful for him.

"Come here." I reluctantly get up out of his lap and pull him toward the bed. "I want you to get some more sleep," I say, as we reach the side of the bed and I move to unbutton his jeans.

"How about we sleep later?" Andrew whispers in my ear, which is hard to resist, but my inherent need to take care of people wins out.

"And you say *I'm* insatiable?" I tease him, as I remove his jeans and t-shirt, and then force him into the bed and under the covers.

I go over to close the curtains so the room is dark, and I return to lie next to him on the bed. "Turn over," I instruct him, so he's now resting on his stomach.

His face is turned toward me, as I begin running my fingernails slowly and softly up and down his back.

"Mmmm...that feels good," he says, closing his eyes.

"My mom used to do this to get me to sleep when I was younger. I still love it."

"I'll repay the favor someday," he says, but it's all garbled up in a yawn.

I smile and keep scratching his back. He's sound asleep in less than a minute.

After I'm sure he's resting well, I get up to take a shower. I'll go out for a bit and look around so he can get some rest. I'll find Abby the perfect souvenir, maybe stroll through Times Square? Our flight out isn't until almost nine o'clock tonight. I have plenty of time.

I take my time in the shower. It feels amazing and helps to soothe my sore muscles from all the monkey business last night.

I finish up in the bathroom and head back into the room to get dressed. I smile to myself, excited that I now have flats to stroll around in today, rather than heels.

Andrew seems to be sleeping like a baby as I get ready, and I try to stay as quiet as possible so I don't disturb him.

I pull on my new jeans from last night, along with the white and black patterned blouse I brought from home. It's a bit dressy for the jeans, but it's the only thing I have to match the flats. To my delight, the new suit jacket from last night will work with the outfit as well.

I grab the jacket and the little purple clutch from last night and start to head out the door. Then I realize I should probably leave Andrew a note.

I sit at the desk where Andrew has his computer set up. Surely there's a notepad around here somewhere.

Andrew's Blackberry goes off as I'm searching for paper and a pen. I find it quickly so I can turn off the ringer. When I pick up the phone, I see it was his messenger that beeped. It is still up on the screen, and when I see who it's from, I can't resist reading it.

> *Why haven't you called me? I miss you.*

A second message from Bitchy Bitchface pops up as I'm holding his phone.

> *Please tell me you're not fucking your secretary, Andrew. So cliché. Hope you let her down easy.*

Tears prick my eyes. I hope this woman burns in the fiery pits of hell.

Just as I'm about to turn down the ringer – and toss his phone in the toilet – he gets another message.

> *Call me, lover.*

Lover? Oh no she didn't.

I turn down the ringer, skip the note writing and head for the door. I'm crying before I get to the elevator.

Let her down easy? Lover? What the hell is going on?

Sadly, I have no answers. Has Andrew slept with her? Why else would she call him *lover*? The thought makes me gag.

Andrew seemed sincere last night when he said he would never be with someone like her. Of course, it could have been a lie. It all could have been a lie. Maybe I'm the one being used here.

Careful what you ask for, Jules.

And after I poured my heart out to him? I told him I *loved* him, for God's sake!

I wipe at my tears as the elevator doors open. There's no one there, which I'm once again thankful for. However, my reasons are a little different this morning.

Damn you, Andrew! Why do you keep making me doubt you?!

I reach the hotel lobby, still crying. I head immediately to the doors and ask for a cab. I wipe again at my tears, willing myself to stop, but I can't. The thought of losing him…

I can't lose him. Not now.

"Where you headed, Miss?" the doorman asks me as the cab arrives.

I give him the first spot that comes to my head.

"The Empire State Building," I say, as a fresh set of tears start to flow.

I get in the cab, as the doorman tells the driver where to take me. We start to drive down Fifth Avenue, and I try again to stop crying. This is not worth my tears. I don't have all of the facts. He admitted to me last night that he's playing games with her. This may all be just a misunderstanding.

But my efforts to convince myself otherwise are in vain. My tears finally start to slow as I reach my destination, but I can't seem to cut them off completely. I thought I was okay with all of this last night, but maybe I'm not. Maybe I was just so excited about Andrew flirting with me, that I didn't take the time to think about how hard this whole thing with Victoria may be.

I pay the cab, thankful I had some cash on me. I didn't even think about needing it before I jumped in at The Plaza.

I walk into the Empire State Building, and the memory of the trip here last night has my eyes wetter than ever, as I step over to the side and stare at one of the displays on the wall.

Calm the hell down, Jules! Since when are you this insecure?
Since Andrew.

Since Andrew kissed me. Since Andrew made love to me. *Since Andrew.*

Just when I feel like I may never stop crying, *she* suddenly pops into my head again, and my tears instantly cease. That's enough. I will not shed tears over that bitch. She doesn't deserve it.

Good. That'll work. I'll just be pissed at Whorebag for now. I'll deal with Andrew later.

I stare at the display a little longer as I dry my face with my hands. My heart is aching, but there's nothing I can do about it right now. I'll find out some answers soon enough, but first things first. I have to get the hell out of this place.

CHAPTER 21

Walking around Times Square, with all of the lights, people and chaos, is rather relaxing. I'm used to chaos. It's no surprise it comforts me.

I was eventually able to clear my mind of the Blackberry Messenger ordeal, and two hours later, I have Abby a shot glass that says "Bada Bing!" and even picked up a small souvenir for me.

As I'm walking now, trying to figure out how the hell I'm supposed to get another cab back, my cell vibrates in my pocket.

I know who it is before I look at it.

> *Where are you? I've now decided I don't like waking up without you next to me.*

I close my eyes. *Don't start crying again, Jules. You may never stop.*

I don't know whether to respond to him or not, so I put my phone back in my pocket and resume my search for a cab. As soon as I see a vacant one, I do my best New Yorker impersonation and wave him down. To my surprise, it works! I feel so empowered!

I hop in and look at my phone again, trying to think of a reply. I still haven't thought of anything by the time we reach The Plaza, and Andrew's texted me again.

Jules? You're starting to worry me.

What do I do? If I tell him I saw the messages, he'll think I'm spying. How embarrassing!

But I have to say something. I can't let this go on between us, thinking he may be playing me with a side of Bitchface. No freaking way. I will not play second fiddle to that heifer.

I get out of the cab and head toward the door. My phone rings in my hand. It's Andrew.

I look at it a moment, and then reject the call. I need to see his face.

I give myself one of my famous pep talks in the elevator, but it doesn't do much good. They worked a lot better when Andrew didn't know how I felt about him. That's not the case anymore…not by a long shot.

I finally reach the door to my room and close my eyes.

You're going to be fine, Jules. No matter what happens, you're going to be fine.

I pull out my key and open the door. Andrew's staring out the window but turns around immediately as I open the door.

"Hey," he says, moving quickly toward me. "You had me nervous for a second there."

"I'm fine," I tell him, trying to hide the sad eyes for now, but I know I'm failing miserably.

"What's wrong?" he says, rubbing his hands up and down my arms. "Did you forget your phone or something?"

"Andrew…"

I can't do this. How do I do this? I'm such an idiot!

"Jules?" Andrew's eyes are full of concern. "Please tell me what's going on. Have you been crying? You're scaring me."

I look into those beautiful eyes and find my answer. I have to be honest with him. It's the only way.

"I saw your messages from Vic—Ms. Hamilton," I blurt out, and look away from him. This is so hard, for so many reasons.

Andrew drops his hands from my arms, and I step back from him. I have a sudden urge to run from the room, but I know I can't. I have to know the truth.

"I'm sorry." His voice is hushed, anguished. "I'm sorry you saw that."

I look back up at him. "I was going to leave you a note," I say, feeling the need to explain. "I was at the desk, and your phone went off, and I was going to try to turn it down so it wouldn't wake you..." And I'm crying. Again. "That's how I saw the messages."

Andrew makes a move toward me, and I step back.

I need to know the truth, Andrew. Please tell me the truth. And please let the truth be you're not sleeping with her.

Andrew stops abruptly in his tracks. "I told you about this last night." He clears his throat. *What are you nervous about, Andrew?* "I told you my plans for her. It's nothing, Jules. I promise."

I have to look away. His eyes are weakening my resolve.

"Are you sleeping with her?" I ask, staring at the wall.

Andrew moves toward me again, and this time, I allow his advance. I want him to hold me - I'm so pathetic – but he doesn't touch me. I look up at him and there's so much pain in his eyes, I nearly stop breathing.

"I have not, and never will, sleep with that woman," he says, his voice severe. "I'm using her to get information on my dad. End of story."

Why do I feel like I just got in trouble?

"Andrew, this is too hard," I admit.

I can't compete with his father, his work *and* Bitchy Bitcherson.

"What's too hard?" his face is anxious now. "What are you saying?"

I pull myself away from the wall I've been leaning against and move toward the bed. I drop my bags and sit on the end. Now, *I'm* the tired one.

"You have a lot going on in your life right now," I tell him, looking down at my shoes. "Perhaps we should put this thing with us on hold for a bit, until you get things worked out."

Andrew is in front of me in a flash. He kneels down and takes my chin in his hand, lifting my head, forcing me to look at him.

"This *thing*?" he repeats, his face incredulous. "What exactly do you think this *thing* is?"

I sigh. "You know what I mean," I tell him. "I'm just not sure I want to be in the middle of all of this."

Even though the idea of not being able to hold you again – or kiss you again – makes me feel like I'm drowning.

Andrew takes my face in his hands. "Jules..." he starts slowly. "First, I need to make sure you know that there is absolutely nothing going on between Victoria and me, and there never will be. I do plan to use her possible feelings for me to get to my father. I'm not proud of it, but I will do what I have to do to save the company." His eyes lock with mine. "Do you believe me, Jules? Can you trust me?"

I nod slowly. I don't think I ever really believed he had feelings for Victoria. I do trust him. He's never given me a reason not to.

"Secondly," he says, his voice softer now, "I've been waiting for you for a long time now, and if you think I'm letting you go that easily, you're mistaken."

I look into my favorite hazel eyes. *A long time*? Is he serious?

"I'll do whatever you want, Jules," he continues. "But I can't let you go. I won't. I thought I made that more than clear last night."

He drops his hands from my face, as I continue to stare at him in shock. Have I honestly succeeded in ruining what is possibly the best morning of my life?

Good God, woman!

Andrew's face is so nervous I quickly put my lips on his to try and rid him of his anxiety. He kisses me back eagerly, and I smile to myself, thinking about how I felt just a couple of hours ago. Looking back, I never fully believed Andrew would lie to me, but the tangled mess that is him, his father, Victoria and the company is a bit daunting.

However, I can't let go of Andrew either. Nothing has been successful in cutting my binds to him in the past, and that was before last night.

"Are we okay?" Andrew asks, his voice tentative.

"I'm sorry," I say, smiling. "I'm normally a pretty confident woman, but for some reason, my insecurities seem to rear their ugly heads around you."

Andrew smiles, finally. "You have nothing to be insecure about, and don't think you're the only one."

I laugh. "Andrew Mercer? Insecure? Right!"

Give me a huge break, Andrew. Who are you trying to kid?

"I can be insecure too," he whispers.

I put a hand on his cheek. "What do you mean?"

He looks up at me, his eyes sad. "This morning, for example, I thought you went back home or something," he says. "I thought maybe you got scared, like last night might have been too fast."

I raise my eyebrows at him in confusion. "But my suitcase is still here."

It's all I can think to say. He can't be serious.

"I know." Andrew smiles. "I realized quickly that I was probably wrong, but then you didn't answer my texts or calls." He looks up at me, face serious again. "And then, what you just said, about this being too much, us putting things on hold. Maybe I wasn't wrong after all?"

I sigh deeply before I speak. Could he be any more perfect?

Nope. I think not.

"Andrew, I'd be lying if I said I thought this was going to be easy," I admit. "But if you tell me that you want to be with me," I slide down onto the floor so we're both kneeling, facing each other. "If you tell me that nothing else matters, and that you need me with you, then I'm here. Because being with you? That's all I've ever wanted."

Andrew puts his arms around my waist and pulls me close. "I want to be with you, Jules." He repeats my words to me in a whisper. "Nothing else matters," he says in my ear, then presses his soft lips to my neck.

The way my body responds to him is foreign to me. The pull is so powerful.

"I love you," he whispers, as he kisses me, and I pull away so I can look at his face.

"What?" I ask, and I can barely get the one word question out.

Please say it again, Andrew, and again, and again, and again...

"I love you," he repeats, smiling.

"Are you sure?" My traitor tears are rapidly approaching again. "Or are you just saying this because I said it?"

Andrew smiles, pulling me even tighter against him. "And why would I do that?" he asks, as he starts kissing my neck again. "Have you ever known me to do something because someone else did it? You're going to have to trust me, Jules."

"I do," I breathe, as Andrew starts unbuttoning my blouse. "I do trust you."

"You told me last night you rarely doubt me, but I've found that to not be true in several incidences recently," he says, looking into my eyes. "I believed you when you said you loved me. Why can't you believe me? I treat you better than anyone else in the office, and not just because you're my assistant. I've given you gifts before that I was sure may give me away, but I couldn't resist the opportunity to make you happy. Why do you think I asked you to photograph the garden party? You had no idea? No clue?"

"I think..." I start, but I have to pause as he starts on my neck again, his arms wrapped firmly around my waist. "I've just wanted this for so long now. I'm having a hard time believing it's real."

"I've pretty much been in love with you ever since you called me an 'immature bully'." Andrew smiles against my neck, as he pushes my blouse from my shoulders. "I'm not used to people telling me off."

"That's a shame." I'm breathless now, as Andrew's lips trail down my neck, and onto my shoulder.

"I agree," he says, between kisses. "It was so sexy. I knew immediately I had to have you."

I giggle, as he brings his lips back up to my mouth. "Had to *have* me?"

Andrew smiles at me. "Yes," he says with rather boyish charm. "It only took me two years to get up the courage to make a move, but it was well worth the wait."

I smile widely as he moves his hands to my jeans and starts unbuttoning them.

"So, tell me we're okay," he whispers into my ear. "Tell me you trust me."

"We're okay," I breathe, as he slips my jeans down, then runs his capable fingers down my back and along the inside of my panty line. "I trust you."

"Now..." Andrew pulls away and runs those same fabulous fingers down my cheek. "Tell me you love me."

I smile, and pull his face close to mine. I place gentle kisses on his chin, up his sexy jawline, to his ear before whispering "Bahibbak, Andrew."

Andrew trembles against me, and I smile. Why should he get to have all the fun?

When we pull away from each other this time, Andrew's eyes are positively feral.

"You told me you loved me last night in Arabic?" he questions, seemingly awestruck.

My reply gets caught in my throat. He's just so beautiful.

"Yes," I finally manage, as he moves his fingers slowly through my hair.

Andrew gives me a heart-stopping smile, before pressing his warm lips against mine. "Bahibbak," he repeats. "I'll try and remember that one."

"Actually, if you wanted to say it back to me, it would be 'Bahibbik'," I explain.

"Okay then," Andrew kisses me once more. "Bahibbik, my beautiful girl."

Dear God, my heart.

"I love you, too," I say breathlessly, as Andrew gazes at me with those stunning hazel eyes.

He stands, and pulls me up with him, quickly finishing the job of removing my jeans and then pulls his t-shirt over his head, tossing both recklessly to the floor.

I sit down on the bed, and scoot backward so Andrew can join me. He smiles before crawling on hands and knees to hover above me.

"We can make this work," he says, and something about the look on his face gives me chills. He's serious, deadly serious, and at this moment, I'm not sure I could love him more.

"I know," I tell him. "And I do trust you, Andrew. I promise."

"Good." He starts smiling again. "But now you're in trouble."

"Why?" I ask, but I can barely get it out before his mouth is warm and welcome against mine.

"Because," he says, almost as breathless as me, "now I'm all rested, and we still have several hours before our flight leaves."

I smile up at him and then push him over onto his back. I climb on top and look down at the magnificent man beneath me. He's like the eighth wonder of my world.

"Why do you think I suggested the nap this morning?" I tease.

"Mmmm...I love the way you think," Andrew growls, as he pulls my face down to his, and I can feel the truth of his love for me in this kiss.

I pull my face away and stare down at him. Andrew gently rolls me off him and onto my side. He pulls me close and starts running a soft hand down my back, to my side, and down my thigh.

"I love you, Jules. I truly do," he says quietly, while staring into my eyes, and I feel something powerful release inside of me.

It doesn't matter – his father, Victoria, the company – nothing matters except Andrew and the fact that he loves me. I love this man with everything I am, and I will take him in any way that I can.

"I know," I say with confidence, as I wrap my trembling arms around him. "And I love you too, Andrew. Always."

CHAPTER 22

Andrew and I spent the rest of the day in my hotel room. I wasn't sure anything could trump last night, but this afternoon ranked pretty damn close.

As we sit now in the Oak Room – having dinner, since we were too distracted to be bothered with lunch – I'm finding food is the last thing on my mind. Dressed in khakis, a long-sleeved white button down and loafers with no socks, the beautiful man sitting next to me is more delicious than any meal this fine restaurant could serve.

"What are you thinking about?" Andrew and I have been smiling and staring at each other like idiots for the past twenty minutes. I could stare at him all day.

"The shower," I whisper, and Andrew smiles.

"I was thinking about the sofa in my office."

"What for?" I ask, confused.

"I still think about that night, last week..." He trails off, but he's still smiling. "I remember thinking you looked so beautiful."

I snicker. "Andrew, I had pretty much been crying for the past twenty-four hours when you came stumbling in that night. I looked like death. You were wasted."

Andrew shakes his head. "No, you looked perfect." He leans in and gives me a sweet kiss on the cheek. "And when you came into my office...I remember you holding me while I sat on my sofa, and when I fell asleep, I had a dream about you."

"Really?" I ask excitedly. "What was it about?"

Andrew takes my hand on top of the table. "I dreamt that you were lying with me," he says so softly that I have to lean toward him to hear. "We didn't do anything but lie there, all night, in each other's arms. I was so disappointed when I woke up and you weren't next to me." He's staring into my eyes again, and I smile widely at the love I see there. "I honestly never thought I would have the chance to live out that dream. But I got that chance and so much more." He smiles back at me and sighs. "God, I love that fucking sofa."

This makes me laugh out loud. *Oh Andrew, you just keep getting better and better.*

"I can think of plenty more things we can do on that sofa," I tease, as I reach up to kiss him again. "It's going to be your most favorite sofa ever."

Andrew laughs and kisses me again. "I look forward to that, Ms. Greene."

"I think we have officially taken the job description of me catering to your every need to a whole new level."

"I suppose we have," Andrew laughs again, but then looks at me with serious eyes. "Jules, I have a proposition for you," he says, "and I want your honest opinion. Don't be afraid to tell me how you feel."

I nod, not sure what I'm getting myself into, but I promised to trust him. I'm going to do my best.

"Until all of this blows over with my father," he continues, still holding my hand on the table, "how would you feel about keeping our relationship a secret?"

My initial reaction to this question is to want to curl up into a ball and cry myself to sleep. There's a certain sense of shame and rejection that accompanies this kind of request, and as hard as I'm trying, my insecurities are still there.

I don't say anything, so Andrew continues. "Let me explain, okay?" I nod slowly, still not sure what to think. "The bottom line is that I don't want you to get hurt, Jules," he says, squeezing my hand. "If my father or Victoria find out that we're together, they may find a way to hurt you in an effort to hurt me, and I can't have that. I don't want you to be a part in all of this, and I feel like one of the best ways to make sure that doesn't happen, is if we just pretend like nothing has changed."

"Andrew, I---"

He interrupts me, which I'm kind of glad about. I wasn't really sure what I was going to say.

"Let me finish," he says, and I nod again. "Another more secondary reason is that I do feel like Victoria could be a good resource for me. If she finds out we're together, my plan with her won't work." I shake my head. This is the part that hurts. "Let me finish," Andrew says again. "I would say let's you and me put what we have on hold for a while, like you suggested earlier, but I can't do that, Jules. I'm too selfish and I need you too much. So, if you're not comfortable with the sneaking around, we'll take our relationship public. It's your choice. I'll do whatever you want."

I take a couple of deep breaths as I look down at my half eaten salad.

What to do? What to do?

"Can I think about it?" I ask. All I can think right now is that I need more time.

"Sure." Andrew's face is hesitant. "I understand."

I pull my hand from his and place it in my lap. I look down at my food again and try to quickly reason this out. My mind is reeling.

Don't cry, Jules. Not now, for goodness sake.

Andrew pulls my hand back from my lap and leans in close. "Jules, I want to be very clear about this." His eyes are sharp and severe. "I know this little game I'm playing with Victoria is wrong, and although I'm glad you don't, you should probably hate me for it. But right now, it's the only way I feel like I can get to my father. I don't know what else to do." I stare up at him, still not sure what to say. "But Victoria, and my father for that matter, they are not good people, Jules. They're full of power and greed, and they'll do whatever it takes to get what they want. I want to try and do what I can to keep you as far away from that as possible." Andrew's eyes soften, as he looks down at my hand in his. "But if you have any reservations at all about keeping this a secret, please tell me. I promise that ultimately, the decision is in your hands."

I lift his chin to stare into his eyes once more. I look for something, anything that would make me think what he's telling me is not the truth, but I can't find it. I only see sincerity and trust in those beautiful hazel eyes.

"Okay," I say softly and Andrew's eyes widen. "I promised to trust you, and I'm a girl of my word," I tell him. Andrew smiles and kisses me softly in response.

"If this gets too complicated or too hard, you have to talk to me," he says, desperation in his voice. "You have to tell me what you want. I just want you to be safe and happy."

"I know," I assure him. "And besides, sneaking around may be kind of fun." I wink.

Andrew smiles widely. "It's a beautiful thing when you find someone you can love for their body, as well as their mind."

I dig my fork into a carrot and pop it in my mouth.

Is there anything I wouldn't do for you, Andrew Mercer?

I smile. At the moment, I can't think of one damn thing.

CHAPTER 23

Thursday morning comes fast and super early. Man, I'm tired.

I turn off my alarm clock and rub my eyes. A slow smile spreads across my face. I get to sneak around with Andrew today!

I jump out of bed and head for the shower. To my surprise, Abby comes bounding into my bathroom seconds after I start the water.

"Morning!" she says cheerfully, her mouth full of bagel.

"Morning," I smile at her. "You're up early."

"New J-O-B? Remember?"

Right! Abby got the museum job. Andrew has successfully removed everything but himself from my memory over the past forty-eight hours.

"Yes," I hop into the shower. "The new job! You like it so far?"

Abby pulls the curtain back so I can see her roll her eyes. "To hell with my job! I want to hear about this damn trip! What did I get?"

Abby was working at Marlow's last night, and I went immediately to bed when I got in, completely exhausted. I haven't had a chance to tell her about the trip.

I laugh and pull the curtain back in place. "It's on my dresser," I tell her and hear her run immediately out of the bathroom.

"I love it!" she squeals from my bedroom, obviously finding her shot glass. I'm smiling as she enters the bathroom once again. "So? The trip? The preppy? Spill it!"

I laugh, wanting to tell her the truth so badly, but I know I can't. "It was a work trip, Abby. Nothing special."

"What?" Abby huffs. "You were in NEW YORK CITY! I don't care if you were working or not, something cool had to happen in NEW YORK CITY!"

I smile again. *Oh something cool happened, all right...something pretty freaking cool.*

"I did get to do some sightseeing," I tell her as I lather up my hair. "I saw the International Center for Photography, Times Square, Rockefeller Center. It was awesome."

"What about the Empire State Building?"

I smile again, glad Abby can't see my face. "Yep. It was...my favorite part."

"I'm so damn jealous!" Abby says, and I hear her hop back onto the floor from the sink. "I'm going to get ready, but I need some more details later, okay?"

"Sure," I say, glad to have the time to make up some good lies to tell. I don't like lying, but I guess this is for a good cause.

I'm still a tiny bit bothered by the notion of sneaking around, and keeping our relationship – can I call it that? – a secret. But I love Andrew, and if this is the only way to keep seeing him for now, I'll give it shot.

Abby leaves, and I finish up my shower. Now, what to wear?

I move to my closet and survey the prospects. I still have one new skirt left, so I'll go with that. Hmmm...navy blue, pencil skirt. I choose my navy blue and green patterned blouse and nude heels. I put on the top and remember it's a little tight across my chest. I smile into my dresser mirror. That will work just fine.

I return to the bathroom to finish my make-up and hair. I don't have much time to put into it, so I put my hair up in a loose bun. I was going for the long and sexy look, but I don't want to be late.

I quickly spritz on some perfume and head for the kitchen.

"I'm outtie!" Abby calls, as she rushes to the door. "I'll see you tonight! Love you!"

"Love you too!" I call back, and then notice the time on the microwave. *Crap!*

I grab a cold bagel from the fridge and a Diet Coke – breakfast of champions.

I rush down to my car, climb inside and pull quickly out of my apartment complex. My stomach starts doing somersaults. This morning should be interesting.

I'm so excited to see Andrew again. It was hard to leave him last night, and honestly, the time apart has made me even more nervous about today. Maybe it was all a dream? It certainly feels like it.

I'm still trying to get my head around all of this, but it's going to be important that I keep my cool at the office. That's going to be tough. Even now, thinking about him in one of his fabulous suits, sitting behind his desk, with that damp hair and those clear hazel eyes...and he's mine. All *mine*. Oh good God.

I'm officially on high level freak out mode by the time I pull into the office parking deck.

Breathe, Jules. Just breathe!

I turn off my ignition and lean back into my seat. I can do this. I've hidden my feelings for him for over a year. I'll just continue playing the game. This can work.

I take a few more deep breaths, although they're not working...at all...and open my car door to make my way inside. On my way up in the elevator, the panic seizes me again. What if he's already here? What if other people are here?

I look at my watch. It's not quite seven-thirty. I'll most likely be the only one here.

But what if Andrew decides to come in early so we can spend a few minutes together? That thought puts a quick smile on my face.

The elevator dings when I reach my floor, and my heart rate reaches warp speed.

The lights are off in the lobby, which means that probably no one is here yet. I start to relax a bit now, as I unlock the door and walk inside. As I walk down the hall, I see that Andrew's light is off too. Well, that's a little disappointing.

I put my purse into my desk drawer as I wait for my computer to start up. I checked my emails late last night, and I had a bunch. I'm not looking forward to getting back to reality today. Right now, it seems almost impossible with the past two days fresh on my mind.

I decide to go finish up my duties in the break room and Bitchface's office, before returning to my desk. As I'm daydreaming about Andrew, my instant messenger pops up on my computer. Speak of the devil in a hot suit...

Morning, Ms. Greene.

I smile and move my fingers quickly to my keyboard.

Good morning, sir.

How are you feeling this mornin?

Tired. And you?

Happy.

Dear God. This man is all kinds of perfection.

Will you be late coming in today, sir?

I hope not. I'm not sure how long I can wait to see him. He doesn't have any meetings this morning. I checked last night.

No.

Yay! Happy dance!

When can I expect you?

Very soon.

I smile again. I can hardly wait!
I'm about to type back a response – I need an exact time, before I explode – but Andrew sends another message as I'm typing.

May I see you in my office, Ms. Greene?

I gasp and turn my head quickly toward his door. I'm confused. The light is still off.

I stand quickly, smooth out my skirt, and pray my shaky legs can make the ten foot walk to his office.

Andrew opens the door right as I approach. Now that he's back in the office, I guess his impatience is getting the best of him.

I smile, and he smiles back.

"Ms. Greene, I need to go over a few things with you," he says, as I walk the last few steps toward his dark office.

I look him up and down, as I walk in. He looks gorgeous, in my favorite charcoal three-piece and garnet tie. He seems to have already lost the jacket. Even better.

He closes the door behind me and quickly pushes me against it, his body pressed hard against mine.

"Good morning, Mr. Mercer," I growl into his ear, and then wrap my teeth around his earlobe.

Andrew trembles against me. "God, I missed you," he whispers, as I reach up to run my fingers through his still damp hair.

"I missed you too," I say before pulling his mouth to mine. Oh dear heavens, those lips.

As we kiss, Andrew slowly runs his hands up and down, all over my body, like he's reacquainting himself. *Have at it, Andrew. Take your time.*

"Were you waiting for me?" I ask, when we finally break away.

"Of course," he says, pulling me with him toward his leather sofa. He sits down and pulls me into his lap. "I honestly wanted you to stay with me last night, but I wasn't sure if that would have been asking too much."

"I would have stayed," I proudly confess, before nuzzling my head into the crook of his neck.

"Really?" Andrew seems surprised, so I raise my head to check his expression. "I didn't want to push my luck."

I smile. *Oh, my silly Andrew.*

"I didn't want to leave you either," I say, and kiss his cheek. "I'm glad you came in early today."

"Me too." Andrew takes my face in his hands, and kisses me softly. "Are you sure this is going to be okay with you?"

I look into his eyes, and decide again on the truth.

"I'm not sure, but I'm willing to try," I admit. "I'll do what I can to be with you, Andrew."

Andrew smiles at me. "Good. I want to be with you too."

He kisses me harder this time, as his hand starts moving enticingly up my thigh. I groan, too loudly for where we are, but I'm pretty sure we're still alone.

I look at Andrew and he's smiling playfully at me. "You're wearing my favorite suit," I manage to get out, as his hand moves higher and higher. Oh Lord.

"Yes," he says, pulling me out of his lap and lying me down on the sofa. "Anything for you, Jules," he whispers, as he moves on top of me. "Anything."

CHAPTER 24

"I love this fucking sofa," I tease, as Andrew and I lie next to each other, still breathing heavily.

Andrew laughs. "It's my most favorite sofa, ever."

Andrew's arm is around my waist, his hand gently caressing my bare stomach. We took off only the necessary clothing. I'm lying with my back pressed against him, still in my bra, blouse unbuttoned, skirt on. God only knows where my undies went.

I turn so I can see his face and smile as I look at Andrew – shirt and vest open, beautiful chest exposed, tie still in perfect position. His pants are on, but unbuttoned, unzipped and hanging very low on his hips.

I love my job.

"I apologize," he says, smiling over at me. "I promise not to attack you every morning. I just missed you so much last night."

I frown. "I don't like that promise."

Andrew smiles, and kisses me gently. "We better get dressed."

I look over at the antique clock on his wall. It's just now only eight o'clock. Wow. That was fast, but so very fabulous.

I stand and walk to Andrew's bathroom to put myself back together. I'm happy to see, when I look in the mirror, that it's not as bad as I thought it may be. My cheeks are a little rosier than normal, but my hair and make-up are manageable.

I button my blouse and re-do my bun before walking back into his office. Just one thing missing…

"Have you seen my undies?"

Andrew smiles. He lifts his hand and they're dangling on his finger. His outfit is already perfectly back into place, but his hair is a bit disheveled, with a proper "just fucked" look. Simply irresistible.

I walk over to him, and snatch my undies from his finger, but he pulls me to him before I can put them back on.

"This is going to be harder than I thought," he says, kissing me gently again.

"What is?"

"Pretending." He kisses me again, a little deeper this time.

I smile onto his lips. "It will be tough," I agree. "But I think we can manage."

"How?" It's almost a whine, and it's so adorable.

I kiss him again before backing up to slip my undies back on.

"Well, there's always lunch time," I say, before wrapping my arms around him again. "Coffee breaks? Perhaps we should take up smoking?"

Andrew laughs. "I love you."

"I love you too," I say smiling.

Oh, how I love you Andrew Mercer.

"Jules," his face is serious all of a sudden. "You have to promise you'll talk to me. Okay? If this starts to bother you, or you feel uncomfortable, you have to tell me."

"I will," I say, kissing him again in an effort to release the tension. "I promise."

To my delight, it works. Andrews smiles at me, again. "Good, now go get me some coffee, and make it quick." He turns me around and slaps my bottom.

I scoff, pretending to be offended, but it was totally hot. Yes, I'm so going to Hell.

I open the door to Andrew's office, and Adrian is walking down the hallway toward her desk.

"Morning!" she says cheerfully, and I flush. I'm not going to be very good at hiding this.

"Morning." I smile back.

Adrian stops and looks at me. "Are you okay, Jules?"

Pull it together, Jules!

"Totally fine," I say, pulling out a more genuine smile this time.

Just got ravaged by my new boyfriend in his office. No worries!

Wait, is Andrew my boyfriend? Ugh. No time to think about that now.

Adrian smiles, seemingly unaware, as she continues walking to her desk. I can't believe my smile worked. This is going to take some practice.

I am barely in my chair when I hear a nightmare of a laugh coming from the lobby.

"Yes sir, Mr. Mercer," I hear, her voice dripping with sticky, sweet ass kissing. "I'll get back to you as soon as I know something."

I stare dubiously at my computer, so I don't have to look at her. What are the odds of her not needing to speak with me? I sigh. Slim to none.

"Ms. Greene." Her screechy voice sends chills down my spine.

I look up at her, planting my practiced fake smile on my face.

"Good morning." I'm surprised to see she looks...happy, satisfied.

Is it about Andrew? Did he say something to her? I have to suppress the urge to vomit. This whole scheme he is cooking up with her is not going to be easy to swallow.

"Is Andy in?" she asks, smiling at me. I want to punch her teeth in.

"Mr. Mercer," I correct, "is in his office. I'll let him know you're here."

I don't want that slutty slut calling him Andy, or even Andrew for that matter. She's not worthy.

I pick up the phone and dial his office.

"Yes, Beautiful?" he answers, and I stifle my smile. This is going to be seriously tough.

"Ms. Hamilton is here to see you, sir."

Andrew sighs. He's not happy to see her. Good.

"Send her in," he says and hangs up.

"He'll see you now," I tell Bitchface, and she walks past me directly into his office, without another word.

I look over at Adrian, and she smiles and rolls her eyes. I nod in agreement.

I try to get back to my work, but I'm completely preoccupied by what's going on in Andrew's office.

Jules, jealousy is not a trait you typically adhere to. Lock it up!

I try several times to shake it off, but the gnawing rage inside me, knowing he's alone with her in his office – that yucky smile she had plastered all over her face when she came in this morning – and knowing what his plans are has me riding bareback on the green monster, trying unsuccessfully to tame the beast.

What is he doing to me? I'm a completely different person with him. I'm so insecure for some reason. It's ridiculous.

I laugh to myself. It's because I care. I actually care about him, about what he thinks and how he feels about me. I can't say that for any of the other guys that I've been with. That's the difference. I love him.

After about forty-five minutes of agony, Andrew's door opens, and Victoria walks out, an even bigger grin on her face than the one she was sporting earlier. What the hell?

"Ms. Greene," she nods, as she walks past my desk, her face smothered in victory. What did he say to her?

I roll my eyes at her back as she walks away. This is going to be so hard, and this is only the first day. How many more days before I break?

Deep breaths, Jules. In and out.

Andrew loves me. He doesn't love her. I have the upper hand here. The thought makes me smile.

As I'm basking in my new revelation, I hear the familiar "ping" of my instant messenger.

Miss me?

Oh, this man. I smile widely, and then take a nervous glance up at Adrian. She's looking down at her desk, engrossed in some paperwork.

Of course. Miss me?

I'm grinning ear to ear waiting for his response.

Very much. Dinner tonight?

Dinner? Like a date? I didn't think that would be allowed in our new little secret world.

Are you asking me out, Mr. Mercer?

Yes I am, Ms. Greene. Interested?

Ummm...*hell yes*!

Absolutely, but I didn't think public appearances would be allowed.

Maybe he has something private in mind? Hmmm...I hope so.

If it's okay with you, I was thinking we could have dinner at my place.

My smile widens at the thought of some more alone time with Andrew. Any time, any place, any way I can have him, I'll take it.

Will you be cooking? If so, then count me out.

I happen to be a very good cook, Ms. Greene. You will be missing out.

The man can cook too? Figures. He is perfect, after all.

Sounds wonderful.

You'll love it...especially what I have in mind for dessert.

Oh dear. Warmth courses through my body with that promise, leaving a very pleasant tingly feeling in its' wake.

I can hardly wait.

And that's a fact.

Me either. Meet me at my place? 7:30?

I'll be there.

I sit and wait for another reply, but nothing comes. I think for a moment about asking what his meeting with Victoria was about, but I decide against it. Maybe he'll tell me tonight.
I glance up at the clock and sigh as I settle into my chair, preparing for what is sure to be one of the longest days of my life.

CHAPTER 25

My stomach is rolling with nerves and excitement, as I stare at my closet. What the hell am I going to wear?

I'm trying to figure out how to make "casually sexy" happen, and I'm coming up empty handed. I have work clothes and t-shirts and jeans – not much in between.

I decide to go check out Abby's closet. Maybe she has a fun dress I can borrow.

"Abby? Can I borrow your closet?"

Abby's lying on her bed, ear buds in, a book in her hands, looking as beautiful as ever, even in her favorite pair of "Hello Kitty" pajama pants and Transformers t-shirt.

"What?" she says, removing her ear buds.

I smile at her. "Your closet? I need something to wear."

"Where are you going?" she asks.

Dammit. What do I tell her?

"Just some dinner and drinks with work friends," I say, as I move toward her closet.

I can't look at her in the eyes. Abby's hard to lie to. She knows me too well.

"Go for it," she says. Thankfully, she doesn't question me. I turn back to her, and she has her ear buds back in, her nose back in her book.

I thumb through her clothes, and stumble across a cute, deep red dress that I've never seen before. It's light and frilly and girlie and perfect.

"Where did to you get this?" I ask, pulling it out and turning to Abby.

Abby smiles as she removes her ear buds again. "I rewarded myself for my new job. You like?"

"I love," I say, looking down at the dress, but I notice the tag is still on it. "Have you already worn it?"

"Not yet. But you can wear it. I don't care."

"Really?" I hate to do it, but it's exactly what I had in mind for tonight.

"Sure." Abby smiles at me. "Have at it."

"Thanks!" I hold the dress up to my front and move to look in the full length mirror on the inside of her closet door.

"So…" Abby sits up on her bed and puts her book down on her bedside table. "Can I interest you in a date with a certain bookstore owner?"

Damn. I forgot about that guy. I feel my cheeks redden before I turn to her.

"Ummm…" I have no idea how to handle this. "Abby, I…"

Abby rolls her eyes at me. "Jules, seriously? It's just a date. I'm not asking you to marry the guy."

I smile. "I know. I just…well, you know how I feel about blind dates."

"Look," Abby sighs. "I'll invite him to the bar tomorrow night, you can show up and I'll introduce you. I haven't mentioned you to him at all, so the ball will be in your court. What do you think?"

I turn back to the mirror to look at the dress once more. What could this hurt? It may actually help mine and Andrew's cause. If I'm seen with another guy every once in a while, it may help throw people off our trail. Of course no man could ever compare to Andrew, so what do I have to lose?

"Fine." I sigh, resigned. "I'll meet him, but I'm not making any promises."

Abby claps her hands, and smiles widely. "Yay! So, tomorrow night at the club, say around nine?"

"I'll be there." I turn back to her with the dress in my hands. "Thanks for the loaner."

"No problem." Abby leans back into her bed, smiling at me, before immersing herself back into her book and music.

I turn and leave her room, a sick feeling coming over me, as I think about meeting another guy tomorrow night. I quickly brush it off. Andrew's pretending with Victoria. I can pretend with this Nate guy. No problem.

I walk back into my room, and slip the dress on. It's adorable, and a great color. It sits right above my knees, and the loose and flowy material clings comfortably to my body. The scoop neck is cut low, but not too low. The small, ruffley straps add just the right amount of casual, while the tight bodice and low back give it plenty of sexy. Perfect. Perfect. *Perfect*.

I pull out a pair of gold, strappy sandals and accent with some gold jewelry. I give myself a last look in the mirror. Wait, these earrings are too dressy. I look like I'm trying too hard.

I rummage through my jewelry box to find another pair. I decide on a pair of gold hoops that my mom bought me for my high school graduation. They're perfect with this dress.

I smile in the mirror. This dress is almost the color of Andrew's garnet tie. I can't believe he wore that suit this morning. He looked incredible. I wonder what he'll have on tonight. Casual Andrew in jeans is just as good as business Andrew in a suit.

I add a little lip gloss, grab my purse, and make my way toward the door.

"Have fun!" Abby calls from the kitchen as I pass, scaring the hell out of me. "Why so jumpy?" she asks, one eyebrow raised.

I'm the worst liar *ever*!

"You just scared me," I claim. "That's all."

Abby stares at me, her eyebrow still raised in interest. "Fine. Don't do anything I wouldn't do."

I smile. "That doesn't leave me with many options."

"Shut the hell up and go drink," she says, turning back to whatever she's concocting in the kitchen.

"Love you," I call back, as I walk out the door.

"Love you too!" I hear her yell, as I close the door.

I turn and take a deep breath before walking down the stairs to my car. I'm so excited to see Andrew again, I could burst.

I know where Andrew lives, but I've never been to his place. I pull into his driveway a little before seven. I was aiming for fashionably late, but ended up being early, as usual.

Andrew texted me the code to his gate earlier. I give it a go, and thankfully it works.

The huge iron gate slowly opens and I proceed down what appears to be a long, rather windy driveway. Eventually, I start to make out Andrew's house in the distance.

I've never seen it before, but I know it's custom built. I'm sure it's filled with all kinds of wonderfully expensive amenities, but it's not oversized, or over the top. The design is contemporary, with an exterior covered in tons of beautiful stone, cedar and windows. There's a large front porch, and the house is completely surrounded by woods. It's very peaceful and so different from the monstrosity where he grew up.

I finally make it to the end of the long drive, which leads to his three-car garage. I pull up behind the door on the far right, and take a couple more deep breaths before I open my car door.

I'm not even a foot away from my car when I see Andrew come through his front door and down the steps to meet me.

I smile widely, as I watch his face light up. He really loves me. I can't believe it.

"You look incredible," he whispers, as he hugs me and places a kiss right at the base of my neck.

"Thank you," I breathe, closing my eyes, as he continues to trail kisses along my bare shoulder. His hands move down my back, to my thighs. *God help me.*

"Sorry," he says, breathless, as he slowly pulls away, and grabs my hand, "You have a strange effect on me."

He smiles and I smile too. "I'm used to it," I tease, before giving him a quick kiss on the lips. "I have that same effect on most men – some women too."

"I'll bet." Andrew grins, as he leads me toward the door. "Especially looking like that," he says, as we walk up his front porch steps.

"You don't look so bad yourself, Mr. Mercer." My current view, of his tight backside in a pair of dark tan cargo pants, is not bad – not bad at all. He's wearing an olive green v-neck t-shirt, which hugs him in all the right places, and the same gray Nikes I saw him in last week when he stumbled into the office, drunk out of his mind.

Andrew turns to me, and smiles, as he opens his front door. "Welcome, Ms. Greene," he says, as I step across the threshold.

Oh. My. Goodness.

"Wow," I manage, as I walk into his incredible house. And I thought the outside was beautiful.

Through the front door is a short foyer that leads to an enormous open space, with a huge, sunken living area, a smaller dining area off to one side and a gourmet kitchen. Behind all of that is another large room composed of nothing but windows, looking out over what appears to be a small pond with woods in the back.

All of the furnishings look manly and sturdy, with lots of wood and leather. And everything is covered in deep, rich burgundies, browns or greens.

What I love most about it is how comfortable it feels. The high ceilings, deep colors, and all of the windows make it feel like the house is just an extension of the woods surrounding it. I love every inch.

"Do you like it?" he asks, his expression nervous and expectant.

"I do." I nod. "I love it."

"Good," he says, obviously relieved, as he releases my hand. "Let me get you something to drink."

Andrew makes his way over to the kitchen, and I take another quick look around before joining him.

"This really is an amazing house," I say, as I reach the bar in his kitchen. I sit on one of the stools as Andrew uncorks a bottle of wine.

"Thanks," he says, turning to me and smiling. "But more importantly, have I told you how beautiful you look tonight?"

"Yes," I blush. "Thank you, Andrew."

"I like hearing you call me *Andrew*," he says shyly as he pours our wine. "I know that sounds kind of ridiculous, but I like it."

"It doesn't sound ridiculous," I admit. "I like it when you call me *Jules*. I've tried to get you to do it before, but you never would."

"I know." Andrew sighs. "I had to keep my guard up. It's been hard enough for me to keep our relationship professional over the years."

Andrew smiles as he places our wine glasses on the bar in front of me. He then walks around the bar, pushes my stool around and moves in between my legs. I gasp, as my dress hikes up to nearly my hips. He grabs the back of my head and pulls my mouth swiftly to his. Damn, he tastes so good.

I put my arms around his waist, drawing him closer, eager to have his body pressed against mine. The kiss is deep, long and passionate as he runs his fingers slowly, lovingly through the back of my hair. I feel like I'm about to explode by the time he pulls away.

"Dinner first?" he breathes, and I smile. Oh, this *man*.

"Sure," I say, and wipe some of my lip-gloss from his mouth. He licks his lips and smiles afterward, sending my libido into overdrive.

Andrew moves slowly back into the kitchen, and I discretely pull my dress back down. I'm just now noticing the delicious scent filling his house.

"What are we having?" I ask, as Andrew grabs a pot holder and opens the oven.

"Simple, but always a crowd pleaser," he says, turning back to me, after pulling out two foil-wrapped baked potatoes from the oven. "Steaks, potatoes, roasted green beans and a salad."

"Sounds fantastic," I tell him, and he gives me a proud grin.

"I was hoping you were okay with red meat, but then I remembered our lunch at *21* and that you also like roast beef, so I thought I'd be okay."

I cock an eyebrow. "How did you know I like roast beef?"

"Because I remember you ate it at the company holiday party last year." Andrew turns and leans against his counter toward me. "I was watching you." He smiles.

"You have issues." I smile back, and Andrew leans in further and places a soft, sweet kiss on my lips. "But I don't mind," I add.

Andrew laughs and turns back to his kitchen duties. "I wasn't kidding when I said I've had a thing for you ever since you told me off that day. Honestly, I've had a thing for you since the day I hired you. You're a beautiful woman, Jules, and I am just a man, after all." I smile, as he pulls the steaks from the oven. "But that day you got upset with me, and every day since, I've realized how incredibly passionate you are. It's nearly impossible to resist."

"So, what took you so long?" I ask, dying to know the answer to this one.

I watch as Andrew slices and then puts some kind of sauce on the steaks. He licks a few of his fingers when he's done. I really wish he would stop messing with his mouth. I'm never going to make it through dinner at this rate.

"I was scared of your reaction," he says, his back still to me.

"What do you mean?" This is fascinating to me. Things are never what they seem.

He turns to me, smiling. "I wasn't sure if you had feelings for me."

A giggle escapes my lips. I can't help it. This is so ludicrous. Oh, the irony.

I move off my stool to go stand beside him. I reach up and wrap my arms around his neck. "I hope we've cleared all of that up now."

"You know," Andrew has his arms wrapped snugly around my waist, his forehead pressed against mine, "I was scared that if I told you how I felt, and you didn't feel the same, I would lose you. I couldn't risk that."

I lean in to kiss him. "I hope we've cleared that up now too," I tease.

Andrew smiles, still holding me tightly in his arms. "I never in a million years thought it would feel like this," he says, pulling a hand up to caress my face. "I always thought you were amazing, but you're even better than I imagined," he says quietly, and pulls my mouth to his once again.

This time, the kiss builds in intensity until I nearly stop breathing in his arms.

I pull away and look desperately into his eyes. I need him. Now.

"Screw it," Andrew says, as he picks me up and places me on the kitchen counter. "Dinner can wait."

CHAPTER 26

Andrew's bedroom is just as gorgeous as the rest of the house. The walls are dark. Navy blue maybe? I can't tell now that it's dark outside. They're decorated with very few pictures, but the ones he has hung are all stunning landscape portraits. One looks like an exact replica of the woods behind his house.
He has a huge four poster bed made of worn wood. It's very sturdy looking, like the rest of the décor. There's also a dresser and chest to match, plus a sitting room, with yet another leather sofa and large television. He has a black and white photo of his mother on his dresser. She's beautiful.
"I really do love your house," I say, as I look around his room.
"Thank you," Andrew says, and I feel his sigh as his chest rises and falls under my cheek. "I like it too."
"It's much homier than your dad's house," I admit, hoping I haven't said anything to overstep my bounds.
I feel Andrew chuckle beneath me. "Yeah, my dad's not real big on *understated*."
I laugh too. "Sorry to break up this party, but I'm officially starving."
Andrew moves out from under me, and I roll on my side to face him. His smile, his smooth, muscular body, his messed up hair and his eyes are pleasantly overwhelming.
"Hungry for what?" he whispers, as he pulls me close to him, my chest firmly pressed against his. *Oh my.*

"Screw it." I smile, repeating his words from earlier. "Dinner can wait."

"So..." I'm so hesitant to bring this up, after the amazing experience I just had in Andrew's kitchen, then bedroom, but I have to know. "What did Ms. Hamilton want today?"

I can't look at him because I know my face is glowing with several emotions at the moment – jealously probably the most prominent. I just look down at my plate on his coffee table and play with my green beans.

Andrew clears his throat next to me, and I pop my head up. *Nervous, Andrew? Why?*

Now he won't look at me. This is not good.

He takes another bite of his steak, and I pull his t-shirt down to cover the tops of my thighs, suddenly feeling shy and uncomfortable.

Andrew notices my reaction, and reaches to grab my hand. "Stop it," he says, as he places my hand in his lap. "I told you there's nothing to worry about with her."

I sigh, hating that I can't seem to keep my emotions on lock down around him. He completely disarms me, and it scares me to death.

"I know," I admit, but not with as much confidence I was hoping for. "That woman seriously gets under my skin."

Andrew laughs. "She has that effect on a lot of people, including me."

"Really?" I ask, looking into his gorgeous eyes. "She's a very attractive woman. I've seen some of the men in our office drooling."

"Yes, until they meet her," Andrew scoffs. "And Jules, if you think for one second that woman has anything on you, you're mistaken. I've seen plenty of guys around the office drooling over you as well, before and *after* they meet you."

I roll my eyes and smile. "Liar."

"You know it's true," Andrew says smiling, taking a bite of potato. "But now they'll have to get through me first. And no one wants to mess with the boss."

"Yes, you are rather scary in the office," I admit.

"You aren't scared."

"I was for a while," I tell him, looking down at my hand still in his lap. "But you got better, at least with me."

Andrew's face pales, his bite stopped suddenly in the air before it reaches his mouth.

"Don't bring that up again, please," he says quietly, placing his fork back on his plate. "I can't believe I upset you like that. It's been a rough couple of years for me. That's not who I am."

"I know," I assure him. "I know who you are, and I love you, every part of you, good, bad and ugly."

Andrew smiles. Thank God.

"I love you too, although, I'm yet to find the ugly parts."

I smile, but inside, my stomach turns. *I haven't told you about my screwed up family yet, Andrew. Just wait.*

We both get back to our meals, and I get back to my original question.

"So? Ms. Hamilton?" I start, "If you don't want to, or can't tell me, I completely understand."

Andrew seems more at ease now. "She came to give me some information on my dad," he says. "But she's definitely playing both sides. I'm going to have to be careful."

"What kind of information? Anything you can use?" I ask, hopefully.

"Not yet." Andrew sighs. "She said he plans to try and sabotage my efforts in New York. I assumed as much."

"Really?" I ask, still shocked at the fact that a father could do this to his own son. It's repulsive.

"Of course." Andrew shakes his head, resigned. Poor Andrew. "I thought this was what he wanted, but I've recently found out that he's trampled nearly every attempt I've made over the past couple of months to re-design the company. I just don't understand why." He stares at his plate for a moment before continuing. "Victoria claims she can hold him off this time."

Andrew clears his throat again. I wonder if I should tell him I've clued into his little nervous habit, but I quickly decide against sharing such a useful tool.

"In exchange for?" I ask. May as well get to the heart of things.

Andrew looks quickly over at me, then back at his plate.

"You know what she wants, Jules." He looks at me now, sincerity in those beautiful eyes. "But I'm not giving it to her. Please trust me," he pleads.

"I do," I reply, as I do trust him. It's *her* I don't trust.

Andrew breathes a sigh of relief. "It seems my dad's going behind my back killing the deals. I honestly didn't know what he was up to until recently, and none of the previous investors will admit to his involvement. I thought we were on the same side." Andrew takes another deep breath. "The information I received recently came from a friend of a friend that works for one of the companies I was soliciting. He saw my dad visiting with the president of the company the same day I got the call that the deal fell through. It could be a coincidence, but I have a bad feeling it's not."

I squeeze Andrew's hand that's still holding mine in his lap.

"Why would he do this, Andrew? Doesn't he want to save the company?" I neglected to ask him this in New York. I found myself rather distracted by all the flirting…and the sex.

Andrew looks at me, opens his mouth, and quickly closes it. It's obvious he's wrestling with whether or not to tell me something. I don't press. I just sit calmly and wait for him to respond.

He looks back down at our hands. "Honestly, I'm not sure. He keeps telling me he wants to, but then with the recent developments…well, I'm finding out otherwise. I don't understand."

I shift so I'm turned and facing him on the floor. I grab his hand with both of mine. "I'm so sorry, Andrew, for all of this. What a terrible and exhausting thing to be going through. Is there anything I can do to help?"

Andrew shakes his head. "I want you as far away from all of this as possible. Please stay out of it, for me?"

I nod, but I feel so helpless.

"Okay," I say quietly. "But no one knows about us, Andrew. I could do some spying. No one would suspect a thing."

Andrew looks at up at me, his eyes laced with confusion and something else...admiration? Wonder, maybe?

"What?" I ask nervously, after he doesn't speak for a minute or so.

He shakes his head. "I just think you're..." He looks down again at my hands holding his. "I just can't believe..."

Suddenly, I know exactly how he feels.

"I would do anything for you Andrew," I tell him, leaning in to lay my head on his bare shoulder. "I love you."

"I know," he moves his free hand to my cheek. "It's unbelievable."

I raise my head back up to look at him. "Unbelievable that I love you?"

"No." He shakes his head and smiles, his hand back on my cheek. "It's unbelievable *how much* you love me. I'm not sure I deserve it."

"Yes, you do." I put my hand on his, as he caresses my cheek. "And I really do want to help," I tell him. "If there's anything I can do, please let me help, okay?"

"No." Andrew's eyes are deadly serious. "My father's ruthless and you'll get hurt. I won't let that happen."

I drop it for now. I can see it frightens him, and at least he knows I'm here for him.

"Okay." I look down at our hands again. Why do I keep asking questions I don't really want the answers to? "But how are you going to handle Ms. Hamilton? I mean, she's not going to be easy to hold off for long."

Andrew releases one hand and pulls my chin up so I'll look at him. "Call her Victoria around me, or whatever colorful curse word you choose. No need for the formalities."

I smile. "Fine. What are you going to do about Bitchface?"

"Better." Andrew smiles too, and places a gentle kiss on my lips. "I'm going to hold her off as long as I possibly can. I just need her to keep my dad in line until this New York money comes in. Then I can tell them both to go to hell."

"When will that be?"

How long do I have to suffer through the thoughts of her attacking you in your office?

"Should be within the next few weeks," he says. "They have to push the paperwork through the executive team, but I was assured there would be no issue."

"A few weeks..." I ponder. "I'm not sure she can keep her hands off you for that long."

"Jules," Andrew squeezes my hand. "I'm honestly not sure how any of this will work out, but if me taking her out on a date or two will prevent my dad from sabotaging me and save the company...well, I have to do it. I don't have a choice."

I nod, but I hate this. I freaking hate it with everything inside me. But I have to do this for him. I love him too much to let him go. I don't have a choice either.

"You have to take her on dates?" My mouth is twisted in disgust and Andrew smiles sadly.

"Probably," he says, and I can hear the regret in his voice. "But she's nothing to me, Jules. Just a means to an end. I promise. You have to trust me on this."

"Will you have to sleep with her?" This is the burning question for me. I don't think I could take it.

"Hell no!" Andrew nearly yells, which startles me. "I will do everything possible to avoid touching her in any way."

I smile at his overreaction. "Okay," I surrender, and then I remember the plans I stupidly agreed to tomorrow night. "I have to tell you something."

Is he going to be mad? He can't be mad. It's nothing. Just like this weird thing with Victoria is nothing, right? Andrew can obviously sense my nervousness. It shows on his face.

"What is it?" he asks tentatively.

"Well..." This is hard to say. I never pictured our relationship being such a cluster. "I kind of agreed to go on a blind date tomorrow night with a friend of Abby's."

Andrew's eyes widen in shock. "You did what?"

"Abby asked me to meet a friend of hers earlier this week, before our New York trip," I tell him. "She's relentless, so I just agreed to meet him. It's nothing, really."

Andrew clears his throat a couple of times before he speaks. I have to suppress a smile.

"Who is this guy?"

Okay, so maybe he's not mad. He's...nervous? Jealous? It's hard to tell.

"He's just some friend of Abby's." I try to blow it off, keep it light, but I can tell Andrew's not buying it. "I thought it couldn't hurt – may even help our cause."

"*Our cause?*" Andrew's eyes widen again.

Hey buddy, this whole sneaking around thing was your idea. Not mine.

"You know, if we're both seen out with other people, then it will help solidify the fact that nothing's going on between us," I explain.

"So, you're going to see other people?"

Wow. Andrew's not nervous, or jealous or intimidated. He's hurt. *No, Andrew. It's not like that.*

I smile, trying to reassure him. "Andrew, it's nothing, okay?" I tell him in earnest. "I'm only doing it for the reasons I just mentioned. And it will help keep my roommate off my ass, since I am a shitty liar."

He gives me a poor excuse for a smile, and it breaks my heart. "I'm not in any place to judge, I guess," he admits. "So, I'm going to lie and say I'm okay with it."

"You asked me to trust you. Now you have to trust me. You have nothing to worry about." I try again to reassure him. I move into his lap so I'm straddling him. He's back in his cargo pants, but nothing else – a truly remarkable sight. "Now," I say, wrapping my arms around his neck, and pulling his face close to mine, "I would like my dessert please."

I'm happy to see a more genuine smile spread across his face before I move to kiss his perfect lips.

"I just got you, Jules," he whispers breathlessly as we kiss. "I don't want to lose you."

His words cut to the core of me. "You won't," I promise him, trailing kisses down his neck, onto his bare shoulder.

Andrew pulls my face in front of his with both hands. He holds it there for a moment, staring deep into my eyes, not saying a word.

His probing stare sends heat coursing through my body, concentrating mainly between my legs. Oh dear God. I just can't get enough of him.

I try to move my lips to his, but he holds me still, continuing to try and solve some mystery in my eyes. What does he want me to say? What does he need to hear?

I run my fingers slowly through the back of his silky hair. "I love you, Andrew. I need you," I whisper. "I don't want to lose you either."

I watch his shoulders relax before he pulls my face to his and kisses me softly. "I love you too, Jules," he says and then eases me gently to the floor. A wicked smile spreads suddenly across his face as he hovers above me. "Now let's talk about that dessert."

CHAPTER 27

Good God, I'm so freaking tired.

I didn't get home from Andrew's until around two this morning, and now I'm up at six, trying to keep my eyes open in the shower.

I smile as I think about last night. Andrew begged me to stay, but I didn't think it was a good idea. Abby would have been suspicious, if she's not already.

Ugh. Abby. I have to meet that Nate guy tonight.

I finish washing my hair and get out of the shower. No need to waste any more time trying to let the water wake me up. I need coffee. That's all that will suffice.

I dry off and head to my closet. Have I mentioned that I hate trying to find something to wear?

As my eyes search my closet I think about what Andrew might be wearing today. I can't wait to see him.

With that thought, I reach for the first thing in front of me – a black A-line skirt and a deep red short-sleeved sweater. Andrew seemed to like this color on me last night, which reminds me, I need to drop Abby's dress off at the dry cleaners. Kitchen sex got messy – not that I'm complaining.

I put on a little make-up, grab my black heels and head to the kitchen. I look at the clock on the microwave and see that I'm really early. Oh well. Can't hurt. I could use the time to get caught up on a couple of new proposals. My mind was a bit pre-occupied yesterday after the visit from Bitchface.

"How was your evening?"

I gasp, as I toss my bagel up into the air. It lands with a thud on the counter next to me.

"Why so jumpy lately?" Abby adds with a yawn as she moves past me and grabs a Diet Coke from the fridge.

"I'm not jumpy," I say, trying to catch my breath. "You just scared me."

Abby rolls her eyes. "So, how was last night?"

"It was fine," I say, collecting myself. "Just dinner with work people."

Abby looks suspicious. *Dammit!*

"What work people?" she asks, one eyebrow raised.

I smile at her, blowing it off. *I'll never tell, friend. Think what you want.*

"Just work people," I reply, continuing with the chore of spreading peanut butter on my bagel. "It was fun."

Abby eyes me suspiciously for a moment longer, but decides to give up for now. Thank goodness.

"Are we still on for tonight?" she asks, as she walks back toward her room.

"Yep," I say with a smile, whatever appeases her.

"See you then," she calls before closing her door.

I finish my bagel and wrap it in a paper towel. I'm scowling. Why am I scowling?

Probably because I don't want to do this tonight. It doesn't feel right. None of this feels right. All of this sneaking around, lying, cheating, misleading. It's all very suspect. In all of my years daydreaming about being with Andrew, I couldn't have dreamed this mess up if I tried.

But it's just temporary. Right? Pretty soon, it will be everything I imagined.

I exhale in relief at the thought and my phone rings. I check the clock. Who the hell is calling me at this hour?

I run to get my phone thinking it may be Andrew, but it's not.

"Hi, Mom." I close my eyes, prepared for the worst.

"Hey sweetheart."

I open my eyes wide in shock. She sounds good…and sober.

"What's going on? Why are you calling so early?"

There's still doubt in my voice, which I hate, but I've been burned too many times.

My mom laughs. "I just had a nice walk, and I'm about to eat breakfast. It's bagels today. I thought of you."

"Wait…" This is too good to be true. "Are you in rehab?"

Did my dad actually follow through this time? And she's still there? I feel like crying.

"Yes, I've been here since Monday," she replies, and I can tell she's smiling on the other end.

Since Monday? My mom's longest stint in rehab in the past is about seventy-two hours. This is a new record.

"Mom!" Here come the tears. "I'm so proud of you!"

"Me too, hunny. Me too."

"Where are you?" I ask, eager to go visit her, if allowed.

"I'm at the Watershed this time," she says. "It's nice. I don't remember much about the last time I was here."

I smile through my tears. I'm going to have to redo my make-up.

"This time will be different, Mom," I say confidently. "Just stay, okay? You can do this."

"I know, Jules. I know I can. I want to."

Her words are a comfort. I've heard them before, but they never get old, even when they're not true. I want to believe them so badly.

"When can I visit?" I ask, wanting to see her.

"They say no visitors for thirty days," she informs me, and I can hear the sadness in her voice.

"That's okay." I keep my voice happy, trying to lighten the mood back up. "You can call and chat whenever you want. You need to follow the protocol. They know what they're doing."

"I miss you," she says. "I can't wait to see you."

"Same here. I love you." I start crying harder, but I try to hide it. "I'll see you soon. Call me any time, okay?"

"I will, sweetheart. I love you."

We hang up, and I feel like some invisible weight has been lifted. Maybe it will work this time around.

I smile, as I lay my breakfast down and head back to my bathroom to fix my face. Maybe my talk with her Sunday really worked. It was no different than the other hundred chats we've had, but you never know when it may sink in. She looked so happy when she heard me telling off my dad. Maybe that's what she needed.

I stare into my bathroom mirror feeling like a million bucks. There's no need to worry about work, or Andrew, or anything else for that matter. If my mom can make it through rehab, anything's possible.

The excitement from the call with my mom this morning is quickly overshadowed in the office by the shrill sound of laughter echoing from the lobby.

Andrew had a meeting with his father this morning and he's still not in. I have no idea what the meeting is about. Andrew had me add it to his calendar a couple of weeks ago.

"Where's Andy?" Whore-In-Heels asks as she approaches my desk.

God, I want to punch her in the throat. Hearing her say his name is like ice in my veins.

"He had a meeting with his father," I say, putting on my best fake smile. "He should return within the hour."

I watch as her heavily eyeshadowed eyes roll in my direction. "Fine. I'll just call him."

"Sounds good," I say, willing her to walk away with my eyes. *Leave, Bitch!*

I smile at her back. I guess it worked! She stomps away without another word.

I look over at Adrian, who has a sympathetic look on her face. I shrug my shoulders and look back down at my computer.

Lunch today?

Adrian's messaging me. I think about it for a minute. I wanted to leave my schedule open for Andrew, but maybe I shouldn't do that. *Desperate much, Jules?*

Sure. The Diner?

I'm craving some of their chicken salad for some reason.

Sounds good! 11:30?

Perfect.

I go back to work and Andrew shows up as Adrian and I are about to leave for lunch.

"May I see you in my office before you leave, Ms. Greene?" he asks, as he walks toward his office. He doesn't even look my way as he passes by. He seems upset.

"Yes sir," I say quickly and put my purse back on my desk. "One minute," I mouth to Adrian before walking into Andrew's office and closing the door.

He's sitting on his sofa, his head in his hands. The posture is so familiar, still etched in my mind from his drunken night in the office.

I walk quickly over and take a seat beside him. "Andrew?" I try to pull his hands away from his head, but he's resisting. "Andrew, what's wrong?"

I put my arm around him, and try to pull his face to mine. He's still resisting, and he's shaking.

"Andrew?" I say nervously. "Please talk to me."

I move my arm from around him, thinking maybe he doesn't want me touching him, but as soon as I move away, he lifts his head.

"Are you okay?" I ask, as I take one of his hands in mine. He squeezes it hard, but still says nothing. His eyes are heavy and tired. I bet he got zero sleep last night. Part of that may be my fault.

I wrap my arms around his neck, and hug him close. "I'm here for you," I whisper.

Andrew buries his face in my hair, and kisses me gently on the neck. "I know," he whispers back. "This is all I need."

We sit there, holding each other for I don't know how long. I eventually remember Adrian's waiting, so I reluctantly pull away.

"Are you going to be alright?" I ask, as I hold his tired face in my hands. "I don't have to go."

"Where are you going?"

"Lunch with Adrian. I won't be long."

"I'll be fine," he tells me, but he's not very reassuring. "This is just really hard, all of this lying. He's my father."

"I know." I frown, as I caress his cheek. "I'm so sorry, Andrew. Hopefully, it will all be over soon."

"I'm glad you're here," he says, with a smile on his face. "I really am. So glad."

"Me too," I tell him with a smile. "You're better than him, and you're going to win this the right way. I can feel it."

"It doesn't feel right. It feels awful."

His face is sad again, so I pull him back into my arms.

"I know it does, but I'm here for you, and I love you. I'm not sure if that helps, but it's all I have to give at the moment."

"It's more than enough," Andrew breathes into my neck. "It's everything."

"I have to go," I say finally, and Andrew stands, pulling me with him. "Do you want me to bring something back for you?"

"Where are you going?" he asks, before pulling me toward him and kissing me softly on the lips.

"The Diner. Chicken salad sandwich?" It's both of our favorites.

"Sounds delicious," he agrees, and kisses me again. "What's for dessert?"

He winks at me and I smile. God, he's gorgeous.

"We'll work that out later."

He kisses me once more before letting me go.

"I miss you already," he tells me, as he walks to his desk, and I walk to the door.

I turn to him and smile, before remembering the unwanted guest that stopped by this morning.

"Ms. Hamilton came to see you this morning," I say, not even trying to hide the loathing on my face.

Andrew smiles at me from behind his desk. "*Who* came by?" he asks, cocking a perfect eyebrow at me.

I smile, taking a split second to admire the vision in a black suit, blue shirt and checkered tie in front of me. Have mercy.

"Whorebag Hamilton, sir."

"Much better," he says, and turns to his computer.

I quickly hide my wide grin before completely leaving his office. Can't have Adrian getting suspicious, although something tells me she may have an idea after all she did during our New York trip. I have to remember to thank her for that fabulous outfit.

"Ready?" I ask Adrian, as I grab my bag and start walking toward her desk.

"Yep!" she calls, grabbing her purse and coming to meet me.

We walk to the elevators in silence. I'm still reeling over what just happened in Andrew's office. I wonder what he spoke about with his father.

"Everything okay?" Adrian asks, as we get on the elevator.

"Yeah. I just have a lot on my mind."

"I understand," she nods. "How was your trip to New York?"

"Great!" I say excitedly, maybe too excitedly. *Dial it down a notch, Jules!* "And thanks for the outfit, by the way. It was perfect."

You have no idea how perfect, Adrian. You are my angel.

"It was my pleasure!" she beams. "I'm so glad you liked it. The sales lady I spoke with at Bloomingdales was very helpful. I told her jeans, blouse, and colors, and she did the rest."

I smile at her. "Well, it was a beautiful outfit."

"Thanks," she says, smiling shyly back at me.

We finally reach The Diner, which is just a couple of blocks from the office. That's the beauty of working in town. There are tons of great restaurants within walking distance.

The waitress comes for our order quickly after we're seated, and after some normal office chit chat, we sit and enjoy our lunch in silence for a bit.

"So, you never told me about New York," Adrian says, nearly finished with her soup and salad. "Did everything go well with Mr. Mercer's meetings?"

I'm not sure how much Adrian knows about what Andrew's trying to do with the company, so I keep things vague for now.

"I think so," I tell her. "I'm not really kept in the loop," I lie, but oh well.

Adrian nods, accepting my lie. "I will admit I missed you guys a little. Andrew's busy. I have no idea how you do it."

I smile at her. "You get used to it."

"Plus, I hate having to go through Mercer Senior for all of the invoice approvals," she adds. "It's bad enough that I have to go to him with the few he personally signs."

What? That's odd. I wonder if Andrew knows about this.

"Why would he have to personally approve invoices? Does he do that often?" I ask calmly, trying not to raise too many alarms.

Mercer Senior's been out of the day-to-day for a while now, and even if he was still involved, I'm sure something like signing invoices would be beneath him.

Adrian shrugs. "I periodically get invoices from various departments that require Mercer Senior's approval. The ones this week weren't even that big. I guess it was just something he was personally involved in."

"Who were they from?"

Adrian looks up for a minute, thinking. "If I remember correctly, I think they were from the design group." She shrugs again. "Something about new software, maybe?"

Huh. That sounds innocent enough, but I still make a mental note to pass on this whole invoice thing to Andrew.

"So…" Adrian starts, as I chew and think about what the hell Mercer Senior could be up to. "How was the sightseeing?" she asks with a smile.

Either she's totally suspect, or I'm totally paranoid. Either way, I need to hurry over this subject.

"It was great," I admit. "I'd never been to New York before. It's a beautiful city."

"That was so nice of Mr. Mercer," she says, another huge smile on her face. She's totally on to us.

Shit!

"It was," I say, concentrating uncomfortably on the last bit of my sandwich.

"He's a good man," she continues, and when I look up, I'm surprised to see sincerity in her eyes. "I know a lot of people don't like him, and I won't lie and say that he doesn't scare me a little, but I do respect him. I trust his leadership."

"Me too," I agree, and at the same time, I realize Adrian's giving me her approval without actually saying it. I love this girl. "He's inspiring, really."

"I'm glad he has you," she says, and I nearly choke on a potato chip. "As an assistant of course," she quickly adds. "I think you guys work well together."

"T-Thanks," I stutter, trying but failing to act cool as I take a sip of water to get the chip down. "Thanks Adrian," I say with more sincerity this time, and she smiles.

CHAPTER 28

The rest of my work day flew by. I was extremely busy, as was Andrew, so I had little interruptions. Part of me wanted to be unhappy about that, but oh well. Before I left, I agreed to come over to his place again tomorrow night.

I'm standing in my closet now, enduring the arduous task of trying to find something to wear to meet this Nate guy at Marlow's.

Andrew wasn't very happy this afternoon when I reminded him of my plans tonight, but I decided to hold my ground. For some sick reason that I don't want to think too hard about, meeting this guy tonight makes me feel better about the situation Andrew and I are currently in. Mostly, I think it just helps settle my nerves about the whole Bitchface thing. I mean, if I can go meet a guy and play along, then Andrew can do the same with that slut. No problem. Right?

I decide on skinny jeans, my long, gold silk halter top, and a pair of silver and gold heels I picked up several weeks ago. I haven't worn them yet, which makes me think for a second they may be a bad idea since I'll be walking to the club. But they'll look really cute with my top, so I'll take the fashion risk. I toss my hair up in a bun knowing it will be burning hot in Marlow's anyway, and add a little more make-up to complete my look. *Not bad, Jules.*

I look at the clock, and see it's a little after eight. I decide to go ahead and leave. I may beat him there, but that will give me some time to ask Abby a few more questions about him.

As I walk out the door, my Blackberry buzzes in my small clutch purse.

I pull it out before locking my door and see it's a message from Andrew.

> *Have fun tonight, but not too much. Please?*

Oh good grief. He's adorable.

> *I'll try.*

Why not tease him a little? Gotta keep him on his toes.

> *Not funny.*

I smile. He's obviously not amused.

> *I'll be thinking of you all night.*

Hopefully, that will ease his mind.

He doesn't respond immediately, so I start down the stairs. My phone buzzes again in my hand, as I reach the door to go outside.

> *Please call me when you get in. I'm desperate and pathetic and so not okay with this.*

I laugh, as I walk outside. It feels nice out.

Please don't worry. Love you. Will call you later.

The thought of Andrew Mercer being jealous of someone I'm dating makes me kind of giddy. Life is so very good right now.

I start walking toward the bar and notice the streets are already very crowded. Everybody must be excited about the warmer weather.

I walk leisurely toward Marlow's, knowing I have some extra time. It really is a nice night. I may be a little chilly walking home since I decided against a jacket or sweater, but it's not that far of a walk. I'll tough it out.

My Blackberry buzzes again right as I reach the door to Marlow's.

Seriously not okay with this, but I love you too. Call me.

I smile as I walk in. I'll have a casual drink with this Nate guy, head home and chat all night with my wonderful new boyfriend. *See, Andrew? This can work.*

I will. Promise.

I type back, before I head toward the bar to wait for Abby. I don't see her immediately, so she must be in the back.

"Is someone sitting here?" I ask a guy sitting next to the only empty seat at the bar.

"Looks like you are," he says, turning to face me. *Wow*. Mega hottie.

"Thanks." I smile and slide in next to him.

He goes back to his drink, and I sneak a glimpse of him out of the corner of my eye. I can't help it. He's gorgeous, and totally my type...before Andrew, that is.

His hair is dark, almost black, and his eyes are steel blue – so light that his irises nearly blend in with the whites of his eyes. *Yowzers*.

I try not to stare so I don't catch much, but I can see he's wearing a short-sleeved, button down shirt, and he has a tattoo peeking out of his shirt on his left arm, with a couple more on his lower arm. I don't look long enough to decipher what they are.

"Can I get you something, sweetheart?"

Steve the bartender pulls me away from my discreet gawking.

"Sure." I smile at him. "I'll have a beer, Steve. Blue Moon."

"You got it," he says, as he saunters off to retrieve my beverage.

"Regular here?" the hottie next to me asks, and I instantly feel bad for being excited about the chance to look at him again.

"Sort of."

Damn, his eyes are incredible, and he has a killer smile.

I see now that his shirt is light blue, to match his eyes, and he has a gray t-shirt underneath. He appears very unkempt, but in a hot, rockstar kind of way.

Steve returns with my beer, and I reach into my purse for some cash.

"I got this," Cute Boy says, and I sigh. *Seriously guy? Nice gesture, but a little too soon.*

"Thanks," I say, before taking a sip of my beer, kind of glad I'm now a little turned off by my neighbor.

"Too soon?" he asks, and I turn back to him. His smile is lovely.

"Maybe a little," I admit, smiling back. "But thanks anyway."

"I was just looking for a reason to chat with you," he tells me. He has an interesting accent – not from around here.

"Well played." I guess I owe him a little conversation, so I ask him the first question that pops in my head. "Where are you from?"

"Is it that obvious?" he chuckles, and it's a light, airy sound, very pleasing to the ears. "I'm from Seattle, but I've been here a while. My southern accent is a work in progress."

His smile is contagious. Warning signs start going off in my head. A guy this good looking has to be a player. I know his type. I've dated his type.

Oh well. I have nothing to lose. I already have everything I want. May as well have some fun with Mr. Player here.

"You still have quite a bit of work to do," I tell him, smiling. I wish he wasn't so nice to look at.

"Maybe you can teach me."

I'm temporarily breathless. There's something kind and genuine in those crystal blue eyes – not very *player-like* at all.

"I'm sure there are plenty of women around here that would be more than happy to help," I suggest, no longer interested in playing along.

Don't look into his eyes, Jules! It's a trap!

"Right." Mr. Ocean Eyes looks away from me, and back down at his drink. I sneak a glimpse out of the corner of my eye again, and I'm shocked to see he looks truly hurt. "Sorry to bother you."

I sigh. *No need to be a bitch, Jules.*

"I'm sorry," I say quickly, and he looks back up at me again. "I've had a rough day. Let's start over, shall we?"

I extend my hand, and he grabs it with a smile. "I'm Jules," I tell him.

"Jules?" his eyes widen, and the next thing I know, Abby's beside me holding on to my arm.

"Hey roomie!" she says excitedly. "I see you've met Nate!"

I turn back to the blue eyed beauty next to me, and try to pick my jaw up off the floor.

This is Nate? *Fuck. Me.*

CHAPTER 29

"How's that for intros?" Nate asks, as I continue to try and regain my composure.

I can't believe this is the guy Abby was talking so nonchalantly about a few days ago. He owns a bookstore? He doesn't look like the bookstore type.

I shake my head and take another long swig of my beer.

"I knew you guys would get along," Abby says smiling, her arm still around me. "Isn't he dreamy, Jules?" she teases in a sing-song voice, and I flush.

Abby, some tact? For the love of God.

To my surprise, I catch Nate blushing too. Don't tell me this man is humble. There's no way. Does he have mirrors in his house?

"Abby, why don't you get back to work now?" I say, telling her much more than that with my eyes.

"I hear ya!" She leans in to give Nate a quick kiss on the cheek. "Thanks for coming, Nate."

"My pleasure," he tells her, while looking directly at me.

Oh no. This is bad. Very bad.

Abby winks at me, before skipping back behind the bar. The bar is a huge square, and it appears Abby's working on the other side from where we're sitting. Good. I don't need her distractions tonight. I need to keep a clear head so I can get through this. *Dammit.* Why is he so freaking hot?

"So, Jules," he starts, and I try hard not to look at his perfectly pink lips. "Abby tells me you work for a construction company."

"She does, does she?" I'm sure that's not all Abby said about my job, and Nate's face tells me I'm right. Abby told me she had said nothing to Nate about me. I knew better than to believe that one.

"Well, she actually said you're wasting your time working for a construction company," he admits with a smile, "when you should really be out doing what you love...photography, if I remember correctly."

I smile back. "Well, Abby should be thankful I like to *waste my time*, since *my* job has paid her rent a few times when she refused to waste *her* time with a job."

Nate chuckles again. So pleasant. "Abby's a character, that's for sure."

"How did you two meet?" I ask. I think Abby said they met here, but I can't remember.

"Technically, we met here," he confirms." But shortly after we met, she stumbled across my shop by coincidence. We ended up talking a little more then. That's when she told me about you."

"Really?" I'm betting the shop visit wasn't a coincidence. I'm also wondering why Abby didn't snatch this one up for herself. So far he's kind of fabulous.

"Yeah, I'm not usually one for blind dates," Nate says, "but I haven't really met anyone of interest since I've been here, so I thought I'd give it a shot."

"I don't usually like this type of thing either," I quickly agree. "But Abby can be ruthless."

"That too." Nate laughs again. He's really easy to talk to, once you get past the overwhelming good looks.

We continue our casual banter, and before I know it, it's last call. *No way!* Have we been sitting here that long?

"Do you need a ride home?" he asks politely, as I finish my beer. I don't even know how many I've had. I've just been enjoying the conversation.

"No thanks," I tell him. "Abby and I only live a couple of blocks away."

"Well at least let me walk you home," he offers, and I accept. No harm in that, right?

I get off my stool and take an embarrassing stumble. I think it's these heels, more than the beers, but it's probably a little of both.

Nate grabs my arm to steady me, and I fall into his chest, face first. Mmmm...he even smells pretty.

"Sorry," I say, quickly righting myself, but he doesn't drop my arm.

"It's no problem," he says with a smile, as he moves my arm so it's linked into his. "Ready?"

Not really, but here we go.

I smile up at him as I grab my purse from the bar. He's tall, really tall, and thin, but not too skinny – just right.

"Be safe you two!" Abby yells from across the bar as we reach the door.

I roll my eyes at her, and we leave.

The cold air is welcome, at first. It helps clear my head, but after a few minutes I start shivering slightly as the wind blows. It is a little colder out than I thought it would be tonight.

"If I had a jacket, I'd offer," Nate says, before putting his arm around my shoulders and pulling me into him.

I don't allow myself to feel guilty yet because he's really warm. I'll cry about all of this later.

I wrap my arms around him, hugging him close as we walk – a little faster than I would like in these heels – back to my apartment.

When we finally reach my building, Nate releases me. "I had a nice time tonight," he says with a smile.

"Me too," I admit, truthfully. My brain is currently clouded with beer, but I did have a good time. I think? Sure, Andrew kept popping up now and then and I'm sure to feel horrible about all of this in the morning, but for now, I can say I had a good time.

"Interested in doing it again sometime?" he asks, a shy smile on his face. "Maybe somewhere a little more quiet next time?"

"Sure."

Wait, what did I just agree to?

"Great." Nate looks pleased, and I suddenly feel rotten. Did I just agree to a second date?

"I'll call you then?"

"Sure."

Dammit! I did it again! Stupid beer brain!

Now we're at that awkward moment where there could be a kiss.

Please don't kiss me, Nate. Please, please, please.

"I'll call you soon," he says, and starts walking away.

Thank goodness. He turns back to me and waves before he rounds the corner. I wave back and then hug myself because it's freezing out here and I need to go to bed.

What the hell just happened?

I quickly turn and head into my apartment building. The stairwell isn't that warm, but better than outside.

I finally reach my door and sigh as I enter, soaking up the warmth of my apartment. Now I just need some sweats, and I can pretend like this confusing evening never happened.

But I can't because my dumbass agreed to a second date with him! What in the hell was I thinking?

I put my hands over my face and sink down to the floor next to my door. What am I going to do?

Suddenly, I feel my purse buzzing in my lap. *Andrew!*

I fumble trying to pull out my Blackberry, my brain moving slightly faster than my drunk fingers.

I have one message from Andrew, and it's from about an hour ago.

> *Just wanted to say goodnight. Talk to you tomorrow.*

I close my eyes briefly as the guilt threatens to consume me, but I force myself up and head to my room.

I toss my horribly uncomfortable shoes in my closet and start to pace. Should I call him back? I want to hear his voice so badly right now.

My panic is sobering. What the hell am I doing? I can't believe I agreed to a second date with Nate.

Oh well. That can be easily remedied. I try to work it out as I pace. When he calls, I'll just tell him I'm seeing someone else. That will take care of that.

But I can't really do that because he'll tell Abby, and she'll want to know who my new guy is or why I lied to her friend. This sucks!

I look at my Blackberry, which I'm still gripping tightly in my hand. I need to at least message Andrew back.

> *I'm home. I miss you so much. Sweet dreams. I'll call you tomorrow.*

I do miss him like crazy. The second date blunder was a result of too many beers – and Nate's killer eyes. I can see that now, as my anxiety is slowly starting to overpower my buzz.

My phone going off startles me, and I drop it. I pick it back up quickly, knowing it has to be Andrew.

> *Glad you're safe. I miss you too.*

Why's he still awake? It's nearly two in the morning.

> *Can't sleep?*

My poor Andrew. I don't think he's had a good nights' sleep in months. I suddenly remember the state he was in after his meeting with his dad today. I never even asked him what that was about. I'm a terrible girlfriend!

Nope. Wish you were here.

Dammit! Why did I drink so much?

Me too.

I sit down on my bed, tired of pacing for the moment, and my phone rings.

"Hello?" I answer, before I even look at the caller ID.

"Hi." It's Andrew. "I wanted to hear your voice at least, if I can't see you."

I smile at how he makes me feel like I'm the most important person on the planet.

"I'm glad you called," I admit, as I lie back on my bed.

"So, did you have fun?"

"No," I answer immediately, and I realize it's true…well, maybe half true. Nate doesn't even hold a candle to Andrew, but he was nice to talk to. "I thought of you all night, just like I promised."

Andrew laughs, but he sounds exhausted. "You don't have to lie."

I smile into the phone. "I'm not lying. He was nice," I tell him. "But he was nothing compared to you."

"Glad to hear it," he finally says, before yawning. "You know, I could really use one of those special back scratches right about now."

"I wish I was there. I would gladly oblige." I physically ache for him. *Curse you alcohol!*

"I know. I wish you were too," he says, and yawns again. "But I'm sure you drank a few this evening, and unfortunately, in an effort to fall asleep, I had a few myself. I'll have to settle for tomorrow night, it seems."

"I can't wait."

I briefly contemplate taking a cab to his house. I think I have enough cash.

"Me neither. I love you, Jules. I'm glad you're safe."

"I love you too," I tell him. "And I'll see you tomorrow."

We hang up, and I feel like complete shit. I should have had one beer, chatted politely with Nate for Abby's sake, and then left. I could have gone and spent the night with Andrew, but no. I had to flirt with super sexy eyes for hours like a stupid slut!

I pull my covers over myself, not even bothering to change my clothes. I lie in my bed with the light off, staring out the window of my room, feeling like a horrible person as I start to cry.

CHAPTER 30

"Where are you headed this evening?" Abby asks, as she strolls into my room, the same knowing smile on her face she's been wearing all day. She's so excited about Nate and me she can barely see straight.

"I'm hanging out with my friend Adrian from work," I say, giving her my alibi for staying at Andrew's tonight. I hate lying, but I don't have a choice.

"Oh," Abby pouts. "Okay then."

"What's wrong?" I ask her, smiling.

"Am I being replaced?" she asks, her face like a pouty little girl, which makes me laugh. "You're spending a lot of time with work friends lately."

"Seriously?" I roll my eyes at her. "You're my forever friend. You know that."

"I know. Just checking." Abby smiles. "So, where are you going?"

"Some club near Adrian's house. I may stay the night with her."

"She lives in Gwinnett, right?" Abby yells from my bed, as I start my make-up in the bathroom.

"Yep, so I probably won't drive all the way back home." *Because I'll be staying at Andrew's house! Yay!*

"They have clubs in Gwinnett?" I can hear the judgment in her voice. Abby's become such an intown snob.

"No," I decide to tease her. "We're going to hang out in a cow pasture and drink moonshine from Mason jars."

"Sorry," she says, coming to visit me in the bathroom. "That was rude of me."

I smile at her. "I like Adrian. You'd like her too. She's nice."

"Yeah, yeah." Abby rolls her eyes at me, her sympathetic wave has passed. "So, when are you and Nate going out again?" She wags her eyebrows at me. This is only the twentieth time she's asked this question today.

"No idea," I say, trying not to roll my eyes. "He said he'd call."

"He'll call."

Abby's trying to comfort me, but I honestly couldn't care less if he calls or not. He's not Andrew and he's never going to be.

"Hey, quick question," I start, putting down my mascara to look at Abby. "Why didn't you snatch him up? He seems like a catch, and obviously easy on the eyes."

Abby shrugs. "Dunno. Just not interested in the dating scene right now."

"Okay," I say, but it sounds more like a question.

Abby shrugs again. "Nate is the kind of guy you go out on dates with, much more your type."

I laugh. "Not the one-night-stand kind of guy?"

"Nope." Abby smiles.

"Which is more *your* type?" I smile back and start on my mascara again. "Because you're a dirty slut?"

"Precisely."

"But I love you dearly, and all of your whorish ways."

"I know." She giggles. "I really hope the two of you work out."

I pause again to look at her. "Why?"

"Because you deserve a good guy for a change." I smile at her and she smiles back. "And maybe it will help you get over your whole gay-boss-loving thing."

I swallow hard before tossing my mascara in my make-up bag and zipping it.

"Abby..." God, I want to tell her so badly, but I just can't. "I've been in love with Andrew for a long time. I don't see that changing anytime soon."

Abby's pouting again. "What about Nate? You better not lead him on, Jules."

I raise an eyebrow at her response. Hmmm...she seems overly protective. How well does she know this guy? I thought they just met.

"I promise I won't," I assure her. "He's very nice, and I will not take advantage of that."

"Good." Abby looks satisfied. "Well, have fun tonight. I have to work, so I'm going to get showered. Will you be gone before I leave?"

I take a quick glance at the clock on the wall of my bathroom. "Probably. Be careful tonight, and I'll see you tomorrow."

"See you tomorrow," she calls, as she walks out of my room.

I take a last look in the mirror before grabbing my toiletries and heading back to my room. I went for super casual today – dark skinny jeans, my favorite long, snug-fit leopard print t-shirt, and some strappy flat sandals. Due to our top secret relationship, I assume Andrew and I will just be hanging around his house, so I went with comfort.

I put my make-up and a couple of other essentials in my overnight bag and grab a bottle of water from the fridge before leaving.

"See you tomorrow!" I call to Abby before walking out the door. I'm not sure if she heard me or not.

I start my car and go to pull out, but I stop to check who's buzzing me on my Blackberry.

> *Why aren't you here yet? I'm getting impatient. Love you.*

I smile wide, but rather than message him back, I decide to call. Don't want to text and drive.

"Hi." He sounds excited when he picks up. "Tell me you're in your car on the way to me."

"Yes," I say. "I didn't want to type and drive."

"Good thinking. Sorry for being so needy."

I laugh. *Oh Andrew. Sometimes the irony is just too much.*

"You're not needy."

"Maybe a little?"

"Okay, fine. Maybe a little." I smile. "But I miss you like crazy too. I'll be over as soon as I can."

"Sounds perfect. What do you want to do tonight?"

Hmmm...snarky remark or no?

"I'm game for whatever. Did you have something in mind?"

I'll leave the snarky ball in his court.

"I have a few ideas." I can tell he's smiling. I can't wait to see it in person. "Just get here soon, okay?"

"I will." I love that he seems as desperate to see me, as I am to see him. "I'll see you soon."

"I love you, beautiful girl."

Uh-oh. There went my panties.

"I love you too," I breathe. The man can take my breath away like no other.

We hang up, and I sit in the silence in my car for a second, just letting his voice linger in my head. God, I love that man. I can't wait to see him again. I'm still not happy about the sneaking around, but it sure does make me appreciate the moments we do have together.

I eventually turn up my radio and sing myself all the way to his house.

I'm not far away when my phone rings. I'm surprised to see it's Adrian.

"Hey Adrian! What's going on?" I ask, wondering why she's calling me on a Saturday night.

"Hi Jules. Sorry to bother you."

"No worries," I assure her. "Everything okay?"

"Yes, everything's fine," she says, her voice hesitant. "I actually have a favor."

"Okay. How can I help?" There's a long pause. "Adrian?" I wonder if she's hung up.

Finally, she takes a deep breath before speaking again.

"Well, I sort of have a date tonight, and it's been a long time since I've had a date, and I have no idea what to wear," she gets out in a rush.

I have to try hard not to laugh at how adorably nervous Adrian sounds.

"No problem," I say confidently. "What are the options?"

I hear a sigh of relief on the other end, which makes me smile.

"Well, I have this mauve dress, or I can do jeans and a nice top."

"Where's he taking you?"

"Bailey's Downtown."

"Definitely the dress," I tell her. "Put it on and text me a picture."

"Thanks Jules," Adrian says, and I can tell she's smiling. "I don't have a lot of girlfriends, and I love your sense of style. I really appreciate your help."

"My pleasure, Adrian." I'm so flattered by her compliment. "I'm glad to help."

We hang up, and a few minutes later I'm looking at the picture she sent. I have to take quick glances as I drive, but I know instantly this is the right choice. The color is perfect for her creamy complexion, and the halter style shows just enough skin to drive her man wild. I'm instantly jealous of her sky-high, silver heels. I may need to borrow those.

I quickly call her back. "I won't be surprised to hear the two you ran off and eloped in Vegas after dinner tonight," I tease when Adrian picks up.

"Ugh. No thanks." Adrian laughs. "Besides, wouldn't want to risk running into Mercer Senior there."

Huh? Mercer Senior in Vegas?

"What do you mean?" I ask, my curiosity peeked.

"He just seems to spend a lot of time in Nevada lately," she tells me. "I've seen the airfare and hotel expenses pass through the department. I assume he's working on some business there." Adrian pauses for a minute. "Now that I think about it...that's where the software company was – Winchester, Nevada. The one I mentioned to you? I guess that's what he's been working on."

"The invoices you had to get his approval on?" I ask to confirm.

"Yep." Adrian pauses again, then sighs. "Big business in Winchester apparently, wherever the hell that is." She laughs.

"Sure," I say, smiling. "Well then, definitely steer clear of Vegas."

This certainly seems suspect. I'll make sure to bring it up to Andrew just in case.

"I will. I have more of a beach theme in mind, anyway." Adrian says haughtily, and I laugh at her confidence. It's amazing what a good dress and a hot pair of shoes can do for your self-esteem.

"Have a great time tonight," I say. "And please let me know how it goes."

"I will," she says. "Thanks again, Jules."

Shortly after I hang up with Adrian, my phone rings again. Seems I'm the popular one this evening.

"You're very impatient," I say with a smile as I answer.

"When it comes to seeing your beautiful face, I am," Andrew says, and I sigh. "Forgot to ask earlier if pizza was okay."

I smile. "Sounds perfect."

"Great. I'm starved so I'll go ahead and order. Preferences?"

"I like it all. Surprise me."

"You got it." He laughs. "I can't wait to see you."

"I can't wait to see you either. I should be there in a few minutes."

"Be careful," he says. "I'll see you soon."

"Okay. I will. See you soon."

"Love you."

"I love you too."

I hang up with Andrew, turn up my stereo and roll down my windows. Today has been a great day.

I spent my morning in the gym, which felt great. I haven't been there in forever, and I've missed my treadmill.

I talked to my mom again this morning, and she's still in rehab and sounded happy. I have a good feeling about her this time.

Plus, I'm feeling thankful for mine and Adrian's recent closeness. She seems like a great person, and I just know her man is going to fall in love with her tonight when he sees her.

And now, I get to spend the night with Andrew. The butterflies start fluttering in my tummy just thinking about it.

Life is good.

I sing loudly the rest of the way to Andrew's house. A little 80's alternative was the perfect choice for my ride. You can never go wrong with Depeche Mode.

Andrew's sitting on his front porch when I pull up. My heart starts beating rapidly and my hands are fumbling all over my gear shift as I try to put it in park. I can't get into his arms fast enough.

As soon as I get my car stopped, I jump out and Andrew walks down the steps to meet me. I rush into his arms, and he hugs me close. We stand in the middle of his driveway for several minutes, just holding each other.

I eventually pull away, only because I want to see his gorgeous face.

"Miss me?" I ask smiling.

"Always." He smiles back, and kisses me. *Yummy.*

"Pizza's on its way," he says, and grabs my hand to lead me up to his front door.

He's wearing plain khakis tonight, with no shoes or socks, and another snug t-shirt, navy blue this time. He looks scrumptious.

"You can sit down if you want. I'll grab us some drinks." He kisses me once more before letting go of my hand.

I have a seat on the cushy leather sofa, and Andrew returns soon after with two beers. Blue Moon. And he even poured it in a glass and fastened an orange slice on the rim. How did he know?

"I love Blue Moon. It's my favorite," I tell him, as I take a sip. "Did you know that?"

"Coincidence. I promise," he says smiling. "I like it too. Cheers."

He holds up his glass for a toast, and I clink mine against his. We sit and enjoy our beers on the sofa for a few minutes before the pizza arrives. Andrew goes to pay and I get up to follow him to the dining room table.

"Another beer?" he offers, and I nod.

"Thanks for the pizza," I say, when he returns with our beers, two plates and some napkins.

"Thanks for coming over." Andrew sits, makes his plate and takes a bite of his pizza.

"Thanks for asking me." I take of bite of mine as well. It's loaded with all kinds of goodies, and tastes heavenly.

We eat for a bit in silence, but it's soon interrupted by my phone. I grab it from my pocket and see that it's my dad. I don't want to talk to him right now, but I worry something may be wrong, so I answer.

"Hey, Dad. What's up?" I stand and move from the table, into the huge sunroom in the back of Andrew's house.

"Hey pumpkin," he says cheerfully. "I haven't talked to you in a while, so I thought I'd see how you're doing."

I roll my eyes. "I'm still mad," I tell him, and I am. I'm perpetually mad at my father.

"I know." He sighs. "You made that pretty clear the last time we talked."

"Thank you for taking Mom, though. Glad you listened this time."

"No problem. I want her to get better too, Jules. Honestly, I do."

Yeah, right.

"Well, anyway, she sounds like she's doing well this time."

"Let's hope so."

Dammit. Can't he ever just believe in her? For one freaking second?

"Did you need something specific?" I ask, already eager to let him go. "I'm at a friend's house."

"Oh," my dad sounds taken aback. "I didn't mean to bother you. I just wanted to see how you're doing."

"I'm fine, Dad. I'll call you later."

"Okay, sweetheart. I love you."

I close my eyes and take a deep breath.

"I love you too," I say before hanging up. It's painful to say those words to my father. It's a shame, but it's the truth.

I decide to stand in the room for a minute or two before returning to Andrew. I need to find my happy mood again.

Breathe, Jules. Just breathe.

After a few deep breaths, I turn and make my way back to the table.

"Sorry about that," I tell Andrew as I sit back down.

"Everything okay?"

One more deep breath. I'll have to spill it eventually.

"It's fine. It was my dad. I was just worried something may be wrong. We don't speak very often."

Andrew stares at me a moment, seeming unsure if he should press the issue.

Here we go.

"My family's kind of messed up," I start.

"Join the club." Andrew laughs and I smile.

"But I hate to even tell you the details. You might change your mind about me."

I'm half kidding, half not.

Andrew grabs my hand and smiles. "Good luck making *that* happen."

Damn, he's gorgeous.

"Well, okay…" Where to start? "My dad's an attorney."

I look at Andrew and he nods, encouraging me to continue.

"He's a corporate attorney."

I watch as the light finally comes on.

"No way." Andrew leans in toward me. "Is your dad Richard Greene?"

I nod reluctantly. "Yep."

"Wow. I can't believe I never knew that." Andrew looks shocked, and I wish I knew exactly why. Money? My dad's reputation? I never know. "I've heard a lot about him. It's hard to believe he's your dad."

I sigh with relief and smile. Yes, my dad and I are nothing alike. *Perfect answer, Andrew.*

"We don't get along," I happily admit. "My dad and your dad have a lot in common."

"Sorry to hear that." Andrew's eyes are sincere, and I lean in to give him a kiss, my hand is still in his on the table.

"Thanks," I say, before continuing. "So, the short story is…my dad's a huge, money-hungry asshole. He's ex-military, which made him super fun to grow up with, and he's been cheating on my mom for the past ten years or so, which has led her to a crippling alcohol and drug addiction."

Andrew's eyes are wide. "Okay," he says, leaning back, trying to take it all in.

"My mom's currently in rehab for the…" I pause trying to think of the number of times, but it escapes me. "I don't even know how many times she's been. It never works, or maybe it works for a while, but since nothing ever changes at home – and for some unforeseen reason, she loves my bastard of a father – she always goes back to her vodka and pills."

Andrew pushes his chair back, then grabs my hand and pulls me onto his lap.

"I'm so sorry, Jules. I had no idea." He wraps his arms around my waist, and I put mine around his neck. "I can't believe you've worked for me all this time and I didn't know."

"It's okay." I sigh. "They've always been a mess. It's kind of a deep, dark family secret. I'm used to it."

"No one should have to get used to something like that."

He raises a hand to my face, and I press against it. I can hardly feel the pain when Andrew's around.

"I'm not going to lie and say it probably hasn't done some permanent damage," I tease, trying to lighten the mood back up. "But it's nothing a little therapy can't help."

Andrew smiles. "I'll be your therapist."

"Oh, really?"

"Totally." His face is serious, but I can see the hint of a smile on his lips. "You can lie on my sofa and tell me all of your problems."

"I'm not sure you're qualified."

"I'm not." He shakes his head. "And I can't promise I'll listen because I will be very distracted."

"And why is that?" I smile.

"Because you'll be naked, of course."

"Of course." I giggle. "I'm thinking that would violate some kind of doctor-patient statute."

"Good thing I'm not a doctor then," he says, bringing my face close to his. "May I interest you in some bedroom therapy, Ms. Greene?"

He kisses me before I have a chance to answer. "Or dining room table therapy?" I suggest against his lips.

He answers by picking me up and pushing his plate aside, before sitting me gently down on the table.

"Table therapy it is," he breathes, and I laugh into his mouth.

"We'll have bedroom therapy later," I say.

"And shower therapy? Back porch therapy? Kitchen counter therapy?" Andrew suggests in between kisses.

I laugh again, as his mouth moves down my neck. "We have all night," I moan, as Andrew moves up toward my ear.

He pulls away and puts both hands on either side of my face. "Yes we do, my beautiful girl," he whispers, and my therapy session begins.

CHAPTER 31

"I think I'm cured," I tease, as I lay naked, tangled up with Andrew on the floor of his dining room.

"I told you," he says, still breathing hard. "I'm an excellent therapist."

"I can't disagree." I giggle. I'm dragging my fingertips along his shoulder, watching as goose bumps appear on his arm from my touch.

"We're two of a kind, baby," Andrew kids, but I like the way he just called me "baby".

"It seems that way," I say and then shiver. It's chilly on his floor.

"Cold?" Andrew raises his head, and I raise mine to look at him. He brushes some hair from my face and smiles. "Do you want a blanket? How about some sweatpants and a t-shirt?"

My stuff is actually still in my car, but I'd much rather be in Andrew's sweats.

"I'll take some sweatpants and a t-shirt," I say, as Andrew gently eases me off him and then stands to fulfill my request.

I can't help but get an eyeful as he walks naked to his bedroom. Hot damn.

He returns quickly with a pair of gray sweatpants and a black t-shirt for me. He's put on a pair of dark gray, cotton pajama pants, but no shirt. Double hot damn.

I sit up and slip on the shirt first. Then I pull the pants over my legs and stand to finish the job.

"Very sexy," I say, spinning for him in my baggy outfit.

"You'd be surprised." He smiles and takes me swiftly into his arms.

I reach up to give him a kiss, and we stand there kissing softly, sweetly, lovingly. It's unbelievable how much I love him.

"How about another beer and a movie?" he suggests, brushing my hair from my face again.

I may need to go get my things so I can do some damage control on the hair situation. I should have a hairband in my purse.

"Sounds great," I say. "I need to run out to my car though to get my things."

"I'll do it," He offers quickly. "Where are your keys?"

I think for a second, trying to remember where I left them.

"On the coffee table." I point, suddenly remembering.

Andrew kisses me on the forehead and then releases me to go get my keys.

I move into the kitchen when he leaves to get us another beer. While he's gone, I hear a buzz and notice it's his Blackberry on the countertop. I try not to look. I honestly do, but it's right there!

I glance quickly over and all my worst fears come to life.

I miss you, lover. Wish you were here.

Gross! Why does she keep calling him "lover"?

He claims he's not doing anything physical with her, and I have to trust him, but this is seriously hard.

Andrew's back from my car in record time. Startled, I turn clumsily back to the fridge to retrieve our beers.

Andrew drops my things by the door and comes to stand next to me in the kitchen. "Are you okay?"

"You just startled me," I admit, but Andrew raises an eyebrow. How does he know? "And you got a message from Ms. Hamilton."

Andrew smiles as he picks up his Blackberry, and I kind of feel like punching him.

What about this is funny? We just made love on your dining room table, you tell me you love me, and I have to read texts like that from Demon Spawn Hamilton? What girl would put up with this shit?

I sigh, resigned. I would put up with it. I *do* put up with it. I love him, and I have to trust him. He's doing this with my interest in mind, and he said all I have to do is say the word, and we'll go public. It's up to me.

"Sorry I read it," I mutter guiltily. "It was right in front of me. I feel bad."

"Why?" Andrew shrugs. "I don't mind if you read my messages. And what did I say about formalities?"

"Right." I smile up at him. "The she-devil messaged you."

"Better." He smiles, and leans down to kiss me. "What movie do you want to watch? I've got Netflix or we can rent from Amazon."

"What kind of movies do you like?" I ask, as I finish up our beers.

"Well, let's see." Andrew leans against the bar and crosses his arms across his heavenly chest. "I like a little bit of everything, really."

I roll my eyes. "Crappy answer."

"What?" Andrew laughs. "Okay, I enjoy a good action flick, always appreciate a good comedy and I can even deal with a little romance, but nothing super sappy. No Nicholas Sparks, please."

I frown and turn on my puppy dog eyes. "I was hoping for *The Notebook* or *Dear John*, but oh well."

Andrew smiles and pulls me into his arms. "For you, I would endure it. That's how much I love you."

"That much? Wow!" I tease, and he kisses me again. "How about something fun from the 80's? I was listening to Depeche Mode and The Smiths on the way here. I'm in an 80's kind of mood."

"Nice taste in music," he smiles. "And I'm totally cool with the 80's. Let's go see what we can find."

I go grab a hairband and pull my hair up into a messy bun before we settle into the sofa, and start browsing through movies. Andrew wants *The Road Warrior* and I beg for *The Princess Bride*. We finally agree on *Top Gun*. Andrew gets jet planes and Kelly McGillis, and I get the volleyball scene. It's a win, win.

By the end of the movie, Andrew's leaning against the armrest of the sofa, and I'm between his legs, cuddled into his chest.

The credits start rolling, and I look up to see my sweet Andrew is sound asleep.

His neck is twisted in what looks like an uncomfortable position. I hate to wake him, but he'll be much better off in his bed.

"Andrew?" I whisper, sitting up and lightly stroking his cheek. "Let's go to bed."

He opens his eyes briefly, and smiles. "Okay," he mumbles. So adorable.

He opens his eyes again when I get off the sofa, and I pull on his hand. He stands slowly and follows me into his bedroom. I pull his covers back, and he slides in on his tummy.

I move to the other side of the bed, and take off my sweatpants before crawling in next to him. "How about a back scratch?"

"Mmmm..." He smiles, as I start running my fingernails down his back.

He's breathing heavy again within seconds, and I happily sit and stare at him as he sleeps. I can't believe I'm actually lying next to Andrew in his bed. And he loves me. It just doesn't get any better than this.

Eventually, I fall asleep too. When I wake up, I can see it's still dark out and Andrew's not next to me.

I quickly find his alarm clock. The glowing green digital lights are the only bright spot in the darkness. It's a little after four in the morning. I get out of bed and walk toward the bedroom door to go find Andrew.

I open the door slowly, trying to be quiet. I can't hear anything. He may be sleeping on the sofa.

As I open the door, I notice a light on to my far left in the sunroom.

When I finally reach the room, Andrew looks up at me. He has his glasses on. He's been reading.

"Hi," he smiles. "Did I wake you?"

"No." I smile back. "What are you doing up?"

I move to sit next to him on the sofa. He puts his book and glasses on the table and pulls me close.

"Need another back scratch?" I murmur into his chest, and I feel it rise and fall as he laughs. I raise my head to look at his face. "I feel helpless. I don't like feeling helpless," I admit.

Andrew strokes my cheek with his fingertips. "I know," he says. "But you being here is such a comfort."

I sigh into his chest – such a fabulous place to be.

"Andrew?" I start. "What was your meeting about Friday with your dad, if you don't mind me asking?"

Andrew takes a deep breath. "I had planned to confront him," he says. "I was going to tell him what I know, and try to see if he'd tell me why he was doing it. I wanted an explanation. I have my suspicions, but I wanted him to confide in me."

I raise my head so we're face to face. "Did you do it?"

I can't believe I didn't ask him about this yesterday. Worst. Girlfriend. Ever.

"No." Andrew takes another deep breath. "I chickened out."

"Or maybe you just don't want to know," I say before I think.

Filter, Jules! Filter!

Andrew looks at me thoughtfully for a moment. "You're probably right."

His voice breaks on the last word, and I can see, even in the dim lighting of the sunroom, the tears pooling in his eyes.

I put my hand on his cheek, and turn his face toward mine. I don't know what to say, but I have to comfort him. My family's messed up for sure, but both of my parents love me dearly. That's something I've never questioned.

"Andrew," I start, and then pause a moment so I can keep my own tears in check. "Your father loves you. I'm sure of it."

I don't know if this is true or not, but I want to believe it. I don't know how anyone could not love their child, especially Andrew. He's a parent's wet dream – smart, dedicated, loyal, ambitious.

"I'm not so sure, Jules. Maybe he did at one point, but I'm not sure he does any more." He grabs my hand and moves it from his face to his lap. "I just don't understand. I've done everything he's ever expected of me. I played sports. I graduated with honors. I have a Master's degree. I work for the family business. Why would he be going against me now? It doesn't make sense."

"Maybe the company reminds him too much of your mom," I suggest. "Maybe he wants out of it because he misses her too much."

"Right," Andrew scoffs. "Trust me when I tell you, that's not it."

I honestly know nothing about Andrew's parents' relationship. I was just hoping to maybe find some good in Mercer Senior, but so far, I'm coming up blank.

"Did they not get along?" I ask, just trying to understand what it was like for Andrew growing up.

"In public," he says, with a frown. "But behind closed doors, he was horrible to her." Andrew laughs a sad laugh. "But she didn't take it lying down. She fought back. I loved her so much for that."

"You shouldn't take it lying down either, Andrew. You should fight."

Andrew studies my face. "Easier said than done." He smiles. "But you're right. I'm trying to fight." He runs a hand through his hair. "I just don't have any ammunition at the moment. I'm working on it."

I roll my eyes. "I wish you had another angle."

"If I did," he kisses me lightly on the lips, "I would definitely use it. I'd take whatever I can get right now. I want to make this work so badly. I want to save the company. It's what my mom would have wanted."

So, there it is. He's doing this for his mom. My hearts swells at the notion. He's perfect – perfect in every way.

"Your mom loved the company?" I wish I would have known her.

"Yes," he answers quickly. "She put everything she had into starting it with my dad. She was a hard worker, very dedicated. She told me that she did it all for me. She wanted me to have a legacy, something I could be proud of." Andrew turns and pulls his leg up on the sofa so he's facing me. "I want to be proud of the company, Jules. I want to make her proud."

"You will," I grab both of his hands in mine. "You will, Andrew. I know it. I believe in you."

I see his gorgeous hazel eyes light up as he smiles shyly at me. "Thanks," he says, and I just want to pull him into my arms and hold him forever.

I suddenly remember some things I'd wanted to tell him, and they fit nicely into this conversation.

"Not sure what, if anything, this means," I start, "but I was chatting with Adrian, and she mentioned some things that I thought were kind of odd."

"Really?" Andrew raises an eyebrow. "What did she say?"

"First off, she said that she had to get approval on some invoices from your dad while we were in New York."

"Okay." Andrew shrugs. "That makes sense."

"I know," I continue, "but the weird part was that she said she periodically gets invoices that require her to get approval directly from your dad, and bypass you altogether."

"Interesting…" Andrew turns to look out the window for a moment before turning back to me. "Did she say if they were large sums? Who they were for? Any details?"

I shake my head. "Not large amounts," I tell him. "She only told me about one of the recent ones which was for some new software for the design group."

"Yeah, he was talking to some software guys at the garden party – probably the same company." Andrew looks out the window again and shakes his head. "But I still don't understand why my dad would invest money into the company and thwart my efforts to save it at the same time." I say nothing as Andrew continues to stare thoughtfully out the window. "Anything else?"

"Yesterday she told me your dad's been taking several trips to Nevada – Winchester, I believe. Anything unusual there? Oh, and the software company – the invoices she had to go directly to your dad with – they're located there as well."

Andrew stops and stares at me, before looking back out the window. "Nevada, huh?" He closes his eyes and runs a hand through his hair. "I can't believe it. That fucking bastard."
What the hell?
"What's in Nevada?" I ask curiously.
Andrew sighs and opens his eyes. "I'm not sure yet, but I have an idea." He turns back to me with a sad smile. "I can't believe I didn't think to go to accounting. That's more information than I've been able to gather in a month. You're pretty good."
"My pleasure." He's obviously not going to elaborate on the Nevada thing at the moment, so I leave it alone. "Anything to get Bitchface out of our lives," I say smiling.
"She'll be gone soon enough."
Maybe so, but yesterday wouldn't be soon enough.
I run my fingertips along the dark circle under one of his eyes. "You're so tired, Andrew. Isn't there anything I can do?"
He sighs, seeming content, even though he looks exhausted.
"Stop worrying about me," he orders, smiling. "I'll be fine. Once all of this blows over with the company, I'll either have a company to run, or I'll be collecting unemployment. Either way, I'm sure I'll be sleeping soundly once again."
"But what are we going to do with you, now?" I whine. "You need sleep. This is unhealthy."
"I'll be fine," he says. "But I do love how you always want to take care of me. It makes me feel...very special."
"You are special," I say, reaching up to kiss him, then I smile. "How about I wear you out again with more therapy?" I tease. "I'm really messed up, you know? I think I could keep you busy for a long time."

"Dr. Mercer is happy to help," Andrew says smiling, before pushing me back onto the sofa, and moving on top of me.

I giggle, as he pushes up my t-shirt and starts kissing my tummy. "So, Ms. Greene," he says in between very ticklish kisses. I start running my fingers through his soft hair. "Tell me about this tyrant you work for. I'm sure he's doing a number on your psyche."

"Who? Andrew Mercer, Jr.?" I gasp as Andrew's lips move further north, between my breasts. "He's absolutely incorrigible," I breathe.

"How so, Ms. Greene?" he asks, looking up at me briefly with fiery eyes before exploring each breast in turn.

"Well," I moan, and arch my back as his relentless lips fondle my breasts, kneading and biting. "He keeps coming on to me, for starters."

"Sounds like sexual harassment," he breathes into my neck. "You should call Human Resources. Have that bastard put away."

"I would." I wrap my legs around him, and pull him toward me. "But I'm afraid I find him rather irresistible."

"Is that so?" he whispers into my ear before grabbing my earlobe with his teeth. *Sweet heavens.*

"Yes," I whisper.

Andrew looks up at me. "I think I may have to violate our doctor-patient relationship once again, Ms. Greene." He leans down and kisses me tenderly on my lips. "I find you rather irresistible as well."

I smile and nod in agreement as I wrap my arms around his neck. "I love you, Dr. Mercer."

Andrew smiles back. "I love you too, baby."

There it is again. *Baby.* But this time, the endearment is so sweet and sincere that I could cry.

Oh, Andrew Mercer, my heart is full.

CHAPTER 32

"So, how was last night?" Abby asks, as I go to put my things in my room.

"Great," I say smiling. Thankfully, my back is to her so she can't see my blush.

"How was the hick bar?"

"Abby, honestly." I turn to face her after setting my stuff on my bed. "It's like thirty minutes from our place, not exactly God's country."

Abby smiles. "I'm glad you had fun."

"Adrian's really nice," I admit, which reminds me, I still haven't heard from her about her date last night. I'm going to go with the whole "no news is good news" philosophy for now.

"Yeah, yeah." Abby brushes off my Adrian compliments again for some reason. "Did Nate call yet?"

Now I see why – so eager to chat about Nate. I had all but forgotten about him after last night.

Andrew, Andrew, Andrew.

"No, and I don't expect him to call, at least not until next week."

"You're going to see him again, right?" Abby obviously senses my apprehension and disinterest.

"I don't know," I say, turning back to my things to unpack. I don't want to look at her. I may give something away.

"Jules, look at me," Abby demands, and I can't see her, but I visualize her standing, tapping her foot, hands on her hips.

I turn slowly and meet her gaze. I was dead on about the posture.

"What?" I was going for nonchalant, but didn't succeed.

"You're not telling me something," she says, her eyes squint, probing mine. "What the hell's going on? Are you seeing someone else?"

I shake my head, but find I'm unable to speak. I want to tell her. I want someone to talk to, but if I tell her, then I may feel like it's okay to tell someone else, then where does it stop? It's not a big deal, and it's not forever. I can keep a secret for a few weeks.

"I'm not seeing anyone else," I manage with confidence. I can do this for Andrew. I'd do anything for Andrew. "I'm just not sure I'm ready to move on."

Abby raises an eyebrow. "What do you mean? Please tell me this is not about Andrew."

I roll my eyes. "Abby, look. You don't know him at all. You met him at my art show a million years ago and exchanged names. That's it." I give her a knowing look, and she instantly backs down. "I love him, Abby, and I don't want to lead Nate on. He seems like a nice guy."

Abby nods, such a push over, but sometimes I love that about her. "I understand," she says, ruefully. "I just want you to be happy."

"I am happy." I'm able to say this with loads of confidence. *Abby, you have no idea how happy I am right now.* "So stop worrying about me."

Abby sits on my bed, and I join her. "I just know you've been going through a lot with your mom and your shitty job lately, so I want you to have some fun," she tells me. "And Nate is a really nice guy. I think he'll be good for you."

"My mom's back in rehab." I change the subject, realizing I haven't said anything yet to Abby. "Been in there since Monday," I add proudly.

Abby's face lights up. "Awesome! Tell her I'm pulling for her. You think she'll make it this time?"

"I hope so," I say, smiling. "I had a blowout with my dad last weekend that she caught the tail end of. She looked so happy that someone was standing up for her. Maybe it made an impression."

"I hope so too." Abby reaches out to hug me, and I gladly reciprocate. "Give Nate a try," she tells me again before pulling away. "He's different from the other guys you date."

"He has tattoos. I saw them," I remark, smiling.

"Yes, but he's not a total dick." Abby smiles back.

"What are you saying?" I feign shock, and Abby laughs.

"I'm saying you date assholes. Was I not clear?" Abby smiles and then gets up to leave. "I have to go to work at the museum today, then Marlow's tonight. I'll catch you tomorrow, probably."

"Have fun." I wave and stand to finish unpacking my stuff.

Abby waves back and turns to saunter off back to her room. I do wish I could tell Abby about Andrew, mainly because I want to share my happiness with her, but I know I can't. It will just have to wait.

As I start unpacking my things, my Blackberry buzzes on my dresser. I rush to retrieve it, knowing it's probably Andrew. I smile, as I read the message.

Thinking of you. Hard to concentrate. Miss you like crazy.

I close my eyes, and hold my phone close to my chest. When will this ever seem real? I can't believe after all this time, he's finally mine.

Miss you too.

I type back. I want to see him again. I just left him, but I need him near me, all the time. That's not really anything new. The pull has definitely gotten stronger over the past week...much, much stronger.

I'm rethinking your offer for help.

I smile. I still can't believe he's working on a Sunday. I offered to help him this morning, but he insisted I go home and rest. My hands shake with need, as I try to type him back.

Is that so? What exactly did you need help with?

I sit on the edge of my bed, knee bouncing, waiting not so patiently for his response.

What have you done to me, Ms. Greene?

Oh, my heart. The man is better than I ever thought possible.

However, he needs to work, and as much as I would like to strip him down and do very naughty things to him on his desk, I'll have to wait.

> *No, Mr. Mercer. It's what you've done to me. I can't seem to get enough.*

I type, still smiling. Then I work to type another message before he has a chance to respond.

> *But you have work to do, so I'll have to wait.*

I continue typing...

> *Perhaps I'll come in early tomorrow. I can help you with whatever you need then.*

I stop typing and wait eagerly for his response. I hope he doesn't think I'm blowing him off.

> *Regretfully, I'll admit that you're right. I'll sleep here tonight. Come in as early as you'd like. I'm sure I can find something for you to do.*

Oh boy. That promise results in a delicious, tingly sensation between my thighs.

> *Yes sir. P.S. I love my job.*

I type, smiling widely.

I love you, Jules.

He types back and I sigh.

I love you too. Very much.

Honestly, what *has* he done to me?

See you tomorrow.

I'm still smiling.

Can't wait.

And I'm not sure I can. I didn't even know it was possible to feel this way about someone. I want to be with him every second of every day.
I lie back on my bed, clutching my phone against my chest. I look at my watch. It's a little after noon. I smile as I ponder what Andrew considers "morning".

I wake up and the sun is shining bright in my eyes. I feel disoriented. Where the hell am I?

I open my eyes fully and see I'm in my bedroom, still in my clothes, on top of my covers.

Then the panic sets in. I glance quickly at my clock. It's seven thirty.

In the morning? *SHIT!*

I jump up and run to the bathroom, then back out to my room, then back to the bathroom.

I run back to my night table. Phone. Where the hell's my phone?

It's not on my night table, so I start shuffling through my covers. I finally find it, beneath the pillow on the other side of my bed.

I have several messages, all from Andrew, and two missed calls. Those are from Andrew as well.

I run my fingers through my hair and sit down on my bed, as I read the messages. They start innocently enough, around four this morning, and then they progressively get more anxious.

I type him back quickly, my hands trembling, just to let him know I'm okay.

> *So sorry. I passed out last night and forgot to set my alarm clock. Will call you shortly.*

I rush back to the bathroom. I have to shower. I didn't shower yesterday, so it's a must.

I quickly turn on the water, rip off my clothes and jump in. I start washing my hair with record speed, trying to remember what the hell happened last night.

I was alone in the apartment and bored for most of the night. I did some cleaning, some laundry, watched some TV, and then went to my room to clean out my closet. I've been meaning to do it for a while, but hate the process, so I've been putting it off.

I remember lying on my bed, just to rest a bit, and I must have fallen asleep. That was around nine o'clock! I must have been beat from the past couple of nights with zero sleep.

I hurry out of the shower and rush around like a Tasmanian devil to finish getting ready.

I toss on some light brown pants and a cream colored blouse. Nothing special, but I don't have time for special right now.

I put on minimal make-up and dry my hair just enough before throwing it up into a haphazard looking bun. I'll fix it later.

I pick up my phone but don't look at it yet. I grab my purse and laptop case and rush toward the door. I'm glad Abby's not around to distract me.

I wait until I get in my car to look at my phone.

Glad you're okay.

That's not good.

I dial his number to call him, but it goes straight to voicemail. Oh dear.

I drive way too fast to the office, but because there is a wreck on the highway, I don't get there until around nine.

In the two years I've worked for Mercer Construction, I've never been this late. Never. I'm not a late person. What's happening to me?

Don't be mad at me Andrew. It was an honest mistake.

I'm trembling as I wait for the elevator. I feel like crying. I can't believe I missed an opportunity to spend time with him this morning.

Stupid Jules! Stupid!

The elevator finally arrives, and I hop on. This morning the elevator seems like it's moving at a snail's pace. Does it have to stop on every floor?

Andrew never called me back and no further messages.

I finally make it to my floor and rush off the elevator. I walk quickly back to my desk, and Adrian gives me a puzzled look. I roll my eyes and shrug. *Don't ask, Adrian.* I feel like crying again.

Andrew's light is on, but of course, I already knew he was here.

I go ahead and start up my computer and put my things away. Should I go into his office? Do I knock? Should I wait for him to ask for me? This new work dynamic is so confusing!

My computer finally comes to life and I open my emails. I wait a moment to see if Andrew messages me, but there's nothing. I look aimlessly around my desk wondering what to do. That's when I notice the foreign object on my veranda next to my desk. It's a dark blue vase, full of wild flowers. Flowers? Who would send me flowers?

I close my eyes. That's why he's pissed.

I stand to go read the card, and when I turn back around, I catch a glimpse of Adrian. She wags her eyebrows at me and I smile tentatively. *Damn!* I need to ask her about this weekend. I survey her for a moment. She looks happy.

I shake my head and get back to the task at hand.

I take a deep breath before opening the card.

> *Had a great time Friday. Just wanted you to know.*
> *Call you soon.*
> *Nate*

Oh dear God. Andrew probably saw them. I'm sure he didn't read the card, but knowing they're not from him, it would be an easy deduction.

I glance uneasily toward his office before sitting back down at my desk.

Still no message, no email, nothing.

I take another deep breath. I won't allow him to scare me. I've done nothing wrong here. It was an honest mistake, me oversleeping. And the flowers? Well, I'll nip that in the bud. Why would Andrew even worry?

I stand confidently and walk toward his office door. I notice Adrian watching me, but I ignore her.

I knock once and wait. A couple of seconds pass that seem like hours before I finally hear. "Come in."

One more deep breath, and in I go.

"Morning," I say, my confidence wavering when I see him. Damn, he looks good. He's totally disarming. I feel so vulnerable around him. Part of me loves it, and another part hates it.

"Ms. Greene." His voice is cold, and even though he's focused on his computer screen instead of me, I can tell he's hurt. I can see it on his beautiful face.

I close the door behind me, lock it and walk purposefully toward him. I spin his chair around so he'll face me.

"That was not a very pleasant greeting."

His face is a mixture of shock and amusement. "Good morning," he says, and I can tell he's suppressing a smile. "How was your evening?" he asks, as he stands to face me.

I smile and instantly start moving backwards, away from him, until I'm pressed firmly against his wall of windows. I can feel the sun's warmth on my back through my thin blouse as I watch him. His approach is slow and stealth-like.

Andrew is close, very close, but not touching me. His eyes are amused and full of longing. I guess he's not *too* mad at me.

"I'm so sorry," I say, as I stare into those glorious eyes. "I overslept. I didn't mean to."

"I missed you," he says, moving closer, but still not quite touching me. He lifts a hand and puts it on the window next to my head. I'm suddenly reminded of the Empire State Building, and my insides quiver at the thought.

"I missed you too," I whisper.

His gorgeous face is centimeters from mine. I stare deeply into his eyes, trying to convince him how sorry I really am.

"Nice flowers," he says, his mouth close to my ear. I shiver, and he pushes his whole body against mine, pressing me hard into the window.

I put my arms around his waist, under his suit jacket, so I can feel his warm skin through his shirt. He's not wearing a vest today, but he still looks gorgeous in a light gray suit, white shirt and his red and black striped tie. God, he feels so good.

"They're just flowers," I whisper, before placing a wet kiss directly beneath his ear. His answering groan vibrates into my neck.

Andrew raises his head to look at me. "You stood me up this morning. Then you got flowers from another guy. I'm not having a very good day."

I giggle, and reach up to pull his face to mine. He moves his arms around my waist and pulls me close to him as we kiss. I feel like crying again for my missed opportunity this morning.

"Were you mad?" I ask, as I stroke his cheek.

"No." He looks down, and takes just my hand to pull me toward his sofa. He sits, and I settle in beside him. "With everything that's going on..." He pauses and puts a hand on my knee. I lean my head on his shoulder. "I just haven't felt like myself lately."

"Am I causing problems, Andrew?"

I look up at him. I'm not sure I want the answer to this question, but I don't want to be a distraction.

Andrew immediately laughs. "Are you kidding? You're the best thing I've got going at the moment." I smile, and he reaches with his other hand to touch my cheek. "I didn't like seeing the flowers."

"Jealous?" I ask, still smiling.

"Insanely."

"You have nothing to be jealous of. You know that." I grab the hand stroking my cheek, and turn it over to kiss his palm. "It's nothing."

Andrew sighs and smiles a sad smile. "Why do I feel like I'm going to lose you?"

Okay. Where the hell did that come from?

"Why do you feel that way?"

Andrew shakes his head. "Everything is so shitty right now, Jules," he starts. "You're the only bright spot in all of this, but it feels too good to be true. And everything I'm doing...to try and save the company..." He looks guiltily at me, and I know he's referring to Bitchface. I try not to show the disapproval on my face so he'll continue. "It doesn't feel right. None of this feels right."

"None of it?" I frown.

"Except you, of course," he says, his face serious as he looks deep into my eyes. "I just don't feel like I deserve to have this right now," he says, squeezing my hand. "I don't know if it's what's going on in my life at the moment, or because I've never really felt this way about anyone before, but I'm so insecure about this, about us."

I don't like the way this conversation is headed. Is he trying to break up with me? I feel the tears pool in my eyes with just the thought of him leaving me.

"Andrew..." I sit nervously next to him, holding his hand tight in mine, trying to push down my tears. "I'm not sure what you're trying to say."

One tear escapes. Yuck. I'm turning into such a girl.

Andrew looks horrified, as he wipes the tear away.

"Oh God, no." His voice is anxious. "I'm just trying to tell you how lucky I feel and how I need you in my life, but apparently, I'm not doing a very good job."

A relieved giggle escapes my lips. "Oh. Yeah. I wasn't getting that."

"I'm so sorry," he says, smiling. "I love you, Jules."

I put my hands on either side of his face. "I love you too, and I'm sorry again for this morning." I laugh. "I think I'm crying more over that missed opportunity than anything."

"Well, we have all day. Last I looked, my schedule's open."

I smile. "Lunch then? Perhaps we need to go over a few things." I run my finger under his collar and pull, effectively bringing his lips to mine.

"You're such an ambitious young woman, Ms. Greene," he teases against my lips. "I think you have a bright future at Mercer Construction."

"Thank you, sir," I breathe. "Just doing my job."

"And you're excellent at it," he whispers, as he pulls me onto his lap, so I'm straddling him. He leans up and quickly removes his jacket, loosens his tie and undoes the top button. "I'm thinking a raise may be in order."

I smile down at him, admiring my view. "All I want is you." I lean in to kiss him again. "Just you."

He grabs my hips as I start rocking slowly against him. I move my mouth to his neck, excited to make up for what I missed this morning.

"Jules," Andrew growls my name, which only fuels my already blazing need for him.

I continue trailing kisses down his neck, as I unbutton his shirt and push it off his shoulders. I pull away, but only to remove his tie. I quickly return my lips to his neck, down to his shoulder, all while moving slowly, back and forth in his lap. Andrew's grasping my hips for dear life, pushing me down onto him. The sensation is incredible, but not enough.

"Come with me," I say, my voice ragged, as I climb off him. He stands quickly and pulls me into his arms.

He grabs the back of my thighs and lifts me. I wrap my legs around him, so I'm pressed against him once again. I put my arms around his neck, and hold on tight as he carries me over to his desk. He doesn't even bother moving anything. He sits me down gently, removing my blouse before he starts unbuttoning my pants.

"Desk therapy?" he smiles, and I have to take a deep breath to steady myself. *Good gracious.*

I quickly start unbuttoning his pants, anxious to have him. All of him.

Andrew's kissing me hard, as he pulls me off his desk so he can fully remove my pants. I take the opportunity to remove his as well.

We're both standing now in our undies, and I'm pressed hard against him, his lips moving urgently against mine. The heat and the excitement of doing this here – the office crawling with people just outside his door – is overwhelming.

And so very hot.

Andrew pulls away and we're both breathless. I need him. He needs me. It's a beautiful, wonderful, extremely sexy thing.

He turns me around so my back is to him, and puts his arms around me.

"I love you," he whispers in my ear, before moving his hands slowly upward from my stomach toward my breasts. "I missed you so much," he breathes, as he pulls down my bra and cups my breasts in each of his hands.

I close my eyes, unable to find any words. I reach around and move my hand into his boxer briefs, grabbing him, stroking, caressing. His face falls onto my shoulder, his soft moans once again vibrating against me.

I reach my other hand around and push down his boxer briefs so he's naked, pressed against me. He moves his hands quickly down to remove my undies, and I start to pant. I want him so badly. I need him. Now.

Suddenly, he spins me around, and moves his hands to either side of my face. He kisses me sweetly, tenderly, before grabbing my waist and lifting me onto his desk.

He moves slowly inside of me, and I wrap my arms and legs around him, pulling him close. I kiss his cheek, his jaw, his neck, his shoulder, as he sets a steady pace, holding me close, loving me.

"Jules," he whispers, and the warmth of his breath on my neck finally sets me free.

I cry out softly, as my legs squeeze tightly around him. He moans into my neck before finally stilling in front of me.

Neither of us move for a few minutes. He's breathing hard against my shoulder, and I'm breathing hard as well, my cheek pressed firmly against the back of his hair.

I'm thankful his arms are wrapped snugly around me, or else I would probably fall backward onto his desk. I feel wiped.

Eventually, Andrew lifts his head and looks at me.

"Do you think anyone heard that?" I ask, suddenly horrified, but I can't force anything other than a smile onto my face.

"Who cares?" Andrew brushes a piece of hair behind my ear that must have fallen from my loose bun.

"You care," I remind him, still smiling.

"Not right now," he says, breathlessly. His eyes heavy, but I can still see the fire there burning just for me. It's a glorious feeling.

We hold each other a moment longer before Andrew pulls me gently off his desk, and bends to grab my undies off the floor.

"I think that meeting went very well," he teases, handing my undies to me.

I smile and pull them on, and then fix my bra. "I agree. We should probably discuss the situation further though."

"Still on for lunch?" He smiles widely, as he puts his underwear back on, and I reach down to grab the rest of my clothes.

"Sofa therapy?" I suggest, gesturing toward his leather sofa.

"Yes, indeed." He grabs my face and kisses me. "My beautiful girl."

I melt into his arms, dropping my clothes back to the floor and wrapping my arms around his neck to kiss him again. Oh, those lips.

"Ms. Greene," Andrew smiles against my mouth, "I will never get anything done today at this rate."

I pull away and give him a pouty smile. "Fine."

I grab my clothes again and start putting myself back together. Andrew does the same.

"Mind if I use your bathroom?" I ask, knowing my hair has to be a mess.

"Of course not," Andrew says, as he finishes buttoning his shirt. "But you look beautiful."

"You're biased," I tease as I walk toward the bathroom.

"Very."

I turn to him and smile before shutting the door to his bathroom. Luckily I'm not a huge mess, but my cheeks are crazy red.

I pat a little cold water on them, hoping to remove some of the heat. Lord, Andrew is too much.

I finish up and open the door to walk back out into his office. He's sitting at his desk, in the same position he was in when I walked in earlier – just as put together and absolutely breathtaking.

He looks up when he hears the bathroom door open and smiles at me.

I walk slowly back over to his desk, and his appreciative, hungry look makes me smile.

"Will that be all, Mr. Mercer?" I ask, letting his name roll seductively off my tongue.

Andrew blinks and swallows hard before smiling up at me.

"One more thing," he breathes, and gestures for me to lean in close to him.

I put my hands on his desk and bend over, moving my face close to his.

He reaches up and runs his fingertips along my cheek. I close my eyes briefly as his touch resonates through my body. *Good God.* I am so obsessed with him.

"Come closer," he orders, and I open my eyes and move in closer.

"I love you," he whispers and then reaches up to kiss me softly. Yes. Totally and completely obsessed.

"I love you too," I say and smile before standing back up and walking toward his door.

"See you at lunch," he calls, as I unlock and open his door. "I think we'll order in."

I smile back at him and then leave his office, dazed and deeply in love.

CHAPTER 33

Andrew and I didn't get to have our lunch date. It was interrupted by The Skank Ho, who showed up a little after eleven.

She's been in his office ever since, approximately two hours, fourteen minutes and twenty-seven seconds, but who's counting?

I try for the millionth time to get back to my work, but it's just not happening. I can't concentrate with that heifer in his office. What have they been doing in there for so long?

He sent me an email shortly after she arrived to ask that I hold all his calls until they were done.

What the hell?

I got forty-five minutes of his time this morning, and she gets over two hours? My face feels hot, and I want to leave.

Everything okay?

Adrian. Damn, that girl's perceptive.

Fine. Just the usual.

I hope she reads into that properly.

Totally understand. I hate unexpected guests.

I look up at Adrian and smile.

Ditto.

I hurry to type something else, realizing again I never asked her about this past weekend. I'm a terrible friend.

So, how was the date?

I look up to gauge her reaction to my message. Her face instantly blushes and she smiles.

Incredible. We should do lunch one day this week. I'll tell you all about it.

Yay! I smile hugely as I look up at her again. She's still blushing.

Can't wait! I'm so glad it went well! Sorry for not asking sooner.

I'm so happy for her. She deserves it.

No worries. You've been busy.

My turn to blush, and I glance up just in time to see Adrian wink and smile. Yep. She's totally on to us. Oh well. I don't think she'd say anything, but I'm going to continue to deny it.

How about lunch tomorrow?

Let's roll right over that other subject for now.

Sounds great! Rose's?

Yum. I skipped lunch today, hoping Andrew would have time for me, so now I'm starving.

Perfect.

Adrian and I both get back to work, and a few minutes later, The Ho Bag walks out of Andrew's door.
I look her up and down, as discreetly as possible, checking for any signs of change. Is her shirt buttoned? Is her skirt straight? Is her hair ruffled? Make-up smudged?
I don't notice anything but her lack of lipstick, which causes bile to rise instantly in my throat.
"Ms. Greene," she says, turning slightly as she walks away, a sinister grin on her ridiculously beautiful face.
Now, I'm fuming.
My knee starts bouncing involuntarily under my desk. Damn that woman. I take a few deep breaths trying to calm down.
Oh screw the breathing!
I stand up quickly and walk away. I'm not sure where I'm going. I need to scream. I need to hit something.
The first door I come to leads to the stairwell, and I take it. I have to get some fresh air. Maybe that's what I need.

I walk quickly down the eight flights, heels and all. My feet are the least of my concerns at the moment.

When I reach the lobby, I move toward the back of the building, where the smokers take breaks. There are a few benches out there.

I'm relieved to see there's no one outside. I sit on one of the benches, and my knee starts in again.

I can't do this. I can't pretend like this. Andrew was right. This doesn't feel good. And it's her. Does it have to be *her*? Of all people!

I put my head in my hands and pray I don't start crying. I don't feel like crying at the moment, but lately my over eager tears have been surprising me.

I'll just scream in my head, until I can get to the gym later. Maybe there's a kickboxing class tonight. I make a mental note to check online when I get back upstairs.

I sit in silence for a moment and jump suddenly, as a hand touches my shoulder. I half expect to see Andrew, but it's Adrian. *Oh God.* What have I done?

"I just wanted to see if you were okay," she says, her eyes full of genuine concern, as she sits down next to me.

"I'm fine," I lie. "Bit – I mean, Ms. Hamilton just gets to me."

"I know," Adrian sighs. "She has that effect on everyone."

"Except Andrew," I say sullenly, before I can stop myself.

Adrian acts like she doesn't even notice. "She has that effect on him too. I'm sure of it."

I look at her thoughtfully. "How do you know?"

Adrian smiles shyly at me. "Because I don't think Mr. Mercer would do that."

"Do what?" I ask.

I'm going to make you say it, Adrian. Please just say it, so I'll have someone to talk to about all of this.

Adrian breathes deeply, looking into my eyes, as she steels herself. "I don't think he would do that to you."

Oh, thank God.

My relief quickly turns to panic. "Adrian, you can't tell anyone, okay? Mr. Mercer doesn't want anyone to know. Not yet."

"My lips are sealed, Jules." Adrian smiles. "I promise."

I smile back. *Thank you Adrian. For everything.*

"How did you know?" I have to ask. Is it obvious to everyone else too?

"Don't worry. I'm pretty sure no one is suspicious, except maybe Victoria, but she'd be jealous regardless." Adrian smiles as she answers my unasked question. "Everyone knows me as the quiet one, but it's because I'd rather spend time listening than talking."

"Not a bad quality," I remark, smiling to myself.

"Your secret's safe with me, Jules, and I'm here, if you ever need me."

"Thanks, Adrian," I say, sincerely. "I really appreciate it."

Adrian leaves, and I sit a few minutes longer, staring at a small patch of grass in the concrete jungle that is our office complex before finally getting up, smoothing out my pants, and walking back toward the elevators.

This thing with Andrew is so confusing, but the bottom line is that I love him. I'll just take this day by day, and hope that soon, we can start leading relatively normal lives.

I remember our conversation in New York in the Oak Room and how he told me the decision was in my hands. I think for a moment about whether or not I'm ready to play that card. Am I? I don't think so. I think I can keep this up a little longer. If it means Andrew gets the company, I can do that for him. As long as I know he loves me, and not *her*, I can do this.

By the time I reach my floor, I've actually managed to find a smile.

I walk back to my desk, and before I can even sit down, I get an instant message from Andrew.

Everything okay?

I sigh, as I sit and type him back.

Fine. Just needed to clear my head.

I wince. Maybe I shouldn't have typed that.

Would you come here, please?

Yep. Shouldn't have typed that.

I slowly rise, and move toward his office. I knock before entering. Not sure why, but I do.

"Come in." His voice sounds close to the door.

As I open the door, I realize I'm right. He's standing to the left, just inside of his door.

He closes the door behind me and immediately takes my hands in his. "Are you okay? Did she say something to you?"

"I'm fine." I try to smile, but his beautiful eyes are like probes into my soul. "I promise."

Andrew studies me. "You're not fine. What happened?"

I hang my head. I feel ashamed that I don't have more confidence in him than this. I can't believe I don't have more confidence than this in myself.

"This is hard," I reluctantly admit.

Andrew lifts my chin to peer into my eyes once more. "I know, and I'm so sorry," he says, his eyes sad. "But I promise you, she is nothing. She's a pawn in this ridiculous game I'm playing with my father. It makes me feel like shit because it's hurting you, not because it may hurt her." He pulls me into his chest, and I breathe him in. Now I feel better. Now I feel safe. "I'll do whatever makes you happy, Jules. Remember that."

"Thank you, but I'm okay," I say into his chest. "It's just hard. I dislike her very, very much."

Andrew chuckles. "Me too."

We stand there a moment longer, and I try to bury it, but my curiosity is burning.

"Did you kiss her?" I ask, and he pulls me away to look at my face.

"Yes," he says, quietly, and I feel the ground fall away at my feet. "I have to give her something, Jules. And that's all I'm willing to give."

Dammit. Stupid tears.

"Please don't cry, Jules. I'm so sorry," he breathes, as he wipes my tears away. His face is pained and utterly exhausted. "I'll stop it," he promises urgently. "I'll end it now. I'll come clean. I can't lose you. I won't."

I push him away, walk toward his wall of windows and stare out. What do I want? I'd resolved everything in the elevator. What was that conclusion again? I can barely remember – my mind foggy with the thought of her disgusting mouth on *my* Andrew, and mere hours after we made love on his desk. *Slut! Slut! SLUT!*

Andrew doesn't approach me, and I'm glad. He keeps his post by the door, and I stand in front of the windows, until I'm all cried out.

I finally turn to see Andrew sitting on the floor, next to the door. His knees are up, and his head is in his hands.

I walk slowly back over to him, wiping the remaining tears from my cheeks.

"Andrew?" I call to him, as I hover above him, still a few feet away. My heart constricts as he looks up at me and I see his tired eyes. "I may be the dumbest woman in the world, but I will do this. I'll stay with you, while you do what you need to do with that...person." I can't even bring myself to say her name. Andrew pulls himself slowly up from the floor, his eyes wide now, hanging on my every word. "I love you. And if it means you'll save this company, then I'll suffer through this." And I emphasize the word "suffer", in case he didn't pick up on it. "But after all of this is over, no matter what happens I have to know I can trust you. Please tell me you will never touch her again. Flirt, hold hands even, but kissing or anything else more physical is too hard to take. Can you promise me that?"

"I won't kiss her again. I swear," he says in a rush, eyes wide with panic. "I'll do anything you want, Jules. Just tell me what to do, and I'll do it. Anything."

Oh God. His face is heartbreaking. *Hold your ground, Jules!*

"I just told you my rules. Do what you have to do, Andrew, but I can't sit by and let you have your way with her *and* me. It's not right, and I'm better than that."

So there!

"You *are* better. You're everything." Andrew comes close now, and reaches tentatively for one of my hands. I let him take it, and I see his shoulders relax a bit. "I just don't know what to do, Jules." *Oh my.* He's whispering, and his voice is breaking. This conversation is no longer just about Bitchface. "Please tell me what to do," he begs. "Please."

Damn you, Andrew. Damn you for making me love you.

I pull him into my arms, and he quickly buries his face into my shoulder. "I'm so sorry," he breathes. "I don't want to hurt you. You're the last person I want to hurt. I'm so sorry."

I rub my hands soothingly up and down his back. He's so tired, mentally and physically. Just so damn tired.

"It's okay," I say, trying to calm him. "I'm here, and I love you Andrew. No matter what happens, I will always love you."

I can say that with certainty. As mad as this situation makes me, I still love him. Maybe I shouldn't, but I do.

"I love you too," he says, lifting his heavy eyes to mine. "So very much."

I reach up and kiss him, and try not to think about the bitch's lips being there only hours before.

I pull away first and move to leave, but Andrew grabs my hand and pulls me toward him.

"I'll never touch her again," he promises, and his eyes are glowing with intensity. "Please believe me."

"Fine." I sigh, resigned, as I reach up and kiss him again, this time on the cheek. "Go brush your teeth." I smile, as I move to walk out the door.

Andrew smiles too, and releases my hand slowly as I walk away. "I love you, Jules," he says quietly before I open the door.

"I love you too," I say, and turn away.

CHAPTER 34

Andrew asked me to stay at his place last night, and those beautiful, pleading eyes made it extremely hard to turn him down. But with everything that happened yesterday, I felt like we may need a night off.

Plus, I'm worried Abby's getting suspicious. She texted me yesterday on a rampage about me working late again and how I should "quit that shitty job like yesterday".

And to add insult to injury, I received a voicemail from Nate yesterday afternoon that went something like…"Just calling to see if you got the flowers. I hope it wasn't too much. I had a great time, and hope to do it again soon. Call me."

But it turns out that an evening away from Andrew did nothing but make me miss him like crazy.

I missed the way his sheets and pillows smell like him – the perfect catalyst for dreaming about him. I missed his strong arms around me, keeping me safe. I missed his warm, soft lips stealing kisses on my neck, my cheek, my shoulder, in the middle of the night when he thinks I'm sleeping.

I miss him every minute that I'm not with him. It's becoming quite unhealthy, I fear.

As I make my way back into the office now, I'm thinking about yesterday again and everything that's happened over the past week. It's been a whirlwind.

Just to think, this time last week, I had never even kissed Andrew and had no idea he had feelings for me. Knowing where we are now, already saying "I love you", it's hard to fathom.

It should seem too fast. It should seem crazy. I've never told another man I love him. I barely tell my own father that anymore.

But it's not too fast. I've loved him for so long. Saying it out loud doesn't change anything.

I just can't believe he loves me too. The fact that he's had feelings for me, and I've had feelings for him, and neither of us could muster up the courage to say anything is rather comical. What a waste of time!

I finally make it to the office around eight. Traffic was a bear, due to an accident, making me late. I texted Andrew a while ago to let him know but never heard back. He may not even be in yet, or he may be stuck in traffic as well.

I park, having to drive a while to find a space since I'm late, and then make my way to the lobby. As I get on the elevator, my heart flutters with the thought of seeing Andrew again. God, I'm so pathetic.

I exit the elevator and walk through the lobby, down the hall to my desk. I glance over at Adrian, and her face is serious.

I shrug my shoulders, and she gestures with her chin toward Andrew's office. I look over and see the door is closed, the light is on. Nothing seems amiss.

I sit down at my desk, and switch on my computer. As soon as it starts up, I type a quick message to Adrian.

What's going on?

I look up at her anxiously, waiting for her to respond.

Unexpected guest.

I look back up at her after I read her response, and she nods her head, apologetically.

When did she get here?

I wait impatiently again. I can feel my bagel from this morning rising up into my throat.

About an hour ago.

Really? Three hours yesterday, and again this morning? What the hell are they talking about? And why the hell was Andrew here so early? To meet with her?

Thanks.

I type back angrily and then go to check my emails. *He promised you, Jules. He promised he was done with her, physically at least.* I have nothing to worry about.
I try my patented breathing technique, but it does absolutely nothing. I hate this. I hate her.
I'm looking down at my computer, trying to concentrate on my emails, when I see a figure coming down the hall toward me. Awesome. Mercer Senior.
"Ms. Greene. Is my son available?"

Normally he just walks in to Andrew's office. Thankfully, not today.

"I'll check for you, sir."

I pick up the phone to dial Andrew, but he doesn't pick up. *Come on, Andrew.*

I know my face is red, but there's nothing I can do about it.

"He's not answering," I say sweetly. "He may be on his cell. I'll go check."

"Ms. Greene," Mercer Senior stops me before I can stand up. "I don't remember seeing those photos from the garden party as requested."

I cringe as I look up into his beady eyes. "I gave them to Mr. Mercer, sir. I'm sure he chose some appropriate images for the PR Department."

Mercer Senior nods, but the irritated look is still on his face. I'm thinking it's permanent.

I get up quickly, and take a quick glance over at Adrian. Her face is panicked, and she shakes her head "no", right before I open Andrew's door. What's that about?

For some reason, I don't knock. I don't know why. I always knock.

As I open the door to his office, I hate myself for my lapse in knocking etiquette. I hear them before I see them.

"Oh, Andrew." Her sick, screeching voice whispers his name, and I stop breathing. "You know you want me."

For some bizarre reason, maybe hoping my ears are deceiving me, I continue to push the door open and walk inside.

"I'm so sorry," I say when I finally see them, trying very hard to keep my voice level as I stare at them in horror.

Andrew's pressed against his desk, and The Slut is pressed against him, chest to chest. She's kissing his neck, and she doesn't stop, even when she hears my voice. The position is almost identical to when I caught them at the garden party, and like that time, I'm absolutely heartbroken. But unlike that time, I have a right to be angry. He promised me.

Andrew shoves her away immediately and stares at me. His eyes are unreadable. I feel like I'm going to puke.

"Your father's here," I choke out, and that seems to get Victoria's attention.

She turns to me and starts straightening her clothes, wiping at her lips. I can't take my eyes off Andrew.

"Send him in," he whispers, still staring at me, pleading, trying to make me understand with his eyes.

Too late, Andrew. I try to convey with my own eyes. *Too fucking late.*

I finally gather the strength to turn away. I walk out of his office and close the door.

"You can go on in," I say to Mercer Senior with the best fake smile I can muster. I can't believe I'm still standing.

Mercer Senior walks past me and moves to open Andrew's door.

"Some coffee, Ms. Greene," he demands before he walks in.

"Sure," I smile sweetly. Too sweetly.

I have no idea how to feel, but currently, I'm going with anger. I stomp purposefully to the break room to get Mercer Senior his coffee. I think about spitting in it, but then decide not to. He's not the one I'm mad at, not currently at least.

Maybe I should take the other two some coffee as well. One big happy family. I could spit in theirs.

I decide against that too, and move to bring Mercer Senior's coffee to him. He's such a prick. He likes a cup and a saucer, on a tray, with sugar and cream on the side. He doesn't like anyone else putting his cream and sugar in. They just can't get it right, he says. Prick.

Less than five feet away from Andrew's office door, I stop. I can't go any further. My shaky legs won't allow it, or is it my heart?

Adrian's at my side in a flash. "Here," she says, grabbing the tray from my trembling hands. "I'll do it."

I look at her, and I feel like crying, but I can't even do that right now.

"Thank you," I mouth and she smiles sadly, before walking the tray into Andrew's office.

I fall into my office chair. What am I going to do?

I don't have to think about it long. I know what I have to do. I should've done it a long time ago, in hindsight. It sure as hell would've saved me a lot of grief and heartache.

I open my email and click "compose".

> *Dear Mr. Mercer,*
>
> *I regret to inform you that I will be resigning from my position as Executive Assistant, effective immediately.*
>
> *Thank you for the opportunity you have given me. It was a pleasure to work for such a passionate and forward thinking company.*

I will be eternally grateful for the time I spent here, and I wish you all the best in your future endeavors.
Sincerely,
Julia Greene

There. That should do it. I can't believe I'm still not crying. The thought scares me a little.
I hit "send" just as Adrian comes out of the office.
"He asked me to make sure you don't leave before he's done," she tells me, her face sad.
I giggle. I can't help it.
"Well, too bad," I tell her. "I'm leaving. For good."
I pull my purse out of my desk, and check for a few other things I may want to take. I don't see anything immediately, other than some snacks, which I could currently give two shits about. With the way my stomach feels right now, I don't know if I'll ever be able to eat again.
"You're quitting?" Adrian finally says, shocked. "You can't quit."
I look over at her. "Why not?"
I go back to shutting down my computer, and other than my tacky Elvis clock, I see the one thing I'll take with me – my snow globe souvenir from New York. It has the Empire State Building inside. It will feel good to break it into pieces later.
"B-Because," Adrian stutters. "You just can't."
I grab my cardigan from the back of my chair and start moving toward the lobby.
"I'll call you Adrian," I say as I walk away. "I'll take a rain check on our lunch."

"Jules," Adrian calls after me, but I ignore her. I can feel the tears brimming now, and I need to get out of here before tear Armageddon starts.

I take the stairs again, eager to leave this place and every memory of it behind me.

I'm in the parking deck when my phone starts blowing up. I ignore it too. Whoever it is can wait. I can't talk to anyone right now.

The tears are flowing so hard by the time I reach my car, I'm not sure I can drive, but I will myself to start my car and put it in reverse. What if Andrew decides to come chasing after me? Not likely, but what if?

I can't see him again. I don't want to see his lying face.

I peel out of my parking space and tear out of the deck. There's no traffic going home, thankfully, so I make it home in less than fifteen minutes.

I nearly run up to my apartment, hurrying before my legs officially give out.

I fumble with my key in the door. My hands are shaking so badly.

I just quit my job.

And I just quit Andrew.

Oh, dear God.

I finally get my door open and sprint to my room. I'm not sure if Abby's here or not, and I don't care.

I slip out of my shoes as I walk into my room. I throw my stuff on the floor and fall face down in my bed.

And here come the sobs.

I can't believe it. He promised me. He promised me he wouldn't touch her again.

And I sob some more.

Either way, I was just a distraction. He doesn't need that in his life right now. I did the right thing.

Still sobbing.

Please God, make it stop.

The next thing I know, I'm waking up – groggy from all of the crying and completely disoriented. I fell asleep?

I'm still lying on my stomach, in my black pencil skirt and light blue button down, and it's daylight. Oh, right. I quit my job. I roll over and cover my eyes with my arm.

As I start coming to, I hear raised voices outside my room. Is someone here? I jump up and place my ear to my closed door.

It's Andrew! Oh my God!

And it's Abby. They're fighting?

"What did you do?" I hear Abby yell, and I can picture her stance – arms crossed, legs apart, one eyebrow raised.

"Just let me talk to her," Andrew pleads. I feel the tears resurfacing just from the sound of his voice. "I need to talk to her."

"No way," Abby says. "She can talk to you when she wakes up if she wants, but right now, you can't come in."

"Please," Andrew begs, and even through my door, I hear his voice break. "It was a misunderstanding. I have to explain."

Misunderstanding? I was there, Andrew. Everything came across loud and clear to me.

"Look, you and I are not friends," Abby says. "I don't give a damn what you want at the moment. You can't come in. Good bye." And I hear the door slam.

I move back to my bed and sit. Abby must have heard me crying. I guess she *was* home.

I look at the clock. It's a little after eleven. I wasn't asleep that long. Good.

I slowly make my way to the bathroom, tears still pouring down my face, but I barely notice. It's as if I'm immune at this point.

I look at my horrific face in the mirror. What am I going to do? About my job? About Andrew? What am I going to do without him?

I fall to my knees in my bathroom, and shortly after, Abby's by my side.

"Jules?" There's panic in her voice, but I can't make out her face through my tears. "What the hell happened today, Jules? And why is your boss coming by our house? Did he do something to you?"

She has me by the shoulders, trying to get me to look at her, but I can't. I can't confess. What's the point now, anyway?

"I quit," I manage to get out somehow.

"Okay," Abby sounds puzzled. "That's a good thing, right? I wanted you to quit that damn job before you got it."

I don't say a word. *I quit him too, Abby. I quit him too.*

"Jules, you're freaking me out. Is it the money?" she asks.

I shake my head. Who gives a damn about money?

"I can totally float you until you find another job," she continues. "Don't worry about it. I'm making pretty decent money now. We'll figure it out."

"It's not the money," I whimper, my tears finally subsiding, if only by a small amount.

"Well then what is it?" Abby drops my shoulders and sits back on her heels. I look up at her, finally able to make out her face. I wipe away the wetness from my cheeks with the back of my hand.

"I love him, Abby," I whisper. "I love him, and it hurts, okay? It freaking hurts."

Abby stares at me, and I watch as her face turns from anger to sympathy. "I'm sorry," she says, grabbing one of my hands in hers, as we sit on our knees facing each other on my bathroom floor. "I'm so sorry, Jules."

"It's okay," I lie. "It's over now."

"Do you want to tell me what happened?"

I shake my head. "Not right now."

"Do you want to take a shower or something?"

I shake my head again.

"Hungry?"

I shake my head quickly. Even the thought of eating makes me feel like puking.

Abby squeezes my hand and smiles.

"Wanna get drunk?"

I nod. Now that sounds like a plan.

CHAPTER 35

I decided to go ahead and take a shower when Abby left me in the bathroom, and I'm glad I did. It felt great, and helped to wake me up a bit. I'm trying to pretend I washed all my tears down the drain too, but I know that's a falsehood. I could breakdown at any moment. I can feel it.
I get completely dressed in my favorite faded jeans, a black tank top and flip flops before looking at my phone. *Holy missed calls, Batman!*
I scroll through them...and ninety percent are from Andrew. There are a couple from Adrian, a couple from Abby, and one from a number I now recognize as Nate's. Hmmm...Nate.
No, Jules. He's a nice guy.
I have several voicemails too, so I start to listen to them. I start crying again as I listen to the ones from Andrew.

> *Please Jules, you have to let me explain. Call me. Please.*

> *Jules, I have to know you're okay. This is killing me. Please call me.*

Well, sorry Andrew, but I don't want to talk to you right now. My life's already messed up. I don't need your shit dragging me down.

Good. Looks like the anger is back. Anger I can manage. Anger doesn't hurt so much.

I grab my purse and a cardigan, put my phone inside, and head out my bedroom door.

"Where do you want to go?" Abby asks.

"Don't care," I say, strolling into the kitchen to meet her.

She sighs. "You know your boss is still sitting in his car outside. Creepy bastard." She rolls her eyes. "What happened, Jules? I mean, I've quit jobs before, but my bosses certainly don't pay me personal visits, looking like they just lost their best friend, practically on hands and knees begging to speak to me."

I bow my head, forcing the tears away. I'm going to have to talk to him. He's not going to give up.

"Fine," I say through my teeth, trying to find my anger again. I toss my purse on the kitchen counter and move toward the door.

"You're going to talk to him?" Abby asks, incredulous.

"I have to. He won't give up. I know him."

Abby shrugs. "Okay, but you take that job back, and I'll kick your ass."

"Don't worry about that," I assure her. I won't be going back there. Hell no.

I stomp down the stairs and outside.

Andrew's out of his car and walking toward me before I'm barely out the door. I stop on the sidewalk when I see him, and he stops when I do. The tension in the air is tangible, as we stand and stare at each other.

Andrew looks like hell. He's still in his work clothes, minus his jacket and tie, and one side of his shirt is untucked. His hair is a mess. He's obviously been running his fingers through it. His eyes are heavy and sad, and it looks like he hasn't slept in months.

And even with all that, he still manages to look absolutely beautiful to me.

My anger starts subsiding the minute I see him, but I hold on with a death grip. It's the only way I'll get through this.

I finally will my legs to move and start walking toward him again. He starts moving slowly toward me, but I bypass him and go directly to the passenger side of his Land Rover and get in. I suddenly feel contempt for his pretentious car.

Yes. Good. Anger.

I watch from the car as he stands, staring into the direction I came from for a moment, before he finally turns and comes to join me.

Andrew gets into the driver's side slowly, and I cross my legs to help control my bouncing knee.

"Andrew, you need to leave," I tell him, without looking at him. I can't look at him. Instead, I stare out the front windshield. "Just go. It's over."

"Don't do this, Jules." He reaches for one of my hands in my lap, but I quickly move them. "Please don't," he pleads.

"Just go," I say again. "There's nothing left to say, and you're freaking out my roommate. *Go.*"

I move to open his car door, but he grabs my arm.

"Let go, Andrew," I whisper, and he immediately releases me.

To my surprise, he chuckles before he leans down and covers his face with his hands. Is this funny? Or has he officially lost it?

"Jules, please," he mutters from underneath his hands. "Don't do this. I can explain."

I sigh as my apparently never-ending tears surface yet again. I can't bear to see him like this. This is not the man I fell in love with. He seems so broken, so insecure.

"Andrew, look," I say, reaching to remove one of his hands from his face, but he fights me. "Andrew, the bottom line is that I'm not good for you right now. Okay? Figure out this stuff with the company, and maybe we can work things out down the road. I don't know. I just can't be around it anymore. I have enough to deal with. I don't need this."

Andrew finally pulls his hands from his face, and I see now why he was fighting me. He looks out the window and wipes his tears away with the back of his hand.

"You don't *need this*?" he says, still looking out the window, and I get his meaning.

"I love you Andrew," I try to assure him, because it's the truth. "But this is too much for me. It's too complicated. It's too hard."

Andrew turns to me, and his face is angry, not what I expected. "You may not need *this*," he says gesturing to his chest, "but I need *you*. I love you, Jules, and I want you in my life. I told you to tell me. I told you I would do whatever you wanted me to do, but you said it was okay."

Really? Throwing stones are we? Two can play this game.

"You said you would never touch her again," I remind him, holding my ground, even though tears are still flowing liberally down my face.

"And I didn't!" he yells. "She was pushing herself on me for an hour!" He closes his eyes and runs a hand slowly through his hair. "You happened to catch my weak point when I caved. It was one moment, a one second lapse. I was about to push her away. I don't know what else to say. I'm just so sorry. I'm sorry I ever thought about this messed up idea to begin with. It never should have happened."

I close my eyes and sigh. "Andrew, just figure this mess out with your company, okay?" I don't want to fight with him. "Just work things out, and then we can talk. I promise."

"I can't lose you Jules," he whispers. "I can't do this without you."

"Yes you can," I say, crying harder now. "It's only been a week. I'm a distraction, Andrew."

He turns quickly in his seat to face me. "No you're not. You're not a distraction." He reaches for my hand again, but I pull away.

"Just get your life together, and then we'll talk." I move to open his car door, eager to get away from him before I officially cave.

"But what if you're not there?" he asks, his voice soft. "What if you decide not to wait for me?"

I turn around and give him one final glance. Oh God, it hurts. It hurts so damn much.

"I will always love you, Andrew," I whisper, and he looks up at me, his eyes once again filled with tears. "No matter what. That will never change."

I get out quickly and close the door. I half expect Andrew to chase after me, but he doesn't. It's better that way.

I walk quickly back to the door to my building, and once I'm out of sight, I sit down on the stairs as my tears overcome me once more.

A few seconds after I sit, I hear Andrew peel out of the parking lot and out of my life.

That's it then. It's over. I have no job. I have no Andrew.

Maybe he'll come back to me. Maybe after everything is over he'll come back.

This thought, this hope, allows me to breathe a little easier. I close my eyes and concentrate on stopping the crying. I have to get myself together. I've never let a man get to me like this, not even my shithead father, and I won't start now.

I sit for a few more minutes until I'm finally breathing semi-normally again. I wipe my face one last time, and make my way back upstairs.

"So, everything good?" Abby asks from the sofa when I walk in.

"No," I admit truthfully, "but it will be."

"What happened, Jules?" she asks again, but I'm still not ready.

"I'll tell you later," I say, walking back to my room to fix my face before we leave. "I'm going to go freshen up."

"I'll be here," she says softly, and I catch her double meaning. I love my friend.

"Thanks," I say, half smiling at her, before I head into my room.

My hands are shaking as I try to add a little color to my cheeks. I can't believe it's over. Twenty-four hours ago I had everything I ever wanted. I've dreamed of being with Andrew for so long, only to find that actually being with him was better than I ever thought possible.

Now, it's gone. He's gone. Maybe for good.

I drop my make-up brush and put both hands on my sink to steady myself. Am I going to make it through this?

I look up and into my mirror. *Yes.* Yes, I will make it through. Andrew will come back. He will. And I'll be waiting, and we'll pick up right where we left off.

Things are better this way. He may not see it now, but he'll understand in the end. Now he can do what he has to do to save his company. At least I don't have to watch it anymore.

Gathering myself once again, I add some lip-gloss and walk out of my bathroom back toward the living room.

"Let's go get hammered," I tell Abby.

She smiles, grabs her purse and follows me out.

CHAPTER 36

"I can't believe you won't tell me what happened," Abby slurs. We've been at it for almost four hours now, and we're on our third bar.

"I don't want to talk about it," I say. I'm drunk, but honestly, with the amount of alcohol I've consumed, I should be worse.

"Fine." Abby rolls her eyes at me. "How about Nate then? Can we talk about Nate?" Abby has a huge smile on her face, which makes me smile.

Sure. Let's talk about Nate. No harm in that at this point, I guess.

"Why don't we call him?" Abby asks, getting her phone out.

I grab her hands to prevent her from digging in her purse. "I don't think that's a good idea."

Abby gives me a disapproving look. "You're done with Andrew," she says. "It's over. You quit, and even though you won't tell me what the hell happened, I'm guessing it didn't end well." I try to interrupt, but she holds up a hand to stop me. "So, I vote we call Nate, have him join us – maybe bring a hottie friend along," she adds with a smile, "and we have a few drinks. What's going to happen?"

I study her for a moment. The only good that could come of this is that it will probably help get my mind off the obvious, if only for a moment. And it would help get Abby off my back, which would be nice. She gets incorrigible the more she drinks.

"Fine." I sigh, closing my eyes. "But I can't date him, Abby. And you told me yourself not to lead him on."

"Just give him a chance," she begs, grabbing my hand. "He's great, Jules. Much better for you than that preppy asshole from work. I promise."

I smile. She's probably right, but it doesn't change the fact that I'm in love with Andrew and always will be.

"I said it was fine," I repeat. "I needed to call him back anyway. He sent me flowers yesterday."

Abby's mouth drops. "When the hell did you plan to tell me about that?"

I laugh. "Sorry. I've had a crazy couple of days."

She shakes her head at me, as she dials his number. "Unbelievable. Such a good thing, right in front of her face," she says, talking to herself, "and she doesn't even want it. Did I mention he's like ridiculously hot?"

I laugh again. "I met him, remember?"

But Nate obviously picks up before Abby has a chance to comment.

"Hey! What are you doing?" She's looking at me while talking to him on the phone. "Well we're at Mick's if you want to meet us…Yeah, Jules and I…Okay great!…See you then!"

"He'll be here in about ten minutes," she tells me excitedly, putting her phone back in her purse. "He's already downtown."

"What about his shop?" I ask, looking at my watch. Certainly a bookstore doesn't close this early.

"He has some other people working for him," Abby explains. "I guess he's not working today. He owns the place. He can do whatever the hell he wants."

Ten minutes later, Nate strolls into the bar. Right on time.

Damn. He is incredibly beautiful – dark, worn jeans, a snug black t-shirt to match his dark unruly locks, and black boots. *Good-ness.*

I watch him as he looks around for us. Finally his baby blue eyes meet mine and he smiles. Abby's back is to the door, so she hasn't noticed him yet.

"Nate's here," I tell her, as he approaches.

She turns and finds him then waves, as his long and lean body weaves through the happy hour crowd.

Abby turns back to me. "Sexy fact number five hundred and seventy-two about Nate..." she whispers. "He drives a motorcycle."

I gape at her. That is so hot, and she knows I have a thing for motorcycles.

"For comfort or for speed?" I ask, as Nate gets closer.

"He has a Ducati." She winks.

Oh holy hell.

"Hi," Nate says, as he finally reaches us with his killer smile.

"Hi," I say, my smile matching his. It's kind of contagious.

He turns to the table next to us to ask if they're using an empty chair there. Obviously not, as Nate grabs it and pulls it up next to me at our small table.

"Thanks for having me," he says, sitting down. He looks oversized at our table. He's not big, just really tall.

"Thanks for coming," Abby says, taking another sip of her Mojito. "Jules had a shitty day. We're drinking it off."

Nate looks at me. Good God, those eyes are crazy blue.

"What happened?" he asks, genuine concern on his face.

"I kind of quit my job," I admit. Andrew's face flashes briefly before my eyes, but I quickly block him out.

"Oh," Nate says, surprised. "I'm sorry?" He's obviously not sure whether this is a good or bad thing. Honestly, neither am I.

I laugh. "It's okay. I'll find another one."

Just then the waitress pops up and Nate orders a Heineken. "So, how long have you ladies been at it?" he asks after the waitress leaves. We both look over at Abby who's swaying in her chair as she smiles at him.

"A few hours," I admit, smiling at him.

"I gotta pee," Abby says suddenly, before stumbling out of her chair.

"Want me to come?" I ask, getting up to help her.

She steadies herself at the table, and smiles at me. "I got this," she says, and starts making her way slowly through the crowd.

"She's been drinking liquor," I explain to Nate. "I stuck with beer. I figured she would make it a marathon, and I need to find a job tomorrow."

"Gotcha," he smiles. "Sorry to hear about the job thing."

And there it is. Andrew on the brain again.

Alcohol is a depressant. Suddenly getting drunk doesn't seem like such a good idea.

"No worries." I quickly try to think of something to change the subject. "Thank you for the flowers," I blurt. "They were beautiful."

Nate smiles. He has great teeth.

"Glad you liked them. It wasn't too much too soon?"

"No." I shake my head. "It was nice."

"I had a good time chatting with you the other night," he continues. "I wanted to call on Saturday, but I'm not sure how the rules work with the whole calling-after-you-meet-someone thing." He laughs. "I haven't done this in a while."

I laugh and stare at him. He is seriously hot, so I wonder why he hasn't dated in a while. Damaged? I have to ask.

"Why not?"

"Why not what?"

"Why haven't you dated in a while?" I ask, as the waitress shows up with Nate's beer.

He takes a sip before answering. "Took me a bit to get over the last one."

"Oh," I say, kind of embarrassed I asked now. "Sorry for being so nosey."

Nate smiles again, and I smile back. "It's not a problem," he says. "I put over two thousand miles between us. I think that oughta do it."

"That's why you moved here?"

"Part of it." He takes another sip of his beer. "I needed to get away from a lot of things. She was definitely the most painful to let go."

Yikes. Nate is damaged goods. Good to know.

"I'm sorry to hear that," I say sincerely. "Trying to get over someone, even when they've wronged you, is no easy task."

Nate, I understand you more than you may know.

"Agreed." He nods. "I was angry for a long time and just didn't want to deal with the relationship thing anymore, but that gets pretty lonely after a while."

"Well, we've all had our share of terrible relationships." God knows, I've had more than most, due to my inability to date decent men. "But the important thing is to keep trying."

"That's exactly why I'm here," Nate says, voice low, his baby blues darkening as he stares into my eyes. *Shit.*

"I better go check on Abby," I say, anything to change the subject.

"Need my help?"

"No," I smile at him. "I'll be right back."

I take off toward the bathrooms, already knowing what I'm going to find before I get there.

Sure enough, Abby's locked in one of the stalls, puking her brains out. This is not like her. Something must be bugging her. She only drinks until puking when something is bugging her.

"Abby, let me in," I coax from outside the stall door.

"I wanna go home," she whines, before opening the door to let me in.

She looks like hell. I pull her out of the stall and take a minute to wipe her mouth and face. I straighten out her outfit, and then fix her hair back into the neat ponytail she started the night in.

"I'll take you home, babe. Ready?"

She nods, looking like she may puke again at any moment.

I walk out of the bathroom, toward the door, and then I remember Nate.

"Can you sit here a second, while I tell Nate we're leaving?"

She nods again, as I sit her down on a stool near the door. "Don't move," I tell her, but I'm pretty sure she's not going anywhere.

I walk quickly back over to our table. It's gotten really crowded for happy hour, so it takes me a while to get through the crowd.

I finally reach Nate. "I have to get Abby home," I say apologetically. "She's a mess."

Nate immediately stands. "Let me help. Do you need a ride?"

"No, we only live a few blocks from here."

"Right," he says, obviously remembering walking me home last Friday night. "Well then can I walk you?"

Damn! Persistent!

"Okay," I reluctantly agree, not wanting to be near Nate, his killer smile or his beautiful blue eyes in my seriously tipsy state.

Nate follows me back to Abby, and she's exactly where I left her, slumped over on the stool.

Nate grabs one of her arms and puts it around his waist. He puts his arm around her, and she cuddles in to him. I don't blame her. I remember him being warm and smelling nice the other night.

"Lead the way," he says to me, as we leave the bar.

I start walking toward our apartment, slowly so Nate can keep up with Abby. However, I find I have to take two steps to his one to keep up with his long legs.

I look over at Abby, and she looks totally content against Nate. I feel bad for her. I wonder what's wrong. It's not like her to get this wasted, especially not during the week. I hope she doesn't have to work tonight.

I take out my phone quickly, and call Marlow's. Nate looks at me questioningly.

"I'm seeing if Abby has to work tonight," I tell him. "Hey," I say, when someone finally answers. "This is Jules. Does Abby work tonight?"

Steve tells me on the other end that she's not on the schedule tonight. Good thing.

"Thanks Steve," I say and hang up.

Nate's leading the way now. I guess I fell behind a little while on the phone. I rush to catch up, as he enters the parking lot of our building. I open the door for him so he doesn't have to let Abby go. Surprisingly, she's still on two feet, but she will be out like a light when she hits her pillow.

Abby staggers a bit when we hit the stairs, so Nate lifts her with ease and cradles her. *Wow*. That's so sweet. And kind of hot.

We walk into our apartment, and I lead Nate to Abby's room so he can lay her down.

"Is she going to be okay?" he asks, once he gets her in the bed. Her eyes are already closed.

"She'll be fine," I assure him. "I'm going to get her out of these clothes and let her sleep it off."

Nate recognizes his cue to leave. He smiles at me and turns to walk out the door, closing it behind him.

I disrobe my roomie, slip on some cotton shorts and a t-shirt and get her under the covers. I grab her trashcan from her bathroom and bring it to her bed side.

"Abby?" I shake her a little and she opens her eyes.

"Yeah?" she croaks.

"In case you get sick again..." I hold up the trashcan and then put it back down on the floor beside her bed.

"Thanks, Jules," she says, rolling over. "Love you."

"Love you too," I say before turning on her ceiling fan – to make sure she stays cool – and leaving the room.

"She'll be out a while," I tell Nate, as I walk back into our living room. He's sitting on our sofa, and moves to the edge when I walk into the room.

I go to the kitchen, grab her a glass of water, take it to her room, and come back to sit by Nate.

"Thanks for your help," I tell him. "She honestly doesn't get like that often. Something must be bugging her."

I feel bad that I don't know what's eating her. I've been so consumed in all of my bullshit. I've been a terrible friend.

"I'm glad we got her home," he says.

I smile at him, and we sit in somewhat uncomfortable silence for a moment.

"Are you hungry?" he finally asks.

Actually, I'm starving, but my stomach is still in knots from this morning. Was that really just this morning?

"I could eat," I say, not because I actually think I can, but because honestly, I don't want to be alone.

"Great." Nate smiles. "Do you want to order a pizza or something? I guess we probably shouldn't leave Abby."

I smile at the sweet gesture, but I don't want to be here.

"Abby will be fine," I tell him. "Let's go out, if that's okay with you."

"Fine by me," he says. "Anything special in mind?"

After some deliberation, we decide on a sushi place near our apartment, and to my surprise, I end up having a nice time.

Nate truly is one of the good ones, it seems. He's warm, smart, witty and obviously gorgeous. I found out over dinner that we have a few things in common. For example, Nate comes from money as well. His dad's a surgeon in Seattle, and Nate was pressured to go to medical school, which he tried and hated. He's always had a passion for literature and writing, but his parents weren't fans of the starving artist career path. So, that was another reason he moved away. He said he just didn't want to deal with the pressure anymore.

I can so relate. I wasn't necessarily made to go to Law school, but my father was not very happy with my photography major. The most surprising thing about dinner was that I was able to keep all Andrew thoughts at an arm's length for the most part. I wasn't able to get down much sushi, of course, but the fact that I made it through the dinner without breaking down was a win, I think.

"That was great," Nate says, as we walk out of the restaurant. "You barely ate a thing. Did you want something else?"

"I'm fine," I say. "I've just had a rough day."

"I understand," Nate nods. "I truly am sorry about your job. I could offer you something at the bookstore, if you get desperate." He smiles.

"Thanks," I say, genuinely loving his sincerity.

We walk a couple of blocks into town, with no real destination in mind, just continuing the conversation from dinner.

"Do you still talk to your parents often?" I ask.

"Probably not as often as they would like," he admits. "It's always the same conversation. And it gets really old."

"I wish I could avoid mine." I sigh. "My mom has…problems, so I feel obligated to stick around. I only talk to my dad when absolutely necessary."

Nate smiles at me, and stops in his tracks. "I have an idea," he says. "You wanna go for a ride?"

His motorcycle! Oh dear God yes!

I nod enthusiastically. "Sounds good."

Nate takes my hand in his, as he moves to cross the street. It makes me kind of uncomfortable, but I don't pull away, mostly because I don't want to hurt his feelings. He's been so nice to me tonight. Holding hands seems like a small price to pay, but he doesn't let it go when we get across the street. Now it feels wrong.

He looks down at our hands as I remove mine, but keeps walking. He looks over at me, and I give him a sad smile.

"Sorry," he says. "Again, not sure how all of this really works."

"Would you hate me if I said it's not you, it's me?"

I'm sorry Nate, but I'm the most recently damaged here.

"Not at all." He gives me a reassuring smile, and then stops walking. "But could you give me a little more detail?"

Ummm....

"Well, I kind of recently had my heart broken too," I start, with no idea what else to say.

"Oh." Nate looks surprised. "When?"

How about today?

"Recently. Very recently," I continue. "And I don't want to be unfair to you. You seem like an incredible guy. I'm just not in a good place right now."

Nate nods and thinks for a moment.

"Look, Jules." He takes both of my hands in his, and bends to look into my eyes. "I like you. I like hanging out with you. That's about all I know at the moment," he says confidently. "So how about we just leave it at that for now? Friends. Does that work for you?"

I smile and nod. "Friends I can do."

"Great," he says, smiling. "Now, let's go blow off some steam."

He drops my hands, and we start walking purposefully through a few more blocks before turning onto Highland. I'm happy the conversation is still light and tension free. I can be friends with Nate. No problem.

"Are we going to your store?"

"Yeah. That's where my bike's at, and I need to get you a helmet," he says.

A couple more blocks, and we're at his store. It's already closed for the night. Nate unlocks the door, and I follow him inside.

"I have an extra helmet upstairs in my office. I'll be right back," he tells me, and starts up the wooden stairs to the left of the door.

I wait downstairs, and browse the books in the front of the store. Nate's back in a flash, carrying two helmets, and a leather jacket. He also has what looks like a sweatshirt.

"This is for you," he says, handing me the sweatshirt, as he puts on the black leather jacket. "You'll probably get cold."

It's a hooded sweatshirt with the University of Washington emblazoned on the front. I slip it on, and it's huge on me, hanging down to my knees.

"A little big." Nate laughs, "But it will keep you warm."

"Thank you," I say smiling, as he hands me the helmet.

"Come on. My bike's out back."

Nate locks the front door, and I follow him through the dark to the rear of the store.

Sweet Mary, the bike is a beauty. I'm no connoisseur, but I would think any motorcycle lover would be jealous of this fine piece of black steel and smooth leather.

"Did you know I have a bike?" he asks, as I slip my helmet on and he helps with the chin strap. The helmet's a little big too, but it's better than nothing.

"Abby," I say, and he nods.

"I assume from your enthusiasm earlier about taking a ride," he finishes buckling me up, "that you've been on a motorcycle before."

"Yes," I nod. "I love motorcycles."

"Well, I like to drive fast, so hold on tight." His smile is wide, and rather breathtaking, as he hops on, and I hop on behind him. "Just pull the visor down if the wind gets to be too much."

He starts the engine, and eases us out of the small parking lot behind his store.

He drives slowly through town, while I do as I'm told and hold on tight. I'm instantly thankful for the sweatshirt. A few minutes in, and I'm already cold, even pressed against Nate's warm body.

When we finally reach the interstate, Nate takes off. It's positively exhilarating. I've gotta get me one of these!

I have no idea how fast he's going, but we weave in and out of the cars with ease, and I'm smiling so wide, my face starts to hurt.

The speed, the wind on my face – no matter how chilly it may be – the sheer power of the Ducati engine roaring between my legs, it's exactly what I needed. I feel awake, elated and alive.

Thank you, Nate. Thank you with all of my heart.

I have no idea why, maybe it's the adrenaline, but I feel my eyes fill with tears. Am I crying from happiness or sadness? I honestly don't know, and I don't feel like questioning it, as the warm tears run down my cheeks.

I reach to pull down the visor on my helmet before wrapping my arms tighter around Nate's waist. I feel the bike slow, when I lay my head against his back. He removes one of his hands from the handlebar to place it on both of mine around his waist.

I give him a gentle squeeze to let him know I'm okay, and he puts both hands back on the handles, and picks up speed again.

I close my eyes, and let my tears fall, as Nate powers on. I keep my arms around him, my cheek pressed against the inside of the helmet, and my eyes closed, until my tears finally stop. I look up again, just in time to see Nate getting off at the Tenth and Fourteenth Street exit. He must have turned around at some point. I didn't even notice him slow down.

Nate puts a hand on mine again when I lift my head, and when he stops at a light, he turns to look at me. I can barely make out his eyes through his dark visor. I smile, but then realize he also probably can't see me through my dark visor. So I nod, and he nods back before turning back around.

Pretty soon, the light is green and we're moving slowly again through the downtown traffic. I raise my visor to appreciate the sights. It's a really nice night, and the streets are crowded, even though it's Tuesday.

I don't often have the opportunity to be a passenger while driving through the city, so I'm surprised to see things I've never even seen before, and I've lived here my whole life.

I also notice several people drooling over Nate's bike when we stop at traffic lights. It really is a great bike. I would probably never get off of it, if it were mine.

When we finally arrive at my apartment building, Nate parks and helps me off first. I watch as he hops off the bike with ease and grace, unlike me. He takes off his helmet, as I try to fumble with mine.

"Let me help you." He laughs, as he places his helmet on the seat, and then reaches to help me.

"That was amazing," I tell him. "Do you do that a lot? I know I would."

"I do it often," he says smiling. "I'm glad you liked it."

"I really did. Thank you so much."

"You're welcome." He removes my helmet, and places it on the seat next to his. "I'll walk you up," he says and gestures for me to lead the way.

Nate follows me up the stairs, as I run my fingers through my bushy helmet hair. I take the hairband from my wrist and quickly pull it up and off my neck. Much better.

I unlock the door, and think for a minute about asking Nate to come in. It's still kind of early, but I'm sure he has to work tomorrow. I don't want to wear out my welcome with him today. I can't deny that I've really enjoyed his company.

"Another fun night," he says, as I turn to him before opening my door. "I hope to do it again soon."

"Me too," I say, truthfully. If we can truly be just friends, then I'm okay with that.

"Good night, Jules," Nate says, and leans toward me slowly. I panic for a moment, but he just kisses my cheek, and then pulls away. "I hope Abby's okay."

Damn. I had almost forgotten about poor Abby.

"I'm sure she's fine." I smile, and Nate starts down the stairs. "Nate?" I call to him, and he turns. "Thank you for tonight. I really did have a great time. It was exactly what I needed."

Nate smiles and nods, before continuing his trek down my stairs. I watch his descent for a minute before opening my door and going inside.

It's still dark in the apartment, which means Abby's still passed out cold. I go to check on her, glad to see she's still breathing, before going to my room.

I toss my purse on my bed, and change my clothes. *Ahhh.* Pajamas feel great.

As I sit down on my bed, I hear my purse vibrate. I have purposefully avoided my phone all day. The last time I looked at it was this morning.

I think for a moment about leaving it alone until tomorrow, but then I realize I probably shouldn't do that. Maybe it's my mom. Maybe something happened.

I sigh and pull out my Blackberry. The buzzing was a text, so I check that first. It's Adrian.

> *I hope you're okay. Please call me soon. Take care.*

I smile. Adrian's so sweet. I wish I would've started hanging out with her sooner.

I also see that I have a voicemail message. I check it quickly. It's my mom.

> *Hey sweetheart. Just calling to see how you're doing. It's lonely in here. Call me when you can.*

Dammit. She didn't sound good. I make a mental note to call her first thing tomorrow.

Last thing I check are my instant messages. I have two, and I know they're both from Andrew. He's normally the only one that Blackberry messages me.

I scroll to the first one. It was sent around two this afternoon.

> *I'm so sorry, Jules. I think we can work this out. Please call me.*

I scroll down to the next one, sent about a half hour ago.

miss u

No caps? And abbreviations? He's probably drinking.
Oh Andrew. I'm sorry too.
I lie down on my bed, and toss my Blackberry aside. Even with my nap this morning, and even though it's only a little after ten, I'm exhausted. With all the drinking, all of the stress and all of the adrenaline from the unexpected motorcycle ride through Atlanta, I'm completely spent.
I turn on my side, curl into a ball on top of my covers, and cry myself to sleep.

CHAPTER 37

I've spent all week trying to find a job with absolutely zero luck – not even as much as an interview. It looks like I may have to take Nate up on his offer after all.

It's Sunday now, and I'm trying to force my depressed ass out of bed. It's been a long week.

I haven't heard from Andrew since his "miss u" message on Tuesday night. I've wanted to call him, just to hear his voice. I've ached to see him every minute of every day since I left, but I can't give in, even though my decision to leave is starting to seem more and more like a bad decision...a *very* bad one.

I'm also worried about my mom now. She's still in rehab, and even though I've called every day this week with words of encouragement, I'm thinking she's about to break. She told me yesterday when we spoke that she thought she was ready to come home, and that she would be fine. I stayed on the phone with her an hour to try and convince her otherwise, but I'm not sure I succeeded.

How did my life go completely sideways this fast? Less than a week ago, I had a great paying job, a mom working hard to turn her life around and a wonderful, beautiful boyfriend. Today, I have none of those things, and I can't help but to feel like all of the failures are my fault, even my mom's.

I should have called her more. I should have sent her some care packages. I should have spent more time with her over the past few years, instead of trying to do anything and everything to forget what was happening. I thought once I moved out and made a life of my own, I would stop worrying about her twenty-four-seven. I thought if I wasn't around it all the time then it would be easier, but it's the opposite.

And Andrew....

I curl back up into a ball in my bed, and hug my knees to my chest. How long will it hurt like this? I miss him so much.

"Getting out of bed today?" Abby's standing in my doorway with two cups of coffee.

I raise my head to look at her, but quickly drop it back down on my pillow.

"Haven't decided yet," I mumble into the covers.

Abby comes to sit next to me on the bed and puts the mugs on my nightstand. She runs her fingers through the side of my hair.

"Jules, you have me a little worried," she says, and I can hear it in her voice. "I've known you a long time, and I've never seen you like this."

I stay quiet. I still haven't said anything to Abby about Andrew. I'm holding up my end of that bargain and keeping our secret.

"So you quit your job," she continues. "Big damn deal. You'll find another one soon."

I nod and close my eyes.

"Jules, is there something else?" she asks quietly.

She's asked me this question more than once in the past few days, and I've avoided it every time.

"I'll understand, Jules," she pleads, "whatever it is, but I can't help you feel better unless you talk to me."

I uncurl myself, and sit up slowly in my bed.

"Don't worry, Abby." I try my best to give her a reassuring smile. "I'm going to be fine. I'm just anxious about the job thing, about my mom...my brain feels very full at the moment."

Abby studies me through squinted eyes. She knows I'm lying, but I don't care.

"Okay," she says finally, with a smile. "Why don't we go out for breakfast? Nate's already called. He said he wants to come. His treat."

Nate.

Nate has definitely been a ray of sunshine in all of this. He's turning out to be a great friend.

"Okay," I nod. "I'll get dressed."

"I knew the mention of Nate would get you out of bed," Abby says smiling.

"Whatever," I scoff. "I want to have breakfast with your sexy ass. Who cares about Nate?"

Abby laughs, takes her coffee and leaves to let me get ready.

Honestly, I'm worried about Abby too. I asked her what was up after her drunken night last week, and she was very close-lipped – very un-Abby like. She seems better now, but I can still tell something's bugging her. I guess she'll tell me when she's ready. I can't judge. I'm keeping things from her too.

I skip the shower and toss on jeans and a t-shirt. It's probably warm enough for shorts today, but I go with jeans.

I walk out into the living room, where Abby's ready and waiting. She has on a sundress and flip flops – a little overdressed for breakfast in my opinion, but whatever.

"Nate's meeting us at The Diner," she tells me, standing and grabbing her purse. "You want to drive, or do you want me to?"

"I'll drive," I say. It's a good day to put the top down on my beat up BMW. At least that function on my car still works.

It's a nice drive to The Diner. We pull into a spot right next to Nate's fantastic bike. I've ridden on it several more times this past week, and it gets better each time. My next mode of transportation will definitely be a motorcycle.

Nate's sitting on a bench outside the front door of the restaurant waiting for us. He has another guy with him that I've never met before. I look over at Abby and she shrugs. Guess she's never met him either.

"Morning ladies," Nate greets us, standing as we approach.

"Morning," I reply, as I lean in to kiss him on the cheek. Abby does the same.

"Ladies, this is my brother, Charlie," he tells us, introducing the stranger sitting next to him. "He flew in last night. He's going to be staying with me for a few days. Charlie, this is Abby and Jules."

Damn. Good looks run in this family. Charlie's not quite as tall as Nate, but they share the same dark hair and the same gorgeous blue eyes. Their different personalities are reflected in their clothes – Nate in dark jeans, a dark gray t-shirt and his black boots, while Charlie's wearing baggy, worn jeans, a vintage t-shirt with some muted design on the front that I can't make out and flip-flops.

"Nice to meet you," Charlie says, extending a hand to shake both of ours.

I glance over at Abby, and her smile is wide as she appraises Charlie.

"Shall we go get a table?" Nate suggests, as he opens the door and gestures us inside.

Abby immediately cozies up next to Charlie, as I walk beside Nate. Nate looks down at me and winks. I smile at him. He's just such a likable guy.

Normally this place is packed in the mornings, but we get seated right away today. I scoot into one side of the booth, half expecting Abby to slide in next to me, but she takes the other side, forcing Nate next to me and Charlie next to her. She discreetly raises her eyebrows at me and I smile.

"What's good here?" Charlie asks. "I'm starving."

"The pancakes are famous." Abby smiles at him, and he smiles back. *Yay for Abby!*

Abby and Charlie continue their conversation about breakfast, while Nate and I peruse the menu.

"And how are you today?" Nate asks, closing his menu. Obviously, he's made his breakfast decision.

"Good," I reply with a smile. "You?"

"Not bad," he says. "Better now."

Luckily, the waitress comes by to take our drink orders, before I can analyze that comment too much. We all order coffee, except Charlie, who orders an orange juice.

"I don't drink caffeine," he informs us, and Abby gasps.

Nate and I laugh, as they launch into another conversation about how Charlie is remarkably able to survive without caffeine.

"I was thinking of taking Charlie out for dinner tonight," Nate says to me, and the other two stop talking to listen in. "Would you guys like to go? Maybe some place fun, like Luna?"

"I'm free!" Abby says, a little too excitedly, but the look on Charlie's face tells me he's more than pleased by the idea of her being available.

"Sounds good." I have no plans tonight, but then I suddenly remember I have no money either.

"What's wrong?" Nate asks, when he sees me frown.

"It's nothing," I say. How embarrassing. I'll just put it on a credit card.

"Okay," Nate says, eyeing me suspiciously, but I brush him off with a smile. I'll get a job soon enough. I have to stay positive.

The waitress comes back with our drinks, takes our orders and we chat lightly throughout the rest of breakfast.

"What are you guys up to today?" I ask as we head back to our cars.

"Home first, then we're going to go do some touristy stuff," Nate tells me. "Maybe the Aquarium, walk around downtown a bit. How about you?"

"Laundry." I frown, and we both laugh.

"Sounds like a blast."

"I can't wait."

"Hey, can you ladies give me a ride?" I hear Charlie ask Abby.

"I don't really want to cuddle up to my brother again, if I don't have to."

"I'll take you home," I offer, and then I look at Nate. "Hey, why don't you borrow my car today?" I suggest. "I know it's nothing special, but at least it has plenty of room, and a convertible top."

I grin as Charlie nods his head enthusiastically.

"Okay," Nate agrees. "I'll follow you guys back to your place. We can take your car from there."

I smile excitedly at Nate and toss my keys to Abby. "Abby can drive my car back. I'm riding with you!"

Abby takes my keys and she and Charlie get in my car, as Nate hands me the extra helmet. I hurriedly strap it on – I have it down to a science now – and then I hop on the bike behind Nate.

"We're going to go for a short ride," Nate tells Charlie. "We'll be back soon."

Charlie looks over at Abby, before looking back at Nate. He nods and smiles, and I see Abby smile too. She's a beauty. It's no wonder he's excited about the company.

Nate slips on his helmet, and I wrap my arms tightly around him, as he backs out of the parking lot and starts through the streets of Atlanta. In no time, we're zooming down I-85, and I delight in my new favorite method of escape.

Definitely must have a motorcycle. And soon.

Nate and I don't stay out long. We're back at my place in less than thirty minutes. Abby and Charlie are on the sofa talking when we come in.

"Ready to go?" Nate asks, and Charlie turns and smiles at us.

"Sure."

If I'm not mistaken, he looks sad to leave. Abby has entranced him in only a few hours. She's good.

"Nice to meet you, Charlie." Abby extends her hand, and Charlie brings it to his lips and kisses her knuckles. Nate and I give each other a sideways glance and a smile.

"It's been a pleasure," he says to Abby, before walking toward Nate and me. "Nice to meet you too, Jules," he says, but I just get a smile, no hand kissing.

"Same here. See you tonight," I tell him.

Nate leans down and gives me a quick kiss on the cheek. "See you ladies around eight," he says, and I nod. "Bye Abby." He waves at her, and she waves back.

"Bye guys," Abby says, and Nate and Charlie both turn and smile at us as they start walking out the door.

Damn. Those are some pretty brothers.

I go sit by Abby on the sofa. "So, Charlie, eh?" I tease and she smiles widely. "Whatcha think?"

Abby smiles back at me, her eyes wistful. "He's gorgeous. That's what I think."

"And nice," I add. "Must run in that family."

"That's some good DNA. That's for sure," Abby says, making me laugh. "Seems like you're feeling better," she adds. "I'm happy to see it."

I nod, and sigh. "I'm getting there, but I still have my moments."

"That's to be expected," she says. "And it may take a while, but you'll pull through. I know you will."

"Thanks friend."

We hug, and then Abby releases me but keeps her hands on my shoulders. "So, let's go pick out some fabulous outfits, shall we?"

I smile at her, enjoying her excitement. "Sure. Your closet first."

"Sounds like a plan." She jumps off the sofa, and takes my hand to pull me up.

I follow her into her room, and she starts talking idly about what color she wants to wear tonight, jeans vs. dresses, etc. I start to tune out for a minute as yet another image of Andrew pops unwanted into my head. My chest takes on a familiar empty feeling, and it's like last Tuesday is happening all over again.

This has occurred several times a day since I quit last week. I keep thinking it will stop, or at least get easier, but it's getting worse. Every time I get struck by some memory of him, I'm left breathless and in agony.

I sit on Abby's bed, trying to smile as I work my way through the pain. Luckily she's caught up in the outfit search, so she isn't paying too close attention. I clutch at my chest, trying to discreetly catch my breath as the pain slowly subsides.

What was I thinking? I'm never going to get over him. He has somehow woven himself into my person, and now I feel like losing him means I've lost a part of me. I understand that expression now more than ever. I feel lost, hopelessly lost, and no amount of friendly chats or motorcycle rides are going to change that fact.

"I have to go to the restroom," I tell Abby, as she buries herself further into her closet.

I get up quickly, not giving her a chance to comment and nearly run back to my room. I go into my bathroom, lock the door behind me and sit on the floor. I manage to pull my knees up and bury my head in my hands before the sobbing starts.

Oh Andrew. How am I supposed to live without you?

CHAPTER 38

I eventually made it out of my bathroom. Luckily, Abby didn't seem suspicious of anything. I'm getting pretty good at hiding things. That's a scary thought.

After we finally decided on some outfits for the evening, I finished the super fun task I had in store today – laundry – and spent the rest of the day lounging around, doing absolutely nothing... very similar to what I've been doing the past few days.

I'm glad we made plans to go out tonight. I may die of boredom, otherwise.

Abby comes out of her room wearing the red dress that I wore to Andrew's that first night I had dinner at his place. It will be hard to look at that dress all night, but there's not a lot I can do about it. Plus, I couldn't discourage her to wear it because she looks incredible.

"Hey sexy lady," I tease, as she walks runway-style toward me in the kitchen.

"You like?"

"I love."

"You look mighty fabulous yourself."

Since Abby's wearing a dress, she demanded that I do the same. I decided on one of my own – an oldie but a goodie. It's my favorite little black dress –silky, short and sexy. I feel great in it, and after my episode earlier today in my bathroom, I wanted to do something to try and lift my spirits. The dress helps a little, but I still feel pretty tired and worn down.

"Thanks." I manage a smile, despite my weariness. "I do love this dress."

The halter neckline is my favorite, but I fear the low back may be chilly tonight. Oh well.

"I'm sure Nate will love it." Abby winks.

"Whatever. You're one to talk." I roll my eyes at her. "Charlie will be eating out of your hand before we leave for dinner."

Abby gives me a devilish smile. "Let's hope so."

Nate and Charlie arrive, just as Abby and I are about to make some drinks.

"It's open!" I yell, and pretty soon, Charlie's joining us in the kitchen.

"You look gorgeous!" Charlie booms, and Abby giggles. She turns then and gives me a conspiratorial wink.

"Work it," I mouth, and Abby smiles before leading Charlie toward our patio.

Nate finds me in the kitchen soon after and stares at me a moment. I watch as his lips part before he breaks into a smile. "Wow," he says, and walks slowly toward me. "You look amazing."

"Thanks." I smile back, and he leans in to kiss my cheek. "Do you guys want to have a drink before we leave?"

"Sure," Nate says, still smiling.

"We can take a cab to Luna, if you want," Charlie suggests from the patio. "My treat."

"That sounds good," Nate agrees. "I actually have a card in my wallet for a service I've used before. We'll call them in a few."

I turn back to the job of fixing our drinks. "Everyone okay with Pinot Noir?"

I get a mutter of agreement from the crowd, so I open the bottle, grab some glasses and pour.

"You really do look beautiful tonight, Jules," Nate says, standing rather close to me now. My, my, he smells nice.

"Thanks," I say again, before looking him up and down. "You clean up pretty well yourself."

He's in his signature dark jeans and black boots, but he has on a dark gray button down with the sleeves rolled up – exposing those sexy tattoos – and a black suit vest. *Yummy.*

"Thanks," he smiles and blushes. He really is so easy to like.

He takes two of the wine glasses, and I grab the other two, before following him out onto the patio.

I notice Abby and Charlie standing close, leaning against the railing, watching the already crowded streets below. Even on Sunday night, the nightlife is busy in Atlanta.

As we drink our wine on our tiny patio, the conversation is happy and light.

Seems Charlie didn't follow in his father's footsteps either. He lives in San Diego and owns a surf shop, which explains his more laid back style and killer tan. Charlie's just as likable at Nate though, and it's obvious he's enjoying Abby's company very much.

We eventually make it to Luna, where the night remains relaxed and very enjoyable. Dinner is delicious, and Nate is as sweet as ever. He even got me to dance a little, which is usually a feat. I'm not big on dancing, but after my forth gin and tonic, I decided what the hell.

We all managed to get a little tipsy this evening, I realize, as we try hard to concentrate on a story Charlie's telling about his most recent surfing adventure in Mexico. He's passionate about the experience, and I watch Nate and Abby laugh in turn at his story – everyone's cheeks flush and everyone's smiling.

"How about we go?" Nate suggests, and I welcome the idea. I'm drunk and feeling really tired.

"I vote we keep up the dancing!" Charlie says excitedly, and Abby agrees.

"Yes! Awesome idea! I know a great place!" she says.

I shake my head at them. "Sorry guys. Not tonight, but you have fun."

I look apologetically at Nate, and he smiles. "I'll get you home, and join them later."

Abby's frowning at me. "Sorry," I mouth, and she smiles and nods, letting me know she understands.

Nate signals for the check, and the waiter brings it a few minutes later. I reach for my small clutch to grab my credit card, but Nate puts a hand on mine to stop me.

"It's on me." He smiles.

"But you got breakfast," I whine.

Yikes. Why am I so drunk? Oh right. *Maybe it was the bottle of gin you just consumed over dinner.*

Nate laughs at me, and I pout. He puts a finger on my forehead to smooth it, and I relax at his touch. "I asked you guys out. I would never expect you to pay," he says, and then looks over at his brother. "Besides, I'm celebrating my baby brother being in town for a visit. It doesn't happen often."

Charlie smiles at him. "Thanks, big bro."

Nate takes the bill and places some cash inside. "Let's go. I'll call the cab company when we get outside."

Nate hops off the high top chair before offering me a hand down. I hear Abby and Charlie talking about where they may go next, but I stop listening. I just want to go to bed all of a sudden. I've been fighting Andrew out of my head all night, and it's getting exhausting.

We walk outside and the air is cold, but nice. It wakes me a little at first, but the drunken drowsiness slowly creeps its way back in. I shiver, and Nate puts his leather jacket around my shoulders. He pulls me close as he calls the cab company.

"I need two, actually," he tells whoever he's talking to on the phone. "Yeah, at Luna…Ten minutes?…Sounds great."

He hangs up and puts his phone back in his pants pocket before wrapping both arms around me.

"It will be about ten minutes," he tells Charlie and Abby, and I snuggle eagerly into his chest.

He's so warm and smells heavenly. I close my eyes in an effort to stop the spinning. It's not working. I'm about to open them again, when someone calls my name.

"Jules?"

Is this a nightmare or a dream? I have no idea, but either way, please don't let it be real.

Nate doesn't release me. He actually squeezes me tighter, as I hear a throat clear and then my name once again.

"Ms. Greene? Is that you?"

Andrew's voice is low and disbelieving. *Holy shit*. This can't be happening.

I open my eyes and raise my head slowly. Nate loosens his grip, but still doesn't let me go completely. I look up at Nate's face. "It's ok," I tell him, and he looks down at me and frowns before releasing me.

I take a deep breath and turn to face Andrew. He's standing several feet away, looking as gorgeous as ever in his charcoal three-piece and garnet tie. Oh dear God. My heart catapults into my throat, and all I can think is that I hope my legs don't give out. Maybe I should have held on to Nate a little longer.

"Hi," he says, looking at me, then Nate, his face impassive.

"Hi," I manage. The tension couldn't get any thicker between us.

I turn to my friends and see Abby and Charlie are looking from Andrew to me and back again. Charlie looks confused. Abby looks like she wants to rip Andrew's throat out, and when I look over at Nate, he only has eyes for Andrew, and they are far from impassive.

I move toward Andrew so we no longer have an audience. We stare at each other a moment, and it takes everything inside me not to burst into tears at the sight of his beautiful face.

"It's good to see you," he says finally, jaw tight, and his gorgeous eyes are burning holes into mine. "You look…great."

Great? What?

This should be a sobering experience, but I'm so tired I can't seem to fight off the fuzziness from the alcohol.

"Thanks," I say, which sounds like a question. "What are you doing here?"

Luna is more for a fun night out than a business meeting.

"I'm meeting Zach from accounting at Cline's for a drink," he says, gesturing toward the wine bar two doors down from Luna's.

"Oh," I say, not sure what else to add, and suddenly Andrew's resolve breaks, and he looks irritated.

"Nice jacket," he hisses, and for some reason, it pisses me off.

I look down at Nate's jacket wrapped around my shoulders, and then look back up at him. "Thanks," I say again, with a little more confidence this time.

When Andrew sees I'm going to fight back, he seems to cower a little. I notice then how tired he looks. His face is pale, and the dark circles under his eyes are nearly black. He's still beautiful though, absolutely beautiful, and my heart aches to touch him, but I don't.

"I knew you wouldn't wait for me," he whispers, and I nearly lose it, but even with all the alcohol in my system, I somehow manage to hold it together.

"It's not like that," I whisper back.

"You deserve to be happy, Jules. I want you to be happy."

No Andrew. Why are you saying this? I feel panicked.

"I'm not happy," I admit. "I'm miserable."

"You didn't look miserable a minute ago." He gives me a sad smile, and I have to wrap my arms around myself to keep from touching his face.

"Nothing's changed," I tell him, as our cabs pull up.

Andrew looks at Nate, then at the cabs, before leaning slowly toward me. I freeze, as he places a soft kiss on my cheek. My eyes close involuntarily, while heat runs through my body, warm and satisfying.

"You're right," he whispers into my ear. "Nothing's changed. I still love you, Jules. Always."

He pulls away and looks at me briefly, before walking quickly toward his destination. I stare after him in a daze – dazed from the alcohol and the kiss.

I see Nate coming toward me and I turn quickly and walk toward our cab. Nate opens the door for me and I slide in.

"You okay?" Nate asks, as he slides into the seat beside me.

"No," I admit honestly. I look over at him, the tears pooling in my eyes. "I'm sorry, Nate."

And I am. So sorry. Nate doesn't deserve this. He deserves someone else, someone who's not as screwed up as I am – someone who's not still hopelessly in love with someone else.

"I assume that's the heartbreaker," Nate says ruefully, pulling me close.

His arms are friendly and welcome, and I slide into them and let my tears fall. I can't believe that just happened. I hate myself. I hate myself for leaving my job over this. I hate myself for doing this to Nate. And most of all, I hate myself for leaving Andrew. I feel like such a coward.

It's a short drive back to my place. Nate gets out first, and then offers a hand to me. "Come on," he says, pulling me out of the cab and wrapping his arm around me. "I'll walk you up to your place."

I nod into his chest, and before we start walking toward my building, he asks the cab to wait for him. I'm not sure why he's still being so nice to me after what just happened, but I'm not questioning it right now. I'm just so thankful he's here.

I fish my keys out of my purse, and go to unlock the door. "Are you going to meet Abby and Charlie?" I ask him, as I wipe my tears away with the back of my hand.

"I think I should," Nate says softly and pulls my hand away from my face.

He moves toward me, and I step back so I'm pressed against the door to my apartment. He cups my cheek and uses his thumb to finish the job of wiping away my tears, his blue eyes burning into mine.

My head's not clear enough to handle this. I have no idea what to do, so I just stand perfectly still. Nate moves his hand from my cheek, dragging his fingertips behind my neck, before pulling my face slowly to his.

I know I shouldn't do this. Just the thought of it makes my stomach hurt, but for some reason, I don't stop him, as he presses his lips tenderly against mine.

I remain still, my arms at my sides as he kisses me, and I kiss him back. It's gentle and appreciated, and the next thing I know, my arms are around his neck, and I'm on my tip toes as the kiss gains momentum. Nate moves his arms around my waist and pulls me close.

It feels so good. It's such a release. I feel like myself again, like this kiss is making me whole.

I continue kissing him, deepening it, moving my hands through his silky hair at the back of his neck, as he moans softly onto my lips.

And all of a sudden it hits me. My gin-filled brain finally registers that it's Nate I'm kissing. I'm not kissing Andrew. I'm kissing Nate.

I drop my arms from his neck and gently push against his chest. "Stop," I whisper breathlessly, and Nate backs away immediately.

I'm a horrible person. A horrible, horrible person.

"What's wrong?" he asks, his eyes concerned and wary, but still burning bright from our kiss.

"I can't do this," I confess. I close my eyes and shake my head. "Oh God. I'm so sorry Nate. I can't do this to you."

Nate keeps his arms around me and pulls me close, as I start to cry again into his chest. He holds me for a minute before opening the door behind me and walking me inside.

He sits me down on the sofa and then takes a seat beside me, pulling me into him again.

"I understand," he says finally, and I look up at him in disbelief.

"Stop being so nice," I say through my tears. "I'm a terrible person."

"No you're not," he says smiling, wiping my tears again with his fingers. "I've been there. It's confusing and hard, and it absolutely sucks. I shouldn't have kissed you. I just hate seeing you so sad."

I stare at him. *Maybe in another life, Nate...I could definitely fall in love with you.*

I put my hand on his cheek. "I can't do this to you Nate. You're too good."

Nate smiles again. "I'm not going to lie. I was hoping for something more, but after tonight, I can see that's not going to happen."

I try to smile at him, but I just can't make it happen. "I'm not good enough for you," I admit. "I'm way too messed up. You deserve better."

"I'm not sure about that." He laughs, as he wipes more tears from my cheek. "But you can't let him do this to you, Jules. Don't let him bring you down. You're better than that. I promise."

I finally manage a smile. "Thanks Nate. Thanks for everything."

"Still friends?" he asks, and I wrap my arms around his neck and hug him.

"Always," I say with sincerity. "You really are amazing, you know?"

I pull away from him and he's still smiling at me.

"Yeah, I know," he teases.

"And you're one hell of a kisser," I add and smile as I watch the blush form on his cheeks.

"You're not so bad yourself."

"You should go meet Abby and Charlie," I suggest. "I'll be fine."

"You sure?" he asks. "I'm happy to stay a while."

"I'm fine. Go."

Nate leans in to kiss my wet cheek before standing up. I stand too, and give him another hug.

"Have a good time," I say to him, before he leaves.

"I'll see you again soon," he says and walks out my door.

Damn. Nate.

If he would have been around a couple of years ago, things may have been a lot different.

I grab my purse and move into my room. I sit down on my bed and fish out my phone. I should probably text Abby, if she hasn't texted me already.

I find my phone, and see that Abby has sent me a couple of texts, all of them wondering what the hell happened at Luna.

I quickly text her back.

> *I'm fine. Nate's coming to meet you. Will explain everything tomorrow. Have fun. Love you.*

I put my phone on my nightstand, and then move to change my clothes and wash my face.

As I'm brushing my teeth, my phone rings. I'm sure it's Abby.

I put my toothbrush away, and go grab it. I'm surprised to see who's calling.

"Hello?"

"Hi sweetheart." It's Bessie, and for the second time tonight, I feel my heart come up into my throat. I already know what's she's going to say.

"Hi Bessie," I say quietly.

"She came home this afternoon," she starts. "She got a cab to the house, and your dad was here with Rebecca. I thought she was going to be okay at first, but she and your dad got into a fight, and a couple of hours later, she was in the liquor cabinet."

You've got to be kidding me!

"Where is she now?" I ask Bessie, as I plop down on my bed and close my eyes.

"She's here," Bessie says, "already passed out. I just wanted to let you know."

I want to go see her tonight, but I'm still way too drunk to drive, so I'll just have to pay her a little wake-up visit in the morning.

"I'll be over tomorrow," I tell Bessie. "Thanks for calling me."

"Okay sweetheart. I'll watch after her."

"Thanks Ms. B. See you tomorrow."

I hang up and lie down on my bed. I turn on my side and pull my knees to my chest as I start crying again into my pillow. I'm thinking of my mom when out of nowhere, Andrew's weary face from tonight pops into my head like a nightmare, and I sob uncontrollably into the night.

CHAPTER 39

I'm so tired of dealing with this shit. I just don't understand why my dad won't get with the program.

I turn my radio up full blast, hoping Thom Yorke can help ease my mind. My head's still aching a little from all the gin last night, or is it just the unrelenting stress that's built up over the last week? Either way, my head freaking hurts.

Mom, Mom, Mom. What am I going to do with you?

I pull up into the circular drive and sit for a minute letting the song finish. Thom works for me every time.

I get out and walk toward the door, and Bessie meets me.

"Morning, sweetpea," she says and kisses me on the cheek.

"Morning, Ms. B. How is she?"

"I checked on her a couple of hours ago." Bessie frowns. "She's just gotta sleep it off."

I close my eyes and take a deep breath. I feel like crying. Again.

"Are you okay?" Bessie asks, and I can't help but smile.

"Far from it," I confess. "I quit my job last week."

"What?" Bessie asks in shock. "Why?"

Do I tell Bessie? No. I haven't told anyone, so why start now?

"Just wasn't working out," I say.

Bessie nods apologetically. "Want me to make you some breakfast?"

"No thanks," I say turning my nose up. Food sounds repulsive.

"Something to drink?" she offers. "Some coffee?"

"It's okay." I smile at her. "I'll just go check on Mom."

"Okay," she says, smiling back. "Let me know if you need anything."

"Thanks," I tell Bessie before walking up the stairs. Of course my dad is nowhere to be found.

I take another deep breath. I can't think about my dad right now. I'll have to deal with him later. This week's been hard enough, with everything that's happened. I just may have to swear off men permanently this time.

I reach my mom's bedroom, and open one of the French doors. She's lying on her side, facing away from me. God, she's so small. If she's not careful, she's going to waste away.

I walk quietly over to her bedside, not wanting to startle her. I notice the usual spread of liquor and pill bottles on her nightstand.

"Mom?" I whisper, knowing this probably won't work, due to the amount of pills and alcohol she apparently consumed last night.

As suspected, she doesn't stir. "Mom?" I try again, but still nothing.

I reach a hand out and place it on her shoulder. She's so frail, and cold...wait...too cold.

"Mom?" I say louder now, urgent. Something's not right. Something's definitely not right.

"Mom?!" I'm screaming. She's too cold.

I turn her over, and her eyes are closed, her mouth slightly parted. I put my face to hers. She's not breathing.

"Mom?!" I try again, as I shake her. I'm vaguely aware that Bessie's walked into the room. "Mom?!"

NO! NO! NO! NO!

I turn her all the way over, and try CPR.

1,2,3,4,5,6,7.....all the way to 30.

I pound on her chest.

Come on, Mommy! Breathe!

1,2,3,4,5....This is taking forever!...28,29,30.

I breathe into her mouth. Once. Twice.

Come ON!

"I'll call an ambulance!" I hear Bessie say before leaving the room, but I don't stop.

1,2,3,4,5,6,7,8,9,10...

Please Mom. Come back to me. Please.

I keep trying. She has to come back. She has to.

I put my face to hers again. She's still not breathing.

I'm pushing harder now. I can't believe I'm not crying. Why am I not crying?

I shove the thought away. If I'm crying, I can't give her CPR. She's going to make it. I have to save her. I have to help her.

"Mom!" I scream. "Mom, please!"

I shake her again, but there's nothing. There's nothing there.

I don't stop my efforts. I can't. I won't. She's so cold, so pale.

1,2,3,4,5,6,7...

I pound on her chest, and then breathe into her mouth – just like I learned in class so I could start babysitting some neighborhood kids for extra money in high school.

Come on, Mom. Please!

The next thing I know, there are strange men in my mom's room. They're pushing me away, trying to get to her, but I won't leave her side.

Oh God, my head hurts so freaking bad.

"Miss, please step aside!" one of the strangers says to me, and I want to punch him, but I don't.

One of the men quickly, but gently pulls me away. I stand behind them and watch. I can't move. I can't breathe. It's too surreal. I don't understand what's happening.

I watch as they try doing the same thing I've been doing for the past...however long it's been. I want to tell them I've already tried, but I can't. I'm crying too hard now. I can barely see them through my tears.

Someone's arms are around me. Bessie? I have no idea.

"Come on, baby," Bessie says gently, and tries to move me even further away from my mom.

"No!" I manage to shout at her. I hold my ground. I'm not going anywhere until her eyes open.

I stand and stare at the strangers in navy blue and white, trying to help my mom. They seem to know what they're doing. They'll be able to help her.

They get a machine out. I've seen it before on TV, but can't remember the name. They turn it on, and place the two circles on my mom's chest.

"Clear!" one of the strangers shouts, and it startles me. I stop crying. This will work. She'll open her eyes any minute.

But she doesn't.

I wait in anticipation.

Mom, please!

"Clear!" the stranger shouts again. I wait, but my mom doesn't move. Her eyes don't open.

I have no idea how long these men are in my mom's room, but eventually, they stop trying to help her.

"I'm sorry, Miss," one of them says to me.

No, no, no! You're giving up?

"Get the hell out!" I scream at him, and rush back over to my mom's side. If they can't help her, then I will. I have to. It's my job.

I start CPR again. I haven't forgotten, even after all of these years.

1,2,3,4,5...13,14,15...

Someone's arms are around me again. I don't know who it is, but I push them away. I don't need their help. I don't need anyone's help.

"Mom?!" I shake her, and nothing.

Back to CPR.

1,2,3,4,5,6,7,8...28,29,30. Breathe.

"Jules." It's Bessie. "Jules, baby, she's gone."

"No."

I shake my head. She's not gone. I can save her. I can bring her back. I always do.

"Come here, sweetheart." Bessie's trying to pull me away.

"No." I push at her. "Go away!"

Bessie doesn't understand. She can't help her. Only I can help her.

"Ma'am." It's one of the strangers. I glare at him, as I continue to tend to my mom. I thought I told them to leave. "Ma'am, I'm very sorry. There's nothing left to be done."

"Fuck off!" I yell, and turn back to my mom.

Come on, Mommy. Please!

Suddenly, I'm being pulled away from her. These arms are not Bessie's. These arms are strong.

"No!" I wail, pushing and kicking whoever's pulling me. "No!"

"Come on, Jules. She's gone."

I stop fighting so I can turn and look at the person holding me. "You did this," I seethe at my piece of shit father. "You did this to her!" I scream.

"It's not the time or place, hun," he says, trying to pull me away again.

"No!" I start kicking and screaming. "I want to stay with her!"

I watch in horror as they wheel a stretcher into the room and the strangers start picking my mom up to place her on it. I don't like those strange men touching her. Can't they see how frail she is? They're going to hurt her!

"Put her down!" I scream at them. "You're going to hurt her!"

They don't listen, and my dad keeps pulling me away. "No!" I scream and struggle in his arms. "Let me go!"

But he doesn't. He pulls me into the hallway, and I finally still, shocked by what I see. They put my mom's small body on the stretcher and cover her up with a sheet.

"She can't breathe!" I yell, but again, no one listens.

"Jules…" It's my dad again, in my ear, too close. Way too close. "Jules, please."

I turn my head and see him crying. Bastard.

He releases me, and I turn to face him. I stare dumbfounded into his eyes, as they take my mom away from me, down the stairs and out of the house.

"Jules," my dad sobs. "I'm so sorry."

Sorry? Is he telling me he's *sorry*? Oh, I already knew that.

My tears have stopped. I'm numb. I don't understand what the hell's happening. Where did they take her?

"Jules, please," the asshole in front of me pleads again. I'm tired of listening to his voice, so I slap him. Hard. Across his lying face.

"Fuck you," I say before running down the stairs to catch the ambulance.

They're not taking my mom away from me.

By the time I reach the front steps, they're putting my mom into the ambulance.

"I'm coming," I say, daring one of the strangers to refuse me.

"Yes ma'am," one of them says, looking a little scared. Good.

I take a seat by my mom and uncover her face. She can't breathe.

One of the strangers looks at me, but I glare at him, and he quickly turns away.

I pull her hand out from the sheet, and hold it. "It's going to be okay," I say, and the stranger looks at me again.

"What?!" I yell at him, and he scoots away from me.

I look back to my mom. I stroke her cold hand. "It's going to be okay," I repeat, over and over.

I'm crying again. I can tell the strange man next to me is still looking at me, but I don't care. I don't care about anything.

Oh God.

I stop crying as I look at her face. She's not there. I can tell she's not there. She's gone.

It hits me like a tidal wave, and I drop my mom's hand.

"It's going to be okay," I say again, before the world goes black.

CHAPTER 40

When I wake up, I'm not in my bed.//
I blink, confused, and look around. It's dark, and I'm alone. Story of my life.//
Then it rushes back to me – the strangers, the ambulance, my mom.//
Mommy.//
I start sobbing in the darkness.//
A few minutes later, I realize I'm in a hospital bed. I still have my clothes on. I must have passed out.//
I hug myself, trying to stop the tears, but I can't. They won't stop. They just keep coming, harder and harder.//
"Mom," I whisper to no one. "Oh, Mom."//
All of a sudden, there's light in my dark room. Someone opens the door.//
I still don't stop crying, because I can't.//
"Are you okay sweetheart?" Bessie comes rushing to my side. "I didn't know you were awake. I went for some coffee."//
She's frantic, touching me, trying to hold me. I don't want her to, but I just don't have the strength to push her away.//
My eyes are closed, but I feel her sit beside me on the bed. She starts rubbing my arm.//
"It's okay, Jules. You're going to be okay," she assures me, but it makes me mad.

I am NOT going to be okay! I want to scream at her, but I can't make the words come out. I'm crying too hard, and I can't stop.

I feel so empty. I feel like I have nothing left. There's nothing left.

I hug myself tighter as the sobs continue to wrack my body.

Andrew.

I want Andrew.

I *need* Andrew.

The thought of him makes me cry even harder.

"Andrew," I whisper, and Bessie's hand tightens around my arm. I feel her breath on my cheek, as she leans down trying to hear me better.

"What sweetheart?" she asks frantically. "What did you say?"

But I don't repeat his name. No one is supposed to know. No one will ever know. It's like it never really happened.

Andrew.

I squeeze my eyes shut, wondering if I'll ever stop crying. I'm shaking, violently. It hurts so much.

I can feel Bessie's hands on me, trying to soothe me, but it's not what I want. I just want *him*.

Please, Andrew. Please come and save me.

I have no idea when the crying stopped, or when I fell asleep. I'm awake again now, and it's still dark outside.

I close my eyes, before the tears can come back. I'm still curled up in the hospital bed, but I'm alone again. Did Bessie leave me?

I feel a tear run down my face. *Great.*

I move my arms around my waist to brace myself for the inevitable sobbing, but I stop short when I feel a warm arm already wrapped around me. I freeze, panicked. Someone's in the bed with me?

I start to move out of the bed, but then I smell him – that familiar, intoxicating scent. *Could it be?* I tentatively run my fingers along the arm wrapped around me. It's covered in a long sleeve shirt. A dress shirt, maybe?

Am I dreaming? If so, I don't want to wake up.

I open my eyes wide, as the arm tightens around me, responding to my touch. I feel a face nuzzle into the back of my neck, and I smell him again.

Andrew. Please, please God. Let it be Andrew.

"Jules?" his voice is low and cautious.

I'm not sure if I want to turn around. I want to see his face more than anything in this world at the moment, but I'm afraid it's a dream or some kind of hallucination. Will he take his arm from around me, if I move? What's he doing *here*?

I turn slowly around in the bed to face him. Thankfully, he doesn't move his arm.

I stare into his beautiful eyes, shining bright, even in the darkness.

"Andrew?" my voice is hoarse, barely a whisper.

He moves his arm from around my waist, but only to put a hand on my cheek. *Oh God.* The warmth, the smell...I close my eyes to absorb it all.

My sweet Andrew.

He's here. He's here with me.

I quickly wrap both of my arms around his neck and start sobbing immediately as he pulls me against him.

"Baby, I'm so sorry," he says, but I barely hear him. He's here, and my arms are around him, and I'm never letting him go again.

"Oh God, Jules. I'm just so damn sorry," he continues, as I sob into his neck.

These sobs feel better for some reason, cathartic, relaxing almost. Andrew's here. I'm not alone.

"I'm here for you," he whispers into my hair, as if he can read my thoughts. "I'll always be here for you. I love you so much, Jules. I'm so sorry."

"Stop," I finally manage between sobs.

I don't want to hear his apologies anymore. I don't care. It doesn't matter.

"I love you," I say, and Andrew holds me tighter, soothingly rubbing my back, up and down, up and down.

I feel like I could drift back off to sleep, but I don't want to. I want to stay like this forever. I want to stay with him forever.

"Please don't leave me," I beg, my sobs slowly starting to ebb. "Please."

"Never," Andrew answers quickly, as he continues to run his fingers down my back. "I will never leave you."

His words are the air I need to start breathing again. My sobbing eventually stops, but tears continue to run endlessly down my face.

I pull back from Andrew, but only a tiny bit. I have to see his face. I want to see his beautiful, perfect face.

His eyes are hesitant, understandably. We've been through a lot over the past few weeks.

I can see now he's in work clothes, a dress shirt and pants with no tie. He must have come from work. How did he know?

I reach a hand up and put my fingertips on his forehead. I drag them slowly down the side of his face, over his cheek, along his jaw, to his lips. They part at my touch, and he closes his eyes.

I want to kiss him. I want to pull his mouth to mine and get lost in him, lost in my Andrew.

But I don't. Not yet.

I let my fingertips linger on his bottom lip. Andrew's breathing picks up, but he doesn't open his eyes.

I move my fingers from his mouth, back along his jaw, down his neck, to the back of his hair. I run my fingers through it slowly, enjoying it, cherishing this moment with him.

Andrew moans softly and hugs me tight. "Jules," he breathes, as he opens his eyes. His voice is so sad. It brings on a fresh set of tears for me. "Will you let me take you home?"

I'm surprised by the question. "I can leave?" I ask through my tears.

Andrew nods slowly, still hesitant. "Yes," he says. "You only fainted yesterday in the ambulance, but they wanted to keep you here for a while, just to make sure you're okay."

Yesterday? How long was I asleep?

Suddenly, everything comes back to me. Another tidal wave crashing into me, hard. I gasp as a sob wracks violently through me.

But it's different this time. Andrew's here now. He grabs the back of my head and pulls me into his chest.

"It's okay," he whispers. "I've got you, baby. It's going to be okay."

I finally catch my breath, but I don't want to move. I breathe him in. *Sweet, sweet Andrew.*

"I want to leave," I say into his chest. "I want to go."

"Okay," he answers quickly, and I pull my face up so my eyes meet his. "You want me to take you home?" he asks, and I shake my head. I don't want to go home.

Andrew's eyes turn sad. "I understand," he says, and I want to make the sadness go away, but I'm not sure what I did. "I'll call Bessie or Abby. They can take you."

Wait. *What?* No.

It takes a second for my cloudy brain to figure out why he's upset.

"I don't want Bessie or Abby," I say quickly.

"Oh, okay." Now Andrew looks confused.

"I want you," I tell him.

I want you on so many different levels right now, Andrew. You have no idea.

A small smile appears on his face. The sad eyes are gone. I'm so grateful.

"But you don't want to go home?" he asks me, gently stroking my hair.

I shake my head again. I'm having a hard time articulating my thoughts. Luckily for me, Andrew seems to be in a pretty patient mood.

"Do you want to go to your parents' house?" he asks, and I shake my head quickly. *No, no, no.* "Do you want me to take you to my place?"

I nod and sigh, as he finally figures it out. That's the one I've been waiting for.

"You got it," he says, and kisses my forehead.

He moves to get up, but I stop him, pulling him close to me. No way. He's not leaving.

Andrew chuckles softly. "Baby, I have to get your things and talk to the nurses, so we can go, okay?"

I look up at him and reluctantly nod. Andrew kisses my forehead again before he gently slides out of bed. I watch him walk out of the room, the feel of his lips still tingling on my skin.

Andrew's here. He's here. I can't believe it.

And he'll be right back.

I have to keep telling myself this so I don't break down again. My body's sore from all of the sobbing.

In what feels like an eternity, Andrew walks back through the door. I exhale the breath I was holding, as he returns to my side.

"A nurse is going to come in and check your vitals one more time before we leave, okay?" Andrew's brow is furrowed, still so much anxiety in his eyes. I want to make it go away, but I can barely sit up.

Andrew sees me trying to sit and rushes to put an arm around me. He's so warm, so sweet, so Andrew.

He pulls me up slowly, and I wince. My ribs really do ache, I assume from the crying.

"Are you okay?" he asks, seeing me tense. I look over at him but don't answer. I don't know if I'm okay or not.

The nurse shows up a few minutes later and does what she needs to do. Andrews stays with me in the bed the entire time, holding at least one of my hands when it's available.

"You're free to go," the nurse says, as she removes the blood pressure cuff from my arm. "You can sign out at the front desk," she adds, looking at Andrew.

"Thank you," Andrew replies, and then looks at me. "Ready?"

The nurse leaves us, and I take a couple of deep breaths. I'm not sure if I can stand, but I certainly want to get the hell out of this place.

As I start to get out of the bed, another vision of my mom's frail body from yesterday floods into my mind. I close my eyes as I stand, trying to push it away, but I can't. I feel the tears coming back at the same time that my legs give way. I can't do it anymore. I'm just so tired.

I'm vaguely aware of Andrew's arms around me as I start to fall. "I've got you, baby," I hear him say, but I can't see him. I can't see anything through the tears.

Suddenly my legs are no longer on the ground, but I'm moving. My arms are around Andrew's neck. He's carrying me, quickly it seems.

"You're okay," he tells me again, his voice is strong and confident. It's exactly what I need.

My sobs stop, but I don't let Andrew go. *Never. Never again.* But I'm having such a hard time staying awake. I don't want to fall asleep. I don't want him to leave me, but I keep drifting in and out, in and out, as my tears continue in a steady stream down my face.

Is Andrew still carrying me? I try to open my eyes to see where we are, but I just don't have the strength.

I finally manage to open them a bit as Andrew sits me in the passenger seat of his car. Did he carry me all the way through the hospital?

He looks gorgeous, even in his wrinkled dress shirt and pants. His hair's a mess, just the way I like it, but he looks so tired.

I stare up at his face, as he fastens my seatbelt. God, I love him so much.

After he has me all buckled in, he leans down and brushes a piece of hair from my forehead. There's so much worry in his eyes.

No, Andrew. Don't be worried. I'll be fine, as long as you stay with me.

I want to tell him how I feel, but I'm once again speechless.

Andrew shuts my door and moves quickly to the driver's side. He pulls my hand to his mouth and kisses it before starting the engine.

"Get some sleep, Jules. I love you," he says, and with that, my eyes close and I'm gone.

CHAPTER 41

When I wake, it's still dark outside. *Again?* It seems like I haven't seen daylight in weeks.

I have no idea what time it was when we left the hospital. I had my eyes shut most of the time we were outside and Andrew was carrying me to the car. I don't remember anything after that.

I sit up a bit and look around. I'm in Andrew's bedroom, but he's not here. A now familiar empty feeling threatens my chest. I can hardly remember anything about last night...or yesterday, maybe? What the hell day *is* it?

I lean back into the pillows. My head's killing me, and I feel a little hungry, though the thought of eating makes me want to hurl. When's the last time I ate? I have no clue.

Mom. The sudden thought of her brings everything back to the surface.

I need to find Andrew.

I will myself out of the bed before the sobbing starts again. I'm not sure how much more of that my body can take.

I step out of the bed, and notice for the first time that I'm in a pair of Andrew's boxers and a t-shirt. Andrew must have changed my clothes. I lift the collar of the t-shirt and inhale his scent.

I need to find him. *Now.*

I walk slowly out of the bedroom, my legs feeling very unsteady. Luckily, I don't have to go too far. Andrew's sitting at the desk in his living room, focused on his laptop.

He doesn't notice me at first, or at least he doesn't turn around. I stay where I'm at, and lean on the doorframe for balance.

Even though the living room's not well lit, it's still brighter than the dark bedroom I just came from. I squint my eyes in Andrew's direction. His back is to me, and he seems engrossed in whatever he's doing.

I take a moment to stare at him, while I let my eyes adjust to the light. Just looking at him helps me relax. His presence, knowing he's near me, that's all I need.

My nerves pick up a bit as I start slowly walking toward him. I don't remember much about last night. Are we okay? I'm not even one hundred percent sure how I got here or why I'm here.

When I'm about halfway to my destination, Andrew hears me and turns in his seat. I stop immediately in my tracks.

Are we okay, Andrew? I want to run into your arms so badly it hurts.

Andrew stands up, but stays by his chair, an unreadable look on his face. I feel all the air leave my body. Oh God. We're not okay.

I don't want to cry, but I feel the tears pooling in my eyes. I want to say something, but what? How do we reconcile this?

Thankfully, Andrew starts talking.

"Jules..." His voice is soft, like he's scared, like I'm a vicious predator about to pounce. "How do you feel?"

I cock my head at him. I have no idea what to say, how to react. My bottom lip starts to tremble, as I try hard to hold back my tears. I just want him to come to me. I want him to close this gap between us in his vast living room, and hold me close.

I shake my head slowly. It's the only answer I'm capable of giving at the moment.

Andrew starts walking toward me slowly, tentatively. It's killing me. The tears finally brim over.

Andrew stops his advance and his face looks pained by the sight of my tears. What does that mean? I feel like my legs are about to give out again.

Please just hold me, Andrew. I don't give a damn about what happened last week. I need you.

Then it hits me. Is he waiting for *my* permission?

Without another thought, I walk determinedly toward him, as fast as my weak legs will go. I fall into him, my arms around his waist, my head on his chest.

He holds me close, and I hear him exhale a long, shuttering breath. "My beautiful, Jules," he whispers, and I relax even further. I feel so weak, but I use every bit of strength I have for this homecoming. The hospital starts coming back to me in pieces, as I breathe him in.

I remember his arms around me when I woke up. I remember his smell. I remember him telling me he was sorry and that he loved me. I love him too, and I want to make sure he knows.

"I love you," I tell him, as I nuzzle further into his chest, his shirt now soaking wet from my tears.

"I'm so sorry, Jules. I'm so sorry about your mom."

Mom. I start crying harder, but it's not as bad as before. I think the initial shock has worn off now. I'm not fully ready to accept that she's gone, but I know it to be a truth now, whether I like it or not.

"It's okay," I say, and Andrew hugs me tighter. "I'm just so glad you're here."

Then some more of yesterday skims across my mind. "How did you know?" I ask him, lifting my head so I can see his face...his perfect face. He's wearing his glasses.

Andrew gives me a small smile, and kisses my cheek. "Let's go sit," he suggests. "Do you want something to drink? Something to eat?"

I nod as he walks me over to the sofa. "Something to drink would be nice." My mouth is horribly dry. I wish I had my toothbrush.

"Water? Coke? Whiskey?" he asks, as he plants me on the sofa. I don't want him to leave me.

He starts to take his hand out of mine, and I squeeze tight. *No.* I get back up off the sofa, and Andrew raises an eyebrow. "I want to be with you," I tell him, as I wipe the tears from my cheeks with my free hand.

Andrew smiles. "Of course," he says, pulling me into his chest again as we walk to the kitchen.

I decide on a Coke. The carbonation tastes good and helps to settle my stomach a bit.

Andrew and I are standing hand in hand in the middle of his kitchen while I drink my Coke. It should be awkward, but it's not. He's like a breath of fresh air, standing there in his jeans, gray t-shirt and glasses, looking every bit the gorgeous, passionate, preppy geek that he is.

My geek.

"Do you want to go back to the living room?" he asks "Or do you want me to make you something to eat?"

I look up at him. I'm definitely hungry, but nothing sounds good. I pull on his hand, leading him back toward the living room. I'm not ready to eat.

Andrew follows me, as I sit back down on the sofa with my tasty beverage. Andrew sits next to me, never letting go of my hand. Good. Let's keep it that way. I feel safe with his hand in mine.

"So, how did you know?" I ask him again, "About my mom...how did you know?"

Andrew gives me a shy smile. "Abby called me."

My eyes widen in shock. *What?* Does Abby know? I didn't talk to her. Did I?

"I believe your housekeeper, Bessie, called her yesterday while you were asleep," Andrew continues. "And then she called me."

That's weird. "Why would Bessie call Abby?" I ask Andrew, but I don't really expect him to have an answer.

I look at Andrew, and he looks embarrassed. "Abby said..." he pauses and clears his throat. "Abby said that you were asking for me in the hospital."

Oh. Well, okay.

Now I'm the embarrassed one, and I can feel the heat rise to my cheeks. I don't remember asking for him out loud, but I'm not surprised one bit that I did. Bessie must have called Abby to see who the heck Andrew was.

"Am I in trouble?" I ask, feeling guilty. I hope I haven't ruined our little secret.

Andrew furrows his brow. "Trouble?"

"I mean, I don't think Bessie or Abby will say anything to anyone." Oh God, have I blown this? "I can call them now to make sure."

Please don't be upset at me Andrew. I can't take it.

To my surprise, Andrew laughs. "Are you serious?"

I look at his smiling face, and I suddenly feel like I may explode if I don't have his lips on mine soon.

"I just needed you," I confess. "I knew you would be the one person that would help me get through this, and I was right."

Andrew raises his free hand to caress my cheek. "Beautiful girl," he whispers "I could care less who knows. I'm never letting you go again."

I can't resist his lips anymore. I reach up and put a hand on his cheek before I remove his glasses. There are those beautiful hazel eyes I've missed so much.

I lean to put his glasses on the coffee table, but I don't take my eyes off him. I barely have his glasses on the table before Andrew pulls me into his arms and his lips are on mine.

Oh God. It feels so good.

I wrap my arms around his neck. This is what I need. Him. All of him.

"I'm so sorry, Jules," he whispers again, as we kiss, his hands flat against my back, pulling me close.

"Stop it," I breathe. "I don't care. It doesn't matter."

And it doesn't. I couldn't care less about what happened last week. In hindsight, it was a stupid and rash decision on my part. I was using my head, not my heart. And the heart should always win.

Now, as he moves his mouth against mine, his love for me is unmistakable. I called out to him in my time of need, and somehow, he found me.

Andrew pulls away to look at my face. "I've missed you so much." His voice breaks at the end.

I move my arms from around his neck to either side of his face. "I've missed you too," I tell him. "But we're here now."

"I'm sorry I wasn't there sooner," he says.

"Where?"

"At the hospital." He looks down, but I pull his eyes back up to mine. Those eyes...those beautiful, beautiful eyes.

"How could you have known?"

"I nearly wrecked my car on the way to the hospital." He gives me a sad smile. "I couldn't get there fast enough."

I manage a chuckle. "Thank God you made it in one piece."

Andrew smiles briefly. "I was so afraid you wouldn't want me back," he admits, and there's so much pain and heartache in his expression that it brings yet another set of fresh tears for me.

Andrew starts frantically rubbing the tears from my face. "I can't watch you cry anymore, baby," he says. "Why are you crying?"

"Because..." I sniff. "Because I actually made you think I didn't want you anymore."

What a travesty. What a falsehood.

"Oh, Jules." Andrew pulls me close again, and I happily nuzzle into his chest. "I deserved it. I made you doubt me. I lost your trust. It was my fault. I was just so scared for you. I don't want you messed up in my crazy life."

I laugh. "Your life isn't the only one that's crazy."

"True, I guess." Andrew's chest shakes, as he laughs too.

I look back up at him, and I'm glad to see the pained face is gone. "I'm a big girl," I tell him, even though I'm certainly not at my strongest at the moment. "I can handle whatever happens, as long as I get to be with you."

Andrew puts a hand through my hair, which must look a huge mess.

"I promise to do everything in my power to make sure you never have to doubt me again," he says, before kissing me once more. The feel of his lips on mine is pure bliss. We kiss for a while longer, lost in each other, reconnecting.

"You have to be hungry," Andrew says eventually.

Hmmm...I'm hungry all right, but not for food.

I nod reluctantly, knowing it will probably make me feel better if I eat.

"I have stuff for sandwiches," he offers. "Or I have leftover Chinese from last night."

I smile. "A sandwich sounds good."

Andrew gets up to leave me, but I hold tight to his hand, and stand when he does. He's not getting away from me. No way.

He smiles down at me before kissing me softly on the lips. "Do you plan to hold on to me all night?" he asks and I smile again.

"If you don't mind."

"Nothing would please me more." He offers his other hand to me, and starts walking backwards toward the kitchen, pulling me along with him.

I can't believe how much better I feel – all because of Andrew. He looks adorable, pulling me toward the kitchen, a boyish grin on his face.

I feel bad for being momentarily happy, as an image of my mom comes bursting into my head, but I push it away. I've cried enough for now.

Andrew keeps hold of one of my hands as he gets the sandwich ingredients from the fridge. I help, but we still have to make a few trips, since I refuse to let him go.

He puts everything on the counter, and then looks at me before he starts. His face is puzzled.

"How do I do this?" he asks, and holds up our interlocked hands.

I smile but don't say a word. I'll let him figure it out.

He thinks for a moment before wrapping one of my arms around his waist, and then the other, so that I'm behind him, holding on tight.

"Don't let go," he says, and I lay my head on his back, as he starts making my sandwich.

He periodically reaches down and touches my hands or rubs my arm while he works. I close my eyes and practically melt into him. He's so warm, and that smell…I could breathe it in for hours and hours, days and days.

He finishes up my sandwich, and takes one of my hands back in his, as we walk over to his dining table.

Once again, we face the conundrum of me not letting him go while I eat, but he doesn't think long this time. He puts my plate on the table, sits and then pulls me onto his lap.

I smile widely at him. "Thank you for the sandwich."

"It's the least I can do," he says into my neck, as he wraps his arms around me. *Wow*. The sandwich is now the last thing on my mind.

I turn toward him, and pull his face to mine. He kisses me briefly – much shorter than what I had in mind – and then chuckles. "You should eat. You have to be hungry."

I give him a reluctant smile. "Fine," I huff, and turn toward my food.

I pick up my turkey sandwich on whole wheat and take a bite. It's actually delicious. I didn't realize how famished I was. I honestly can't remember the last time I ate something. Yesterday morning maybe? I'm still not entirely sure what day it is.

Andrew holds me as I eat, rubbing my back, my leg. His touch has me relaxing more and more by the minute.

"All done?" Andrew asks, as I finish the last bite. "Want something else?"

I shake my head and turn to wrap my arms around his neck. "How about a shower?"

"You can have whatever you want," he says, and my pulse quickens.

Once again, I feel guilty for feeling happy, but I push it aside. I don't want to think about that right now. I want to forget. I want Andrew to help me forget.

"How about you join me?" I ask before leaning in for a kiss.

Andrew smiles. "I was hoping you might say that."

Andrew lifts me easily in his arms, as he stands and carries me out of the kitchen toward his bedroom.

"Did you carry me through the hospital?" I ask, still remembering bits and pieces as they come to me.

"Yes." Andrew's face is sad. "I wanted you out of there."

"I wanted out of there, too," I admit. "Thank you."

"Anything for you," he says with a smile.

When we get to his bathroom, he places me gently on the floor and takes my hand. I smile. He's really not going to let me go. God, I love this man.

He pulls me over to the shower, and as I watch him start the water, something occurs to me.

"Where's my purse?" I ask. I'm sure I have a million missed calls.

Andrew turns back to me. "It's in the living room," he says. "Your phone is charging next to my computer. Abby said she'd handle letting people know. You've had several calls from your dad."

Ugh. My dad. I close my eyes and take a deep breath. I'm going to have to deal with that shit storm eventually, but not right now.

"Anyone else?" I ask, after I regain my composure.

"Someone named Nate has called a few times." Andrew clears his throat again and looks away from me. "Abby said she called him – even let him know where you were." He opens the small closet in his bathroom and starts fishing some towels out, still not looking at me. "But I guess he wants to make sure you're okay. I assume he's Mr. Leather Jacket from the other night?"

I nod, and look down at my feet. *Nate.* The thought of him makes me sad. He may have possibly saved me from the loony bin last week, and I will be eternally grateful, but he's not even a contender when Andrew's in the running.

I look back up and smile, as I tug on Andrew's hand. He stops his miscellaneous plundering in the closet, but still doesn't look at me.

"You should call him," he says, obviously still hurting over this.

I pull his face toward me so I can see his eyes. "I don't want to call him," I say confidently.

Andrew's face is sad again, anxious. "He's probably worried about you," he says. "There's nothing wrong with that."

"I don't want to call Nate. " I wrap my arms around his neck. "I don't want to call anyone. I just want you."

I reach up to kiss his sweet lips, and Andrew drops the towels in his hand to pull me against him. He pushes me into the wall, his hands roaming eagerly down my back.

"I want to be with you too," he breathes. "I've missed you so fucking much, Jules."

He hitches my legs up around him, and pulls me up, pressing me hard against the wall.

Yes. I want him. Every part of him. All of him. I want to forget about everything and get lost in my Andrew.

His kiss is desperate now, his mouth hungry, as it moves up and down my neck. I close my eyes and toss my head back, surrendering to him completely.

I can't believe I wasted the last week without him. I feel like my senses have been closed down since we've been apart and they're now reawakening. I can finally feel again.

Andrew releases my legs, and pulls his body away slightly, letting my feet fall slowly back to the floor. He drags his hands up my legs to the bottom of my t-shirt and slides it up. The touch of his bare hands on my skin is pure heaven, and he keeps going – up my sides, over my breasts.

Oh God, how I've missed him.

I lift my arms, and he pulls my shirt off. I quickly reach for his, eager to heal the ache inside.

Andrew is the only drug I'll ever need.

And I'm glad to see he seems to be just as addicted to me.

After a few minutes, all of our clothes are off, and we're moving into the shower. It feels like the warm water is washing away everything bad that happened between us. I can't deny it happened, but I can try to put it in the past and start fresh.

For what seems like hours, Andrew and I are all mouths and hands as we kiss and touch and reconnect with every inch of each other's bodies. By the time we finally move back toward the stone bench inside his shower, the water is running cold, a stark contrast to our overheated skin.

Andrew sits and quickly pulls me on top of him, as eager for this particular connection as I am. He groans into my neck, as I wrap my arms around him and slowly slide myself down. I pull him close, my fingers running lovingly through his wet hair.

"Andrew," I whisper his name, and he lifts his head to look at me. His eyes are dark, fervent and reeking with desire. I still on top of him to catch my breath. He's just so beautiful.

Andrew takes that opportunity to lift me once again. I keep my legs and arms around him, as he walks out of the cold water, kneels and lowers me slowly onto one of the several plush rugs on his bathroom floor.

"I love you, beautiful girl," he whispers into my ear, and takes me immediately back to the place I need to be – clinging to him, loving him – unhurried and blissful.

I never want to leave.

CHAPTER 42

"What time is it anyway?" I ask, as Andrew and I lay in the bed, wrapped around each other.

I'm showered, loved and feeling surprisingly content for now, back in Andrew's boxers and one of his t-shirts. Andrew's lying next to me, in nothing but black, cotton pajama pants – sexy as hell.

"It's a little after ten," he says. He sounds so sleepy.

"What day is it?" I chuckle.

"It's Tuesday."

Has it already been over twenty-four hours since I found her? I'm going to have to face this again soon…but not now. Not right now.

"Did you work today?" I ask. I know I may be jobless, but Andrew still has a company to run.

"From home," he tells me, stroking my cheek with his fingertips. "I couldn't leave you."

I snuggle into him. "Thanks for taking care of me."

"I wanted to," he says. "I wouldn't have it any other way. I'm just sorry I wasn't there sooner. If I would have known…"

"How could you have known?" I ask, and I feel him tense beneath me. I raise my head to look at him. "What's the matter?"

He closes his eyes and takes a deep breath. What did I say?

"If I wouldn't have been such an ass…" he starts, and I try to interrupt, but he stops me. "If I would have treated you like you should have been treated from the start, I would have been there."

Why is he so hell bent on apologizing still? I told him to forget it.

"We should have never kept our relationship a secret," he says quietly as he runs his fingertips down my back. "I should never have done that to you. It didn't feel right in the beginning. I should have known."

"Andrew," I sigh. "It's over. It doesn't matter now."

Andrew stares into my eyes as if trying to pull the truth from them.

That is the truth, Andrew. I love you, and I never want to be apart, ever again.

I meet his stare, willing him to believe me. Eventually, his eyes soften, and he pulls my face to his. I gladly accept his lips on mine before sinking back onto his chest.

We sit for a moment in silence. I feel Andrew's breathing start to even out, and I assume he's gone to sleep, so his voice startles me.

"Do you want to talk about your mom?" he asks quietly.

Mom. I feel the empty feeling start to spread slowly through my chest.

"If you're not ready, I understand," he adds. "But I wanted you to know that I'm here for you. The situations were very different, but I've been through it. I just want to help you in any way that I can."

I wrap my arm tightly around his waist. Do I want to talk about what happened? Can I?

The tears come before I even say a word, and Andrew pulls me close against him. "I'm sorry I brought it up. I just thought…"

"It's okay," I say quickly, so he doesn't feel bad. "I just can't believe it."

"I know," he says soothingly. "I'm so sorry, Jules."

"I can't believe I couldn't save her," I admit. "Believe it or not, that never occurred to me. I brought her back so many times. I got over confident."

"Jules, she had to want to help herself. It was never your responsibility."

For some reason, this stings.

"She needed support, Andrew. She needed help," I snap back. "My dad certainly wasn't around to provide it. That left me."

Andrew sits up quickly, and looks down at me.

"No, baby. I'm sorry. I didn't mean to upset you." He wipes some of the tears from my face. "I just don't want you to try and take this on. This was not your fault."

I'm crying hard now into his pillow. Doesn't your body eventually run out of tears?

Andrew pulls me up and onto his lap. "Shhh," he whispers as he kisses my forehead. "I'm sorry for bringing it up. I really ruined our moment, didn't I?"

I laugh. I can't help myself.

"That would be a yes," I say, and Andrew pulls me tighter against him. I wrap my arms around him and bury my wet face in his neck. "I should have been there. I could have stopped her. I knew all the tricks. I used to hide her stashes. I could have saved her, Andrew. I could have."

Andrew doesn't say anything this time. He just rocks me in his lap to soothe me. I don't know what I would do if he wasn't here with me. The thought makes me shudder.

"It's okay, baby," Andrew says, and I eventually start to settle down.

My mother dying is pulling at the only thing inside me that keeps me grounded – the one thing in my life that I pride myself on. I take care of people, and I'm damn good at my job, but I failed her.

After all of these years of bringing her back from the dead, I couldn't do it this time. I couldn't save her.

I cry harder into Andrew's neck, as he continues to try and soothe me – holding me, rocking me, loving me.

Andrew holds me until I finally cry it out, at least for now. Eventually, I wipe my face with my hand and raise my head to look at him. He smiles at me, but he looks horribly tired. I suddenly feel so guilty.

"You need some sleep," I tell him, and kiss him on the cheek.

"Please don't worry about me," he says, still smiling. "I'm fine."

"I know you're *fine*." I wink at him, and he smiles wider. "But you need some sleep."

As if on cue, Andrew yawns. I crawl out of his lap, and push him gently down on the bed.

"Turn over," I tell him, and he obliges, sprawling out on his tummy next to me.

I lie on my side and prop myself up on my elbow. I use my free hand to start slowly scratching his back.

"Mmmm..." Andrew closes his eyes and moans softly. "I've missed you so much."

"You only want me for my back scratches," I tease, and he opens his eyes.

"I want *you*." He smiles. "The back scratches are just a bonus."

I smile back. "Go to sleep."

He closes his eyes again, and he's asleep within minutes. I look at the clock. It's almost eleven.

I get out of bed, and walk into the living room to get my phone. It's charging by Andrew's computer, just like he said.

I take it off the charger, and dial, disregarding the million missed calls, messages and texts.

"Jules? For fuck's sake! Are you okay?"

"Not really," I tell Abby, "but I'm a little better thanks to you."

"You're a shitty liar," Abby says. "I'm still not sure he deserves you, but I wanted you to have whatever you wanted. I'm so sorry, Jules."

Her voice breaks, which starts some new tears on my end. "It's okay. I'm sorry I waited so late to call."

"It's understandable." Abby's definitely crying now. "Is there anything I can do?"

"I don't think so," I tell her. "Not right now. I'll talk to you more about everything later. I just wanted to hear your voice."

"I'm glad you called," she chokes. "I miss you, love you."

"Miss you, love you too," I say, choking through my own tears. I sit for a second and catch my breath. "Actually, Abby, there is one thing."

"Anything," she says.

"Have you spoken to Nate? Will you tell him I said thanks for checking up on me, and I'll call him later?"

"Sure," she says. "I've already spoken to him a couple of times. He's worried about you."

"I know." I smile through my tears. "He's a great friend."

"He's a good guy," Abby agrees. "Will you be home tomorrow?"

"Not sure," I sigh. "I may come home in the morning. I don't have any clothes here." Then something hits me. "Are you at home? What are you doing home?"

"Yeah," she says, "I took tonight off. I wasn't sure if you would need me or not."

I smile. "Thanks again Abby, for everything. I love you."

"I love you too, Jules. I'm here for you whenever you need me."

"I know," I assure her. "I'll see you soon."

I hang up and feel a little better after getting at least one phone call out of the way. I can't call anyone else tonight, since it's already kind of late, but I'm not tired at all. It probably has something to do with the fact that I've basically been asleep for the past twenty-four hours.

I stroll into Andrew's kitchen, and look around in his cabinets. I find some Chamomile tea, which sounds fabulous.

I fill a mug with water and put it in his space-age microwave – it takes me about five minutes to figure out how to heat up my water – and once it's done, I add my tea bag. I shuffle around again in his cabinets until I find some honey, and I have to look through every drawer in his kitchen for a spoon, but I eventually find one.

I take my hot tea out into Andrew's sunroom, and sit on the sofa. The view is amazing. There are no lights on out here, but the room is well lit by the reflection of the moon shining off the pond in his backyard. It's incredible. I wish I had my camera.

I sip on my tea, and take a moment to contemplate everything that's happened over the past couple of weeks.

I smile as I realize I finally have my Andrew back. What happened between him and Bitchface doesn't matter to me anymore. Maybe it should, but it doesn't. It seems insignificant, compared to what happened with my mom.

And I love him. I love him with everything that I am. It's a certainty that feels so good to hold on to, particularly right now. He's like the one string left, tethering me to the ground.

I feel awful as I realize I haven't asked Andrew about his life. I wonder what the latest is with his job. He's still not getting any sleep, so I'll assume nothing's changed. I'll have to make sure to ask him tomorrow, see if there's anything I can do to help.

And just like that, my mind drifts back to my mom. A funeral. How does one plan a funeral? I have no idea. I start tearing up again thinking about it. My mom barely has any friends. Everyone that shows up to her funeral will be friends of my dad's.

My *dad*.

I frown as I remember slapping him across his face. Honestly, he deserved it, but he's still my father, and I'm still his child. I remember him crying over my mom. That surprised me. I didn't think he cared at all. I guess I was wrong.

I pick up my phone from the coffee table in front of me, and type a quick text to my dad.

> *Just wanted to let you know I'm okay. Will call you tomorrow.*

That's about as sympathetic as I'm capable of right now. I'll call him tomorrow so we can deal with her funeral.

I put my empty tea cup and my phone on the coffee table, and lie back on the sofa. There's a blanket over the back, so I pull it over me, and look out at the beautiful pond. I have no intentions of falling asleep, but before I know it, my eyes are closed, and I'm out.

What feels like only seconds later, I hear Andrew's voice. At first, I think I'm dreaming, but I start slowly coming to, as he puts his arms around me and lifts me from the sofa.

"Come on, baby."

He's carrying me again, just like he did in the hospital. I wrap my arms around his neck, and breathe him in.

"Mmmm...I like it when you call me *baby*," I tell him.

"Do you now?" he asks softly, and I smile against his neck. "I love you, *baby*."

"I love you too," I whisper, as Andrew lies me down on his bed.

He crawls in behind me, putting his arm around my waist, nuzzling his face into my hair. "I missed you," he whispers. "You promised you wouldn't let go of me the entire day."

I turn in his arms to face him. "You needed some sleep."

"I need you more," he says, and the next thing I know, his lips are on mine, and I'm lost in him again, never wanting to be found.

CHAPTER 43

Andrew's voice wakes me again, but it's not close this time. It sounds far away, muffled.

I open my eyes. I'm in his bedroom, and he's not here.

I look over at the clock. It's a little after eight in the morning. Andrew's pulled the curtains in his room, so it's dark. I can't believe I slept another eight hours!

I smile as I stretch in Andrew's bed. I did have one very pleasant interruption last night, but still.

I move to get out of the bed, and find Andrew's boxers and t-shirt I had on last night still lying in a pile on the floor – exactly where Andrew threw them after ripping them off of me. Still smiling, I put them back on and make my way toward the sound of Andrew's voice.

As I reach the bedroom door, his voice becomes clearer and I can start to make out more of the conversation. I listen for a moment, to make sure I won't be interrupting anything if I walk out of the room.

"But sir, I thought we had agreed..." I hear him say, panic in his voice. "I understand sir, but I thought this was a done deal. I just don't....yes sir...Thank you for your time."

Then there's silence. What's happened *now*?

I open the door to find Andrew sitting in front of his computer, elbows on his desk, head in his hands. As I watch him, he takes his glasses off, and flings them sideways across the room.

His back is to me, so I wait a moment, deciding whether or not to bother him, but I can't resist the urge to try and comfort him, to try and help him.

I walk slowly toward him, and he turns when he hears me approaching. He offers me a sad smile.

"I'm so sorry if I woke you," he says.

I slide onto his lap when I reach him, and he quickly wraps his arms around me. I put my arms around his neck, and hug him close.

"What happened?" I ask, but I'm pretty sure I already know the answer.

Andrew sighs deeply and doesn't answer immediately. Instead, he presses his cheek against my shoulder and holds me.

"It's over," he says finally. "He wins. I'm done."

I pull away, but keep my arms around his neck. "What do you mean? New York fell through?"

Andrew sighs again. "It's over."

"What about Victoria? She turned on you?"

He looks up at me. "I turned on her," he says. "I came clean with my dad the day you caught us together."

Wait. *What?*

I'm shocked into silence, staring at Andrew with wide eyes. He lifts me easily and carries me once again over to the sofa. He sits me down, and takes his place beside me, pulling my legs onto his lap.

Andrew's looking at me, waiting for me to ask questions, but I don't even know where to start. "Ummm...so, you told...?" It's all I can manage.

Andrew nods, takes a deep breath, and starts.

"The day you left, I told my dad what I knew. I told him what I was doing with Victoria."

I hold up my hand. "Wait, you told your dad you were pretending with Victoria to spy on him...in front of *her*?"

"Yes, and he fired her."

I sit up straight and pull my legs from Andrew's lap. "What?" I ask, in disbelief. "He fired her?"

Andrew shrugs. "I guess his ego was a little bruised. She was using him, just like I was using her."

"He had no idea?" Surely he knew a girl like that wouldn't really want him for anything other than his money.

"I guess not," Andrew says, seeming just as shocked as I am.

"Go on," I say, eager now to hear more.

"Well, I asked him why he was fighting me. I already knew the answer, but I wanted to give him a chance to admit to it." Andrew shakes his head. "He denied everything, of course, but I wasn't willing to give in this time."

I feel my chest tighten as Andrew looks down at his hands clenched into fists in his lap.

"When you told me about Nevada," he continues, "that's when I knew for sure what was going on. I should have thought of it before, but I guess I hoped he'd keep his promise when he told us he quit." Andrew runs a hand through his hair. "I did some research before I even spoke with my dad, so I already knew about the trouble he was in. It only took a couple of calls, once I figured him out."

I stare at him confused. "What kind of trouble?"

"My dad used to have a bit of a gambling problem. That's *our* deep, dark family secret," Andrew confesses, and I quickly nod in understanding so he'll continue. "It's never been out of control, really – never big money, until now."

"*Until now?*" I repeat, still in shock.

Andrew sighs deeply again. "I didn't know he'd been going to Nevada, or Las Vegas, if we're being honest. He'd lied to me about his trips. So, I confronted him. Told him everything I know – the amount of his debts, the people involved, even how he's been using company money to front his bets – and do you know what he said to me?"

I shake my head, unable to speak.

"He said he couldn't believe I'd turn on him like this – his own son. He said after everything he's done for me, he couldn't believe this is how I would repay him." Andrew takes a deep shuddering breath. "He said I was no better than my ungrateful mother. Bastard."

Oh, Andrew. Your dad may be worse than mine.

I grab one of Andrew's hands from his lap, smooth out the fist, and interlock his fingers with mine. He looks at our hands together a moment before continuing.

"He told me..." he trails off, and I use my free hand to pull his face up so he'll look at me. "He told me that my mom ruined me," he says, his eyes sadder than ever. "He said he tried to make me strong, but she babied me too much. And then I said something awful." He shakes his head as he relives the memory.

"What did you say?" I ask when he doesn't continue after a few beats.

"I tried to keep it professional at first, but then all of the years of disapproval and hurt got in the way. I ended up telling him he was a horrible father and he was just pissed because...because she loved me more."

Andrew looks at me, eyes tight, as if he's afraid I may think less of him for this comment. I give him a half smile. I've said a million times worse to my dad. Andrew has nothing to worry about.

He continues to stare at me, waiting for a response, so I decide to appease him.

"Andrew, I told my dad to fuck off multiple times the other day when everything was going down with my mom, and if I remember correctly, I even slapped him. Hard. Across his face." I smile at him. "I'm not sure your comment to your father is really that detrimental."

Andrew tries a smile too, but it falls short. He's so upset about this, and with reason. He's worked so hard.

"So," I continue. "What did your dad say after that?"

"Actually, he laughed," Andrew tells me, his smile gone. "But I could tell I hurt him. Because it's the truth, and he knows it. That's why he fights me. He's been fighting me for her attention my whole life. I guess he really did love her, in his own sick, twisted way." Andrew pauses, and I squeeze his hand in mine. "If he would've just tried being nice to us," he says. "If he would've tried a little TLC, instead of trying to mold everything to fit his standards, things may have been different. But that's the way it's always been. And the worst part is that no matter how much of a dick he is, I always wanted his approval. I still do."

Andrew lays his head back on the sofa and closes his eyes.

"He's your father, Andrew," I'm quick to explain. "That's totally understandable."

Andrew rolls his head to the side and opens his eyes to look at me. "But he's a shitty one, Jules. And now he's beat me. It's over."

"What happened exactly?"

Andrew sighs again. "Honestly, I have no idea, but suddenly the guys in New York aren't interested. I have no doubt my father's involved." He looks at me and pauses before continuing. "He's trying to sell the company to this slime he's working with out in Nevada, if you can believe it. It seems corporate buyouts are one of the several shady businesses they run. I'm certain my dad's selling at a rock bottom price, just to get his ass out of this jam, hence the reason he's so against my efforts to make the company profitable again. And the worst part is that he has our advisory board convinced selling is the best option, discouraging my ideas left and right, which I didn't know until recently. I could maybe convince some of them to change their minds, but not all. A lot of those guys have been with my dad since the beginning. And he doesn't need a unanimous vote to sell, just a majority."

I pause to process this information for a moment. I can't believe Andrew doesn't have more say than this.

"You don't have any stake in the company?" I ask. Surely Andrew must be invested somehow.

"Not enough." He shakes his head. "We're a private company and family owned. When my mom died, her shares had to be offered back up to the company. Of course my father managed to buy the majority, so unless I plan to kill him – which I may or may not have thought about this morning – he's the boss."

"But if you had an investor," I start, eager to find a way around all of this, "If you had someone interested in your re-design of the company, someone who had the money, maybe you could make the advisory board listen?"

"I guess there's always a possibility, but I can't seem to make anything happen without my father intervening. I've exhausted every possibility," Andrew reluctantly admits. "I don't think there's any hope at this point. He's going to sell, and there's nothing I can do about it."

I smile, cooking up a plan. "What if I have an investor in mind – someone your dad would never suspect?"

Andrew sits up and furrows his brow at me. "What are you getting at?"

I lean in and give him a quick kiss on the lips. "I've got an idea." I smile, before jumping up and heading to Andrew's room to get dressed.

Andrew stands up quickly and follows me. "Do you know something I don't?" he asks.

"Not yet," I say, as we reach his bedroom. I find my clothes from the other day, and start changing into them. "But there has to be a way to convince the advisory board, Andrew. No offense, but your father's not that likable of a guy."

"None taken," Andrew scoffs and sits on the side of his bed while I quickly get dressed.

"I don't have everything worked out, right now," I tell him as I finish pulling my jeans on, "but I'll call you later this afternoon."

"Can't I come with you?" he asks. I turn to look at him, and he's pouting like a little boy. Man, that's adorable.

I smile and walk over to him. I push between his legs, and put my hands on either side of his face. "No," I say, "but I'll call you as soon as I can."

Andrew wraps his arms around my waist and pulls me close. "Will you at least tell me where you're going? I'm not sure I'm comfortable with you leaving me." He smiles.

I smile back. "I'm not comfortable with leaving you either, but I have to face this one alone."

"Where are you going?" Andrew looks at me, puzzled, and I sigh.

"I have to go see my dad."

CHAPTER 44

I pull up to my dad's ivory tower around ten thirty and take a few deep breaths before I get out of my car. I didn't call before I came, but I know he'll be here. The Apocalypse wouldn't stop my dad from coming to work.

I get out of my car and tug at my clothes. I'm in the same jeans and t-shirt he last saw me in on Monday when I found my mom. The memory momentarily takes my breath away. I stop and steady myself at my car before I start walking slowly to the lobby. I move toward the elevators, and press the button for the thirty-third floor.

I try a pep talk on my way up, but it's no use. This isn't going to be an easy meeting. I just have to keep it professional, focusing at the moment on my love for Andrew and forgetting about the rest. I take a deep breath in and out, as the elevator opens into the lobby of my dad's office.

Rebecca is sitting at her usual perch at reception. She stands and walks around the desk when she sees me, and I instantly panic. Is she coming to hug me? I clasp my hands together in front of me. I'm afraid I may haul off and hit her if she touches me.

Lucky for her, she stops a foot or two away.

"Oh, Jules, I am so sorry," she says. Her face looks sincere, but I'm not fazed. I don't even smile at her.

"Is my dad in?" I ask blandly.

"Of course." She gives me a head tilt, like she's trying to express her deepest sympathy for what's happened. I tighten the grip on my hands. "He's with someone. I'll let him know you're here."

I turn and take a seat on one of the leather sofas in the ridiculously posh lobby. I keep my fingers interlocked. My knuckles are white at this point.

I want to hit that woman.

So very much.

I'm only seated a minute or two before two men exit my father's office. "I'll have Rebecca set something back up for us this afternoon," my dad says, trailing behind them into the lobby.

They all shake hands, and my dad sneaks a glance over at me.

"Hi sweetheart." My dad gives me the same sympathetic head tilt that I just received from Rebecca.

I stand, not saying a word, and walk into his office.

I sit down in one of the chairs in front of my father's desk, and he follows shortly behind me, after I hear him tell Rebecca to hold his calls.

"I wasn't expecting you," he says, as he takes the seat next to me, rather than behind his desk.

This throws me off guard. It's too personal. I would prefer him to be in corporate attorney mode, rather than dad mode right now. It would make things easier.

"I guess we have some things to discuss," I start. "I'm sorry I've been kind of M.I.A."

"It's understandable," he says, smiling a sad smile at me. "But I have all of the funeral arrangements in the works, according to your mother's will." He's so business-like about it. It's making me edgy. "She wanted to be cremated, but we're having a memorial for her at our church on Friday, then a reception at our house."

"She requested a memorial?" I ask, knowing my mom would have never wanted this.

"Well, no," my dad says, looking down at his lap. "But it's the proper thing to do."

I roll my eyes. "You just want the sympathy votes, and an excuse to mingle with your rich friends. Mom never would have wanted this."

My dad stands and moves behind his desk. *Thank you.* Much better.

"Jules," he says my name sternly, like only a father can. I roll my eyes again. *Puh-lease.* "I know what you think of me, but contrary to what you believe, I loved your mother."

Oh? That's news.

I stare impassively at him, as he continues. "There were many times we thought about separating, but she was always so unstable, and we didn't want you to be a part of a broken home."

"Seriously?" I roll my eyes one more time for good measure. "She let you get away with whatever you wanted to get away with. It was like having your cake and eating it to."

"Jules..." My dad sighs and runs his hands through what little hair he has left. "I loved your mother," he says softly. "When we first met, she was so vibrant and full of life. She loved to have a good time." I watch as he smiles fondly at the memory, and my heart aches for my mom. "I know I did wrong by her."

"Understatement of the century," I seethe.

"I know," my dad looks tired, but I don't really care. This is his fault. "And I know I'll never be able to make it right – not with her, or with you. I just wanted you to know that I did love her, and the past couple of days haven't been easy for me either."

That's it. Now I'm pissed.

I stand up. I have to pace. I can't sit still. I'm too unnerved.

"What good does it do now for you to tell me you loved her?" I ask, as I start making a path in the carpet. "You could have helped her. You could have stayed by her side through all of this. But you didn't. You just decided to sleep with half the population of Atlanta so you wouldn't have to deal with her."

I stop my pacing and go back over to his desk to face him.

"And you're right. I will never forgive you," I hiss through my teeth. "I will never forgive you for not being a better husband or a better father. You've had years...*years* to try and make things right, and yet you decided that work and your temporary sluts would be a better option."

My dad stands now, and I take a step back. His face is red from anger, his eyes fuming. I've never seen him like this.

He walks slowly over to me, and his look alone makes me instinctively cower into my seat.

"Now you listen to me," he says softly, menacingly. "I may not have been the best father or husband, but I will not sit here and have you speak to me that way. Do you understand?"

I roll my eyes again, and look down at my hands.

In a surprise move, my dad grabs my chin and lifts my face to his. "Do you understand?" he repeats.

I push his hand away and stand up to meet him. "Don't you ever fucking touch me again. I'm twenty-four years old. I don't have to listen to a damn thing you say. I don't have to respect you. I don't want anything from you. You've never been a father to me. So don't think you can start now."

My father stares at me, and I watch as his anger subsides, and he falls into the chair next to me. He puts his head in his hands, and to my utter astonishment, he starts to cry.

My heart is still pounding from my recent outburst, but I sit back down in my chair, and stare at him. I don't know what to say.

"I was the best father I knew how to be," he finally says, his voice choked with tears. "I'm so sorry, Jules."

I feel the tears surface then start falling quickly down my face. I sit and stare at my normally larger than life father, now crying like a baby in a chair in his office. Maybe he did love her. Maybe this has shaken him more than I ever would have thought.

Either way, I can't forgive him. Not yet. I know he wasn't wholly responsible for what happened with Mom, but he wasn't any help either.

I reach for one of his hands, still pressed against his face. He releases it to me, but doesn't look up.

"Dad," I say softly, my voice rough from my own tears. "Look, things have been wrong between us for so long. I can't forgive you. Not in a day." I sigh, and wipe some tears away from my face with my free hand. "But maybe we can try a different road. Only time will tell."

My dad looks up at me, and pulls his hand from mine to wipe his face. "I'll take that," he says, looking at me with a sad smile. "I'll take whatever I can get. You're all I have left, Jules."

I close my eyes and breathe in, as that realization hits home. Mom is gone. It's just the two of us, now.

My dad grabs my hands, and I open my eyes.

"Jules, I'll do whatever it takes to make things right between us. I want to try," he pleads. "I know I don't deserve it." He shakes his head. "Believe me, I know. But I'll do whatever you want. If you want me to skip the memorial for your mom, I'll do it. I just wanted her to have a sendoff of some kind. I felt like she deserved at least that from me. I wanted to do something. I'll never be able to make it up to her, Jules. I'll never have that chance."

Dammit, Dad. You're breaking my heart here.

"But she wouldn't have wanted a memorial," I tell him. "She would hate a big fuss over her. It should just be the two of us." I know where she would want her ashes scattered, and so does my dad. "Have her cremated, and I'll go with you to take the ashes."

"You will?" My dad looks shocked. "You want me there?"

I manage a smile. "No, but she would have."

"Work in progress."

"*Slow* progress."

My dad gives me a small smile. "If it takes the rest of my life, so be it."

"Careful what you wish for."

My dad continues to smile as he stands up, reaches into one of his desk drawers and withdraws a box of Kleenex. He passes a few to me, before taking a couple for himself.

"So, when do you want to go to St. Simons?" he asks. "This weekend? Next?"

I blink, suddenly remembering the other reason for my visit today. "Soon, but I actually have something else to talk to you about."

My dad looks up at me from behind his desk again now. "Okay. What's up?"

"Well," I sit back in my chair and cross my legs. "You can consider this part one in the multi-part plan to fix things between us."

"I'm listening." Dad's back in business mode now, which makes me happy. This will make things easier.

"I've never asked you for anything in my adult life, and I'm sure I don't have to explain my reasons for that." He shrugs and nods, and I continue. "But right now, I need your help."

"My help?" My dad looks incredulous, and I sigh.

Yes, I realize me asking you for help is a foreign concept, but humor me, please?

"I have a friend that's in trouble, and I want you to help him."

"And how would I do that?"

Here goes nothing.

I launch into the story about Andrew, the company and Mercer Senior. I tell him all about what's going on, Andrew's ideas for redesigning, his dad stopping his efforts at every turn and now his dad holding his power over Andrew's head so he can sell the company.

I then launch into my currently not-well planned out plan.

My dad doesn't look as shocked as I expected. He stares at me a moment, a hand on his chin, like he's contemplating the idea.

"This isn't typically my area, Jules."

"I know," I admit, but don't say anything further, as he continues to ponder my idea.

I just sit and wait for him to respond, letting my proposal sink in.

"How much money are we talking here, exactly?"

I smile at my dad. He's actually considering this!

"I don't have that with me," I tell him. "But I can get everything together for you, no problem."

My dad's lips form a hard line when we start talking about money. "Get back to me with a figure, and I'll see what I can do."

I smile widely, and for the first time in a long time, I rush to my father's side to hug him. I try to release him immediately, but he tightens his hold.

"I'm sorry, Jules," he whispers, and I can feel the tears forming again in my eyes.

"I know," I assure him. "Just give me time, Dad."

He releases me, and stands. "Just call me with a number," he smiles.

"Thanks." I hug him quickly once again before heading toward the door. "Mind if I tell Rebecca to go to hell?" I ask with a straight face before I open his office door.

My dad looks uncomfortable. "I would prefer you not."

I shrug and smile. "I'll call you later."

"Bye sweetheart." I walk out of my dad's office, and Rebecca is ready and waiting.

"Everything okay?" she asks, with that same stupid, sympathetic smile on her face.

Higher road, Jules. Take the higher road.

"Go to hell, Rebecca," I say with a smile, and turn from her open-mouthed stare to walk toward the elevators.

Seems the higher road's just not for me.

CHAPTER 45

As soon as I'm in my car, I get out my phone to call the one person I hope can help me.

"Hey Jules!" Adrian says. "Long time, no talk!"

"Hey Adrian." I smile. "I'm sorry I haven't called."

"It's okay. I figured you've probably been busy. What's going on?"

"Is it too early for you to meet me for lunch?"

"Nope. Mr. Mercer's not here, so I can go any time," she tells me. "I've been taking over some of your stuff since you left," she explains.

"Damn. Sorry Adrian. I didn't think about the fact that you'd probably be the one to bear that burden."

"No worries," she says happily. "Mr. Mercer's been locked in his office for the most part since you've left, if he even comes in. Jules, I have to tell you something about the day you left."

I smile into the phone. "I know."

"What do you mean?"

"If you're talking about Victoria getting fired, and Andrew fighting with his dad, I already know," I explain.

"How did you know?" Adrian sounds shocked.

"Lots to tell," I tease. "Meet me in 15 minutes at Rose's?"

"I'll be there," she says excitedly, and hangs up.

I decide to message Andrew before I leave.

Just wanted to say I love you. So much to tell you. Will call you soon.

I start my car, and before I can even reverse out of my space, I get a message back from Andrew.

Love you too. Dying to hear. Miss you.

I smile, pull out of my space, and head to meet Adrian.
"Hi Jules!" She waves excitedly as I get out of my car.
"Hi Adrian," I say, giving her a hug before we go inside. "How have you been?"
"Not bad." She smiles. "How about you?"
I sigh. "I've been better." I'm not sure I want to launch into my problems quite yet, so I keep quiet for now.
We quickly find a table, and then place our orders.
"So, did you need to chat about something specific?" she asks.
"I thought maybe you wanted to check up on Mr. Mercer, but I'm assuming that's not the case since you said you already knew about last week."
Adrian looks happy for me, likes this means Andrew and I are back together. I smile. I'm happy for me too.
"Andrew told me all about it," I confess, and Adrian grins wider. "We kind of made up."
"I thought so," she says. "It was only a matter of time. He's crazy about you."
"Do you really think you're the only one that knows?"
"I think so," she nods. "Like I said, I prefer to listen. It's amazing what you'll learn."

"That's actually what I need to talk to you about…" I start, and then launch once again into everything I know about what's going on with the company, but I leave out the part about Mercer Senior's gambling problem for now.

I'm not surprised that Adrian already has the majority figured out. She's been with the company long enough to have a wealth of useful information, and she gladly agrees to help our cause.

"Mercer Senior can't get away with this. I'm happy to know Mr. Mercer is willing to fight. It would be a shame if he had to sell. He's worked so hard to keep things going."

I smile. "I'm not sure yet if this will work, but we'll see."

"Great," she says smiling. "Mr. Mercer would be able to turn things around."

"I know he would," I agree, "and I'm hoping he may have the chance."

Adrian and I finish our lunches, and then spend some time talking about her and her new man, Leonard. Apparently, they are everything short of an engagement ring, which a new, beautifully confident Adrian says she expects by Christmas.

Despite everything that's happened with my mom, I find myself in a pretty good place as I drive back to Andrew's house. And I don't feel guilty for that happiness. Unlike my dad, I did everything I could to help my mom. Andrew's right.

She had to want to help herself, and that's the one thing I could never do for her.

I will miss her terribly, and I'm sure there are many more tears to come, but I hope that wherever she is now, she's healthy, happy and carefree, like my dad said she used to be when he first met her. I wish I would have known her then.

I pull into Andrew's driveway, and hop out, excited but nervous to tell him my news. I want to talk to him before I called my dad to make sure he's okay with my plans.

Andrew must have heard me pull up. He opens the front door, as I'm walking toward the steps.

He grins as walks toward me, and then takes me in his arms and kisses me hard. I melt into him. I've missed him so much over the past week. It may take a lifetime to make up for it. I smile onto his lips at the thought.

"Something funny?" he asks, pulling away, but not letting me go.

"No," I say, still grinning like a lovesick schoolgirl. "Just happy to see you."

"The feeling is mutual, beautiful girl."

I reach up to kiss him one more time, before he takes my hand and leads me inside.

He's showered, wearing army green cargo shorts, a white v-neck t shirt and that's it. Damn, my man is fine.

"Hungry? Thirsty?" he asks, as he pulls me into the kitchen. It looks like he was in the process of making himself a Coke on ice when I pulled up.

"No, I'm good."

"So," he turns to me, and takes a sip of his drink. "I've been dying over here. What have you been up to?"

I bite my lip nervously, and pull him toward his living room. What if he gets mad at me for meddling?

He sits on the edge of the sofa, so I sit on the edge too, and turn toward him.

"I went to my dad's office to talk to him," I start.

Andrew looks sad, and takes one of my hands in his. "Are you okay?"

"I'm fine." I smile, and lean to kiss him on his cheek. "We actually had one of the best chats we've had...well, probably ever."

"That's good to hear," Andrew says, smiling back at me.

Here comes the good stuff. I hope he doesn't freak out. I can't lose him again.

Breathe, Jules. Breathe!

"We talked a little about my mom, but I sort of talked to him about you as well," I say, and carefully watch Andrew's expression.

He clears his throat. "About *us*?" he gestures to the two of us with his free hand. "What did you tell him?"

I smile. "Are you scared of my dad, Andrew?" I tease. "I'm a big girl. I hardly need his approval. Besides, that's not what I meant."

"Oh," Andrew visibly relaxes. I have to stifle a giggle. "What did you mean then?"

"I spoke to him about what's going on in your company." I take a deep breath. "I asked him if he would help you."

Andrew lets go of my hand and leans back into the sofa. "Okay," he says, clearing his throat again.

Dammit! I knew I went too far. I was just trying to help!

"Andrew, I'm sorry," I say quickly. "Have I overstepped my boundaries?"

Andrew stares straight ahead. "What did you tell him exactly?"

I swallow hard before I begin. "I told him everything," I admit.

Andrew's eyes sling quickly in my direction. "You did what?"

"Andrew, I know you love your father, but you can't let him take this company from you. You've worked too hard, and it's not fair," I explain.

Andrew sighs and leans his head back on the sofa. "What did your dad say?"

"He said he'd think about my proposal. I have to get back to him with some figures."

"I assume you need some help from me?" he asks, seeming kind of impressed with me now, but I could be mistaken.

I nod. "I also had lunch with Adrian today. She's willing to help any way she can. She has some pretty incriminating evidence against your dad, if we have to go there."

"You told her everything too?"

"Not everything," I quickly amend. "I didn't tell her anything about your dad's...situation."

Andrew looks away from me again, and runs his hands through his hair. He's silent for a while, and I don't say a word, terrified I've gone too far.

"It's just an option," I finally say. "You don't have to do it. I know going up against your father like this is not what you had in mind. I was just trying to help."

Please don't be mad at me, Andrew. I just want you to have this. I want you to have everything.

Andrew looks over at me, quickly. "Do you think I'm mad at you?" he asks, eyes wide with shock.

"Well, yes...maybe?" I admit.

Andrew leans up and grabs my face. "I'm so far from mad at you right now," he says, looking deep into my eyes. They're smoldering. *Oh my goodness.*

"Y-You're not mad?" I stutter, as my body responds in usual fashion to his heated gaze.

"Jules," he breathes my name, before pulling me onto his lap. "You may have just saved my life."

My smile is wide. "I did good?"

"You're incredible," he smiles back, and I lean down to kiss him.

Andrew wraps his arms around my waist and leans up so we're nose to nose. "I can't believe you did this for me," he whispers, breathless from our kiss.

I tilt my head and smile at him. "I'd do anything for you."

Andrew kisses me again and then lays his forehead against mine. "I know he's an ass, but I don't want anything bad to happen to my dad," Andrew admits, and the sadness in his voice tugs at my heart.

"I understand," I say, caressing his cheek. "And I'm sure we can come up with a way that will benefit and protect everyone."

"I think so too." Andrew lifts his head and he's smiling again.

"So," I kiss Andrew again briefly on the lips. "I think it's time I introduce you to my father."

Andrew looks instantly panicked, which makes me giggle.

"Your dad," he clears his throat. "He has a reputation for being rather..."

"I know," I say, reaching up to smooth out his furrowed brow with my fingers. "But I promise he's not that bad. Just let me take care of it."

I wink at him, and he pulls me close.

"God, I love you," he declares and kisses me hard this time.

"You know," I say, after I catch my breath. "My meeting with my dad today was very troubling. I'm thinking a little therapy session may be in order."

Andrew smiles before kissing me again. "Dr. Mercer, at your service."

CHAPTER 46

Today is the day.

Andrew and I have met with my father several times over the past forty-eight hours. To my delight, my dad really came through for us big time. And so did Adrian. That woman missed her calling. The FBI would have been proud to have her.

We managed to come up with a perfect plan that will allow Andrew to save the company, while keeping his family's deep, dark secret securely in the closet.

Today, Andrew plans to confront his father with the news. Then he has a meeting scheduled with the advisory board to inform them of the new direction for the company.

I can barely contain my excitement, but Andrew has understandably been a nervous wreck. His sleeping patterns have gotten worse. I don't think I've seen him eat more than a meal or two in the past two days. But it will all be over soon, and I'm keeping my fingers crossed that everything goes smoothly…for Andrew's sake.

"I can't do this," Andrew says, while pacing determinedly in his living room.

"You'll be fine, son," my dad tells him, in one of several attempts to try and calm him down.

Andrew wanted my dad here today to help handle things. I'm still struggling a bit with our new effort at a more traditional father/daughter relationship, but if it helps Andrew to have him here, then I'll suffer through it.

"What if he freaks out?" Andrew asks, running a hand through his hair, still pacing. "He's in bad this time. What if he panics?"

"We have everything in place," my dad assures him. "There is no way he can refuse. And if he does, we have an outlet for that as well."

"Let's hope we don't have to go there."

"I'm certain we won't," my dad says with confidence.

Andrew nods and continues pacing. I'm standing in his kitchen, arms crossed, trying to decide if I should even be here. Andrew insisted, but I feel so uncomfortable. Personally, I thought this was something Andrew should do on his own, but I guess he felt he needed the support.

A minute or two later, the doorbell rings. Andrew and I both jump, but my dad seems calmer than ever – just another day at the office for him.

Andrew looks at me, eyes wide with uncertainty and fear. "I love you," I mouth at him, and smile reassuringly. He smiles back and takes a deep breath before opening the door.

"What's this?" Is the first thing Mercer Senior says as he walks in and sees me and my father.

"Come in, Dad," Andrew orders him. "Sit down."

I know Andrew's hanging on by a thread, but you would never know it from the outside. He's radiating confidence. I couldn't be prouder.

His father eyes us speculatively before walking to Andrew's sofa and taking a seat. Mercer Senior is looking as evil and smug as ever. "I didn't know we would be having company," he remarks, and I can tell he's trying hard to maintain his composure.

My dad stands and introduces himself. "Richard Greene," he says, extending his hand.

Mercer Senior stands and looks at my father in admiration before shaking his hand. "Richard Greene?" he questions, and even I can see the awe in his face. Figures. They're really two of kind in a lot of ways. "To what do we owe this honor?"

Andrew takes a seat next to his father, and my dad sits down and begins. "Mr. Mercer, I've recently been made aware of some problems your company's been experiencing. Andrew sought my advice, and we've worked out a solution that's sure to benefit everyone involved."

Mercer Senior's smile quickly disappears. He looks at Andrew. "Why would you seek legal advice for the company without informing me?"

I watch as Andrew's confidence wanes under his father's glare. *Stay strong Andrew.* I will him with my mind. *You can do this.*

"Just listen to what Mr. Greene has to say," Andrew tells him, and looks back to my father for reassurance.

Mercer Senior looks over at me suddenly. "What's she doing here?" he asks, and cuts his eyes at Andrew once again. "Or do I even want to know?"

"She's here because I asked her to be here," Andrew says, his confidence back. "Mr. Greene is her father."

I look quickly over at my dad from the kitchen. He almost looks bored with this whole conversation. I kind of love him for it.

Mercer Senior's laugh pulls my attention back to him. "Oh, I see," he chuckles, before his eyes begin darkening as he stares at his son. "Did you hire her knowing who her father was? Have you had this planned all along?"

"Mr. Mercer," my dad interrupts. "Your son only found out about that connection recently, and honestly, it's absolutely irrelevant to what we'll be discussing today." He's looking sternly into Mercer Senior's eyes, and I once again find myself appreciating my father. Wow! Twice in one day! "I will tell you, Mr. Mercer," my dad continues, "that there are a couple of ways things can go today – the easy way, or the hard way. It's your decision, and we're prepared for either."

"Are you threatening me?" Mercer Senior is livid.

"No sir," my father says, with a hint of a smile on his lips. "I'm only here to provide the facts surrounding your unfortunate situation and help choose the best possible solution. I assume you want what's best for the company, and of course what's best for your son. Am I correct, Mr. Mercer?"

Mercer Senior looks uncomfortable now, probably realizing for the first time that we have a lot of incriminating evidence – which we do – and that he better listen a little more carefully.

"Of course I want what's best for my son," he says quietly, but it's obviously a lie. Prick.

"Good." My father smiles. "So, here's what we're proposing."

I stay in the kitchen and watch as my father relays our brilliant plan to Mercer Senior. Andrew periodically glances at me, and

I try to smile each time, to help ease his nerves. I'm not sure if it's working, but it makes me feel better at least.

"So, you're forcing me to *retire*?" Mercer Senior looks over at his son. "This is blackmail!"

I can't read his eyes. It's almost as if he's hurt, but that can't be possible.

"Yes, I want you to retire," Andrew says, his voice firm and unwavering, as he skips over the other accusation. "You've been out of the day-to-day for some time now, and I think this decision is the best thing for the company."

"Best thing for the company," Mercer Senior scoffs, "or the best thing for *you*?"

Andrew looks down at his feet and then back up at his dad before responding. "Both."

"And if I refuse?" Mercer Senior asks. I definitely think he's hurt. *Oh God*. This must be torture for Andrew.

I look over at my dad, and the ghost of a smile is back.

"Well," my dad starts, "if you refuse, Andrew's willing to reveal your indiscretions to the advisory board, which will not only ruin the reputation you've built for yourself over the years, but it will also most definitely force your resignation. We're asking for retirement, Mr. Mercer – a much more civilized way to go."

Turns out, the sleazy people Mercer Senior was with at the garden party were the people trying to buy the company. They held his largest debt from horse racing. As for the software supposedly purchased for the design group? The design group never received their new software, because Mercer Senior decided that money would be better used to pay off another portion of his increasing debts, payable to another sleazy group that ran a dog racing track just outside of Vegas. The so-called software company just ended up being a front for the guys he owed. Mercer Senior has been doing business like this – funneling company money to pay his debts – for months. And thanks to Adrian, we had all the proof we needed.

"You would do that to me?" Mercer Senior looks angrily over at his son. "You would do that to your own father?"

"Yes," Andrew tells him, without hesitation, which both shocks and delights me at the same time. "It's for your own good," he adds. "You will retire. I'll take over the majority of your shares – as our by-laws state, you can transfer them to an heir at retirement – and my silent partner will invest in our re-design, as well as front me the money to pay off your debts. End of story."

GO ANDREW!

"You will also start going to Gamblers Anonymous, so you don't run yourself or our family into the ground once you retire. And if you choose not to get help, then you can use your own money next time instead of the company's and I can promise you, I won't be there to bail you out again. This offer of help – to pay off your debt – will only happen once. Know that."

Andrew's breathing hard after his little outburst, and Mercer Senior has the decency to look embarrassed.

Andrew sighs and turns toward his father. "Dad, you have to know this is the best way. You don't want the company anymore. We'll pay off your debt, and you'll have plenty of money from your investments and remaining shares to live very comfortably for many years." He puts his hand on his father's shoulder, and Mercer Senior takes a deep breath, as he looks from Andrew to my father.

Am I imagining things or does he look defeated?

"When will all of this supposedly happen? When are we to tell the board?" Mercer Senior asks.

"I have a meeting scheduled this afternoon," Andrew tells him, his voice perfectly confident now.

Mercer Senior looks at Andrew. "This makes you happy. Doesn't it?" he seethes. "You finally think you've won. You think you've beaten me?"

Andrew frowns. "Dad, it's not about winning and losing."

"Of course it is!" Mercer Senior stands and hovers above Andrew. "That's the way it's always been!"

Andrew stands as well, meeting his father eye to eye. "For you, maybe." He points a finger at his father's chest. "Not for me. I just wanted a father, but what I got instead was an enemy. You could have made that right, but you still refuse, even after all of this time. You still want to fight me. Why?"

Andrew's dad stares at him for a moment before his rage finally subsides. He sits down and looks at his feet, seeming years older. Definitely defeated.

"I'll accept," he says quietly, and Andrew sits back down next to him. "I'll retire. I just want to be done with this."

"That's good to hear," my father says. "We have some paperwork for you to sign to make everything official."

My dad pushes the papers across the coffee table toward Mercer Senior. He looks briefly at Andrew before taking the pen and signing.

I can't believe it worked. I want to be happy, but the look on Andrew's face is tearing me apart.

"Thank you, Dad," Andrew says, gently. "This really is the best way."

Mercer Senior won't look at him. "I just hope you're happy now," he mutters, without affection, before getting up and walking toward the door. Andrew gets up to follow him.

I watch as Mercer Senior turns to Andrew, his smug look back in place. "You know," he starts, "you're really no better than me. Taking what you want, no matter who you have to hurt in the process – even your own family." Mercer Senior's smile is deadly. "Maybe I did manage to teach you a thing or two."

Andrew shakes his head. "You'll never learn, Dad. It didn't have to be this way," he says, but Mercer Senior's expression never changes. "I hate that I had to stoop to your level. I hate myself for it. But I couldn't bear to see anything else perish because of your selfish ways. It's over."

I watch as a frown comes slowly to Mercer Senior's face.

Andrew opens the door. "See you in the office at two," he adds before his father leaves. "Have your farewell speech prepared." Andrew's father turns and stomps toward his car, and Andrew slams the door behind him.

He stands stock still, staring at the closed door. I can tell even from my perch in the kitchen he's shaking.

I look over at my dad. He's already packed up and ready to go.

"When will I see you again?" he asks, as he approaches me in the kitchen.

"I don't know," I say, peeling my eyes off Andrew. "I'll call you."

"Okay. I love you sweetheart."

He reaches for a hug, and I oblige, but it's still awkward. This is going to take some time.

"Andrew," my dad says to him as he reaches the front door. "You did well today, even though I know it was hard."

He extends his hand to Andrew and Andrew shakes it – the first sign of movement since his father left. "Thank you again for all of your help and for being here today," Andrew says, his voice barely audible. "I couldn't have done that without you."

My father smiles before walking out the door. "Oh, I think you could have," he tells Andrew. "See you at two."

After my father leaves, Andrew turns and when our eyes meet, we both rush toward each other, eager to be in each other's arms.

"I'm so sorry," I tell him, my arms wound tightly around his neck. "I know that was awful, but you did the right thing, Andrew. I promise."

"I know I did." His voice is quivering, like the rest of him. "I'm just glad it's over."

We stand and hold each other a little longer in silence. "So, you did it," I eventually tell him. "You saved the company, and even though he doesn't realize it yet, you saved your father too." I place my hand on my precious Andrew's cheek. "You got everything you ever wanted."

Andrew smiles, and pulls me close. "That's not everything," he says, and kisses me softly. I snuggle into his neck and inhale his delicious scent. "I love you, my beautiful girl," he whispers. I smile back, and hold the man of my dreams tight against me. "I love you too, Andrew Mercer. And I always will."

EPILOGUE

Three months later...

As I sit alone on the beach near my mom's favorite lighthouse, I think back on my recent past and smile. I can't help it.

The past few months have been riddled with stress and tragedy, but they've also ended up being some of the best times of my life.

I'm still trying to come to terms with some of the unbelievable events in my head, but not today.

The beach is surprisingly deserted for this time of year, which is a good thing. Today, I welcome the peace and solitude.

I look down at my hands and squeeze the urn holding my mom's ashes. I can feel her all around me. She's going to be happy here. I'm certain of it.

My mom loved this place. We took many family vacations here. Unfortunately, most of the time my father was working, but my mom and I always managed to have a blast – just being girls, playing in the sand, soaking up the sun. She was always at peace here, and now she always will be.

"Hi, Mom," I say to the urn, tears rolling down my cheeks. "So, Andrew got the company. The advisory board agreed to everything, no questions asked, even though we were scared at first. They had followed Andrew's dad's lead for many years, and despite his evil ways, a lot of them were friends and thought he was doing what was best for the company. Andrew's dad is a good salesman. There's no denying that."

I sigh as I think about the meeting that day.

"I was worried they would be reluctant to accept the 'changing of the guards'," I continue speaking to the urn, "but they weren't. Like the rest of the company, they'd come to respect Andrew, and everyone thought his plans for a company re-design were brilliant."

I swell with pride at the memory. My man is a genius.

"And now that Andrew's plans have been funded – by Dad, believe it or not – and are in motion, the company's already seeing changes for the better. Everything at Mercer Construction is definitely looking up.

"And remember the woman I told you about? The one I lovingly referred to as 'Bitchface'? It turns out her name wasn't 'Bitchface' after all, or Victoria Hamilton, for that matter. A quick background check informed us that her real name is Patricia Conners, and just a few short months ago, she was going by the clever alias of 'Trixie Toy' – the Flamingo in Vegas has never seen a cocktail waitress with so much potential. I'm sure she has a bright future ahead."

I smile, thinking about the day Andrew and I found out that fabulous news. It made my millennium for sure, but I actually felt kind of bad for Mercer Senior. I think he really did love her, and she broke his heart. He was honestly trying to help her out, but she had other plans.

Mercer Senior was dumb enough to include her in all of his dealings, and she was not only playing him and Andrew, but it seemed she was tied in with some of Mercer Senior's "business partners" as well, trying to bleed everyone dry. Andrew could have pressed charges, but he was adamant about nothing coming back on his father, revealing his gambling problem.

Andrew did threaten Bitchface with a lawsuit if she ever returned, but we're pretty confident "Trixie" won't be bothering us again. She's back in Nevada, last we heard, probably trying to charm the money out of some other poor sap's pockets.

Unfortunately, Andrew and his father have yet to reconcile, but I'm holding on to hope. If my father and I can make it happen, surely there's hope for the Mercer men too.

"Dad and I are trying, Mom." I know this will make her happy. "I definitely appreciate all of his help with Andrew and the company, and we've made some good strides over the past few weeks, but we're still surfing in shark-infested waters. It's going to take some time, but I do want to fix things between us. I know that's what you would want."

The ocean breeze blows at my long curls. I close my eyes and relax into it.

Mom. I feel you, Mommy.

"Abby's doing well," I tell the urn.

My mom always did have a soft spot for Abby and her crazy antics.

"She loves her job at the museum, and she's painting again. I hate that we don't spend as much time together anymore, but you know Abby. She's never without a shortage of friends...or men," I add with a smile. "Her fear of commitment remains, but I'm confident there's a man out there that can break her. I'm kind of hoping it may be a certain book store owner we know, but Abby keeps blowing off that suggestion any time I bring it up. You never know."

I smile at the thought of Nate and Abby. Sometimes I think there's something going on there, but she's constantly denying it. Either way, they've become good friends, and if Nate is half as good to her as he was to me, I'm certain Abby will eventually see the light.

"Everything happens for a reason. Right, Mom?"

My mom used to say that to me all the time. *Everything happens for a reason.* I believe it now more than ever.

"I managed to find a job at an art supply store in town," I say happily. "It's nothing luxurious, but it's nice to be around artists again. I'm starting to feel truly complete.

"And then there's my Andrew..." I close my eyes and smile. "He's perfect, Mom. He's everything I ever wanted, and everything I never knew I needed. He loves me. He takes care of me. And I take care of him. I just hate that the two of you never met. I know you would have loved him."

I look down at the urn. "He surprised me yesterday with two tickets to Italy," I say excitedly. "I'm finally going, Mom. I'm going to Italy, and even better, Andrew's coming with me. I can't wait to get my camera out again full time. It's what I've always wanted to do, and I'm not giving up this time, Mom. I promise."

Another gust of wind nearly knocks me off the wooden spindle I'm sitting on, and I laugh through my tears.

"Enough talking for now? Eager to blow in the breeze, I see? I understand. Doesn't sound half bad, actually."

I go to take the top off of the urn, but I hesitate. It's taken me three months to bring her here. I could've waited even longer, but Andrew urged me to come.

"You have to put the past behind you and say goodbye," he said. "Trust me. The sooner you do that, the sooner you can move forward."

I smile, and look down at the urn once more, then out to the horizon. A random memory of my sweet mom when I was around thirteen years old pops into my head, and a fresh set of tears come quickly to my eyes.

We were on a shopping trip, and she was uncharacteristically sober. We went to Macy's downtown, ate lunch at the Sundial on top of the Peachtree Plaza, and then she took me to an afternoon movie. We talked. We laughed. I'll never forget that day. I remember feeling so loved, so special. My mom had a knack for making me feel like I was the most important thing in the world, even when she was at her lowest. She always thought of me first.

"I owed it to you, Mom," I tell the urn. "All of those years, you treated me like a princess. You took care of me. I don't regret taking care of you. I'm just sorry I couldn't help you in the end."

I cry a little harder, but it's good. It's a release. I'm ready to let her go.

"I know you're healthy and happy now, and that's all that matters."

I stand and move down to the edge of the water before taking the top off the urn, tilting it on its side, and watching as my mom blows slowly into the breeze.

"I miss you, Mom, but you'll always be with me," I whisper, as the last of the ashes leave the urn. "Bahibbik."

After enjoying the breeze a moment, and the feel of my toes sinking into the wet sand, I turn and move back to my makeshift seat. I sit and watch the ocean a little longer, until my tears finally stop.

"Hey, beautiful."

I turn and instantly smile. "Hi there, handsome."

"Everything okay?" Andrew asks, as I stand and walk toward him, leaving the empty urn in the sand.

"Everything's great," I tell him, looking into his beautiful eyes as I wrap my arms around his waist.

Andrew leans down and kisses my neck, and I close my eyes. God, how I love this man.

"Your father's waiting for us."

"I know." I sigh and hug him closer. "Just a few more minutes."

I feel Andrew's smile on my neck, as we stand and let the wind blow all around us. I can still feel my mom, and her wild spirit. It's stronger than ever, and I smile too as a calm peace runs through me.

"I'm ready," I say eventually, pulling slightly away, but still holding Andrew close. "Let's go."

Andrew places a warm hand on my cheek. "You're so strong, baby," he tells me. "Just one of many things I love about you."

"You make me stronger," I tell him. "You make me better."

"Funny," he smiles, "I feel the same way about you, my beautiful girl."

I reach up to kiss his perfect lips. "I love you, Mr. Mercer."

"I love you too, Mrs. Mercer."

I gasp and grab Andrew's shoulders as a strong gust of wind nearly blows us both off our feet.

"Forget to tell your mom about the wedding?" Andrew teases, and we both laugh.

Sorry, Mom. Forgot to mention that one.

As soon as I get the thought out of my head, another soft wind blows around us, like a caress, like an embrace. I smile at my beautiful husband and sigh contentedly, as he takes my hand and leads me back toward our car.

Don't worry, Mom. Andrew and I eloped. In Vegas. With Elvis as our witness.

You would have loved it.

THE END

ACKNOWLEDGMENTS

Something I was reminded of while writing my second book, even more so than with the first, is how very personal writing can be. The stories may be fiction, but I promise there are tiny bits of my soul woven into each and every word. And sharing your soul is not an easy business, my friends.

However, after releasing my first book, I received an overwhelming amount of love and support. It was completely unexpected, but positively wonderful, and it has definitely made putting my second story out there a little bit easier.

That being said, I have to start by thanking you incredible readers for taking a chance on me and another one of my crazy stories. You humble me daily, and I couldn't possibly appreciate you more. I hope you loved the world of Andrew and Jules as much as I loved writing it, and with you guys by my side, I'm so looking forward to all of the exciting adventures to come.

My next thank you has to go to my loving husband. He is wonderful is so many ways, but the amount of patience and support he shows me in regards to my writing is unparalleled. He's my champion, my rock and most importantly, he makes me laugh on a daily basis. Thank you for everything, H. I love you.

I want to make sure and thank all of my friends and family that always seem to be there to love and support me when I need it most, especially my parents. Mom and Dad, your unconditional love throughout the years is the main reason I have the courage to write. Thank you for believing in me, even when I don't. I'm so lucky to have you both.

Thank you again to my dear friend, Kara, for the incredible cover art. She's so genius, it took all of ZERO rounds of edits to fall in love with this cover. She nailed it on the first go. I only pray that one day my writing can live up to her beautiful designs. Thanks for making me look good, K-Dog.

An important thank you needs to go out to my dear friend, Maya. You are gorgeous on the inside and out, you're full of spunk and I'm so proud to call you my friend. Maya, you inspire me in more ways than one, but mainly…I just dig your swagger. Bahibbik.

This time around, I decided to solicit a little extra help with editing. These ladies not only took on my request for help with smiles on their faces, but their brilliant ideas and feedback made this book a million times better than I ever dreamed it could be. Dawn, Kristi, Maya and Summer: Thank you from the bottom of my heart, from the depths of my soul and from everywhere else in between. I hope that someday I'll find a way to repay the favor, but until then, know that I worship at your alters of fabulousness. Shut.Your.Beautiful.Faces.

And last, but certainly not least, I once again have to thank all of my fangirl soul sisters out there. You are the most loving, passionate, loud, crazy, beautiful group of ladies I have ever met. You were the ones that by far showed me the most support when I started this journey, and I know, without a shadow of a doubt, you will be there with me until the end. You have no idea how much that means to me. I love you all.

ABOUT THE AUTHOR

Melinda Harris is an aspiring author, currently residing in the great state of Georgia with her family. When she's not writing, she likes to spend rainy nights with her nose in a good book and sunny days on a playground chasing her son. And most anytime – rain or shine – she can be found engaging in her favorite pastime, which of course is eating ice cream...lots and lots of ice cream.

To learn more, please visit Melinda's website: www.melindaharrisauthor.com

Or, you can find her on the following social media sites:

www.goodreads.com/MelHarris

www.facebook.com/melindaharrisauthor

twitter.com/MelHarrisAuthor

Made in the USA
Charleston, SC
10 October 2013